THE CHEATER'S WIFE

CN MABRY

ACKNOWLEDGMENTS

To my mother, thank you for planting the seed. You believed in my stories before I even knew how to finish one, and that spark never left me.

To the love of my life, your support is my steady ground and your love unlocked a whole new level of creativity in me. Thank you for being both muse and anchor.

And to every reader holding this book, thank you for letting me take up space on your shelf, your kindle, and in your imagination.

PROLOGUE
PROLOGUE

MAYBE IF I had bashed my husband's brains in years ago, I wouldn't be the one lying here, my own blood pooling around me.

But I didn't. And now I can't move. My body is broken, my life leaking out onto the cold floor. Pain splinters through my skull, sharp and unrelenting. Every breath is fresh agony. Even blinking feels like a hammer strike behind my eyes.

The weapon glistens beside me, slick with my failure. It stares back, lifeless but victorious.

I hear Ryan's footsteps drag along the hallway—slow, deliberate. My heartbeat stutters, each second stretching too long. Will he finish the job? Or just watch me rot?

I close my eyes, waiting. Listening.

I deserve this. Don't I?

There were moments—so many moments—where I could have changed the course, but I was stubborn. I had to love him. Had to prove something that was never worth the effort. And now I'm paying for it. We all are.

Memories flicker through my mind, unrelenting. Ryan and me at fifteen. The way I loved him before I even understood what love could cost. Every mistake, every second chance, every time I swallowed my pride, it led me here. Bleeding out on the floor.

And my children—our children. Tainted by my choices. Infected by the same disease that has finally taken me down.

I feel myself slipping, fading. But there's still time. Just enough to save them.

If I can hold on. If I can fight.

If…

CHAPTER ONE

NOW - CAMILLE

QUITE OFTEN, I'm convinced Ryan gave me the wrong son.

It's an ugly thought, one I'd never say out loud, but it festers where a mother's love should be.

I know how awful that sounds. What kind of mother thinks something like that? But I can't help it. Not when I'm standing here, watching RJ dominate the field while Gideon barely glances up from his phone. Not when I see the same fire in RJ that made Ryan great. The same presence. The same ability to take up space and demand the world bend to his will. And Gideon... Gideon is just—there. Existing. Taking up air, but never making an impact.

And then, as quickly as the thought comes, the shame follows.

Gideon is my baby. No matter how imperfect. No matter how much he frustrates me. I love him with all of my heart. And I know that he's the way he is because of me. I'm capable of loving him better. He deserves a fully present parent, now that Ryan can no longer step up. It's just difficult when RJ takes up so much of my time.

They are both seniors in high school, but one requires many more resources than the other. One has a bright future, but the other one's future isn't so certain.

Despite it being December, the midday sun is relentless, beating down on the turf, turning the players' helmets into shining orbs of light. The air is thick with the scent of sweat, hot rubber, and the distant aroma of overcooked concession stand pretzels. The bleachers tremble with the energy of the crowd. I have a blue fleece poncho covering me. A pair of dark blue denim jeans and a pair of Chloé camel-colored knee-high boots keep me warm. These boots are leftover from Ryan's heyday. There's no way we can afford anything like this now.

I catch a glimpse of my daughter Olivia sitting with her best friend, Bailey Diggs. Unlike Gideon, she's caught up in the moment, clapping and cheering, her voice nearly drowned out by the roar of the crowd. They're rooting for RJ, for Thurgood Marshall, for this final game that will cement his place in history.

A mixture of pride and envy swirls through me, thick and suffocating, curling around my ribs like smoke. I didn't give birth to him—no, that honor belonged to *her*—but I shaped him, molded him, made him into the star he is today. The same way I had done for Ryan, propping him up when he stumbled, smoothing out his mistakes, making sure the world only saw the strong, infallible man they all worshipped.

On the field, RJ moves like someone born for this. He's confident, commanding, in control. He steps into the pocket, scanning the field with the same precision Ryan once had.

"That boy is unstoppable!" Maci Diggs exclaims beside me, gripping my arm. She's my good friend and wife of Quenton Diggs, the team's coach. Maci's short curly bob is blowing freely in the wind as she cheers the team on.

I barely register her words. I already know what's coming.

"Did you see that?" she gushes. "He's better than Ryan was at this age."

I force a smile. "He's had an easier life than Ryan."

And he has. Ryan had to claw his way up, fighting for every opportunity. RJ was born into a name that already carried weight before he even had to prove himself. He plays with a freedom Ryan never had—unburdened by desperation, untouched by fear.

The roar of the crowd swells as RJ launches a perfect spiral across the field. My breath catches.

The receiver snatches it midair. Dodges two defenders. Storms into the end zone.

Touchdown.

The stadium explodes. Players flood the field, lifting RJ onto their shoulders. Cameras flash. His name is chanted in waves of celebration.

And me?

I clap, I smile, I cheer. But inside, something twists. This is what I wanted for RJ. I wanted him to be great, to stand outside his father's shadow. To give me the life Ryan promised but failed to deliver.

Maci squeezes my hand, pulling me back to the present. "I'll see you all at Luigi's!" she calls, already jogging toward Quenton.

I nod, even though she's not looking.

I turn to Ryan and Gideon. "Let's go."

Gideon pockets his phone with an exaggerated sigh, moving behind Ryan's wheelchair. He doesn't complain—he knows better. But as he grips the handles, his entire body hums with resentment, shoulders tight with the weight of unspoken words.

Ryan sits in the front passenger seat, his body rigid, his face stuck in a pleasant haze. His fingers twitch slightly in his lap—small, involuntary movements that remind me of how much he's lost. But his eyes... his eyes are sharp.

Lucid in a way that makes me nervous.

He's watching. He's absorbing.

He's fully here today. He saw his son play better than him. And he's pleased.

That doesn't always happen. Some days, he stares off into nothing, trapped in a mind that no longer functions the way it should. Some days, he gets stuck, confused, frightened by his own body's betrayal. But not today.

Today, he knows exactly what's happening.

The verbal aphasia chains his tongue, but his smile says enough. He knows RJ was great. He knows his son just made history.

I glance at the backseat. Gideon is hunched over his phone, knees bouncing, fingers gripping the device like it's the only thing keeping him tethered. Olivia rode with the Diggs—probably laughing, chatting, enjoying herself. Unlike Gideon, she's able to be happy for RJ. She's able to be normal. Even though Gideon is her full-blooded brother, she is closer to her half-brother. They have an undeniable bond, one that I've tried to forge between them and Gideon.

He and Olivia couldn't be more different.

She is social, well-liked, the kind of girl people gravitate toward without effort. Gideon is the opposite. A loner, an outcast, angry in ways that I don't fully understand.

The silence in the car is heavy, broken only by the low hum of the tires against pavement. RJ and his teammates are ahead of us, still buzzing with celebration. The championship trophy is probably being passed around, their voices ringing through the closed windows.

I glance at Ryan, force lightness into my tone. "That was some game. It reminded me of the first time you played first string against Virginia A&T our sophomore year." I smile at him, reaching for a moment of nostalgia, a connection to the man he used to be. "RJ looked so much like you."

Ryan's head turns slightly, his lopsided grin stretching. His hand trembles as he lifts it from his lap, patting my hand in acknowledgment.

And then—I hear it.

A noise. A struggle.

Ryan's mouth works against the words, his throat tight, his lips forming unfamiliar shapes. His tongue fights against the barriers of his own body, and then, after what feels like forever—

"I... prooouuud..."

His voice is raw. Broken. A fragment of what it once was.

And then—

Gideon sucks his teeth.

The sound cuts through the moment like a jagged rip, slicing through Ryan's triumph before it even has the chance to settle.

I don't turn around. I don't need to.

I already know.

The time bomb is ticking. It always is.

And soon, it's going to explode.

I just don't know when.

"You care more about RJ's games than you do about me or anything I like."

Gideon's voice is low, but it's laced with something sharp, brittle—like a crack in a windshield just waiting to spread.

I press my lips together, tighten my grip on the wheel. "Are we doing this today?"

I already know the answer.

Gideon drops his phone into his lap, his jaw clenching so hard that I can see it in the rearview mirror. "Yes! You never even apologized for missing my play."

He's referring to the school's performance of *Mean Girls*. Gideon has always been more of the moody, artsy type—which I did support. I like that about him. He's an amazing writer, kind of like how I used to be. And he's deeply interested in theater. While he would have preferred to perform in a Shakespeare play, he swallowed his pride and auditioned for *Mean Girls,* the musical the high school put on this year.

I inhale through my nose. Slowly. Steadily. Don't react. Don't let him get to you.

"I was there," I say, keeping my voice even. "I came on Friday."

"It opened Thursday!" he snaps.

"It ran for two nights, Gideon," I say, glancing at him again. "I came to one of them."

"The problem," he hisses, "is that I had a lead role. I was Principal Duvall. And you weren't there to see it."

His voice catches at the end. Just slightly.

And that—that is what makes my stomach twist.

I don't want to feel bad. But I do.

I swallow. "I told you, baby. I had to work. Marguerite called out, and I couldn't afford to lose the Serene Horizons contract."

The words taste bitter in my mouth.

I shouldn't have to explain myself. I shouldn't have to defend doing what I had to do to keep us afloat.

When Ryan's health collapsed and the money dried up, I became the breadwinner. I started a cleaning business. The glamour was gone, but it kept us alive.

Typically, I ran the administrative side, hired others to do the physical labor.

But that night? That night, I was down on my hands and knees, scrubbing some rich lawyer's shower, trying to make sure we didn't lose another damn contract.

Gideon lets out a bitter, cutting laugh. "Right. Because cleaning old people's toilets is more important than your son's play."

Something inside me flares—anger, shame, exhaustion.

My breath hitches. And then, it slips out.

"Cleaning old people's toilets is why you get to live in a nice house, eat every single day, and wear the designer clothes on your back!"

Gideon exhales sharply through his nose. His fists clench.

"You've never once missed a game for RJ."

The words land like a gut punch.

I open my mouth. But nothing comes out.

Because he's right.

I haven't.

The car feels suffocating now. Ryan shifts in his seat, his breathing heavier, the weight of it pressing against his fragile body.

And then, in a hoarse rasp—

"Stop."

Ryan's voice barely registers. But it's enough.

Gideon goes still. His entire body burns with resentment.

The red light ahead glows like a warning, casting the interior of the car in a deep, ominous red.

I barely stop before the door swings open.

"Gideon—"

But he's already gone.

The door slams shut behind him, and then he's disappearing down the sidewalk, fists clenched, shoulders tight, head low—walking like a boy who has been carrying his anger for too long.

The light turns green.

I don't move.

Ryan exhales, heavy and uneven beside me.

I swallow past the lump in my throat, gripping the wheel so hard my knuckles ache.

It's a good day for Ryan. A bad day for Gideon. The best day for RJ.

And for me?

Another reminder that no matter what I do—

I will never be enough.

CHAPTER TWO

THEN - RYAN

MY BODY IS BEAT, but that won't stop me from showing out at the party tonight. I put in work on that field today. *Work hard. Party hard.* Greater words have never been spoken.

Today was the first time I played first string for Golden Belt University's Minotaurs. I'd proven myself to be better than the starting running back, and we had won our homecoming game. I could still hear the roar of the crowd, the way they screamed my name when I bulldozed through the defense for that final touchdown. My body was sore, my legs heavy, but the high of victory was still pumping through my veins.

I couldn't wait to celebrate tonight.

But before that, I had to see her.

Camille had come to the game. Despite the excruciating pain she was in, she sat in the stands with a couple of her girlfriends, showing up for my first starting game. She had been in my corner for years. Even when it cost her. Even when she had every reason to stay in her dorm, curled under the covers, trying to forget.

I felt bad that she'd have to stay behind tonight, though. I knew she was exhausted, but I was forever grateful that she showed up for me.

She was one of one.

We'd known each other since we were freshmen in high school. Puppy love that had grown into something ferocious, something unbreakable. Something that maybe—if I was being honest—should've been tamed.

She was the good girl, the daughter of a pastor who led a small church outside of Atlanta. I was the bad boy, the son of Jamaican immigrants who barely scraped by. And yet, we found each other.

From the moment I saw her, I was locked in. She wasn't like any other girl I'd met. She wasn't loud or flashy, didn't try too hard to be seen. And yet, there was no way to ignore her. Her warm, golden-brown skin glowed in the sun, caramel undertones catching the light. But it was the eyes that did it—the green that shifted from moss to honey depending on how the sun hit them. And then there was the hair. Sandy-blonde, thick, soft. She was different, and I wanted to know why.

The first time I met her, I walked up to her like I had every right to.

"What are you mixed with?"

She sucked her teeth, rolled those pretty eyes, and said, "Black with Black."

Then she walked off. Like I was nobody.

I remember watching her go, trying to figure out if I should be pissed or impressed.

She didn't give me the time of day until we were forced to spend it together—when she got assigned to tutor me in Language Arts.

The girl was smart as hell. Beautiful, too. Everybody liked her. All the dudes wanted her.

But she only had eyes for me.

And now, she was mine.

Since I was fifteen, she'd been my rock. She was the only

one I could talk to about my abusive mother, my lack of a father. The only one who never made me feel like I could be more than what I was.

I was the star of the football team, destined for the NFL. And Camille? She was always saying, Let's get you there.

Now that we were in college, we were well on the way.

We had been high school royalty. The prettiest girl in school with the best athlete. And even though I was young, I knew then—I wanted her forever.

I took the stairs to her dorm two at a time, jogging past a group of girls laughing by the vending machines. Camille's room was near the end of the hall, the door slightly cracked.

I knocked lightly, stepping inside when I heard her soft, "Yeah?"

She was curled on her side, facing the wall, wrapped in her thickest orange comforter. The only light in the room came from her desk lamp, casting a soft glow over the small space. The air smelled like vanilla and the faintest trace of lavender lotion.

"Hey, superstar," she murmured, not turning around.

I smirked and slid onto the bed behind her, wrapping my arm around her waist, pulling her close. She was so damn small. I could feel the warmth of her body even through the blanket.

"You came," I said, pressing my lips to the back of her neck.

"Of course I did," she whispered. "You played great. The best I've seen. I'm so proud of you, baby."

I exhaled against her skin. I knew she'd been there, but hearing her say it, knowing she'd dragged herself out of this room, put on a brave face, and sat through the entire game for me? That meant something. That's why she was a keeper. She would do anything for me—*anything*. And I would do anything for her.

I slid my hand over her stomach, feeling the soft fabric of her t-shirt beneath my palm.

It wasn't lost on me what she had endured just yesterday. The weight of it clung to the air between us, thick and unspoken.

We made our first impossible choice together—the kind that burrows under your skin and festers. A decision to end a life before it had a chance to begin. I sat beside her, gripping her hand like it was the only thing tethering us to this reality. And then they called her name. She let go. She walked away.

When she returned, something about her was missing.

The silent, trudging walk back to campus stretched longer than it should have, the cold pressing against us like a punishment. She curled into bed without a word, small and still, as if trying to make herself disappear.

And me?

Guilt coiled inside me, thick and merciless, wrapping around my lungs, making every breath feel stolen.

"I'm sorry," I murmured, rubbing slow circles against her stomach. This was the hundredth time I had apologized but there was no apology that could un-break her heart.

She tensed for half a second before relaxing into me. "It's okay," she said, but her voice wavered.

It wasn't okay.

We both knew that.

I pressed my forehead against her shoulder, breathing her in.

"I promise you—when the time is right. When I can give you everything you deserve… We'll have babies. I swear to you, Camille. I promise."

Her breath hitched, and then, finally, she broke.

A sob wracked through her, and I held her tighter, kissing her temple, whispering soft *shhh's* as she cried into the pillow.

She had given up so much for me.

She had done so much for me.

Kept my secrets. Made the hard choices. Carried the weight of me, even when it wasn't fair to her.

"You're gonna get everything you want," I promised her. "I'll give you the world, Camille."

She nodded against me, her breath shuddering as she wiped at her eyes.

"Stay," she whispered. "Please."

I wanted to.

I really did.

But—

"You know I can't. Dorm curfew is soon," I murmured.

"You can," she sniffled. "My RA is at the party."

I hesitated.

Yeah... that's where I'm trying to get to.

I kissed her softly, my lips lingering before I pulled away.

"Get some rest, baby," I whispered.

As I left, I knew one thing for sure.

I didn't deserve her.

But I was grateful for her. Always.

I step out into the hallway, rolling my shoulders as I let out a slow breath. The air out here is cooler, less heavy. Inside that room, it felt like I was drowning—wrapped in Camille's sadness, in the weight of everything she never said out loud but I knew she felt.

I run a hand down my face, trying to shake it off. I'm supposed to be celebrating tonight. Not standing here feeling guilty, not thinking about the sound of Camille crying into her pillow.

As I move down the hall, I catch a familiar set of eyes locked onto me. It's a chick named Addie.

She leans against the vending machine, arms crossed, her lips tugged into that sly little smile. She knows what she's doing. She always does. Addie is the kind of girl who walks like she owns whatever space she's in. Legs long, long wavy hair cascading, lips glossed just enough to catch the light. And then there are her eyes. Those baby blues, that lured me in. I had a thing for light eyes. But I tried my best to not look her in hers.

CHAPTER
THREE

NOW - CAMILLE

ONCE WE ARRIVE at Luigi's, I park behind the restaurant, away from the front door. I could've parked closer so that Ryan wouldn't have to travel far, but I'm too tense, too angry. I need to relieve some of this pressure, and I don't want an audience.

My fingers curl into a fist before I release it, flexing, stretching. The irritation is alive in my body, itching beneath my skin, begging to be let out.

With quiet precision, I reach for him, pinching Ryan deep. Sharp. Right in the soft flesh of his arm.

He flinches. A flicker of pain dances across his slackened face before fading into vacant stillness.

That's what I hate the most—the way he can't even fight back anymore.

I wish he could fight back.

I wish he would yell at me. Tell me to stop. Do something—anything—to make me feel like I'm not a monster. Or that I'm not alone. But he won't. He just takes it. He takes everything now. And I guess it's all he can give me now.

I'm ashamed, but barely, to admit that this has become my

I know what she wants.

I could go over there, let her flirt, let her laugh at my jokes, let her lean in just a little too close. It wouldn't be the first time she tried it.

But it doesn't matter.

I belong to Camille.

She might not have my last name, not yet, but she has *me*. She's had me since we were kids, since she was that quiet little church girl sitting in the front pew while I sat in the back, sneaking looks at her. She's the one who knows me better than anyone. She's the one I can always count on.

And I'd never hurt her.

I nod at Addie, nothing more, and keep walking.

I'm tempted but I will always stick with Camille.

I'll do anything for her.

Because she would never hurt me.

favorite way to unlock my angst. It's petty. Vindictive. Small. But I like to put him through at least a fraction of the pain he's put me through. A minimum of the suffering I've endured, carried, swallowed whole.

His body twitches, his lips parting in an unfocused moan. For a brief second, it almost feels like control again. Like balance.

Then it's gone.

I exhale sharply and step out of the car, slamming the door a little too hard.

The cold air bites at my skin, but I welcome it. Let it cool the fire still simmering inside me.

By the time I round the car to his side, Ryan is staring at me. He watches me the entire time, his eyes following me from the moment I step away from my door until I reach his side.

That stare used to hold so much. Heat. Desire. Anger. Passion.

Now?

Nothing but dull remorse.

That's all that's ever there these days. Guilt and the rotted-out remains of the man I used to love.

I open his door, crouching down to adjust the footrests of his wheelchair. I can see the apology in his gaze. The silent *I'm sorry* he gives me every single day. But sorry doesn't fix anything. It doesn't undo what's been done.

"Ready?" I ask, my voice softer now.

He doesn't respond, just gives the smallest nod.

I push the chair out of the car, set the brakes, and help him into it with practiced ease. My hands are firm, but my touch is gentle now. The moment has passed. I got what I needed.

Ryan stares straight ahead, as if nothing happened. As if he never even noticed.

He takes my abuse in stride.

It's the least he can do.

I grip the handles of his wheelchair and push him toward the entrance.

The moment we step inside, the warmth of the restaurant wraps around me, filled with the scent of garlic, melted cheese, and tomato sauce. The sounds of laughter, chatter, and clinking glasses echo through the bustling space. Christmas music is playing in the background and there are holiday decorations all around.

The private room is packed. The entire team, their families, friends—everyone who wants a piece of RJ's victory is here.

And there he is, right in the center of it all.

RJ sits with his teammates, his grin lazy, confident, completely at ease. He owns the room the way only young men with the world at their feet can.

I guide Ryan toward a table near RJ's. A deliberate choice.

I want him to see me. I want everyone to see me.

But then, my gaze shifts, catching movement near RJ's table.

Violet.

All soft blonde hair and wide blue eyes, her figure tight and toned. She leans forward, laughing just a little too much at something RJ says. Her lips are glossy, her hand resting lightly on his forearm as she giggles at a joke I'm sure wasn't *that* funny.

She knows exactly what she's doing.

She reminds me of myself at that age. She reminds me of the types of girls Ryan likes. The apple doesn't fall far.

She's popular and only dating athletes. Knowing exactly how to move, how to make them feel special, how to make them *need* her.

Violet played Regina George in the high school musical—Mean Girls. The same play Gideon was in. Apparently, RJ went both nights.

Not just to support Gideon. Not just to see Olivia who danced in the chorus.

But to see *her*.

He did bring Olivia and Violet flowers. He was such a gentleman.

I press my lips together.

I know exactly what kind of distraction girls like Violet can be.

And RJ does *not* need distractions.

He's got a future. A path that has been carefully paved, each stone placed with precision and purpose.

And I'll be damned if I let some blonde-haired, blue-eyed distraction throw him off course.

Why couldn't she like Gideon instead? I knew that Gideon had a crush on her, but of course she prefers RJ.

And RJ is just like his father. He likes light eyes. The girl could've looked like a troll, but if those eyes were any color other than brown, he would be smitten. I've read his messages to and from *Pretty Eyes*. That's what she's saved as in his phone. I only got to skim the messages once, a few weeks back. When I went to search through his phone again, the messages and her contact name had vanished.

"Mom."

I blink, snapping my gaze away from RJ and Violet as Olivia and Bailey appear in front of me, their hands clasped together in the way only teenage girls with secrets and plans do.

"Can I spend the night at Bailey's?" Olivia asks, voice syrupy sweet.

I arch a brow, glancing up just in time to see Maci standing a few feet away. She meets my gaze and gives a small, approving nod.

I nod in return. "That's fine."

Olivia beams, squeezing Bailey's hand like they just got away with something. Internally, I feel nothing but relief. With Olivia and Bailey out of the house, I know RJ will be at Tyler Brown's party tonight. The girls will be gone. And that just leaves one problem.

Gideon.

I don't know where he is, and for once, I don't care. I just need him to be somewhere else. Because tonight? Tonight, I want an empty nest. I want silence. I want to breathe. And for just a few hours, I want to pretend I don't have to be a mother.

The pizza party is going well. Voices are overlapping other voices. I sit next to Ryan, who chooses not to eat in public. He hates the looks of pity that he gets. With half his face paralyzed, chewing is awkward and he has too much pride. I make sure to order a pizza to go for him at home. And one for my problem child. I watch as Olivia and Bailey chitchat and scroll their phones. They were such good girls. Maci and I didn't have to worry about them.

The girls have their plates piled high—Caesar salad, three slices of pizza each, and enough garlic knots to feed a small army. I don't dare touch any of it. Just the salad for me. No croutons, and a vinaigrette dressing. Just sad, almost naked lettuce.

I gave up simple carbs the moment Ryan got drafted. It was my marriage vow to myself. I wanted to keep my body exactly the way it was when we got married. I used to think that if I stayed fine, if I looked just as good as I did when he met me, his eyes wouldn't stray. That he'd see me every day and think, *Wow, what a prize! What a woman! Why would I ever cheat on her?*

I was wrong.

Turns out, no matter how much salad you eat, men can still be trash. How slim you kept your waist and thighs, they would still want more. I was so naive and I didn't want that for Olivia.

But at 45, I'm still trim, toned, and disciplined as hell. I've come too far to let a single breadstick ruin my streak. And if I've learned anything from my husband's wandering eyes, it's that no amount of self-sacrifice guarantees loyalty. But hey, at least I still look amazing in a little black dress.

down to a high school sweetheart. I already know the damage that can bring for the both of them.

The restaurant noise dulls as I push open the bathroom door, letting it swing shut behind me with a soft click. The space is small, the air thick with the artificial lemon scent of cheap disinfectant. A slow drip echoes from the farthest sink, the flickering fluorescent light overhead casting a cold, washed-out glow.

I move to the wall near the paper towel dispenser, folding my arms, keeping my posture relaxed.

And then I wait.

The toilet flushes. A few seconds pass, then the stall door creaks open.

Violet steps out, head tilted down as she fiddles with the rings on her fingers, completely unaware of me at first. Then she looks up, and her breath catches.

For a split second, I see the thoughts race across her face —*Is she waiting for me? What does she want?*

She recovers quickly, offering me that polite, social smile that all pretty girls learn early.

"Hey, Ms. Bell."

I don't smile back.

"It's Mrs. Bell."

I keep my tone sharp, just enough to make her stomach drop.

Violet's expression falters, her shoulders going stiff as her eyes dart side to side.

"Oh… right. Sorry."

She shifts on her feet, the first crack appearing in her confidence.

I take a step closer, closing the distance between us in a way that makes her have to tilt her chin up slightly to meet my gaze. She smells like vanilla body spray and mint gum. It's an innocent scent, young.

I was her once.

And that's why I know exactly how to handle her.

My eyes study my baby girl. Olivia was the spitting image of me with the same caramel complexion, honey-green eyes, and a mix of sandy blonde and brown hair. Right now her hair was in braids with deep purple extensions. She's always exploring fun looks. She was much taller than me, courtesy of Ryan's genes. But rather than use her leanness and natural muscle tone for sports, she chose dance—ballet, jazz, and modern. She wanted to go to either Juilliard or The New School for dance.

Had we still been living off Ryan's money, I would have been more encouraging. She could have been a free-spirited dancer, chasing her dreams without worrying about the bills. But Daddy didn't have any money for her. And I didn't have the heart to tell my baby girl that it was time to be practical—to think about a fallback career. Dancers don't make much money.

Instead, I fed her dream because maybe, just maybe, RJ would make it all the way. And if he did, he would take care of her. Barring any major injuries, he was a shoo-in for the league after college. Bigger than Ryan was at his age. Faster. Stronger.

He had to avoid injuries and other distractions.

Violet pushes back from the table and stands, flicking her hair over one shoulder as she makes her way toward the back of the restaurant. I watch her navigate through the crowded space, moving with the kind of practiced ease that only a certain type of girl possesses. The type who has always been watched. Admired. Wanted.

She doesn't check to see if anyone's following her. She doesn't have to. Girls like her are used to assuming they're safe.

I give it a few seconds before I rise from my seat and follow *Pretty Eyes*. The texts they sent before he deleted her used to be all about how they can't wait to graduate so that they can finally be together. I was not allowing RJ to be tied

"I wanted to tell you that I thought you did a wonderful job in Mean Girls," I say smoothly, my voice warm. "Regina George suits you."

Her brows flick up, caught off guard.

"Oh... uh, thank you."

"And you're very pretty."

Her lips part slightly, then close. A flicker of uncertainty passes through her eyes.

"Which is why I need you to leave my son alone."

Silence.

It's thick. Tense. The kind that settles in the lungs and makes it hard to breathe.

Violet's throat moves as she swallows hard.

"I—"

"No," I cut her off gently. "I'm not asking. I'm telling you."

Her face blanches.

She shifts again, adjusting the strap of her purse over her shoulder, suddenly unable to hold my gaze.

"RJ has a future," I continue, my voice calm, measured. "A real future. He doesn't need the distraction of some high school fling. I know your type, Violet. I used to be your type."

I let the words settle, let her feel them.

Violet blinks rapidly, her hands twitching slightly as she grips the sink behind her.

"I—I wasn't—"

"Stop," I say, my tone firmer. "We both know exactly what this is. You think you're special. That your laugh, your smile, your body will keep him wrapped around your finger."

Her eyes widen, a slight tremor shaking through her frame.

"But you're not special."

Her lip trembles, and her eyes shine with unshed tears.

I sigh softly, tilting my head as if I feel sorry for her.

"Oh, baby girl... don't start crying."

She blinks quickly, trying to stop the tears before they fall.

I grab a paper towel and press it into her trembling hand.

"Wipe your face before you walk out of here."

She hesitates, but takes it, dabbing at her eyes.

I lean in slightly, just enough to make my presence loom. Just enough to make sure she'll never forget this moment.

"Because if you walk out there with tears in your eyes," I whisper, my voice soft, almost soothing, "I'll make sure everyone knows your little secret."

Do I have any idea if she actually has a little secret? Nope. Not a clue. This is a total crapshoot. But I know high school girls well enough to bet that she's hiding something—and whatever it is, she probably thinks it's life-ruining. Teenage girls are like that. They think the world will end if someone finds out they texted an ex or wore knockoff designer shoes.

I hit my mark.

A breath shudders out of her, and she nods frantically, pressing the paper towel harder to her face like she's trying to blot out her existence.

I watch as she squares her shoulders, takes a deep breath, and smooths her hair, her hands shaking just the tiniest bit. Then, finally, she pushes past me and exits the bathroom, head high, expression carefully blank.

Good girl.

I let her go.

I'll give her twenty-four hours.

If she's smart, she'll take my warning seriously.

If not... well.

She'll learn.

They always do.

CHAPTER FOUR

THEN - CAMILLE

IT'S BEEN a month since the abortion. Ryan and I went back and forth about it for two weeks before we decided that ultimately it was the best decision for us. I didn't want him to drop out of school and hurt his chances of going pro. And he didn't want me to raise our baby alone until he could go pro. Besides, if my father knew I were pregnant without being married, he would cut me off.

Physically, I'm fine. My body has healed, the cramps that used to wake me up in the middle of the night are gone, my appetite is back, and my energy is better. I look the same in the mirror—mostly. Maybe a little paler. Maybe my eyes are a little more tired. But overall? I'm fine.

Or at least, that's what I tell myself.

The truth? The sadness still lingers. Not in the dramatic, weeping-into-my-pillow way. No, it's sneakier than that. It shows up in the pauses between conversations, in the quiet moments when I should be happy but I'm just…not. It lurks in the background, waiting.

But I don't have time to be sad.

I have things to do.

Ryan needs me.

I lean forward, fingers flying over the keyboard as I type the final sentence of his paper—*A Critical Analysis of Gothic Themes in 19th Century American Literature.* A truly riveting subject for a class Ryan could not care less about. But he needs to pass. He needs to keep his GPA up. He needs to stay eligible to play. And I'm going to make sure that happens.

Because if I don't, who will?

This isn't the first time I've saved Ryan. And let's be honest—it won't be the last.

I click save and sit back, stretching my fingers. The words on the screen are crisp and well-structured, a paper that will get him at least a B, maybe even an A if the professor is feeling generous. He won't even have to skim it before turning it in.

I should feel exhausted, but I don't.

This is what I do.

Ryan needs me, and I show up.

I always show up.

I close my laptop, shove my things into my bag, and push back my chair. The computer lab is mostly empty now, just the faint hum of fluorescent lights buzzing above me. I step out into the dimly lit hallway, adjusting my bag over my shoulder.

And that's when I hear them.

Laughter.

Light, sweet, the kind of giggles girls do when they want attention but also *pretend* they don't.

I know that sound.

I follow it without meaning to, my eyes flicking toward the vending machines up ahead. Two girls are huddled there, whispering behind manicured hands, casting quick, darting glances in my direction.

I slow my pace, giving them my full attention. They know what they're doing.

Their giggles turn breathy, secretive.

They're talking about me.

I keep walking, casual, deliberate. My eyes land on one of them. Addie Sherwood. High ponytail. Perfectly contoured cheekbones. The kind of girl who looks effortless but actually spends an hour getting ready every morning.

I've seen her before. At games. At team dinners. In the stands, wearing too-tight leggings and a too-bright smile, always positioning herself in Ryan's orbit.

She lingers too long. Laughs too hard at his jokes. Finds excuses to touch his arm.

And now she's here, whispering about me.

I don't have to hear what she's saying to know what it is.

They always wonder why I'm still around.

They think they could do it better.

They think they could have him if they wanted.

If she only knew.

If she knew what I've done for Ryan. What I've sacrificed. What I've given up to make sure he has everything he needs.

She wouldn't be giggling.

She wouldn't be looking at me like that.

I tilt my head slightly, locking eyes with her. It's a small movement, but it works. The smirk on her lips fades, just for a second.

And then, she looks away.

Her friend follows.

The giggling stops.

Good.

I have to stay on my toes with that one. Ryan has a type. And her light eyes signify that she's that type.

I keep walking, my posture relaxed, unbothered. Like I never even noticed them. They don't say another word.

Ryan is waiting for me.

And I have a paper to deliver.

By the time I reach Ryan's dorm, the hallway smells like feet, weed, and failure. The usual. The doors lining the walls are cracked open, muffled music and laughter spilling out.

His room is at the end of the hall, past a few guys' rooms where the air is thick with the scent of reheated pizza and whatever cheap cologne college guys think makes them smell expensive.

I knock lightly, then push the door open.

Darkness.

A single lamp is on, casting a dull glow over the disaster zone of a room. Clothes are draped over a chair, sneakers kicked into a corner, loose papers scattered on the desk. His PlayStation controller blinks faintly from the TV stand, still plugged in, waiting.

And Ryan?

Ryan is sprawled across the bed, one arm thrown over his eyes, his breath slow and heavy.

It's another migraine.

I know it before I even get close. His jaw is clenched, his body tense, even in sleep. He's always been like this. He pushes himself too hard, never knows when to stop. Resting feels like failure to him.

If he slows down, he might not make it.

I drop my bag onto his desk chair and quietly pull out the printed copy of his paper, setting it on top of his textbook. He won't thank me, but he'll turn it in. And that's all that matters.

I step closer, careful not to trip over whatever garbage he's left on the floor this time.

The second I reach the bed, his arm shifts. His hand finds me blindly before his eyes even open.

"Hey," he murmurs, voice thick with sleep.

"Hey, baby," I whisper back, sinking onto the edge of the bed.

His fingers curl around my thigh, warm and familiar. He barely has the energy to speak, but the moment he touches me, something in him loosens.

"Did you finish it?" he asks, still half-asleep.

"Of course I did," I say, smoothing my hand over his chest. His breathing slows under my touch.

He exhales a deep, relieved breath, his thumb brushing absently against my knee.

"You're the best," he mutters.

I don't respond.

Instead, I lean in and press a soft kiss against his temple, letting my lips linger for just a second too long.

I don't mind saving him.

I don't mind carrying the weight for both of us.

It's temporary. I know that. My hard work will pay off.

But sometimes, I wonder if he realizes how much I need saving too.

"I'm going to meet with my parents," I say softly.

His brows twitch slightly, but his eyes stay closed. "You haven't seen them in a while."

"I know."

I don't tell him why I've been avoiding them.

I don't have to.

I run my fingers through his hair, feeling the dampness at his scalp from sweating through another headache. He sighs, shifting slightly beneath the covers.

"You want me to come?"

"No, baby." I shake my head. "Get some rest."

He doesn't argue.

Just squeezes my leg once before his hand falls away, his body going slack as he drifts back into sleep.

I watch him for a moment, studying his face, his breathing, the way he only seems to relax when I'm near.

Then, I grab my bag and slip out of the room. I haven't seen my parents in weeks.

And I know they're going to have questions.

CHAPTER
FIVE

THEN - CAMILLE

WHEN I THINK of my future with Ryan, I imagine warmth. The kind that sinks into your skin, that lingers, that wraps around you like an embrace. Not the sticky, suffocating heat of Georgia summers, but something golden and perfect, like the California sun or the ocean breeze in Miami. I imagine him standing tall at a press conference, his name stitched into the back of a jersey, a new contract signed, the cameras flashing. I imagine our home, a sprawling, modern mansion with marble floors and an infinity pool that overlooks the ocean.

We'll have three or four kids, close in age. Strong, athletic boys who will inherit Ryan's talent. A little girl who will wrap him around her tiny finger. They'll grow up knowing wealth, security, and endless possibilities.

I'll design our home with taste and opulence without being gaudy. Chandeliers imported from Italy. Velvet drapes pooling onto hardwood floors. A massive, gourmet kitchen that I probably won't cook in, but I'll host lavish dinner parties and let a private chef handle the details.

During the off-season, we'll vacation in Mallorca or St.

Tropez, sipping champagne on a private yacht, the waves rocking us gently as the sun sets in pinks and oranges. We'll eat at the finest restaurants, dressed in designer clothes, effortlessly belonging to the world of the rich and powerful.

All I have to do is get him through graduation. Get him signed to a team. Make sure he wins a few rings.

With my support, Ryan can go anywhere.

And if Ryan makes it, we make it.

I just have to keep him on the right path.

And I have to stay on it with him.

The drive to my parents' house stretches longer than usual, each mile winding through the dense, dark woods lining the roads outside of Atlanta. This isn't the city with the skyline, the lights, the bustling streets where ambition hums in the air. This is the outskirts, where the roads are too wide and too quiet, where the land stretches in heavy, unmoving stillness.

The houses out here are modest, traditional, small in their thinking just like the people inside them. White siding. Green shutters. A big yard that my father still mows himself every Sunday, as if maintaining this plot of land is some great moral virtue.

This house—this life—is the opposite of what I want for myself.

I refuse to end up like my mother, standing in a kitchen that hasn't changed in twenty years, cooking the same meals, folding the same laundry, pretending not to hear the sharp edges in my father's voice. Pretending that she's his *only* woman.

I won't live in a house where the furniture never changes, where the same tired beige carpet holds memories of arguments that no one dares to bring up. Where dreams shrink to fit the walls.

I won't stay in a place where love is conditional, where one mistake makes you unworthy. Where you're constantly compared to the rest of them.

And yet, as I pull into the driveway, a strange weight settles in my stomach.

The white porch lights glow, casting long shadows on the perfectly cut grass. The scent of honeysuckle and fresh pine fills the air. It's too peaceful, a stillness that I know is about to break.

I step out of the car, my pulse drumming in my ears.

I don't belong here anymore.

Still, I take a breath, smooth my expression, and walk up to the door.

I tell myself I'm ready.

My mother has beautiful mahogany skin and cropped, curly gray hair. Her figure has softened over the years, rounding with time. She is a dedicated wife and mother, having played her role as his First Lady and homemaker with unwavering devotion. Her dreams began and ended with him.

"Mama? Daddy?"

The house smells the same. Fried chicken, lemon-scented polish, the faintest trace of my father's cologne—sharp and strong, like authority bottled up and pressed into his skin.

My mother is in the kitchen, standing at the stove, her back to me. She doesn't turn when she hears my voice.

"Hi, baby." It's quiet, hesitant. Like she already knows what's coming.

And then I hear my father's voice.

"Sit down, Camille."

My stomach tightens.

I turn toward the living room. He's seated in his usual chair, his Bible open on the side table—but he isn't reading it. A single sheet of paper is clenched in his fist.

I know what it is before he even speaks.

My feet feel heavy as I move to the couch, sinking into it stiffly. My hands fold in my lap, my fingers clenched so tightly my nails press into my skin.

"Do you want to tell me what this is?"

"...'ve committed the ultimate sin." His voice is low and sharp.

I force myself to look up.

"Please, Daddy. I'm so sorry."

"No, Camille," he says coldly. "We're done with you."

My vision blurs.

"What?" I whisper.

"I'm cutting you off."

The words don't sink in right away. They hover in the air, unreal, impossible.

"No more tuition. No more money. No more anything."

The finality of it slams into me, knocking the breath from my lungs.

"You want to act like an adult?" he continues, standing now, towering over me. "Then you can figure it out on your own. I'm a man of God! I didn't raise you to be like this. You disgust me Camille."

I suck in a shaky breath, my chest tight, panic starting to creep in.

"Daddy—"

"Get out of my house."

His voice is final.

I turn to my mother again, desperate now.

She still won't look at me.

"Mama—"

"Go, Camille."

Her voice is barely above a whisper.

But it destroys me.

My legs feel weak as I stand, the room spinning slightly.

This can't be happening.

This cannot be happening.

I stumble toward the door, my breath coming too fast, my hands shaking as I reach for the handle. The night air hits me like a slap, cold against my burning cheeks.

And then—

The door slams behind me.

He holds up the paper, but I don't look. It's my credit bill.

My pulse kicks up, a cold sweat prickling along my s[pine]. I was supposed to pay it off before he saw it. I meant to. between my schoolwork, Ryan's assignments, and everyth[ing] else, I lost track.

Now, it's too late.

"I called the number," he continues, his voice ev[en]. Controlled. "Spoke to a woman at the front desk. Asked [her] about the pricing for their... services."

A lump forms in my throat.

"The charge on the card matches the cost of termination."

The words slice through the air, thick with disap[-]pointment.

"Don't lie to me, Camille."

I don't.

Because what's the point?

I stare at my hands, at the faint crescent-moon indent forming on my palms where my nails press too hard. I wan[t] to lie and tell him, I paid for a friend's abortion. But th[e] words won't pour out of my mouth.

"I'm sorry Daddy," I whisper.

"Sorry can't fix this!" my father snaps, slamming the paper onto the coffee table.

My mother flinches.

I turn to her, silently begging for support.

She won't look at me.

She never does.

"You think I raised you for this?" my father continues, shaking his head. His voice is quieter now, but it's harsher, the weight of it settling into my chest like lead. "You think I sacrificed for this family, for you to turn around and do this?"

His disgust is palpable, curling around the edges of his words.

"Do you know what you've done? Thou shall not kill!

33

The sound of it echoes in my head, ringing louder than anything my father said.

And just like that—

I have nothing.

My father was supplementing my tuition since I had gotten a partial scholarship to Golden Belt University. I never even told him I'd been offered a full ride to Clark Atlanta University because I already knew how that conversation would go.

"Clark is a respectable school, Camille. Close to home. Safe. Why would you even consider anywhere else?"

But I couldn't go to Clark.

I needed to be with Ryan.

You don't let a man like that slip through your fingers.

Men like him, gifted, destined, chosen. They move fast. They ascend. And if you're not there, right beside them, another woman will be.

So I did what I had to do. I accepted less money to go to GBU, knowing my father would cover the rest. It was a small price to pay to secure my future.

But now, without him paying my tuition, there was no way I could afford to stay.

My chest tightens, panic curling around my ribs, but I shove it down, refusing to let it consume me.

My father calls what I did a sin.

His voice was filled with disgust, like I had defiled myself beyond redemption, like I was nothing more than a disappointment, a fallen woman. But if my actions are so unforgivable, then what does that make him? Because I've watched him *sin* for years.

I sit in my car, gripping the steering wheel so tight my knuckles ache. My father—a man of God, a pillar of the community, a leader—has spent years bathing in his own sins while condemning everyone else for theirs.

His drinking. His gambling. His adultery.

The things we were never allowed to speak of. The things

my mother pretended not to see. The things I learned to ignore because calling them out would mean tearing apart the illusion we were all forced to live in.

And all those other women?

They sat in the front pews in their tight skirts and high heels, licking their lips as they whispered "amen". They volunteered for extra duties, stayed late at the church office, conveniently missing rides home so that Pastor Stafford could take them instead.

I remember Sister Karen, the choir director, pressing herself against him in the fellowship hall, her laughter too loud, her hands lingering too long. I remember the way she beamed when he complimented her singing voice, the way she clutched his Bible like it was sacred.

I remember my mother's tears over Sister Anita. The woman wore red lipstick to a service one day and my mother saw the exact shade on my father's lapel.

And Sister Vanessa.

Barely twenty. Barely legal. Looking for spiritual guidance. For a mentor. For a father figure. And my father? More than happy to lay hands on her.

My mother pretended not to notice.

She played her role.

Folded his clothes. Cooked his meals. Smiled when women half her age handed him their tithes and called him Pastor with seduction dripping from their voices.

She pretended to not hear him sneaking out at night. To not hear him whispering on the phone in his study.

She never asked twice. She never made demands. She let it happen, the same way she let this happen.

But it's me he's disgusted with. Me he casts out. Me who has fallen from grace.

I don't know how long I sit there, staring out the windshield like a shell-shocked war veteran. But eventually, my body takes over, and I throw the car into reverse, peeling out of the driveway like I've just robbed a bank. My hands are steady. My heart? Not so much.

The road back to campus stretches ahead of me, dark and endless. It's weird—I should feel heavier, like the weight of my father's words are pressing down on me. But instead, I feel… lighter. Not because I'm free. Oh no, I am very much not free. I've just been evicted from my own life.

But at least I still have my car.

I grip the steering wheel tighter, my knuckles white, my foot pressing down a little harder on the gas. I will not cry again. Crying doesn't pay tuition. Crying doesn't find a way to stay in school. Crying doesn't undo the fact that my father just cut me off like a dead limb and left me to rot in the sun.

No tuition. No rent. No safety net. No mother who cares enough to stand up for me. No father who believes in forgiveness, despite preaching about it every Sunday morning.

And definitely no sister coming to my rescue.

Poor Ricki. She's still too young, too indoctrinated to see my father for what he really is. And even if she did, what could she do? Buy me a value meal with her allowance? Slip me an extra twenty from the church's tithe box? No. She doesn't have money. She doesn't have power.

And that means I have no one. Well. No one except Ryan.

My grip tightens on the wheel as my stomach flips. Ryan is all I have left. The only thing standing between me and complete, irreversible ruin. And that means I cannot afford to lose him.

No matter what. No matter what it takes. I exhale and glance down at my gas gauge. Almost empty. Perfect. Rock bottom, here I come.

At least I still have my car. The one thing I own outright, bought with years of babysitting, tutoring, folding overpriced crop tops at the mall while listening to teenage girls complain about their "toxic friends." All those hours, all that work—just so I could have something that was mine.

And now? It's all I have.

But I'll figure it out. I have to. Because men like Ryan don't wait. And I have no intention of letting some cleat-chasing groupie swoop in and steal what I've spent years building.

No.

Ryan is mine.

And I'm not about to lose him.

CHAPTER SIX

NOW - CAMILLE

IT'S BEEN two hours since we got home, and I'm exhausted.

Ryan is in our bed, binge-watching *Vikings* on Netflix. He may be asleep by now. Who knows? Who cares? At this point, I could set the house on fire, and he'd probably just roll over and mumble something about Ragnar Lothbrok.

I sit in the kitchen, sipping my tea, listening to the kids rummage around in their rooms. A rare, peaceful moment. I exhale, trying to let the tension of the day melt away, but my shoulders stay tight.

The kitchen is smaller than the one I used to have. Back in *the house*, my kitchen was the size of this entire downstairs. Marble countertops, a double island, a six-burner gas range I never actually used but looked beautiful in photos. Now, I have laminate counters that peel at the edges and cabinets that creak when I open them too fast. It's nice enough. Functional. Clean.

But it's not *that* house.

This one is in a nice neighborhood, safe, quiet. The kind of suburban Georgia town where people still wave at each other from their driveways and pretend they care. It's a far cry from the gated community we used to live in, where every lawn was professionally manicured and every woman carried a handbag worth more than my mortgage.

That house had stairs that curved like something out of a movie. Now? I have a set of straight, narrow stairs with beige carpet that's impossible to keep clean. That house had a sprawling backyard with a pool and a deck with built-in speakers. This one has a small fenced-in yard where the grass refuses to grow in patches.

Back then, I used to have cleaning ladies. A team of them, coming in twice a week, scrubbing the baseboards, polishing the floors, making everything shine. Now? I *am* the cleaning lady.

I don't complain. I can't complain. My company might not have been enough to maintain *that* life, but it keeps us here. Keeps the kids in good schools. Keeps food on the table and the lights on.

And as tight as things get sometimes, at least we still have a home.

I take another sip of tea. I need something stronger, but I'll settle for this.

Gideon was already home when we got back from the pizza party. He was still sulking about me missing opening night of Mean Girls. I tried apologizing one last time, but he just gave me that look—the one that says he'll be bringing this up in therapy for years.

But when I pulled out the personal pizza I brought him— pineapple and ham, his favorite—his whole attitude shifted. A crime against humanity, if you ask me. Pineapple. On pizza. But he loves it, and whenever I order for the kids, I always make sure to get him his own.

This time, he actually thanked me. His voice was stiff, like he didn't want to, but he did. And just like that, the walls started to crumble.

Boys. So predictable. Feed them, and they forget they hate you.

Now that Gideon's belly was full, he may be in a good mood for what I have planned for him tonight.

RJ is in the hallway, throwing on a hoodie, already halfway out the door.

"You're heading out now?" I ask. It's 9:00pm and there's a party at Tyler Brown's house. He's RJ's teammate and best-friend who lives in a massive home about ten minutes away. This party is a post-game victory celebration and most of the high school will be there.

"Yes," he responds with hesitance in his eyes.

"Take Gideon with you," I say.

RJ stops mid-step and turns to look at me like I just suggested he take Ryan's wheelchair instead.

"C'mon Mama C," he groans. "Gideon doesn't even like that kind of stuff."

"Maybe he doesn't like it because he's never been invited," I counter, crossing my arms.

RJ huffs, running a hand down his face, irritated. "Gideon's the one with the problem, not me."

I say nothing. Just stand there. Waiting.

It works.

He stomps down the hall toward Gideon's room, knocking like it physically pains him.

"Yo, you wanna come to Tyler's?" RJ asks, voice dripping with reluctance.

Silence.

Then—

"For real?" Gideon sounds suspicious, like RJ is setting him up for a prank.

"Yeah, man. Get ready. We're leaving soon."

I hear Gideon's closet door fly open, drawers slamming, movement full of excitement. He's thrilled.

Meanwhile, RJ? He probably thinks he's doing charity

work. He has no idea this was just as much for him as it was for Gideon.

Two birds. One brilliantly calculated stone.

Olivia appears next, bouncing down the stairs with her overnight bag slung over her shoulder.

"Is Maci on her way?" I ask.

"Yep, pulling up anytime now. Bailey is helping me take these out tonight," she chirps, her purple braids cascading over her shoulders like she's starring in a shampoo commercial.

I frown. "Didn't you just get those put in?"

She sighs dramatically, like I'm the dumbest person she's ever met.

" Yes, but Ashanti copied me," she says, flipping her hair over her shoulder with the rage of a girl who just discovered she's been outfit-twinned against her will. "Same color, same style. I refuse to look like her."

I blink. "You did such a good job though. So you're taking them out… because of Ashanti?"

"Obviously."

Teenage girls. This is their version of war. A battle of aesthetic dominance. Olivia has clearly declared mutiny against Ashanti and is ready to burn the whole kingdom down over it.

Honestly? I respect it. I always liked to stand out amongst other girls too. It was easy to do when you had naturally blonde and light brown hair with a pair of honey emerald eyes. Ricki always said that I relied too much on my looks. And perhaps she's right. I should be encouraging Olivia to not care but she's young. I'll let her have fun.

She pauses at the door, waiting for Maci's car to pull into our driveway. Bailey is in the front seat, and they both wave at me.

"Bye Mom." Olivia says before kissing me on the cheek. "Bye Daddy!" She calls out as she races out.

With Olivia gone, RJ at his party, and Gideon tagging along, the house will be completely empty for the night.

And that? That is exactly what I need. I take another sip of tea, savoring the silence as the door closes behind them.

Now, all that's left is Ryan. And now that we're alone, I can play a little.

Once the kids are out of the house, I take my time in the shower.

The water is hot, nearly scalding, the steam curling around me until the mirror fogs over completely, erasing my reflection. Maybe that's for the best. I don't want to see myself right now. Not like this.

Not when I'm about to do what I always do.

I step out, wrapping a towel around myself, letting the steam linger on my skin as I walk into the bedroom. Ryan is lying in bed, propped up against the pillows, his eyes on the TV but not really watching. The glow from *Vikings* flickers across his face, casting him in shadows, but I know better than to think he's lost in the story.

His mind drifts too easily these days, somewhere between the past and the present, stuck in a body that barely works anymore.

It's hard to believe this is the same man I used to chase around the house, the same man who could pick me up without effort, who could pin me against the wall, who used to pull me into his lap and make me forget my own damn name.

Back then, Ryan was a force, all muscle and speed, a powerhouse on the field and in the bedroom. I used to wake up sore from the things he did to me, from the way he took me.

Now?

Now, he's soft in all the wrong places. The muscle is still there, buried under layers of time and sickness, but it doesn't work the way it used to. His right side is nearly useless, his confident stride reduced to a shuffling limp, slow and deliberate. Aphasia has stolen most of his words, and when he does speak, it's often in fragments, his sentences slipping away before he can catch them. Then there's the dementia. Most of the time he's not really here. I've had to hire a nurse to watch over him on the days that I can't tend to him. Sometimes, I take him to an adult daycare. It's demoralizing for him.

But right now, I know what he wants.

Even if he can't say it.

I drop the towel and climb onto the bed, straddling his waist, my bare skin pressing against his. His left hand twitches, reaching for me on instinct, his fingers brushing against my thigh.

"You like that?" I murmur, dragging my nails lightly over his chest, tracing the ridges of his ribs, feeling the way his body stiffens beneath me.

His breathing changes, sharpens. His left hand grips my hip, his fingers digging in, the pressure just a little too tight —like he's trying to remind himself that he can still touch me.

For a moment, I let myself pretend.

Pretend that this is still our thing. That his body still works the way it used to. That he can still take me the way I want him to.

But when my hand drifts lower, trailing down his stomach, my fingers brushing against the soft skin between his thighs—

Nothing.

Not even a twitch.

I pause, waiting. Giving him a moment.

But nothing happens.

Still soft.

Still useless.

A slow, satisfied smirk curls my lips.

I do this from time to time.

Just to remind him.

Just to make sure he knows what he lost. What he threw away.

He should have enjoyed me. He should have kept his hands on me, worshiped me, been satisfied with everything I gave him. Instead, he wanted more. More women, more attention, more ways to make a fool out of me.

And now?

Now he can't enjoy anyone.

Not me. Not them. Not a single woman in this world.

I drag my nails down his chest again, watching the way his body reacts—or doesn't react. My fingers move lower, teasing, playing, giving him one last chance to prove himself.

Nothing.

Still soft.

Still useless.

A wicked little smile plays on my lips.

"Well," I whisper, dragging my nails up his chest again, my voice mocking now. "Looks like somebody isn't up for the challenge."

His jaw clenches, his face darkening with something ugly —shame, frustration, maybe even rage.

Good.

I lean in close, pressing my lips near his ear, letting my breath ghost over his skin before I start to sing.

"Limp, limp, limpity limp..." My voice is sweet, playful, taunting. "Can't get hard no more..."

His left hand tightens on my hip, his fingers digging in painfully now, but I don't flinch.

I just laugh.

I slide off him, slow and deliberate, grabbing the black lace lingerie I had set aside earlier. I pull it over my body, adjusting the straps, letting the fabric cling to every curve.

Ryan watches me, his left hand still clenched into the sheets, his breathing uneven.

I don't say anything as I walk out of the room, the sway of my hips just exaggerated enough.

I don't have to look back to know that his eyes are still on me.

And I don't have to hear him speak to know that he hates me right now.

That's fine.

Hate is better than nothing.

At least it means he still feels something.

CHAPTER
SEVEN

THEN - RYAN

THE CUE STICK glides between my fingers, smooth and steady, as I line up the shot. The bar is dimly lit, all neon beer signs and flickering overhead lights, the kind of place that smells like stale beer and ambition gone wrong. Voices rise over the music—teammates talking shit, girls giggling in tight dresses, someone at the bar already slurring their words.

I exhale, focusing, pulling back—then crack. The cue ball smashes into the cluster of solids and stripes, sending them scattering across the felt.

A good break.

"Nice one, Bell," one of my teammates mutters, clapping me on the shoulder before stepping up for his turn. I barely hear him because my focus shifts—I feel her before I see her.

That stare.

I glance up, and there she is. It's Addie, one of the many jersey groupies at GBU. She was a junior and had already dated a football player, basketball player, and a soccer player. And now she had her eyes on me. She wasn't the only one. Girls throw themselves at me all the time. They have since high school. And I've tried my best to remain faithful to

Camille, but I've slipped up a time or two... or three. There's so much temptation thrown at me left and right that I've considered breaking up with her. Just until I make it to the pros. I want to get this out of my system. But I can't break up with her. She's the reason I've made it this far. I owe her my life.

But Addie's blue eyes have been locked on me since I've walked into this place. She's been hovering near the bar all night, making it a point to be in my line of sight, tossing her hair, flashing smiles, whispering to her friend while barely concealing her glances in my direction.

I catch her this time.

And instead of looking away, she steps forward.

"That was impressive," she says, all breathy confidence as she stops at the edge of the pool table, tipping her beer bottle toward the scattered balls. Her nails are painted white, the kind of shade girls like her always go for—clean, fresh, just enough to remind you they get them done every two weeks. The kind I like seeing wrapped around my dick.

I smirk, leaning against my cue stick, letting her flirt. I shouldn't. But I do. Her icy eyes send a chill down my spine, but they lack the warmth of Camille's. She still has the most beautiful eyes I've ever seen.

"What can I say?" I shrug, letting my eyes flick over her face. "I've got good hands."

She laughs, twisting the beer bottle between her fingers. "On and off the field..."

She's close now, just shy of touching me. She smells like vanilla and something sharp—vodka, probably. I feel the heat of her gaze, the subtle shift in her stance.

And I know exactly where this is going.

But before I can say another word—

"Ryan."

Camille.

Her voice slices through the bar like a blade, cool and sharp.

Addie flinches just the tiniest bit, barely noticeable, but I notice it. She knows Camille's name. Of course she does.

Everyone does. Camille is my girl and I've never hidden her on campus. We flaunt our relationship out in the open. But that doesn't matter to these groupies. I think they want me more because of her. There's something about their competitive spirits that makes them want to steal me away from her. But I was never leaving Camille.

I turn, and there she is.

She's standing just a few feet away, arms crossed, watching the two of us like she's already decided how this is going to end. Camille doesn't do insecurity. She doesn't do pleading or pettiness or whining about other girls. She eliminates threats.

She doesn't look at Addie—not once. Her eyes are on me, and I know that look. Dangerous. Possessive. A challenge.

She tilts her head slightly. "I need to talk to you."

I glance at Addie, offering her a tight smile—a dismissal. "I'll see you around."

She doesn't argue. Just gives me a small, knowing smirk before stepping back, disappearing into the crowd.

Smart girl.

I follow Camille to a quieter corner near the back of the bar, past the pool tables, past the dartboards, to a shadowed alcove near the bathrooms.

"You good?" I ask, even though I already know the answer.

She exhales sharply, running a hand through her sandy blonde and brown hair. "My father wasn't bluffing."

I sober instantly. Shit.

Camille's father always played hardball, but I figured he'd come around. Camille was his. His daughter, his pride, the one he always paraded around as the good girl, the perfect one. She wasn't like her wild cousins, the ones he grumbled about, shaking his head at their fast ways. I guess he still had Ricki to parade around.

. . .

Camille was supposed to be the one who did everything right.

And now, he was cutting her off. Completely.

And it was my fault.

I had gotten her pregnant. I was the first and only man she'd ever been with. The first time we made love was on the night of our prom, and after that, we were always careful—until a couple of months ago.

I'd come home early from a party, drunk, and didn't put the condom on properly. By the time we were finished, I couldn't find it. Panic set in. I had to fish it out of her with my fingers, both of us shifting between awkward laughter and silent dread.

By the time her next period was supposed to come, it didn't.

We talked about keeping it. We really did. But it just wasn't the right time for us to be parents.

I hated that she had to go through with the abortion.

I want kids with her one day—I know that. I know we'll have a family, a future, a life built together the way we always imagined. But not now. Not like this.

She made a huge sacrifice for our future, and I will spend the rest of my life making it up to her.

That, I promise.

"He's really not paying for spring semester?" I ask, jaw clenching.

She shakes her head. "He's not giving me a dime for anything. They won't even take my calls."

I let out a slow breath, rubbing a hand over my jaw. This isn't just a problem. This is a crisis.

Camille had options. She was smart, could've gotten into plenty of schools with scholarships. Hell, she did—but she chose me instead. Chose to follow me here, to Golden Belt.

And now, she was stranded.

She looks up at me, eyes searching mine. "I have to figure out a plan."

A plan.

I know what that means.

Camille doesn't wait for things to work themselves out. She makes things happen.

I step closer, hands settling on her waist, pulling her in. She's tense, stiff, still wound up from what just happened.

I lower my voice, brushing my lips against her temple. "I love you."

She stills.

I feel the tightness in her body ease, just slightly.

"I'm gonna be with you no matter what," I say, meaning it. "We'll figure this out."

She exhales against my chest, and I know she's already thinking—already lining up possibilities, running through options, calculating.

But I don't want her to have to think. Not about this.

So I say it.

"I'll marry you."

She jerks back, her eyes wide.

"What?"

I shrug, squeezing her waist. "Let's do it. I'll marry you, Camille. Make it official. You won't need him. You'll have me."

A beat of silence.

Then—

The pure joy on her face is enough to knock the air out of me.

She lights up, eyes shining, completely forgetting whatever had happened five minutes ago. Forget Addie. Forget the stress. Forget the money.

Because I just gave her the perfect solution.

I know this is what she wants.

What she's always wanted.

Her arms wrap around my neck, and she kisses me—deep, hungry, like she's claiming me all over again.

And just like that—

I've fixed everything.

For now.

We got married at the courthouse. No big wedding, no dress fittings, no flowers, no family gathered to witness it. Just Camille and me, standing before a judge, saying words that should have felt monumental but instead felt like the only option we had left. She wore a white dress—not a wedding dress, just something simple she already owned. I held her hand, looked her in the eyes, and promised to love her for the rest of my life. And I meant it.

Because I owed her.

For everything she'd given up. For everything she'd done for me. For everything she would continue to do for me.

That was the thing about Camille—she never let up. Never stopped sacrificing, never stopped pushing, never stopped choosing me over herself. It wasn't just the abortion. It was all of it. She had a full ride to Clark University. A different life, a different path—one where she didn't have to work herself to the bone just to survive. But she turned it down. For me. She gave up her father's money, the easy life, the security, all because she wanted me more.

And I? I married her because I knew I owed her my life. I convinced myself that if I could just get to the NFL, if I could just make it big, then all of this—the sacrifices, the struggles, the pain—would be worth it. That was the deal we made without ever saying the words. She'd struggle now so I could build us a future. And I promised her, every night in that small apartment, that I would make it up to her. That I would spend my entire life paying her back for everything she had given up.

We moved into a cramped little apartment off-campus right before the start of spring semester. It was a dump, if I'm being honest—thin walls, a tiny kitchen with appliances that had seen better decades, and a bathroom with tiles that never quite looked clean no matter how much bleach Camille scrubbed into them. She hated it. She never said it out loud, but I knew. She didn't grow up like this. She grew up in a nice house, with a father who paid for everything and a mother who made sure everything was in its place.

This apartment? This wasn't in the plan.

But Camille made it work. She got a job at a diner down the street, working double shifts, coming home smelling like grease and exhaustion. She counted tips on the kitchen table, stretching every dollar, making sure we had enough to cover rent, enough to buy groceries. She'd fall into bed next to me late at night, body bone-tired, her hands rough from washing dishes all day. And I'd pull her close, press my lips to her shoulder, and whisper the same thing over and over: *I'll make this worth your while.*

I'd tell her to just hold on—just a little longer. Once I made it to the league, once I got that contract, everything would change. She wouldn't have to work. She wouldn't have to worry. She'd have everything she ever wanted. And she believed me. She had to.

But that didn't mean it was enough.

Because as much as I loved Camille, as much as I owed her, as much as I wanted to be the man she deserved, I couldn't help my wandering eye.

I never meant to.

But sometimes, it just happened.

Like Addie.

Like every other girl who looked at me like I was already a star, like I was already on my way to something bigger, something better.

Camille saw it, too. She saw the way girls looked at me.

And she never let me forget it.

CHAPTER
EIGHT

NOW - CAMILLE

THE THUD of a drawer slamming shut. The drag of his slipper against the wood floor. A grunt of frustration.

Ryan is struggling again.

I don't have to see him to know exactly what's happening. He's up in our bedroom, fighting with his clothes, wrestling with buttons that won't cooperate, zippers that won't slide, his left hand doing all the work his right side refuses to.

This is how every morning starts now. A battle. A slow, tedious war between Ryan and his own body. Some days he lets his guard down and allows me to help him. But I guess he doesn't feel like the humiliation today. Good. I don't feel like helping him.

I'm tired of this routine and can't wait until it's over. I can't wait until our family is free from the burden of his illness. And I do my part in helping along the path, to reach those pearly gates... or the fiery ones.

I stir his coffee slowly, watching the steam rise, thick and fragrant. It's a little strong today. That's okay. He needs it.

I tap the spoon against the rim of the mug, then reach for the sugar. But instead of just sweetening it, I also grab the tiny orange bottle tucked just behind the canister. The label is worn, the print smudged from too many times handling it.

I know exactly how much to use.

The pill crushes easily beneath the back of the spoon, turning to a fine, weightless powder. It disappears into the coffee with one quick stir. Seamless. Invisible. Undetectable.

I smile.

Upstairs, Ryan grunts again, followed by the clink of something small hitting the floor. A button, probably. He must have been trying to fasten a shirt. He always insists on dressing himself first, refusing my help like it's some final act of dignity.

It never goes well.

I take a slow sip of my own coffee, letting the warmth fill my chest, letting the scent settle into my skin.

I missed his dose last night. A mistake. A lapse in judgment. It won't happen again. I need to be consistent to hasten his death.

The stairs creak. He's coming. His slow, uneven shuffle is distinct, the weight of his body shifting awkwardly, his left foot leading, his right side dragging slightly behind. I hear the heavy thump of his palm against the railing as he braces himself, forcing his way down.

I wait.

Some mornings, he makes it to the table on his own. Other mornings, I pretend I don't see him struggling so he has to ask for my help. It depends on my mood.

The coffee is ready.

I lift his mug, watching the steam swirl in delicate ribbons, then turn toward the stairs with a smile.

"Morning, baby," I say sweetly.

Time to start the day.

Ryan finally makes it to the kitchen table, lowering himself into the chair with the careful, deliberate movements of a man twice his age. He exhales, shifting in his seat, adjusting the useless right arm that he refuses to acknowledge as anything less than fully functional.

Then, he looks up at me and gives me that lopsided smile.

I smile back. Sweet. Loving. The perfect wife.

With a slow, practiced motion, I slide his tainted coffee across the table toward him. His fingers curl around the mug, the warmth seeping into his palm. A look of gratitude flickers across his face—pure, unfiltered appreciation.

He trusts me to do what's best for him.

Unfortunately, he still thinks I'm here for him. That I'm *his* Camille. The woman who would do anything for him.

But people change.

Or maybe... maybe they don't. Maybe they just get better at pretending.

He lifts the coffee to his lips, takes a careful sip, sighs in relief. He's 100% lucid today. Let's see if I can change that.

I grab my phone and dial Maci, putting on my best cheerful voice as I press the phone to my ear.

"Hey, girl," she answers, her voice still groggy.

"Hey! Just checking in. How is my baby?"

Maci laughs, the sound light and familiar. "Your baby and my baby were up all night doing Olivia's hair. Now they're sleepily shoveling breakfast into their mouths and begging me for a Starbucks run because they're, quote, 'sooo exhausted.'"

I roll my eyes but chuckle. "I try not to let Olivia have caffeine, but once a month, I cave and let her have her little overpriced sugar rush."

Maci snorts. "Well, today might be the day. Bailey's got that 'if I don't get a Frappuccino, I might die' look on her face."

I shake my head, already pulling up CashApp on my phone. "Fine. My treat. For the girls. And for you. I'll send you a little something so you can get whatever you want too."

Maci gasps dramatically. "Look at you, being all generous. I knew I liked you for a reason."

I laugh, but my eyes flick back to Ryan. He's still sipping, slow and steady, like he's savoring the moment.

Good.

"Of course," I say smoothly. "What are best friends for?"

I hit send.

Maci hums in appreciation. "Well, you just secured your place in heaven, girl. Thank you!"

I smile.

We'll see about that. As soon as I hang up with Maci, I head upstairs to check on the boys.

I'm not sure if either of them made it home last night. I was too far gone in my own little world. But now, with the house settled and daylight creeping through the curtains, a nagging feeling tugs at me.

Did Gideon even come home?

RJ is my first stop. His bedroom door is half-open, and the familiar scent of sweat and laundry detergent lingers in the air. I step inside and find him sprawled across the bed, limbs tangled in his sheets, mouth slightly open.

Out cold.

I glance at the clock—8:07 a.m. Between the game and the party, I'd be shocked if he woke up before noon.

I turn and head to Gideon's room next, expecting to see him curled up in bed the way he always is, earbuds in, blankets pulled up to his chin like he's trying to disappear from the world.

But his bed is empty.

The sheets are untouched, perfectly smoothed, the way they were when I made them yesterday morning.

A prickle of unease climbs up my spine.

I check my phone, scrolling to Gideon's name, and press Call.

It rings. And rings. And rings.

No answer.

I try again. Same thing.

I stare at my screen, willing him to text me back, to give

me some sign that he's okay. He's probably fine. He's always fine.

Except, what if this time he's not?

Ten minutes pass, and my unease turns into full-blown panic.

I march back to RJ's room, about to shake him awake, but then I hesitate.

He deserves to sleep. He carried the entire damn team yesterday. And knowing RJ, he probably tried to bring Gideon home. But Gideon? He's stubborn. If he didn't want to come, there's no forcing him.

I pull my hand back and step out of the room, shutting the door quietly behind me.

Just as I'm debating whether to grab my keys and start driving around town, I hear the front door creak open.

I whirl around and rush downstairs, my heart hammering against my ribs.

Gideon stands in the doorway, looking like hell.

A dark bruise blossoms on his cheekbone, deep and swollen, and there's blood on his shirt. His hoodie is unzipped, his hands shoved deep into the pockets, his expression a carefully constructed mask of indifference.

"Where the hell have you been?" I snap, already scanning him for more injuries.

He rolls his eyes and steps past me like I'm nothing more than a mild inconvenience. "Like you really care."

"Don't walk past me, Gideon," I warn, grabbing his arm.

He yanks away, his face flashing with something unreadable before settling back into cool detachment. "I got into a fight."

I stare at him, waiting for more.

When it doesn't come, I press. "And?"

"And I've been walking around all night. Slept at the park." His voice is flat, like he's just listing facts, like none of this matters.

"You slept at the—" I pinch the bridge of my nose, inhaling sharply. "Why the hell didn't you call me?"

He shrugs, like that's an actual answer.

I grip his chin, tilting his face toward the light. "Who hit you?"

"Doesn't matter." He pushes my hand away. "I need a shower."

He turns, heading for the stairs, his steps heavy with exhaustion.

I clench my jaw, my fists tightening at my sides. I want to keep pushing, to demand he tell me everything, but I know how this goes.

Gideon shuts down when he doesn't want to talk.

I glance toward RJ's room, my irritation flaring. He was supposed to bring his brother home.

But then again, Gideon makes everything difficult.

I exhale, forcing myself to unclench my fists as I watch him disappear down the hall.

Something is off. Way off.

And whether he likes it or not, I'm going to figure out what the hell happened last night.

CHAPTER NINE

THEN - CAMILLE

THE GEORGIA SUN BEATS DOWN, unrelenting, turning the football stadium into a slow-cooking oven. Rows of graduates sit in their stiff navy blue caps and gowns, shifting uncomfortably under the heat. The scent of freshly cut grass lingers in the air, mixing with sunscreen and the faint smokiness of barbecues from tailgaters celebrating outside the gates.

I sit in the stands, fanning myself with the program, trying to keep sweat from ruining my makeup. The plastic chairs are scorching, and my thighs stick to them every time I shift. But none of that matters, because this is the moment we've been waiting for.

Ryan's name booms through the speakers.

"Ryan Bell, Bachelor of Science in Kinesiology!"

The stadium erupts. His teammates hoot and holler, slapping their programs against their knees. And right beside me, his family—the aunts, uncles, and distant cousins who've never given a damn before today—cheer like they're the ones who sat through the late nights, the injuries, the migraines, the stress.

They weren't there for him when his mother was breaking him down piece by piece. They weren't there when his father abandoned him. They weren't there when he needed a hot meal, when he needed someone to tell him he was more than just an athlete, when he needed me.

But now that he's the number one draft pick in the NFL?

Now that he has a multi-million-dollar contract with the Augusta Firehawks?

Now they care.

I force a smile, clapping along with them, even as I dig my nails into the flimsy program. I should be happy. This is Ryan's moment. But I can't stop thinking about how they don't deserve to be here.

Ryan walks across the makeshift stage at the fifty-yard line, shakes hands with the university president, poses for the camera. Even from a distance, I can see it—the easy confidence, the way he carries himself like the world already belongs to him. And in a way, it does.

He catches my eye as he turns back toward his seat, flashing that signature grin.

I smile back, but my chest tightens.

Because this is my moment, too.

I may not be on that stage, but I damn sure earned this degree with him. I was the one who kept him afloat, who made sure his papers were written, his grades stayed high enough to keep his scholarship, his body was fed and cared for. I woke up at five a.m. to meal prep, packed protein shakes in his bag, spent hours rubbing out cramps and icing swollen joints after practice.

I kept his head straight when the migraines hit, when the pressure became too much, when he doubted himself.

I dropped out so he wouldn't have to.

So tell me—who deserves to walk across that stage more?

Ryan promised me a home in Miami—our dream. I wanted warm beaches, ocean views, palm trees swaying in the breeze. But instead, we're moving to Augusta.

The Firehawks gave him the best offer. The most money. The best package.

So, of course, we're staying in Georgia.

But I will get my Miami house. I'll have my vacations, my yacht parties, my designer bags.

Because after everything I've done for Ryan, everything I've sacrificed, I damn well deserve it.

The ceremony drones on, more names, more applause. I barely listen. I just watch Ryan, watch the way he takes it all in, how oblivious he is to the hungry eyes of his family, already scheming, already lining up for their share.

He won't see it coming.

But I do.

And I won't let them take what I've worked for.

This is just the beginning.

Ryan promised me everything—a mansion, babies, a real wedding, a life where I'd never have to lift a finger again. He said I'd never have to work, never have to stress. He said I'd be the only woman in his world.

He owes me that much.

So when the ceremony ends, I stand beside him like I own him. Because I do.

The field is chaos—caps tossed, cameras flashing, families crying and hugging. Ryan's surrounded, his name called from every direction, people wanting just a piece of him. His old coaches, his teammates, the professors he's impressed with my essays—they all want their moment with the Golden Boy. I watch as he shakes hands, flashes that signature grin, soaking in the attention. They treat him like he's theirs now, like his success is theirs to celebrate. But I know the truth.

They weren't there when he was just another athlete on scholarship, struggling to keep up with his grades. They weren't there when he came home, body aching, migraines splitting his skull, needing me to hold him together. They weren't there when he had nothing. I was.

And then, of course, there are the girls.

They hover, standing in small clusters, eyes trained on him like they're waiting their turn. Some are subtle, some are not. They giggle, flip their hair, touch his arm as if that one moment of contact will do something. They think if they play their cards right, they might have a shot.

They won't. I have his last name now. We've been married for over two years and he wouldn't dare divorce me.

I watch them, my lips curved into the kind of soft, effortless smile that hides everything. I don't need to say a word. Let them think they have a chance. Let them think I'm just his sweet, supportive wife. Let them miscalculate.

Then, I see Addie.

She's standing with her family, looking smaller than when we first arrived at GBU. But she has the same bright blue eyes, the same delicate little nose, the same posture that once screamed confidence. But now? Now there's something different. Something off.

I tilt my head slightly, watching. Waiting.

Then, a gust of wind cuts through the crowd, sending caps flying, fluttering through the air like broken birds. People laugh, reaching for them, adjusting their gowns. But one cap —the wrong cap—gets caught in the wind.

And for the briefest second, I see what's underneath.

Bald patches. Jagged scars. Uneven, thin strands of hair that don't quite cover what's missing.

Addie freezes. Her hands fly up too late, grasping for the cap like she's desperate to hide. The movement is clumsy, panicked. People around her are staring. I'm staring.

She catches it, shoves it back onto her head, fingers trembling as she adjusts it. She's breathing too fast, blinking too much. And then, as if against her own will, she turns—right into my gaze.

Her lips part slightly, her face draining of color.

She looks away immediately, turning sharply on her heel, retreating into the crowd with quick, jerky movements, the way someone does when they're trying not to run. Her hands tighten around her gown, gripping the fabric like she's holding herself together. Like she's afraid she might fall apart right here, in front of everyone.

I watch her go, my smile broadening from ear to ear.

She finally learned her lesson.

Ryan's arm snakes around my waist, his grip warm, firm. His voice is close to my ear, light and easy. "Baby, take a picture with me."

I blink, shifting effortlessly into the role of the perfect girlfriend.

"Of course."

The girl currently in the frame—a teammate's sister, maybe, or just another nobody hoping to be somebody—lingers for a second too long. She touches Ryan's arm, lip gloss sticky and pink, looking at him like she's entitled to this moment.

I push closer, pressing a slow, deliberate kiss against Ryan's cheek, my nails grazing lightly over the back of his neck.

A warning.

Ryan chuckles, oblivious, pulling me in. "Just a few more pictures."

I glance at the girls still waiting for their turn.

They should be careful.

Because girls like Addie?

They thought they could touch what was mine.

Now look at her, bald and scarred.

CHAPTER
TEN

NOW - CAMILLE

RYAN IS asleep on the couch in the living room. Again. My little concoction put him out.

The afternoon sun spills through the blinds, casting slanted lines across his slack face, his mouth hanging open, a thin line of drool trailing toward his chin. The rhythmic rise and fall of his chest is the only sign of life. His right hand, useless as ever, twitches slightly against his stomach, his left curled near his head, fingers occasionally flexing in a dream.

I stare at him, my stomach turning.

This isn't the man I married.

Once, he was six feet of raw confidence, charm, and beauty. His smooth brown skin was always glowing, his bright, dimpled smile made people lean in. Ryan could walk into any room and own it without even trying. If football hadn't worked out, he could have been a sports analyst, a commentator, maybe even a TV host. People liked looking at him. People liked listening to him.

Now?

Now, he is this. This half-man, this broken thing sprawled across my couch, drooling onto the cushions.

I turn away, unable to stomach the sight any longer.

Upstairs, I hear the distinct thump of footsteps—slow, heavy, groggy. RJ.

A moment later, my son appears in the doorway, stretching, shirtless, rubbing the sleep from his eyes. He's the spitting image of his father—tall, strong, built for success. He's a better design of Ryan. Bigger than he was at the same age. He even has more charisma, which I wouldn't have thought were possible. He's what I had always dreamed of for a son. And unlike Ryan, he's still untouched by life's cruelty. Still whole.

RJ scratches his chest and yawns. "Man, I'm starving."

I'm already moving toward the stove before he even finishes his sentence.

"French toast?" I ask, already cracking eggs into a bowl.

"You already know," he says, plopping onto a stool at the kitchen island, his face still puffy with sleep.

As I whisk the eggs, I glance at him. "What happened with Gideon at the party?"

RJ hesitates, running a hand over his face. "I dunno. He got too drunk, I think. Tried to fight Hunter O'Neal. Got his ass beat."

I freeze for half a second before continuing. "You didn't step in?"

RJ sighs. "Mama C, the house was huge. I wasn't even there when it happened. And besides, you asked me to take him, not babysit him."

I press my lips together, biting back the sharp words bubbling up. He's right. I told him to take Gideon to the party, not to chaperone him like a toddler. Still, anger simmers low in my stomach.

I plate the first batch of French toast and set it in front of RJ. "After the fight, what happened?"

RJ shoves a bite into his mouth, chewing, thinking. "Didn't even know about it until I saw Hunter icing his knuckles in the kitchen. Asked him what happened, and he just told me to get my weird-ass brother. So I started looking for him, but then PJ, Nick, and Raheem showed up and invited me to IHOP. I tried calling Gideon a few times, but when he finally picked up, he just said to leave him alone, that he'd get home on his own." He shrugs. "So I went to IHOP."

My jaw clenches. "You went to IHOP while your brother was God-knows-where?"

RJ stabs his fork into another slice, completely unbothered. "Ma, he was being a little bitch about it. I wasn't gonna chase him all over town. Raheem dropped me off around two."

Midnight. His curfew is midnight.

I exhale through my nose, forcing myself to stay calm. This is not the battle to pick. Not right now.

Instead, I turn toward the stairs and yell, "Gideon! Come eat!"

Silence.

Then, a slow shuffle. The reluctant creak of footsteps.

Gideon appears, arms crossed, expression sour. He takes one look at the plate on the counter and immediately wrinkles his nose.

Gideon looks a deficient version of Ryan. Scrawny and lanky. He's much shorter than Ryan was at his age. He doesn't have the dimple that Ryan and RJ share. He at least has the same straight white teeth. And although he isn't likable amongst students, he is a decent actor. And I'm proud of him for pursuing acting at school. But of course he gets bullied for being a drama club geek.

"French toast?" he mutters, unimpressed.

I blink at him. "What kind of child doesn't like French toast?"

Gideon shrugs, his eyes flicking to RJ, who is happily devouring his meal. Ah. So that's it. He doesn't hate French toast. He just hates that it's RJ's favorite.

I slide a plate in his direction anyway. "Eat."

He huffs but sits. Picks at the food like it's poison.

I cross my arms. "Tell me what happened at the party."

Gideon doesn't look up. "Shouldn't have gone."

"Why?"

"Because all those jocks are idiots," he mutters, stabbing at his toast. "Hunter got mad because I corrected him about something stupid. And then..." He waves vaguely toward his bruised cheek. "That happened."

My eyes narrow. "What did you correct him about?"

Gideon's jaw tightens. "Doesn't matter. High school is dumb. Everything is dumb. I just need to graduate and get the hell out of this town."

The words are sharp, final. A wall slammed between us.

I know that tone. I won't get anything else out of him.

But that doesn't mean I'm done.

Because something happened last night.

And I need to know exactly what.

The sudden knock at the door breaks the tension. Three sharp raps, crisp and impatient.

Gideon visibly startles, his fork clattering against his plate. RJ barely reacts, too busy drowning his French toast in syrup. But I see the way his shoulders tighten, the way his chewing slows ever so slightly.

Interesting.

I wipe my hands on a dish towel and stride toward the front door, throwing it open to find Maci, standing on the porch with a drink carrier in one hand and an arm looped around Olivia. Bailey stands beside them, clutching a Venti-sized Starbucks cup like it holds the secret to life itself.

Olivia's hair is different.

Gone are the purple braids she put in just a week ago. She begged me for money to order the extensions online because she saw the style on Pinterest. Instead, she's styled it into a Y2K look straight out of a TLC music video—two high pigtails flipped at the ends, a dramatic swoop bang falling over one eye. It's a *statement*.

I blink. "Well, I guess Ashanti won't be copying this one."

Olivia smirks. "She wishes."

Bailey giggles, twirling a pigtail around her finger. "We were watching Aaliyah videos all night. It was inevitable."

I shake my head. These two and their obsession with the 90s and early 2000s. The oversized denim, the glittery lip gloss, the butterfly clips—honestly, it's like raising a pop star from MTV's golden era. I think it's cute though. I enjoy seeing Olivia get creative. As long as her grades remain excellent, she's allowed to experiment with her aesthetic.

Maci lifts the drink carrier. "I come bearing caffeine. And I got you one, too. I figured you could use a little pick-me-up."

I glance over my shoulder at Ryan, still snoring on the couch. Still drooling. Maci has no idea just how right she is.

"Hey Daddy!" Olivia calls out to her father. The boys look at her and roll their eyes. They know when he's asleep he can't hear. He's barely aware when he's awake.

"Hi, Ryan!" Maci also greets. He still doesn't respond. I have him knocked out cold. "Olivia is so sweet to still talk to him like nothing's wrong. I know it hasn't been easy."

Maci and I have been friends since our daughters met in middle school a few years ago. She and her husband have become close family friends. Maci is a brunette with dark brown eyes. She was rather plain in the looks department, but she was lucky to have a husband like Quenton. In his late forties, he had avoided the classic dad bod. He took athleticism seriously since he was the head football coach at Thurgood Marshall High School. Despite his athleticism, he never had a career anywhere near Ryan. He apparently played in the minor league for a few seasons in his twenties. Nevertheless, he was fit and attractive. Maci—not so much.

"Come in and have breakfast," I say, stepping aside.

"Thank you! We already ate, but you make the best French toast."

"Thanks. There's plenty, help yourselves. See, Gideon? Everyone likes my French toast," I direct my words to him. He rolls his eyes and continues to stuff his face.

The girls breeze past me, heading straight for the kitchen.

Olivia and Bailey plop onto stools at the island, pulling out their phones as they sip their drinks. Teenagers. Always half here, half somewhere else.

Maci lingers, setting her purse on the counter. "On the way here, I saw a ton of cop cars outside the Browns' house."

I pause, my grip tightening around my own cup.

Maci continues, frowning. "Like... a lot of them. Lights flashing, people standing outside, the whole thing. Wasn't that where the boys' party was last night?"

I don't respond right away. I'm watching them.

RJ and Gideon both freeze. It's subtle, but I catch it. The way RJ's chewing slows just a fraction of a second too long. The way Gideon's shoulders go stiff, his fingers clenching against the countertop.

My stomach tightens.

Maci is still waiting for an answer, oblivious to the sudden shift in the air. I clear my throat. "Yeah, that's where they were."

RJ finally swallows, leaning back against the counter like this is all casual. "No idea what that's about."

Gideon just shakes his head, muttering, "Me neither."

I don't believe either of them.

The girls continue eating, oblivious to the storm brewing in the silence. Maci takes a sip of her latte, sighing. "Well, I'm sure we'll find out soon enough. Small town gossip travels faster than WiFi."

She's right.

I'll find out.

And when I do, I better not hear it from someone else.

I glance at RJ and Gideon again, noting the way they both avoid my gaze.

Something happened last night.

Something big.

And my sons are lying to me.

Maci and I leave the kids and walk out into the living room to talk. "How are you holding up?" she asks.

"I'm fine."

"You sure? I know you're dealing with a lot. Having to be breadwinner and nurturer all on your own."

"I'm good. I promise you," I reply with a gentle smile.

"How are those sleeping pills working for you?"

"Perfectly."

They were absolutely perfect at helping further along my husband's deterioration in conjunction with the use of other meds.

"That's good to hear..." she says before switching the subject. We chat a while longer, then she and Bailey leave me alone with my family.

The rest of the day drags by in slow, disjointed moments. RJ and Gideon retreat to their rooms, Olivia disappears upstairs with her phone glued to her hand, and Ryan—well, Ryan remains a useless lump on the couch. He wakes up briefly, groggy and confused, mumbling something before shuffling toward the bathroom. I barely acknowledge him.

Instead, I spend the afternoon in my office, scrolling through schedules, making adjustments for the upcoming week for Silver Bell Cleaning. I don't do the physical work anymore—not unless I absolutely have to. My job is to oversee the operations, manage the employees, and ensure that everything runs smoothly so that I can focus on my real work.

Still, I feel a headache pressing at the back of my skull, the tension from the morning lingering like a bad smell. My mind keeps circling back to Maci's words.

A bunch of cops at the Browns' house.

Something happened.

Something serious.

And RJ and Gideon both know what it is.

I drum my fingers against the desk, staring blankly at the numbers on the screen, but all I see is the look on my sons' faces when Maci mentioned the police. The stiffness in RJ's shoulders. The slight twitch in Gideon's jaw. The way neither of them could meet my eyes.

They're hiding something.

I just don't know what.

By the time the sun dips below the horizon, the house is blanketed in the kind of stillness that always makes me restless. Olivia and RJ are holed up in their rooms, and Gideon is God-knows-where in the house, probably avoiding me.

Ryan is awake now, but still slow, sluggish—lethargic, like his body is working extra hard just to keep up with basic functions.

I watch him from the kitchen as he stares blankly at the television, the remote resting in his lap, untouched. He hasn't even changed the channel. The news drones on in the background, the anchor's voice calm, detached, discussing some local crime reports.

Then I hear it.

"A teenage girl was found dead this morning at the home of well-known businessman Joseph Brown, following a large house party held by his son, Tyler Brown, a senior at Thurgood Marshall High School. Police have not yet released the identity of the victim, but sources say—"

I don't hear the rest.

The blood in my veins turns to ice.

Dead? A girl died at the party?

I whip around, my stomach lurching, but before I can even call RJ and Gideon downstairs, a sharp knock echoes through the house.

Three slow, deliberate bangs.

I don't move right away.

Neither does Ryan. For once, he's paying attention. His head tilts slightly toward the door, his brows furrowing, confusion flickering across his face. He recognizes the sound.

I walk to the door with measured steps, my fingers tightening around the doorknob as I pull it open.

And then—

There they are.

Two men stand on my porch, side by side.

Neither in uniforms.

Both wearing unreadable expressions, but badges around their necks.

Detectives.

"Mrs. Bell? We need to speak with your sons."

And just like that—my world shifts.

CHAPTER ELEVEN

THEN - RYAN

THE THREE-YEAR ITCH. That's what they call it. The point where most guys either break through or break down. The average NFL career is three years. After that, they're either injured beyond repair, shoved into irrelevance, or clinging to some desperate comeback that never happens.

But I made it.

I didn't just survive. I thrived. Rookie of the Year, MVP, franchise player. I signed a contract so big my grandkids will still be living off it. I proved them all wrong. And today, I'm standing in a luxury suite in Jamaica, staring at my reflection, about to give the woman who's been by my side since I had nothing the wedding she deserves.

I should feel on top of the world.

Instead, my skull feels like it's being cracked open from the inside.

I grip the edge of the marble sink, closing my eyes as the pain pulses behind my right eye, radiating down my neck. I've been getting migraines since I was a kid. Nothing stops them. Not water, not magnesium, not the endless treatments I've tried. I know exactly what causes them.

Head injuries.

Years of helmet-to-helmet collisions, the kind that rattle your brain like a loose marble in a glass jar. But even before football, I was used to getting hit.

My mother made sure of that.

She called it discipline. Tough love. Said she was making me a man. But the truth? The truth is that nothing ever pleased her. If I fumbled a ball in the backyard, I got slapped. If I talked back, she'd grab whatever was closest—a wooden spoon, a belt, the back of her hand—and make sure I *felt* my mistake.

But the words? The words cut deeper than anything.

"You think you special? You think you somebody?" she'd hiss, her cigarette burning low between her fingers. "Boy, you ain't gon' be nothing but another washed-up athlete, broke and useless."

She was wrong.

I shake the memory away, straightening my tie. Would she be proud of me now? If she were alive, would she be here, watching me marry the woman I love? Or would she still look at me with that same sneer, waiting for me to fail?

I rub my temple, trying to push the migraine down, to focus on what matters.

I thought of Camille who had been the nurturer and supporter my mother had never been.

She's been with me through everything. She was there in high school, helping me with my schoolwork, making sure I ate right, rubbing my temples when these damn headaches got so bad I thought my skull would split in two. When I got drafted, she was the only one who didn't suddenly change, didn't start treating me like a walking ATM.

I owe her everything.

So why the hell can't I keep my eyes from wandering?

I love Camille. I do. But temptation is everywhere. Women throw themselves at me like I'm the last man on Earth. They don't care that I'm married. They don't care that I have a life outside of football. And sometimes... sometimes, I don't care either.

It's not that I go looking for it.

But when they come to *me*...

I always keep my dirt out of town and on the road. I never mess with women in the city we live in.

I force the thought away, adjusting my cuffs, ignoring the guilt gnawing at the back of my mind.

Today isn't about that.

Today is about Camille. About the life we're building.

Outside, I hear the ocean crashing against the shore, the distant sound of music from the reception hall, my teammates' voices laughing down the hall. The wedding is about to start.

I take one last look in the mirror, at the man I've become, at the man my mother swore I'd never be.

Then I push everything else down—the pain, the doubt, the guilt—and step out of the room.

Today, I give Camille the dream she's waited for.

And tomorrow?

Tomorrow, I deal with everything else.

As I stand at the altar, the sun dipping low over the Caribbean Sea, casting golden light over the crowd gathered on the pristine white sand, I remind myself of one thing—Camille saved my life.

And now, I'll spend the rest of mine saving hers.

The salty breeze ruffles the white fabric draped over the wedding arch, the waves rolling in slow and steady behind me. The music starts, soft and elegant, and the guests turn their heads in unison, waiting for Camille to appear.

I shift my weight, my fingers flexing at my sides. My migraine is still there, lingering beneath the surface like an old wound threatening to split open.

But I don't think about the pain.

I think about her.

I think about everything she's done for me. Every sacrifice. Every moment she held me together when I should have fallen apart.

Because the truth is—this isn't the first time my head has felt like it was caving in.

My first real head injury wasn't on the football field.

It was in my mother's kitchen.

I was ten years old. Standing too close when she was drunk and in one of her moods, the air thick with the scent of rum and sweat. She was yelling about something—I don't even remember what. I think I'd left the door unlocked when I came home from school. Or maybe I didn't wash the dishes. Either way, it didn't matter. When she was like that, any excuse would do.

I didn't see the wine bottle coming.

One second, I was standing there, taking it like I always did. The next, there was a flash of pain, the thick glass colliding with my skull, the world tilting, and then —darkness.

I woke up on the floor, head throbbing, my fingers sticky with blood. My mother was still standing over me, eyes wild, chest heaving. But she wasn't sorry.

She never was.

I looked too much like him. The man who got her pregnant, promised her everything, then left her in a foreign country to fend for herself. She worked long, grueling shifts as a CNA, barely making enough to keep the lights on, and I was just another burden. A constant reminder of the life she should have had.

I wasn't her son.

I was her punishment.

She went upside my head more times than I could count—bottles, belts, whatever was within reach. And as I got older, bigger, stronger, I stopped flinching. I stopped crying. I learned to take it. Because what else was I supposed to do?

Football saved me.

Camille saved me.

And now, as I stand here, waiting for her, I know I owe her everything.

The music swells. A hush ripples through the guests.

Then I see her.

Camille steps onto the sand, her dress cascading around her, the soft Montego Bay breeze catching in her curls. She's breathtaking. Regal. The kind of woman who looks like she was born to be worshipped.

And she's mine.

A slow smile tugs at my lips. The guests are staring at her, but she's staring at me.

I grip my hands together in front of me, keeping my face calm, steady, every bit the picture of a man deeply in love. But my stomach knots.

Because I know—if Camille ever found out about the other women, there would be hell to pay.

She looks at me like I'm her world. Like I'm the man she built, the man she sacrificed for.

And I love her. I do.

But some things?

Some things, she can never know.

CHAPTER
TWELVE

NOW - CAMILLE

THE WORDS SINK like a stone in my gut, heavy and suffocating.

We need to speak with your sons.

I keep my face neutral, my grip tightening subtly on the doorknob. "About what?" My voice is smooth, calm. The perfect mix of motherly concern and casual curiosity.

Detective Amber Winters, a tall, no-nonsense woman with sharp cheekbones and cold blue eyes, folds her arms. "There was a death at the Brown residence last night. A teenage girl. A student at Thurgood Marshall High School, Violet Kowalski."

Pretty Eyes is dead.

My stomach clenches. Violet was the girl I threatened not even twenty-four hours ago. She's the girl RJ was dating. The girl Gideon once had a crush on.

I screw my features into an expression of shocked disbelief. "Oh my God." I press a hand to my chest, tilting my head just slightly. "That poor girl."

The male detective, Michael Joseph, a stocky man with salt-and-pepper hair, nods. "We're conducting preliminary interviews with everyone who was at the party. We understand both of your sons were there."

I resist the urge to glance over my shoulder. RJ and Gideon. One my pride, the other my burden. My greatest accomplishment and my biggest complication. I should have known this day would come—trouble always finds the cracks we try to seal.

I exhale shakily, carefully calculating my next words. "Are they… suspects?"

Winters shakes her head. "At this time, no. But Tyler Brown confirmed they were both in contact with the victim last night, and we need to get a clear timeline."

I cross my arms, forcing a nervous chuckle. "Can this wait until the morning? It's been a long day, and they—"

"The sooner the better," Joseph cuts in. "Memories are fresh. We'd rather not wait."

I bite the inside of my cheek. They're not giving me room to maneuver. Damn.

I plaster on my best worried mother face and nod. "Of course. Let me go get them."

I shut the door before they can respond, turning on my heel and stalking toward the stairs. My heart is pounding, but my mind is already working, already strategizing.

I reach the top of the staircase and stop outside RJ's room first. The bass from his speaker vibrates through the walls, some rap song playing too loud for him to hear anything outside of his own world. I push open the door.

RJ is lying on his bed, scrolling through his phone, shirtless and careless, exactly as he always is. His life is easy. He makes it look easy.

But not today.

He looks up, immediately clocking my face. "What?"

"There are detectives downstairs," I say evenly.

His phone slips from his grip. His expression barely changes, but his body goes still.

RJ is a lot of things, but dumb isn't one of them.

"They want to talk to you and Gideon. It's about Violet."

His jaw tenses. "What about her?"

"She was found dead this morning."

RJ sits up so fast his head nearly clips the headboard. "What?"

The genuine shock in his voice throws me for a moment. He actually didn't know. Interesting. This is good. He looks both hurt and shocked. That means he didn't have anything to do with it.

"I need you to get dressed and get downstairs," I say. "Now."

I don't wait for a response. I stride toward Gideon's room, knocking once before pushing the door open.

He's sitting at his desk, hunched over his laptop, wearing a hoodie. He doesn't turn around, but I can see the way his shoulders pull tight when he realizes it's me.

"Detectives are downstairs," I say. "They want to talk to you about Violet. She was killed last night."

This time, there's no shock.

Gideon stays still for a long moment before finally turning to face me. His face is unreadable. "She's dead?"

"Yes."

I study him. He doesn't react like RJ. No sharp intake of breath. No wide eyes. Just a slow blink. A quiet nod.

And something else.

Something just beneath the surface.

Guilt?

Fear?

I narrow my eyes. "Do you know why they'd want to talk to you?"

He shrugs. "I was at the party. That's enough of a reason."

He's not wrong. But I'm not totally sure.

I don't push. Not yet.

Instead, I step aside, gesturing toward the door. "Let's go."

Both boys follow me down the stairs, RJ tense, Gideon

unreadable. When we reach the living room, Ryan is awake now, still sluggish from when I drugged him, sitting upright on the couch. His head moves sluggishly between the detectives and me, his foggy brain trying to catch up. Pathetic.

RJ's breath stutters, his shoulders stiff. A single tear slips down his cheek before he can stop it. He swipes at it quickly, his jaw tightening like he's trying to will himself into composure. Across from him, Gideon barely reacts. He just rolls his eyes.

Detective Winters flips open her notepad, glancing between them before settling on RJ. "Let's start with you. Walk us through your night."

RJ exhales and sits up straighter, dragging a hand down his face. "Got to the party around ten. Hung out with my friends. Had a couple drinks. Played beer pong. Nothing crazy." His eyes flick to me, testing my reaction, but I give him nothing. He keeps going, his voice thinner now. "Went to the kitchen a few times for water. Talked to some people. That's about it."

Winters nods, jotting something down. "And you left when?"

"Around midnight."

I can tell she doesn't believe him.

"Did you see Violet Kowalski?" she asks.

RJ swallows. "Yeah, of course. It was a party."

Detective Joseph, standing beside Winters with his arms crossed, cocks his head slightly. "You two dated, right?"

RJ's exhale is slow, measured. "We broke up last night."

The air thickens. I can feel it shift, the weight of the detectives' scrutiny pressing down. They exchange a quick glance, silent communication passing between them. My stomach knots. They're already mapping out a timeline. Looking for motive.

Joseph's tone is casual, but his eyes are too sharp. "And what was the reason for the breakup?"

RJ rubs the back of his neck. "It wasn't working out. She wanted more. I wasn't ready."

It's vague. Smart. The truth, minus the dangerous details.

Winters taps her pen against her notebook. "And you didn't see her after that?"

"No."

She tilts her head slightly. "You sure?"

RJ's nostrils flare. "Yes."

A thick pause. Then, she turns to Gideon. "And you?"

Gideon doesn't even look up. "Same. Got there, walked around, had some drinks. Then I left."

Joseph raises an eyebrow. "What time did you leave?"

"Late." His voice is flat.

Winters sighs, clearly losing patience. "That's not an answer."

Gideon shrugs, leaning back against the chair. "It's the only one I got."

RJ shoots him a look, but Gideon doesn't care. His whole demeanor is a wall—casual disinterest, like this conversation is beneath him. But I know my son. That's not boredom. That's deflection.

Winters doesn't let up. "Witnesses say they saw you talking to Violet."

Gideon blinks, slow and unaffected. "Yeah. I did."

RJ stiffens beside him.

Winters leans forward slightly. "And what did you talk about?"

Gideon exhales through his nose, like he's exhausted by the stupidity of the question. "I don't know, detective. School? Homework? Life? What do teenagers usually talk about at parties?"

Joseph's mouth presses into a firm line, but Winters doesn't take the bait. She just flips her notebook closed. "We'll be interviewing more students at Thurgood Marshall tomorrow. We may have more questions then."

RJ clenches his jaw, the muscles twitching. Gideon, ever the expert at shutting down, doesn't move a muscle.

Joseph slides a business card onto the table. "If either of you remember anything else, let us know."

I pick it up before either boy can. "Of course, detectives. Thank you for stopping by."

I usher them to the door, closing and locking it behind them. The moment they're gone, the silence expands, thick and unrelenting.

RJ drags a hand down his face. "I can't believe she's dead."

Gideon shakes his head. "I'm not talking to them again without a lawyer."

His voice is calm, firm. Too firm. Too sure.

Something is off. There's something I don't know.

I should push him. Demand the truth. But instead, I nod.

Because maybe... maybe that's for the best.

Olivia appears at the bottom of the stairs, her wide eyes darting between us, curiosity practically pouring from her. "What was that about?" she asks, her voice laced with unease.

"Violet Kowalski is dead," Gideon says flatly, his tone devoid of emotion. Then, without another word, he stands and walks past her, heading for the stairs like he just announced the weather.

Olivia blinks. "Dead? Dead how?" Her gaze locks onto RJ, who looks too sick to speak.

"She was bludgeoned to death at the party," Gideon calls over his shoulder before disappearing down the hall.

A sharp inhale from Olivia. "What?" She sinks onto the couch next to RJ, her fingers gripping the armrest. "We just saw her yesterday. At the game. At Luigi's."

RJ says nothing, staring at the floor like if he looks up, the truth might rip him apart.

I step forward, my voice low, firm. "RJ, tell me the truth. Do you know what happened to her?"

His head snaps up, his eyes glassy, but burning with

something close to betrayal. "No! How could you ask me something like that?" He shoves off the couch, storming toward the stairs.

Ryan is watching all of this unfold, silent as ever. The only reaction he gives is the slight narrowing of his eyes, the slow lift of his hand to rub his temple.

Olivia rushes after RJ, her voice sharp with frustration. "Ma, you *know* RJ would never do anything to hurt anyone!" she insists, turning back to glare at me.

And she's right. I do know that. Or at least, I want to believe it. RJ, for all his flaws, for all the ways he reminds me of his father, has never had the kind of darkness in him that would allow something like this.

Gideon, though?

Gideon is different.

A slow, crawling tension swells in my chest, coiling around my ribs. My fingers twitch.

And then—without thinking, without warning—I reach over and pinch Ryan's arm as hard as I can.

He winces, a sharp intake of breath, his left hand instinctively jerking up to rub the spot.

I watch him for a beat, then offer him a smooth, unbothered smile.

"Would you like some water?" I ask sweetly, as if I hadn't just hurt him.

Ryan blinks at me, hurt and confused.

Good.

Let him feel a little pain.

Let him feel something.

CHAPTER
THIRTEEN

THEN - CAMILLE

IT HAD BEEN a year since our extravagant wedding in Jamaica, four years of Ryan dominating the League, and I couldn't have been happier. Life had finally settled into the shape I had always envisioned. I was the perfect trophy wife, perfectly positioned on the arm of a star athlete.

I had everything. The dream. Luxurious cars, sparkling jewels, designer clothes, a sprawling mansion, and a penthouse in Miami with floor-to-ceiling windows that overlooked the ocean like I was some kind of queen surveying my kingdom. Shopping trips weren't just a fun weekend activity —they were an event. I'd hop on a plane to Vegas or LA just to get my hands on the latest couture before it even hit the runways.

And my friends? The WAGs. Wives and girlfriends of the elite, the ones who understood the lifestyle. The pressures. The rules. The ever-present, nagging paranoia of knowing that the moment you let your guard down, some thirsty groupie in Fashion Nova would be right there, trying to sink her claws into your man.

The only exception was my little sister, Ricki. She was the

only regular woman I tolerated. Anyone else? Irrelevant. Women who weren't married to high-profile men just didn't *get it*. They'd pretend to be supportive, but deep down, they were bitter, jealous, secretly hoping for your downfall. And let's be honest, most of them couldn't even keep up. The spa treatments, the constant beauty upkeep, the private chefs, the household staff, the tabloid scrutiny—none of it was for the weak.

And I wasn't weak.

I wasn't common anymore.

And I had no time for *common* women.

Especially the kind who thought they could take what was mine.

Back in college and high school, I wasn't as disciplined as I am now. Back then, I had… solutions. Small, creative ways to handle inconveniences. A dead rat slipped under the covers of a roommate who giggled too much at Ryan's jokes. A little chemical adjustment to Addie's shampoo that left her with patches of raw, angry scalp. And then there was *her*—the one who took a tumble down the stairs. A terrible accident, really. She should have watched where she was going.

Those were the old days.

Now, things were different. I had to be calculated. Sophisticated. Mature.

Now, all I could do was keep an eye on my prize. Make sure he stayed satisfied. Be the woman he fell in love with—the perfect wife, the one who knew how to play the game better than anyone else. I even went to his away games, just to let my presence be known. A little reminder to the sideline vultures that he was *very* much taken.

And still, they tried.

They always tried.

If only they knew.

If only they understood just how far I was willing to go to keep Ryan to myself.

Because if it ever came down to it—if I had to—I wouldn't hesitate.

I'd kill for him.

And I'd die for him.

And if I had to, I'd make sure I was the last woman standing.

Always.

The cameras flash, a steady flicker of white light bouncing off the polished marble floor. Voices blend into one another, a low hum of laughter, clinking glasses, and whispered gossip. The scent of money hangs thick in the air—designer perfumes, expensive cigars, the faint undertone of desperation from people who need to be seen, who need to be somebody in a room full of somebodies.

And I?

I *am* somebody.

I stand tall in my emerald green gown, the silk hugging my curves, diamonds glinting at my ears. My fingers rest lightly on Ryan's arm, a soft, practiced touch that says, *Look, but don't touch. He's mine.*

Ricki stands beside me, swirling her champagne, taking in the scene with the same barely disguised amusement she always has at these kinds of events. She's wearing a sleek black dress I picked out for her, something timeless and elegant. She's beautiful, in an understated way. Not like me—glamorous, polished—but in a way that draws people in without them realizing it.

Although we share the same parents, my sister and I look nothing alike. I take after our father—light caramel skin, honey-colored eyes flecked with green, and sandy blonde hair. Ricki, on the other hand, is the mirror image of our mother—rich mahogany skin, deep cocoa-colored eyes, and dark, coily hair. She's beautiful, effortlessly so, but she has little interest in enhancing her looks at the scale that WAGs do.

But she belongs here.

Even if she doesn't think so.

I invited her tonight because she deserved a night of luxury, a night to forget about them. Our parents. The ones who slammed the door in her face the second she stepped out of their narrow, suffocating mold.

Ricardo Stafford, the respected pastor. The devoted husband. The serial cheater.

How many times had my mother caught him? How many times had she sobbed into her hands, *just this once, he swore it was over, we have a family, Camille, I have to forgive him—*

And she *did* forgive him. Every time.

Yet Ricki kisses one girl, and she's an abomination. A disgrace.

It's laughable, really.

I tried to earn my way back into their favor once. Sent invitations to my wedding. Expensive gifts. A luxury car, the very one our father used to daydream about back when we were kids.

They sent it all back.

Rejected.

Like I was *dirty*.

Like I had done something *wrong*.

They only ever loved us when we obeyed. When we fit into their perfectly constructed image.

And maybe that's why I fight so hard to control everything around me.

Maybe that's why I never let anyone take anything that's *mine*.

Our father is a walking contradiction. Before he became a pastor, he was just another Harlem hustler—a smooth-talking con man with devilish green eyes that could charm the change right out of your pocket. He knew how to lure people in, how to make them believe whatever he wanted them to. A stint in prison for fraud was supposedly his wake-up call, his road to redemption. He moved to Georgia, met my mother—a strait-laced schoolteacher—and launched his greatest con yet: grifting in the church.

He preaches about righteousness and redemption, but that collection basket gets passed around three times at both the 8 a.m. and 11 a.m. services. And let's just say he doesn't just dip into the offering—he dips into the women willing to indulge him too.

"Tell me you're actually having fun," I murmur, snapping back to the present.

Ricki smirks over the rim of her glass. "I mean, free drinks, expensive food, an excuse to dress like I belong in *Vogue*—what's not to love?"

I smile, ready to relax—until I see *her*.

Across the room, wearing a dress so tight it might as well be begging for attention, a woman with light eyes is laughing just a little too loud, angling her body toward Ryan. The way she touches his sleeve, tilts her head just so, it's all so predictable. He has a type. The light eyes get him every time. It's what drew him to me.

A familiar, simmering irritation curls inside me.

I know this game. I've seen it too many times.

Ricki follows my gaze and lets out a low whistle. "She's bold."

"Brazen," I correct, taking a measured sip of champagne.

"Doesn't it bother you?"

I exhale slowly, fingers tightening around my clutch. "Ryan can't help himself."

And I *know* that. I've known it for years.

He's a star athlete, wealthy, powerful, magnetic. Women throw themselves at him. And Ryan? Well. He doesn't always *dodge*.

I could accept it. Pretend it doesn't exist. Be the blissfully ignorant wife who turns a blind eye while he "accidentally" leaves his phone face down.

But that's not me.

Instead, I keep him close. I remind these women, without

saying a single word, that there are consequences for stepping into my territory.

"Be careful not to end up like Mom," Ricki says to me. She's always been disgusted at how much Mama accepted from our father.

"I won't," I reply.

But I am like her. No. I'm worse.

CHAPTER
FOURTEEN

NOW - CAMILLE

IT'S the morning after the detectives visited our home to question the boys about Violet's death.

I haven't slept.

I tossed and turned all night, my mind running itself in circles, but Ryan? He didn't stir once. Not that he ever does anymore. The pills make sure of that. He's blissfully unaware of everything unraveling around him, numbed out of his mind, oblivious to the cracks forming in our family, the ones that are quickly spreading, splitting wide open.

Must be nice.

When I finally drag myself out of bed and make my way to the bathroom, the mirror confirms what I already know—I look like hell. The skin beneath my eyes is dark, sunken, bruised from exhaustion. My face is pale, drawn tight, lips pressed into a thin, bloodless line. I poke at the bags under my eyes. My mother would say I look 'ridden hard and put away wet.'

I turn away. No time to fix it. No time to care.

I have to think.

The detectives' questions replay in my head. I can still

hear their voices, clipped and casual, pretending this was just routine. But it's not routine. Not for us.

Violet is dead.

Murdered.

And my boys were some of the last kids to see her alive. They both have a connection to her.

RJ had a reason to kill her. He was dating her. Until I made sure he wasn't. Until I backed that girl into a corner and forced her to let him go. And Gideon? He's always been in RJ's shadow, never quite measuring up, never quite enough. He had a crush on her, I know he did. And she rejected him, for his own brother.

If either of them did this, it would be my fault. Wouldn't it?

I exhale sharply, gripping the edge of the sink.

I don't blame Violet for choosing RJ over Gideon. Who would? RJ was always destined for greatness. Gideon... he just didn't have it. The presence. The charm. The raw talent.

And if I, the woman who brought him into this world, could see that, then surely, Violet could too.

A thick, sour guilt creeps up my throat. Why do I think like this? Why am I like this?

Gideon didn't ask to be born. He didn't ask to be the product of Ryan's biggest mistake. But still, I can't stop resenting him for it.

This is Ryan's fault. He gave his best to that skank. The woman who came before me, who got the first version of Ryan. The untarnished one. And me? I got the leftovers. I got Gideon.

I shake my head, as if I can physically rid myself of the thoughts.

I try not to play favorites. I do. But RJ demands so much more of my time. His future is bright, bursting at the seams with potential. He's got scouts circling, big names lining up. We have to make a decision by March. Meanwhile, Gideon?

He hasn't even applied for schools.

With his grades, his attitude, his lack of motivation, I should just tell him to forget it. Save us both the trouble and go to community college first.

I press my fingertips to my temples, trying to rub away the headache forming there.

I am a terrible mother.

If Gideon killed *Pretty Eyes* out of jealousy, maybe this is what I deserve.

The frustration is like a geyser inside me, bubbling, steaming, rising, threatening to burst.

I need to release it before it destroys me.

I step back into the bedroom, and Ryan is exactly as I left him—pathetic, struggling, useless. He fights to sit up, wincing, his body betraying him at every turn. His breath comes in short, wheezing huffs. His left hand grips the blanket, his right arm hanging limp at his side, nothing but dead weight.

When he finally manages to pull himself upright, he looks exhausted. Like just existing is too much work.

Poor him.

I roll my eyes. "Let's get you in the shower."

He grunts in agreement, as if he has a choice.

I guide him into our ADA-compliant shower, the one I insisted we have installed when his condition worsened. The one that makes it easier for me to handle him.

I sit him down on the built-in bench, grab a towel, wet it then drape it over his face.

Then, I reach for the shower-head. I turn it on to its highest pulsing setting. It's the setting I used to pleasure myself sometimes or work out a knot in my back.

The second the water hits the towel, he flinches, sputters. His body tenses beneath my hands. His left arm jerks up, but it's weak, uncoordinated, and I easily push it back down.

The water pours in heavy streams, soaking through the fabric, pressing it against his nose, his mouth.

He gasps.

I tighten my grip.

His legs twitch, his chest heaves. The sound he makes is strangled, desperate, a gurgling attempt at breath. His body jerks, but he's too weak to stop me.

It lasts for five seconds.

Then ten.

Then fifteen.

Eventually twenty.

I'm thoroughly amused at him struggling to breathe. I finally pull the towel back, letting him suck in air in ragged, broken gasps. His body trembles beneath my hands, his good hand clawing at the shower bench, his legs twitching.

He looks up at me with wild, frantic eyes.

I smile.

And as if I hadn't just nearly drowned him, I tilt my head and ask, "Would you like some water?"

Then I hear RJ call out from the other side of the door. "Is everything okay?"

"Everything's fine!" I holler to RJ.

"Isn't that right, Ryan?"

Once I'm done showering my dear husband—my burden, my curse—I lead him back to the bedroom. He can struggle to get dressed on his own. He needs to feel useful somehow.

I move through the house, checking on the kids, and find them moving like clockwork, each locked into their morning routine. Olivia grabs a banana, RJ shovels cereal into his mouth, and Gideon—nothing. He sits at the kitchen island, hunched over his phone, detached from the world.

I debate keeping them home from school. The police will be there today, pressing kids for information, trying to piece together what happened at that party. I don't want them speaking to the cops without me. Or without a lawyer.

I clear my throat. "Boys..."

"Yeah, Mama C?" RJ responds, looking up mid-chew. Gideon simply flicks his gaze in my direction, disinterested.

"If the cops try to speak to you again, tell them you will not talk without a parent or a lawyer. Understood?"

RJ gives a small nod, but Gideon smirks, leaning back in his chair. "Already on it."

His arrogance makes my stomach turn.

And then, I remember.

The bloody shirt.

The one he walked into this house wearing the morning after the party. The one I know, deep in my bones, I should have thrown away the moment I saw it.

Could he have done something to her?

The thought is an icy fist gripping my spine.

I need to get rid of it. Now. Before the police come knocking again.

Wait.

Maybe I shouldn't. Maybe I should let them find it. Maybe an arrest would protect RJ. If they're going to come for one of my boys, let it be the one who never had a future to begin with.

No.

I inhale sharply, forcing the thought out of my mind. I'm a terrible mother for even considering it. Gideon is still my son. My responsibility.

I will protect my children. Even from themselves. Olivia finishes her banana and heads upstairs to say goodbye to her father. The boys don't bother. They sometimes forget he even exists.

I wish I could. But Ryan is my burden now. And I made him that way. The boys are bitter about the way Ryan has treated me and Tiffany throughout the years. They think his CTE is his karma. I do too.

The kids grab their bags and head out the door. RJ lingers. His energy is off. The usual spark in his eyes—gone. No jokes, no teasing, just a quiet heaviness pressing against him like an unseen weight. He's grieving. Or he's guilty.

I shudder at the thought.

He cannot be accused of this. An accusation could ruin his future—thus ruining mine.

Once the kids are gone, I waste no time. I pull out my phone and call Ricki.

She picks up after three rings, her voice groggy. "Cami, do you know what time it is?"

"You're a therapist. Shouldn't you be up helping people deal with their traumas?"

"I'm off this week." She yawns. "What's going on?"

I exhale sharply. "A girl from the kids' school has died. The cops came to the house last night to speak to the boys."

That wakes her up. "Wait, what?"

I tell her everything. How both boys were at the party. How the detectives came knocking, asking questions. How they're going back to the school today to interview the other kids.

Ricki sighs, and I can already hear the judgment in her voice before she even speaks. "Cami, you cannot let the police talk to them without a lawyer. Even if it's just a 'preliminary interview.' You know how this goes."

"I already told them not to talk without me or a lawyer."

"Good." She pauses. "I told you letting RJ move in was going to cause problems."

I roll my eyes. "Ricki, that's Ryan's son. I've been there since the beginning."

"Yeah, well, beginning or not, he's still a wild card."

I bristle. "You never liked Ryan."

"Because I've always seen him for what he was—a parasite. He's drained you and turned you into something unrecognizable." I didn't call to hear this lecture from her. She's said this many times before. She needed to drop it, especially when Ryan is the reason she was able to get her degrees. When he was bringing in the big dough, he paid for her school so that she could become a doctor. She's now a psychotherapist and prefers talk therapy over prescribing medication, though she does from time to time.

There's a beat of silence.

I don't need this right now.

"Look, I just called to update you," I say flatly. "Not to get a lecture."

"Fine. But Cami... be careful. And if you need a lawyer's name, let me know. I know a good criminal defense attorney."

"Thanks."

I hang up before she can say anything else.

With a sigh, I sink onto the couch, rubbing my temples. I hope it doesn't get to the point where I need to hire a lawyer for the boys.

I catch a glimpse of the TV. The news is on, the headline in bold red letters across the screen:

TEEN GIRL MURDERED AT HIGH SCHOOL PARTY HOSTED BY FOOTBALL PLAYER

My stomach drops. There's a picture of the pretty blonde, blue-eyed girl staring right back at me. Her story is local right now, but by the end of the week it'll be national. And soon the suspects will be broadcast too.

The newscaster's voice is smooth, practiced. "The victim, identified as seventeen-year-old Violet Kowalski, was found bludgeoned to death early yesterday morning. Witnesses report the party was attended by numerous students from Thurgood Marshall High School, including several athletes and prominent figures in the community. Police are currently investigating—"

I don't hear the rest.

The walls are closing in.

It's only a matter of time before they connect the dots.

Between Violet and RJ.

Between Violet and Gideon.

Between Violet and *me*.

My chest tightens. My hands shake.

And then another thought slams into me, harder than the first.

Money.

We're already stretched thin, and now we *will* need a lawyer. A good one.

How much is this going to cost?

And how far am I willing to go to make sure RJ walks away from this unscathed?

CHAPTER
FIFTEEN

THEN - RYAN

LIFE HAD UNFOLDED EXACTLY how I dreamed. Five years into the league, I was living it up. I worked hard and played even harder. I was untouchable, unstoppable.

The migraines were still a bitch, but medication kept them at bay—most of the time. The wear and tear on my body, though? That was another story. I was starting to feel it. The cracks, the bruises that didn't heal as fast, the stiffness that lingered after every game. Football wasn't forever. And as much as I loved it, I knew I needed an exit strategy before the sport chewed me up and spat me out like so many before me.

I had to get smart.

I loved Camille. I had promised her kids one day, and though I wasn't ready yet, I was getting close. When we did have kids, I wanted them to have everything—the best schools, trust funds, a legacy. But I needed to make sure my money stretched beyond my playing years. Football players weren't like actors or musicians; our shelf life was short. One bad injury, one unlucky hit, and it could all be over.

And honestly? I had been reckless with my money.

The managers, the agents, the lawyers—every single one

of them took their cut. What was left? I burned through it. Fast cars. Mansions. Luxury vacations. Camille got everything she wanted—anything her heart desired. And she wasn't the only one who got what she wanted out of me. I had... *others*. Women who expected gifts, shopping sprees, extravagant hotel suites in whatever city I happened to be in.

Then there were the family leeches. The ones who never gave a damn about me when I was a broke college athlete, but suddenly had emergencies, business ventures, medical bills, school fees—hand out after hand out.

I had to stop.

No, I would stop.

Just... after this weekend.

Because right now, I was in Vegas. Off-season. Throwing my cousin Kevin a bachelor party that was eating through my wallet at a frightening speed. I had promised him a weekend he'd never forget, and I was delivering. The best suites, VIP sections at the clubs, private tables at the casinos. I had even agreed to pay for his wedding. But after this?

Kevin was on his own.

"You don't gotta take care of me, man," Kevin said, exhaling a thick stream of cigar smoke as we lounged poolside at the Bellagio. The sun glared off the water, shimmering like liquid gold. "I can handle myself. But if you really want to set yourself up, I got an idea that's gonna be beneficial for both of us."

I side-eyed him, swirling the ice in my whiskey glass. "That so?"

"There's a prime plot of land in Montego Bay. Right on the beach. Some big-time drug dealer used to own it, but he got locked up, and the government seized the property. It's about to go up for auction. If we buy it, we can build a luxury resort." He leaned in, eyes glinting. "Think about it. *Bell Resort*. A five-star destination in the heart of the island. Your parents' homeland. Don't you wanna own a piece of it?"

I lifted my glass to my lips but didn't drink.

Jamaica.

The place my parents came from. The place I was *supposed* to have roots in, but never truly did.

I'd only been there on vacation and for our wedding.

My father? MIA since day one. Never called. Never visited. Never even pretended to care. Sometimes, I wondered—if he had known how big I'd made it, how famous I'd become, would he have stuck around? Would he have claimed me?

My mother? She was another story entirely. She hadn't abandoned me. Not physically, at least. But she might as well have. She didn't love me. She tolerated me. Raised me with an iron fist and a short temper. Every time she looked at me, she saw him—the man who left her. And she made me pay for it.

She was gone now. A tragedy, they called it. A tragic accident.

I called it freedom.

Maybe owning a piece of Jamaica would make me feel connected to something. Maybe it would fill whatever was missing in me.

I set my glass down. "I need to know more. But I'm intrigued."

Kevin grinned. "I got everything. Facts, figures, projections. This is a sure thing, bro. High-end, all-inclusive, celebrity hotspot. We could be looking at generational wealth."

I listened as he laid it all out, numbers rolling off his tongue like he had memorized every damn detail. It sounded solid.

It sounded like exactly what I needed.

An investment. A safety net. A legacy.

"Alright," I said finally, stretching my legs out and leaning back in the lounge chair. "I like it. I'll run it by Camille, but—"

Kevin snorted. "Why? It's your money, man. You earned it

getting your ass tackled every Sunday. She's already got the designer bags, the mansions, the credit cards. She doesn't need to sign off on this."

I smirked, taking another sip of my drink. "Yeah, well. Happy wife, happy life, right?"

Kevin rolled his eyes but didn't argue.

We clinked glasses.

The money was still flowing in, but I knew it wouldn't last forever.

If I didn't play this smart, I'd be another washed-up athlete with nothing to show for my time in the league.

I refused to let that be my story.

The sun was setting, bleeding deep oranges and purples across the Vegas skyline. The pool deck was buzzing—half-naked women draped over lounge chairs, drunk businessmen laughing too loud, music pulsing low from hidden speakers. The air smelled like coconut sunscreen, cigar smoke, and tequila.

I was already three drinks in, my body loose, my mind riding that perfect wave of relaxation.

That's when she appeared.

She was the kind of woman who turned heads without trying. A walking, breathing thirst trap. Voluptuous, surgically perfected, skin the color of velvety mocha. Her long, dark hair cascaded down her back, sleek and straight, like she had just stepped out of a rap video. Probably because she had —I recognized her. Tiffany something.

Not my usual type.

I had a thing for light eyes. Hazel, green, blue. Camille's green and honey-colored gaze had hooked me the moment I met her. But this woman? She was different. A bombshell. Dangerously beautiful.

And she was looking right at me.

"Ryan Bell?" Her voice was like silk, smooth and practiced. She stopped in front of us, one manicured hand on her hip, a sultry smile curling her glossed lips.

Kevin straightened in his seat, grinning. "Girl, you a fan?"

She barely glanced at him. Her eyes were locked on me.

I leaned back in my chair, letting the moment stretch. "That depends on why you're asking."

"I want a picture and autograph. I need proof that I met you."

Her smile widened. She was good. Knew how to work a room, how to make a man feel like the center of the universe. I could tell she'd done this before.

She pulled out her phone. She slid in close, her perfume wrapping around me—sweet, heavy, intoxicating. The kind of scent that clung to your clothes, your skin, your memory.

We snapped the picture.

"Now, where should I have you sign?"

"Your call."

She tilted her head, eyes flicking toward the hotel behind us. "I have something you can sign… upstairs. Room 2809."

The implication hung between us, thick as the Vegas heat.

Kevin let out a low whistle, shaking his head. "Damn, you don't waste time, do you?"

Tiffany just winked, running a finger down my arm. Then she turned and walked away, hips swaying, knowing full well I was watching.

And I was.

I felt Kevin's stare burning into the side of my head.

"Bro," he said, shaking his head with a laugh. "C'mon now."

I exhaled slowly, dragging a hand down my face. "What?"

"You know what." He smirked, leaning in. "You goin' or nah?"

I rolled my shoulders, stretching out like the conversation was casual. Like it wasn't clawing at the part of my brain that still had some self-control. "Man, I don't know. Camille—"

"Camille ain't here," Kevin cut me off. "And you're in Vegas."

I rubbed the condensation off my glass, staring into the melting ice like it held the answer.

Kevin clapped me on the back. "What happens in Vegas stays in Vegas, man. You know the rules."

I did.

And still—something twisted in my stomach.

It wasn't guilt. Not yet.

It was the thrill. The rush of temptation.

Tiffany had given me an open invitation.

And now?

It was just a matter of whether or not I was going to take it.

CHAPTER
SIXTEEN

NOW - CAMILLE

WITH THE KIDS out of the house, I finally have a chance to breathe. To think. To get some damn work done.

But first, I make breakfast for Ryan. Or rather, I put food in front of him and watch him take forever and a damn day to eat it. It's like watching a sloth chew. Agonizing. He used to inhale food like he was afraid someone would snatch it off his plate. Now, he picks at it, drags his fork through the eggs like he's rearranging furniture. It's exhausting just looking at him. I don't have time for this.

I leave him to his never-ending meal and retreat to my office, where I attempt to throw myself into work. Silver Bell Cleaning won't run itself. I have schedules to finalize, invoices to send, and employees to keep from quitting because these days, nobody wants to work. But my mind? It won't focus.

Because no matter how hard I try to distract myself with spreadsheets and supply orders, one thought shoves its way to the front of my mind, over and over again.

Did Violet tell anyone I threatened her?

My stomach twists. That girl looked genuinely scared when I told her to stay away from RJ but maybe not scared enough. If she went running her mouth to her little friends about it, it could look really, really bad. And not just for RJ.

For me.

I try to push the thought away and do something productive.

I spend the next few hours working, stressing, and Googling everything I can about Violet's murder. I needed to know all there was to know about Pretty Eyes. So far, the internet hasn't exploded yet. The local news is still catching on, but the true crime vultures haven't swooped in. No gossip blogs. Only one Reddit thread. Just speculation.

"It's always the boyfriend."

I see the phrase pop up in a Facebook comment and it makes my skin go cold.

Because they're right. It is always the boyfriend.

And Violet's boyfriend was RJ.

I swallow against the nausea creeping up my throat.

No. No, it's not always the boyfriend. Maybe she had another boyfriend.

That's it. Maybe there was some other guy no one knew about. Someone obsessed with her. Someone unhinged.

I go full internet sleuth and start digging through her socials.

Instagram first. Teenagers love Instagram. Or… do they? I swear Olivia once called it the "retirement home of social media." Kids these days are impossible to keep up with.

Joke's on her, though, because Violet does have an IG. But it's bare. Just five posts. All carefully curated like she was auditioning for an Aerie campaign.

•One of her, holding a boba tea, face tilted just right so the sun hits her perfectly.

•A sunflower field. Classic.

•A skating rink. Cute.

• And two mirror selfies, where she looks exactly how a teenage girl should look—young, beautiful, and invincible.

I move on to TikTok. It's mostly dance trends and cutesy videos. Nothing useful. But the comments?

Disgusting.

Grown men. Creeps. Commenting things like "stunning" and "gorgeous" and dropping heart-eye emojis like she was legal.

They knew she was a kid. Didn't stop them.

One of them could've been obsessed. One of them could've followed her to the party. One of them could've killed her.

I make a note to come back to this later.

Snapchat? Empty.

YouTube? One single video. A review of a Morphe eyeshadow palette. No views, no comments. Barely a blip in the algorithm.

This girl didn't have enemies. Not online, at least.

So who the hell wanted her dead?

Not my sons.

...Right?

Am I in denial?

My throat tightens.

Murder *is* in Gideon's DNA. Because it's in mine.

It's a terrible thought. A mother should never think that about her child.

But it's the truth.

His father is a pathological liar, a serial cheater, a man who left destruction in his wake. And Gideon? He's his father's son.

He came home bloody. He said he had been in a fight but was that all? Was there something else he wasn't telling me? He wasn't above lying to me. What if...?

I shake my head. No. I can't think like this.

But RJ? Who knows what kind of psychotic genetics are hiding in his mother's side of the family?

Ricki once told me she didn't fully trust RJ. "He's too perfect," she said. "People like that? They scare me."

I laughed it off at the time, but now? Now I wonder. Because he's been acting off.

Grief? Or guilt? I don't know. But what I do know is that RJ cannot be implicated in this murder.

If RJ goes to prison, his future is gone.

And so is mine.

The weight of it all settles on my chest like a boulder. I need a lawyer. A damn good one. I storm into the living room and shove Ryan awake. He groans, squinting at me like I'm a demon. I don't have the patience for this. He's probably still mad about the whole waterboarding incident this morning, but I don't care.

"What's the name of that lawyer who got Patrick Jones out of that murder accusation?"

Patrick was one of Ryan's ex-teammates. Great player. But beat a man to death in a nightclub parking lot and somehow walked away with a slap on the wrist.

Ryan rubs his face, his movements sluggish, like his body is weighed down by more than just fatigue. There was a time when he was constantly surrounded by people—teammates, coaches, old friends from the league. They used to drop by unannounced, crowding our house, filling the space with loud laughter, inside jokes, and memories of the glory days. But that was years ago. Before the injuries. Before the decline. Before the money started drying up.

Now? They don't even call.

Not because they don't care.

Because sickness and bankruptcy are contagious.

No one wants to be around a man whose life has become a cautionary tale. The one who had it all and lost it. The one who serves as a reminder that no matter how high you climb, the fall can come just as fast.

I watch as he grabs his phone, his fingers fumbling slightly, slow, unsteady. There was a time when he used to text at lightning speed, handling multiple conversations at once, juggling business deals, social plans, and whatever side chick he was entertaining that week. Now? It takes him too long just to type one simple sentence.

We can't afford it.

That's what he types on the screen before turning the phone toward me, as if that should be the end of the conversation.

I feel my jaw tighten, the anger bubbling up beneath my skin like hot oil in a frying pan. Like hell we can't.

Ryan has no idea what I will do. What I am capable of doing.

My voice is sharp, cutting through the thick, suffocating air between us. "If I have to put this house up to save your son, I will."

And I mean it.

This house, these walls, the roof over our heads—none of it means a damn thing if it means losing RJ. He is our only shot. Our last chance at returning to the life we worked for, the life we deserve. If I have to sell my soul, I will.

Ryan stares at me, something flickering behind his dull, lifeless eyes. Maybe it's recognition. Maybe it's regret. Maybe it's just the understanding that he has no control over this. Over me. Not anymore.

A few moments pass.

Then—

A new text pops up.

Xavier Witherspoon.

I hate that it's come to this.

That I am here, desperate, scrambling, clawing to hold on to what little power I still have.

But there's no other choice.

Because I still have our 401(k)s.

I still have assets I can drain, accounts I can empty, moves I can make.

And I will burn through every last cent if it means keeping my boys out of prison.

Especially RJ.

He is my golden ticket.

My last hope of getting back to the life I deserve.

And I won't let anyone—not the cops, not the media, not the truth—take that away from me.

CHAPTER
SEVENTEEN

POLICE INTERVIEW PART 1

DETECTIVES Amber Winters and Michael Joseph stepped into the front office of Thurgood Marshall High School, the fluorescent lights overhead humming softly. The school was busy, students rushing through the halls between classes, the typical mix of chatter, laughter, and lockers slamming shut. But beneath the normalcy, there was something else. A tension.

The air in the administrative office felt heavier than it should. Teachers whispered among themselves. The secretary's fingers flew across her keyboard as she avoided making eye contact. Everyone knew why the police were here.

Violet Kowalski's murder had shaken the school to its core.

Winters and Joseph had already conducted their first round of interviews—starting with Tyler Browne, the senior who had thrown the now-infamous house party. Tyler, the privileged son of a local real estate mogul, had shown up with his parents' lawyer in tow, clearly prepped for the conversation. He was arrogant but cooperative, answering their questions with a rehearsed ease that suggested he had nothing to hide.

Still, they hadn't ruled him out completely.

A forensic team had combed through the Browne estate, collecting evidence, sweeping for fingerprints, fibers, DNA—anything that could tell them what really happened that night. The house, a sprawling mansion on the outskirts of town, had been packed with over a hundred teenagers, music blasting, alcohol flowing freely. The chaos of the night made it difficult to pinpoint where and when the crime had occurred. But they were closing in.

Tyler had claimed that after the party started winding down, he crashed on one of the massive leather sofas in the living room. He swore up and down that he never left that spot until morning, when his father woke him up in a fit of rage over the state of the house.

The forensic team had collected Tyler's clothing from that night, and while there were no visible bloodstains, his shirt and jeans were still being tested for microscopic traces of evidence.

So far? He looked clean.

Which meant they needed to move on to the next batch of students.

Students who had more direct contact with Violet that night.

Students who may have had motive.

Students like Ryan Bell Jr. and Gideon Bell.

They weren't ready to speak to the brothers just yet. Not until they had a clearer picture of what Violet's last moments looked like. Not until they had enough to push them.

So they started with Melissa Shumpert—Violet's best friend.

She had been too emotional to speak last night, but today?

Today, she would talk.

Detective Winters tapped her pen against her notepad, watching Melissa Shumpert closely as she spoke. The girl had composed herself since last night, her makeup fresh, her glossy dark hair pinned back into a neat ponytail. But grief clung to her like an ill-fitted coat—her eyes were puffy, her voice thick with the remnants of too many tears shed in too little time.

Still, Winters wasn't fooled. Grief had layers. And guilt often hid inside it.

"You and Violet were best friends," Winters prompted, keeping her tone gentle but firm.

Melissa nodded, swallowing hard. "Since we were eight. We did everything together. Dance classes, sleepovers, school projects… and this year, we were in Mean Girls together. We played best friends." She laughed, a short, brittle sound. "It's kind of messed up now, huh?"

Winters barely blinked. "You both auditioned for Regina George, didn't you?"

Melissa hesitated, her lips parting, then closing again. "Yeah. But Violet got it. And she deserved it. She was… perfect."

That hesitation was all it took.

Joseph leaned forward slightly, his eyes sharp beneath heavy brows. "Did it bother you that she got the lead?"

Melissa's gaze darted between the two detectives before she forced out a small shrug. "I mean, sure. Who wouldn't be a little bummed? But it wasn't like I was mad at her or anything. She was my best friend."

Winters noted the slight bite in her tone, the tension in her fingers where they gripped the hem of her sweater. Discontent. Jealousy. A sliver of something sharp beneath the grief.

Winters circled something in her notepad but didn't push. Not yet.

"Did Violet have any enemies?" Joseph asked.

Melissa scoffed. "She was beautiful and popular. Of course, she had haters." She shifted in her chair, rolling her eyes. "Girls like Emma K., Parker, and Samantha—they were always running their mouths, talking behind her back, spreading stupid rumors. But the only one at the party was Samantha."

Winters made a note.

"And what about a boyfriend?"

That question earned a small giggle, a flicker of something almost smug in Melissa's expression. "Violet had a lot of guys who wanted to be her boyfriend."

"But she was dating RJ Bell?"

The smugness deepened, along with a knowing smirk. "Secretly."

Joseph arched a brow. "Why secretly?"

Melissa shrugged. "RJ told her he didn't want the whole school in his business. But honestly?" She leaned forward slightly, lowering her voice like she was whispering some great scandal. "I think he wanted to keep it quiet so he could hook up with other girls. Violet thought so too. And last night? She finally called him out on it."

Winters exchanged a glance with Joseph. Like father, like son.

"So they fought?"

Melissa nodded, tucking her hands under her thighs. "Yeah. At the party. She accused him of cheating. They were yelling at each other, and then he pulled her upstairs—one of the guest bedrooms. I figured they were making up, or... you know."

Winters caught the way Melissa's cheeks pinked slightly.

"You thought they were having sex?"

"I mean... probably? They did before." Melissa wrinkled her nose. "I didn't follow them or anything. That would be weird."

Joseph tapped his notepad. "That was the last time you saw Violet?"

Melissa's breath hitched. Her gaze dropped to her lap.

"I called her. A bunch of times. But she never picked up. And I had to leave because my sister came to pick me up. My parents are insane about curfew. If I was late, I would've gotten in so much trouble."

She swallowed again, her voice faltering. "I didn't want to interrupt RJ and Violet if they were, you know, doing it again. But now? God, I wish I had."

Winters let that settle for a moment before speaking. "Do you think RJ hurt her?"

Melissa's head snapped up, eyes wide. "I—no! I mean, I don't know. He was mad. Really mad. But... RJ's a nice guy, right?"

Winters tilted her head, watching her closely.

Melissa didn't sound so sure.

And that doubt?

That was enough to crack things wide open.

CHAPTER EIGHTEEN

THEN - CAMILLE

THE MIAMI SUN draped itself over the penthouse like it was showing off, golden rays spilling across the balcony where I reclined on a cushioned chaise lounge, oversized sunglasses perched on my nose, a virgin strawberry-mango daiquiri sweating in my hand. The infinity pool shimmered just a few feet away, the water so still and blue it could've been a page from a luxury travel magazine.

This was what I worked for.

Well, *technically*, Ryan worked for it. But let's not get caught up in semantics.

The other wives and girlfriends—my fellow WAGs—lounged around me, chatting lazily about their latest luxury hauls. Birkin bags, diamond tennis bracelets, Chanel's new summer collection. We had just returned from an all-day shopping spree in the Design District, dropping more money in a single afternoon than most people saw in a year. My feet still ached from the effort of strutting through boutiques in five-inch heels, but it was a pain I welcomed. A rich woman's struggle.

I let my head fall back against the chair, closing my eyes

behind my designer shades, and allowed myself to *bask*. To *savor*.

Then my phone dinged.

I ignored it at first, stretching out my legs and sighing in pure bliss. But then it dinged again. And again. Three sharp chimes in quick succession, a distinct rhythm that meant one thing—my little sister, Ricki, was about to ruin my mood.

With an irritated sigh, I snatched my phone from the table and swiped to my messages.

And there it was.

A screenshot of a tabloid article, the headline bold and shameless:

"NFL Star Ryan Bell Spotted at Atlanta Hotel with Video Vixen—Cheating Scandal?"

Beneath it, a grainy yet unmistakable photo. Ryan. My husband. The man I built.

Standing in the lobby of an Atlanta hotel. With Tiffany.

Even in the blurry image, I could recognize that surgically enhanced silhouette. The impossible curves, the weave cascading down her back in thick, perfectly styled waves. The same woman I had caught him with before at an away game in California. The same woman I had confronted him about. The same woman I had been trying to figure out how to get rid of.

And yet, here we were.

The virgin daiquiri in my hand suddenly tasted bitter.

Another message from Ricki popped up beneath the image.

Ricki: Girl. GIRL. Are you seeing this?!

Yes, I was seeing it.

Had been seeing it.

For the past year.

I exhaled sharply and typed back, I'll call you later.

My phone immediately started ringing.

Of course.

I put in my bluetooth earbuds and dropped the phone

onto the table beside me. "Ricki, I am relaxing. What do you want me to say?"

"What do I want you to say?!" Ricki's voice screeched through the earbuds. "I want you to acknowledge that your husband is trash!"

I rolled my eyes. "He's not trash."

"He's not? Then what do you call a man who consistently cheats on his wife?"

I flinched. She didn't understand. No one did, Ryan simply can't help himself. But things will change soon.

"Ricki, I'll handle it," I said, lowering my voice. "This is my marriage. I made him. I built this life. I knew what I was getting into."

"Oh my God," she groaned. "You sound like a pick-me."

I scowled. "A what?"

"A pick-me, Camille! A woman so desperate for a man's validation that she'll excuse any and every one of his sins just so he won't leave her! You're just like Mom!"

I gasped, fully offended. "Excuse me? I am not desperate. That's my husband. I have invested in this man! And—" I hesitated for the first time, running a hand over my stomach, pressing my palm lightly against the flat surface that, soon enough, would not be flat anymore. "—I'm pregnant."

Silence.

Then a heavy sigh. "Oh, Camille."

"Once he knows, he'll stop," I insisted. "This will change things. He won't risk his family for some—some Tiffany."

Ricki scoffed. "You keep saying he can't help himself. Camille, he's not a dog humping a stranger's leg. He can help himself. He chooses not to."

I said nothing.

Because I didn't want to admit she might be right. But she didn't know the truth about him. She didn't know his secrets. No one did.

―――

Ryan stumbled through the door, his movements slow, heavy with exhaustion. He looked like hell—his usually confident, broad-shouldered posture slumped forward, his six-foot frame weighed down by something more than just fatigue. The designer duffle bag he always carried with him after away games slipped from his grip, landing on the marble floor with a dull thud. He barely glanced in my direction before dragging a hand down his face.

"I have a migraine coming on," he muttered, pressing two fingers to his temple, his voice thick with weariness. "I need to lie down."

I had been waiting for him, perched on the edge of the velvet sofa, my legs crossed, arms folded, my entire body a coil of restrained energy. The penthouse was dimly lit, the soft glow from the kitchen casting long shadows across the sleek, modern furniture. It was late, and the city outside was alive—horns honking, tires screeching, the occasional burst of laughter from pedestrians below. But in here, the air was thick, heavy, suffocating with the weight of what I needed to say.

I stood abruptly, cutting off his path to the bedroom, planting myself firmly in front of him. "We need to talk. This can't wait."

His brow furrowed. He exhaled sharply, shaking his head. "Camille, not now."

"Yes, *now*," I snapped, the words coming out sharper than I intended. My pulse was erratic, pounding against my ribcage. My fingers curled at my sides, nails digging into my palms to keep from trembling. "I know you're still messing with Tiffany."

There. I said it.

His entire body tensed for a split second, barely perceptible, but I saw it. A fraction of hesitation. A slight shift in his stance. He flinched, but only slightly. His poker face was decent—he had years of practice dodging press, spinning lies into half-truths. But he wasn't good enough to fool me.

I had been watching him for too long.

I knew every tick, every micro-expression. The way his jaw locked when he was irritated. The way his nostrils flared when he was about to lie. The way his lips pressed into a firm line when he was caught.

I exhaled slowly, forcing my voice into something calm, something controlled. "I've known about her, Ryan. This isn't new. I asked you to stop. You *promised* you'd stop." My voice was steady, but my fingers itched to grab the phone sitting on the coffee table, to shove the screen in his face. Instead, I simply gestured toward it, the article still pulled up—his name bold in the headline, his face grainy in the attached photo, standing in the lobby of an Atlanta hotel. And right beside him? *Her.*

A slow, heavy sigh escaped his lips. He dragged a hand over his face, rubbing his temples like I was the migraine and not the guilt clawing at his insides. *"Camille, I have something to tell you—"*

"I'm pregnant."

The words left my mouth before I could second-guess them.

And just like that, the room changed.

The air thickened.

The space between us shrank into something unbearably heavy, something filled with unspoken things neither of us were ready for.

Ryan's hand dropped from his face, his posture going rigid. His usually relaxed expression froze, his gaze snapping up to meet mine. For the first time since he walked in, he actually looked at me. Not past me. Not through me. But *at me.*

But it wasn't excitement I saw in his eyes.

It wasn't relief.

It wasn't even shock.

It was something else.

Something *dark.*

Something that made my stomach twist into tight, uncomfortable knots.

I swallowed hard, my voice lowering, sharpening, the way it always did when I sensed something was off. "Tell me what, Ryan?"

He hesitated.

And in that hesitation, I knew.

Whatever he was about to say—

It was going to change everything.

CHAPTER
NINETEEN

POLICE INTERVIEW PART 2

THE TENSION IN THE SMALL, windowless office inside Thurgood Marshall High School was suffocating. The air was stale, the fluorescent lights buzzing faintly overhead. Detectives Amber Winters and Michael Joseph sat at a cheap wooden table, their notepads open, their gazes fixed on the door. They didn't have to wait long.

Ryan Bell Jr. walked in, shoulders squared, face unreadable. He was wearing his football letterman jacket over a crisp white tee, his athletic build imposing even as he moved with slow, deliberate steps. He sat down across from them but didn't lean back, didn't slouch. He stayed stiff, posture perfect, hands folded in front of him like he was in church.

Winters watched him carefully. He wasn't nervous. But he was... controlled.

Too controlled.

She exchanged a glance with Joseph before folding her hands neatly on the table. "Ryan, thanks for meeting with us. We know this has been a tough couple of days."

RJ didn't respond. He just blinked at her, his face carefully blank.

Joseph leaned forward slightly, voice calm but firm. "We just have a few questions about the night of the party."

RJ let out a slow breath through his nose. Then, with the same unshakable calm, he said, "I've been advised not to speak to you without a lawyer present."

Winters arched a brow, glancing at Joseph, who exhaled through his nose in mild frustration.

"Advised by whom?" Winters asked, even though she already knew the answer.

RJ's lips curled slightly. Not quite a smirk, not quite a smile. "My mom."

Winters fought the urge to scoff. Of course. Camille Bell. The ever-watchful, ever-controlling matriarch.

"You understand," Joseph cut in, his voice a little sharper, "that we're just trying to piece together what happened to Violet Kowalski. You were dating her. You were seen arguing with her at the party. You were the last person seen with her before she disappeared upstairs."

RJ didn't flinch, didn't shift, didn't blink. "I've been advised not to speak to you without a lawyer present," he repeated, like a rehearsed line.

Winters sighed. "Alright, Ryan. If that's how you want to play it."

RJ stood smoothly, pushing the chair back with a controlled grace that only someone used to being watched could manage. "Are we done here?"

"For now," Joseph muttered.

RJ nodded once, turned, and walked out of the room, his footfalls heavy against the tile floor.

The door shut behind him, leaving a thick, cloying silence in his wake.

Winters tapped her nails against the table, watching the door as if she could still see him through it. "Well, that's not the reaction of an innocent kid."

Joseph scoffed. "Not even a little." He scribbled something

in his notepad. "He's guilty of something. Maybe not murder, but something. That was way too smooth."

Winters nodded. "Most kids his age would be nervous, defensive, maybe even angry if they were innocent. But he? He was calculated. Controlled."

Joseph leaned back in his chair, eyes narrowing. "What does he have to hide?"

There was only one way to find out.

Winters stood, stretching her arms before straightening her blazer. "Call in the brother."

The moment Gideon Bell walked in, Winters knew this interview would be just as fruitless.

He was lanky, much leaner than his older brother, his dark hoodie hanging slightly off his narrow frame. He strolled in with a slower, almost lazy gait, his hands stuffed deep into his pockets, his gaze unreadable. But his energy? It was nothing like RJ's. Where RJ was controlled and poised, Gideon was... detached. Amused, even.

He slumped into the chair across from them, stretching his long legs out in front of him.

Winters exchanged a glance with Joseph before clearing her throat. "Gideon, thanks for coming in. We wanted to—"

"I ain't speaking to the cops without my lawyer," Gideon said flatly.

Winters blinked.

Joseph let out a sigh. He knew this was coming. "We just want to talk about Violet and get any information from you about her. Don't you want to help us find her killer?"

Gideon smirked, leaning back lazily. "Oh... more than anything."

Winters studied him, unimpressed. He heard the sarcasm and it piqued his interest. " We're trying to find out what happened to Violet. You were at the party. You knew her. You—"

Gideon clicked his tongue and shook his head. "I ain't

speaking to you without my lawyer," he repeated, almost mockingly this time.

Winters sighed. Joseph closed his notepad.

"Alright, Gideon. You can go," Winters said, barely suppressing her irritation.

Gideon grinned, standing up. "Pleasure talking to y'all."

He strolled out, slow and deliberate, like he had all the time in the world.

The moment the door shut, Winters let out a sharp breath. "That one's cocky."

Joseph exhaled through his nose. "I don't trust him."

Winters nodded, flipping through her notes. "Neither do I."

The silence in the interrogation room stretched thick between them. Detective Winters exhaled, shaking her head as she flipped her notepad shut.

"Well, that was useless."

Joseph leaned back, rubbing a hand over his face. "Two brothers, same script." He shook his head, tapping his pen against the table. "They're hiding something. The question is—what?"

Winters drummed her fingers against the table, her mind working through the possibilities. "RJ seems scared as if he's about to get in trouble. And Gideon? He's got that cocky, detached energy, as if he's above getting in trouble."

Joseph hummed in agreement. "You see the way Gideon was almost… amused? Like he's watching us try to solve a puzzle he already knows the answer to?"

Winters narrowed her eyes. "Yeah. And I don't like it. We'll get them to talk eventually." She tapped her pen against her notes before pushing up from the chair. "Let's bring in the next one."

Joseph nodded, flipping through the list. "Hannah Cartwright."

They called for her, and moments later, the door opened.

Hannah was a stark contrast to the Bell brothers. Small,

soft-spoken, and visibly nervous. She sat down across from them, her arms wrapping around herself like she was trying to shrink. Her eyes were red-rimmed, the skin beneath them puffy—she had been crying.

"Thanks for speaking with us, Hannah," Winters said, her tone gentler than before.

Hannah sniffed, nodding. "Of course."

"We know this is difficult," Joseph added, watching her closely. "But anything you can tell us about Violet—her friends, her relationships, anything that might help us understand what happened—would be really helpful."

Hannah's throat bobbed as she swallowed. "Violet was my best friend. We... we weren't like super close like Melissa, but we talked every day. We've known each other since middle school."

Winters nodded. "Were you at the party?"

"No." Hannah shook her head quickly. "My parents don't let me go to parties. I wasn't allowed."

Joseph made a note of that. "Did Violet mention anything about the party before she went? Anything unusual?"

Hannah hesitated. "She... she really liked RJ."

The room shifted. Subtle, but Winters felt it.

"She wanted to be open about it," Hannah continued, her voice small. "She was tired of it being a secret. She kept saying, 'If he really cares about me, he'll stop hiding me.'"

Winters arched a brow. "And did RJ want to keep it a secret?"

Hannah let out a bitter laugh. "Yeah. He told her he didn't want the school in his business. But let's be real—he just wanted to mess around with other girls."

Winters felt Joseph shift beside her. They didn't have to look at each other to know they were both thinking the same thing.

Like father, like son.

"Did you like RJ?" Joseph asked, carefully neutral.

Hannah's eyes flicked up, surprised. Then, she let out a

small, embarrassed chuckle. "Who doesn't?" She shrugged, a touch of something wistful in her voice. "Everyone does. He's funny. He's smart. He's the best football player. And he can fight."

Winters' brows lifted. "Fight?"

Hannah's expression faltered, like she realized too late that she had said too much.

Joseph leaned in slightly. "You've seen him fight?"

Hannah hesitated, then nodded. "Yeah. Twice this year. Once with Taj Westin. Once with Josh Cooper."

"Why?"

"I don't really know, you would have to ask them."

Winters jotted something down. "Would you say RJ has a temper?"

Hannah chewed her lip.

"Be honest," Joseph coaxed.

She sighed. "I mean… yeah. I guess. He's been in fights. I've seen him punch and kick lockers when he gets mad. One time, he got yelled at for being late to class, and he flipped a whole desk over before storming out."

Winters' pen paused.

Joseph's eyes flicked toward her.

"What happened after that?" Winters asked.

"Nothing," Hannah said with a scoff. "The teachers don't really do anything to him. He's RJ Bell. He's going D1. One day he'll go pro, like his dad. He's the best player on the team. They just let it slide."

Winters leaned back in her chair, watching Hannah carefully. The girl was still talking, still venting, but Winters' mind was racing.

A short temper. Physical outbursts. A history of fights. A secret relationship with the victim.

And the last person seen with her.

Hannah wiped at her nose. "I should've gone to the party," she muttered. "I should've been there."

Winters took in the way her fingers twisted in her lap, her

knee bouncing beneath the table. "Did you talk to Violet before the party?"

Hannah nodded. "Yeah. She was excited. Nervous. But excited. She thought RJ was finally gonna go public with their relationship."

Joseph tapped his pen against his notepad. "And you last spoke to her when?"

"Around eight. Before she left."

Winters nodded. "Alright, Hannah. You're free to go. We might need to follow up, though."

Hannah sniffed again, nodding, then rose from her chair and walked out.

The moment the door shut, Winters let out a slow exhale.

Joseph leaned forward, resting his forearms on the table. "What are you thinking?"

Winters tapped her fingers against her notes. "Two fights this year. Locker-kicking. Desk-flipping. Teachers turning the other way." She shook her head. "If RJ has a temper, and he and Violet were arguing, and they disappeared upstairs together..."

Joseph blew out a breath. "Yeah."

Winters flipped her notepad closed with a soft *thwap*. "Right now? We're looking at two primary suspects."

Joseph nodded. "We'll know more when the autopsy is finished and forensics is complete. We need to start building a case to get a warrant to search the Bell house. Those boys are involved in some kind of way.

A heavy silence stretched between them.

The pieces were aligning.

And the Bell brothers?

One of them was guilty.

They just had to figure out which one.

CHAPTER
TWENTY

THEN - RYAN

I FUCKED UP.

Bad.

Worse than bad. The kind of bad that changes everything permanently.

Camille is staring at me, her eyes glassy, her hands trembling at her sides, waiting for me to speak. To explain. To tell her why, after everything—after all my promises, all my bullshit reassurances—I've managed to ruin us anyway.

I can't look her in the eyes when I say it.

So I don't.

I brace my hands against the kitchen counter, pressing my palms into the cool marble like it can somehow anchor me to this moment, keep me from floating off into the inevitability of what's coming next. My mouth is dry. My head is pounding. My heart is a steady drum of panic, panic, panic.

I exhale, slow and shaky. "Tiffany's pregnant."

The words drop like an anvil, shattering the space between us.

For a moment, Camille doesn't move. Doesn't breathe.

Then, a sharp, broken inhale.

Her lips part, but no words come. Instead, her fingers press into the counter behind her, knuckles straining to break through her skin. It's like she's trying to keep herself upright, trying to keep from crumbling into a heap on the marble floors of our penthouse.

Then, she laughs. A dry, humorless sound that scrapes against my nerves like a dull knife.

"You're lying."

I force myself to look at her then. To meet her eyes and let her see the truth for herself.

I don't have to say another word.

She knows.

Her breath catches. Her body sways. The hand that was pressed against her stomach just moments ago now curls into a trembling fist.

"You're lying," she says again, but her voice is weaker this time. Fragile. Like if she says it enough times, it'll make it true.

I wish it did.

I wish I could tell her that this isn't happening. That it's all some sick misunderstanding. But there's no escape from this.

I press a hand over my face, dragging it down as if I can physically wipe the guilt off my skin. "I didn't mean for this to happen, Camille."

Her eyes snap back to mine, fury cutting through the heartbreak. "Didn't mean for this to happen?" Her voice is sharp now, trembling with rage. "You didn't mean to keep sleeping with her for a year? You didn't mean to lie to my face, to make me feel crazy for suspecting something was going on? You didn't mean to put another woman in the exact same position I'm in right now?"

I flinch, but I don't respond. Because what the hell can I say?

She shakes her head, a hysterical, disbelieving smile

tugging at her lips. "You act like this is some accident. Like you tripped and fell between her legs. Like you just stumbled into ruining our entire marriage." Her voice cracks on the last word.

I hate myself for doing this to her.

"I swear to God, I never wanted this," I say, my voice low, barely above a whisper.

"But you did it anyway," she spits. "You chose this, Ryan."

I turn away, pressing both hands against the counter, gripping the edge like it's the only thing keeping me from breaking apart completely. She doesn't understand. Not really. She thinks this is about Tiffany. She thinks Tiffany is the problem.

But she isn't.

Tiffany was never the point.

Tiffany was the escape.

Camille is controlled, measured, perfect. She knows how to dress, how to smile, how to say the right things, how to carry herself in a way that elevates me. She's my equal in every way. She's the woman I'm supposed to have. The good girl. The one who fits into the image of what a star athlete's wife should be. She's polished, graceful, and respectable. Even with that dark side of hers, she's my light.

And I love her for that.

But Tiffany?

Tiffany is easy. She's reckless. Wild. She doesn't ask for anything real, doesn't expect commitment or loyalty. She doesn't care if I show up smelling like another woman. She only wants me in the moment. She doesn't care about my career or my reputation. She's a good time.

And the worst part?

I liked that.

I liked having someone who didn't hold me to the standard Camille did. Someone who didn't look at me like I was supposed to be a role model or a good man.

I liked that Tiffany let me be the worst version of myself.

Camille is staring at me, waiting for me to say something, to explain, to fix this. But there's nothing I can say to make this go away.

"How far along is she?" she finally asks.

I hesitate. Just for a second.

It's a second too long.

"Ryan," she warns, her voice shaking.

I swallow hard. "Four months."

Her face twists, something breaking inside of her. I see it happen in real time, the way her chest rises and falls too quickly, the way her lips part like she can't get enough air.

Four months.

She presses a hand to her stomach, as if trying to reconcile the fact that she isn't the only one carrying my child. And that she would give birth before her.

That I put her in this position.

That I destroyed her.

Her breaths turn shallow, rapid. She blinks too fast, her head shaking slightly, as if she's trying to force herself to wake up from this nightmare.

I exhale, closing my eyes briefly before opening them again to find Camille still staring at me, her face unreadable beneath the storm of emotions I know must be raging inside her. Her chest rises and falls in uneven breaths, her lips slightly parted like she wants to say something but doesn't know where to begin.

And then she does.

"How do you even know it's yours?" Her voice is sharp, but there's something else underneath it—something desperate, grasping for a way out of this nightmare. A final sliver of hope that this, somehow, isn't real. That there's still a way to undo it all.

I run a hand over my face, rubbing at the tension gathering between my brows. "I'm going to get a paternity test."

Camille lets out a bitter laugh, shaking her head. "A paternity test," she repeats, like the words taste disgusting in her mouth. "So you don't even trust her, but you trusted her enough to sleep with her without protection?"

I wince.

She doesn't let up.

"Did you ask her?" she presses, stepping closer now, her arms folded tight across her stomach like she's holding herself together. "Did you ask her to get rid of it? Like you asked me to sophomore year?"

That hits me like a brick to the chest.

I flinch, eyes snapping up to meet hers.

She's still holding on to that?

It was over a decade ago. We were kids. I was nineteen, terrified, barely able to handle the pressure of football, let alone fatherhood. I didn't know what to do back then. I thought asking her to get an abortion was protecting her. Protecting us.

I thought we had moved past it.

But clearly, Camille never did.

I hesitate for half a second—too long—because she lets out a choked laugh, her head tilting as realization washes over her.

"You didn't," she breathes. "You never even asked her."

I shake my head slowly, the weight of it settling over me like a lead blanket. "She won't," I say, and I don't need to elaborate. Camille already knows why.

Tiffany sees this baby as a payday.

A guaranteed check for the next eighteen years.

Camille's breath shudders as she inhales sharply, blinking too fast. Her fingers press harder against her arms, digging in, knuckles going white. And then she whispers the words I was dreading.

"She's going to have her baby first."

Her voice is so small. So broken.

And it kills me.

I take a step toward her, reaching for her instinctively, but before I can even make contact—she slaps me.

Hard.

The sound cracks through the air, echoing off the walls, louder than it should be in the suffocating silence that follows. My head jerks to the side, my skin burning, but I don't react. I don't move. I just take it.

I deserve it.

Her whole body is trembling now, her breath ragged, tears welling in her eyes but refusing to fall. "I can't do this," she whispers, voice shaking. "I can't be here with you right now."

I open my mouth, but nothing comes out.

What can I even say?

She turns abruptly, storming toward the bedroom. I don't follow. I just stand there, rooted to the floor, watching as she yanks her suitcase from the closet and starts throwing clothes into it. The sound of fabric rustling, zippers snapping, drawers slamming—it's the sound of my life unraveling in real-time.

She's leaving.

I step forward. "Camille—"

"I'm staying with Ricki," she cuts me off, voice cold, distant. "Don't call me. Don't text me. Don't come looking for me."

She zips up her bag, yanks it off the bed, and strides past me without another word.

And just like that—she's gone.

I let out a long, shuddering breath, my entire body sagging with exhaustion. The weight of everything pressing down on me all at once. The betrayal, the guilt, the shame, the suffocating certainty that I just lost the best thing that ever happened to me.

A dull, familiar ache pulses behind my eyes, creeping toward the base of my skull. My vision blurs at the edges, the pressure mounting. I barely make it to the bed before I collapse onto it, dragging the pillow over my head to block out the world.

The migraine is already settling in.

I don't fight it.

I let it take me under.

Because at least when I'm unconscious, I don't have to face what I've done.

CHAPTER
TWENTY-ONE

POLICE INTERVIEW PART 3

DETECTIVES Amber Winters and Michael Joseph are locked in this suffocating, windowless office for hours, cycling through student after student, story after story, lie after lie.

Teenagers are exhausting.

They're either overly dramatic, withholding for the sake of being difficult, or so obsessed with their own social hierarchies that they can't imagine a world beyond high school gossip. Winters starts the day patient, methodical, carefully taking notes—but now her pen taps against the table in a steady, irritated rhythm.

What they've learned so far is frustratingly... basic.

Violet Kowalski is well-liked. Popular, smart, effortlessly pretty in a way that makes other girls resent her but still want to be around her. Aside from a few frenemies and some petty rivalries, no one has anything bad to say about her. No whispered rumors of deep grudges, no ex-boyfriend with a vendetta, no history of bullying.

RJ Bell Jr. is much the same. Charismatic, athletic, the

golden boy of Thurgood Marshall High. Teachers adore him, girls crush on him, and guys either want to be him or be in his circle. He has no real enemies—at least, not any who'd want to kill him or his girlfriend.

Which leaves them with this:

RJ doesn't want to go public with Violet.

RJ and Violet argue at the party.

RJ is the last person seen with her before she disappears.

And that? That gives him motive.

Winters exhales sharply, tossing her pen onto her notepad and rubbing her temples. "I swear to God, if I have to listen to one more teenager talk about who's dating who and who has the most followers on Instagram, I'm going to lose it."

Joseph grunts, flipping through his notes. "They're a self-absorbed generation. None of them give a damn about anything unless it directly affects them."

"Yeah, well, one of them is a murderer," Winters mutters.

Joseph sighs, running a hand through his short-cropped hair. "We're building a case, but we still don't have anything concrete."

Winters picks up her pen again, clicking it twice. "We have enough to keep RJ as our prime suspect. We just need more."

Joseph glances at his notes, then nods. "Let's bring in Josh Cooper."

Josh Cooper saunters into the room with all the energy of someone pulled away from something far more important—probably scrolling on his phone or doing whatever it is high school boys do when they're not being questioned about a murder.

He flops into the chair, stretches his legs out, chewing his gum like they're the ones inconveniencing him. "What's up?"

Winters stares at him. "Josh, thanks for coming in. We just need some clarity on your relationship with RJ Bell Jr."

Josh blows a bubble, lets it pop, then smirks. "We're cool now."

Winters arches a brow. "Now?"

Josh shrugs, like the details don't matter. "Yeah, we had a thing before, but it's over."

Joseph leans forward slightly. "What kind of 'thing'?"

Josh exhales, clearly annoyed. "I was messing with Gideon. You know, bullying him, giving him a hard time. RJ didn't like it. He told me to stop, I didn't, I swung first—he beat my ass. End of story."

Winters taps her pen against her notepad. "So he was defending his brother?"

Josh nods. "Yeah. Dude doesn't go around looking for fights. He's not crazy. But if you push him? He'll handle you."

Joseph tilts his head. "Did Violet have anything to do with this?"

Josh frowns. "Nah. Why would she? Look, it ain't no secret Gideon liked Violet. And apparently he completely stopped talking to her during the rehearsals for *Mean Girls*. He was salty that she chose RJ. She knew Gideon first."

The detectives exchange a glance.

Winters gives a tight nod. "Alright, Josh. Thanks for your time."

Josh doesn't need another invitation. He's already up, stretching as he heads for the door.

Joseph leans back in his chair, arms crossed. "RJ's controlled in his aggression. But Gideon... he has motive too."

Winters nods. "He's not a loose cannon. If he fights, it's for a reason. Gideon is bitter—and that can make for an impulse killer." She taps her notes. "Let's see what Taj Westin has to say."

Taj Westin walks in with an attitude.

Where Josh is indifferent, Taj is bitter. He plops down in the chair with a scowl, arms crossed like he's daring them to accuse him of something.

"Am I a suspect now?" he snaps.

Winters ignores the tone. "We just need to clarify some details. Tell us about the fight between you and RJ Bell Jr."

Taj scoffs, rolling his eyes. "Oh, you mean the time he broke my nose?"

Joseph stays calm. "Yes. Tell us what happened."

Taj clenches his jaw. "I liked Olivia. A lot. Thought she liked me too. So, one day in the hallway, I grabbed her ass."

Winters' face remains blank. "And RJ saw this?"

Taj snorts. "Saw it? That motherfucker snapped. Didn't even let me explain. He went full-on protector mode. Next thing I know, I'm on the floor, blood pouring out of my nose, and this dude is still swinging."

Joseph jots something down. "Did RJ get suspended?"

Taj huffs out a humorless laugh. "Hell no. You get suspended from school, you get suspended from three football games. And our principal wasn't about to let that happen. They let me take the fall. I got in-house suspension. RJ? Nothing. Walked away like the hero."

Winters tilts her head slightly. "Do you think RJ is capable of murder?"

Taj hesitates.

A flicker of uncertainty crosses his face before he exhales sharply and shakes his head. "Nah, man. He doesn't fight just to fight. He fights when he has to."

Joseph nods slowly. "But Gideon?"

Taj lets out a sharp laugh, shaking his head. "That kid's weird as hell."

Winters raises a brow. "Weird how?"

Taj shrugs. "He had a thing for Violet. Everybody knew it. We were doing rehearsals for the *Mean Girls* musical, and it was obvious. The way he looked at her, the way he followed her around. He wasn't on her level, though. She liked RJ. But that didn't stop him from acting like a lovesick puppy."

The detectives exchange another glance.

Taj stands, already assuming the conversation is over. "Y'all done with me?"

Winters nods. "For now."

The door clicks shut behind him.

They stare at their notes, uncertainty thick in the air.

They don't know which brother killed Violet.

But they know one of them did.

CHAPTER
TWENTY-TWO

NOW - CAMILLE

I PACE THE LIVING ROOM, the floorboards creaking beneath my heels, my pulse hammering against my temples. My arms are crossed, nails digging into my biceps as I stalk back and forth, trying to keep my fury from spilling over.

Ryan watches me from the couch, eyes clouded with confusion and fear, his hands twitching uselessly in his lap. He looks small. Weak. And that pisses me off more than anything.

I stop in my tracks and fold my arms tighter. "That lawyer requires a $20,000 retainer. That's what it's going to cost to protect your sons." My voice is even, but I'm simmering beneath the surface, my skin hot with anger.

Ryan blinks. His brow furrows, like he's trying to process the number through whatever fog of medication and regret he's permanently trapped in. His mouth opens slightly, but no words come out.

I tilt my head. "You think maybe one of your cousins could help us out?" My voice drips with sarcasm.

Ryan doesn't answer.

Of course, he doesn't.

Because we both know the truth.

Those same cousins he threw money at for years, the ones who always had their hands out, always had some sob story about rent being due, about their baby needing diapers, about wanting to flip houses or open a car wash, or a resort, or some other silly investment—they're nowhere to be found now. They took from him until there was nothing left, and the second the well dried up, so did they.

I take a step forward, close enough to see the beads of sweat gathering at his hairline. He stinks of helplessness, of stale breath and faded glory, and it's disgusting.

I lean in, lowering my voice. "Of course not," I say softly.

Then, with quick precision, I pinch the soft flesh of his forearm.

Hard.

Ryan lets out a sharp, pained hiss, his body jolting, but he doesn't fight me. He never does. He just winces, jaw clenched, shoulders tensed like a beaten dog expecting another hit.

I release him, stepping back. "You've wasted so much money," I continue, shaking my head in disgust. "And now, when we need it the most, you've got nothing to show for it."

Ryan doesn't meet my eyes.

Coward.

I sigh dramatically, exhaling through my nose. "I have to fix this, like always."

He swallows, blinking rapidly, his gaze flickering toward me but never quite landing. "Ca...mille..." His voice is raspy, barely there.

The house is thick with tension, the air heavy with unspoken fears and everything left unsaid.

A text comes across my phone and I perk up. It reads, "It's been too long without you. Can you meet me at our spot tonight?"

I want to meet him. I need to meet him. I need to let go of some of this tension. But I can't right now. I have to work on something much bigger. I respond with, "Tonight's no good."

He responds with a sad face emoji. I shrug it off. As bad as I would love to be wrapped up in a man's embrace right now, I can't be distracted.

Hours have passed since I sat in this same spot, staring at Ryan's blank, useless expression, willing him to be something —anything—other than the pathetic shell of a man he's become. But the time has done nothing to settle the knots in my stomach. If anything, they've gotten worse.

The kids are back from school now, their footsteps echoing through the house as they move around, their energy subdued, their voices lower than usual.

I take a slow, measured breath, my fingers gripping the stem of my wine glass tighter than necessary. The lawyer will be Zooming the boys tonight. Then, tomorrow morning, he'll come in person, so we can go to the police station for their official interviews. He said it's better to go before the cops come knocking again, before they start putting pressure on them, twisting their words, making them look guilty even if they aren't.

The thought makes me sick.

I glance over at RJ. He's sitting at the kitchen table, slumped forward slightly, his fingers idly tracing the condensation on his glass. He hasn't touched his food. Hasn't said much of anything.

His shoulders are tight. His jaw clenched. His usual easy-going smirk has been wiped clean from his face.

I haven't seen him this sad since his mother died.

Olivia notices too. She pours him a glass of lemonade, sliding it across the table toward him. "Here," she says, her voice softer than usual. "You look dehydrated."

RJ blinks, looking up at her like he's just now realizing she's there. He takes the glass, offering a small nod. "Thanks, Livvie."

The moment should pass quietly.

But of course, Gideon can't let that happen.

He watches from where he's leaning against the counter, arms folded, eyes sharp with something I can't quite place. Then, with a scoff, he shakes his head.

"She's always nice to you," he mutters. "But never to me. And I'm her full-blooded brother."

His words cut through the air like a knife.

Olivia turns to him, rolling her eyes. "Because you're a creep," she says flatly.

Gideon pushes off the counter, his lip curling. "And you're a spoiled bitch."

"Yo, don't talk to her like that!" RJ jumps up ready to pound on Gideon.

"Okay, enough." I cut in, rubbing my temples. The last thing I need right now is their constant bickering. "You all are family! You don't speak to each other that way."

Olivia flicks her hair over her shoulder, looking away like she's already over it. But Gideon? He's still watching. Still simmering.

I sigh and pour him a glass of lemonade, placing it on the counter near him as a peace offering.

He doesn't take it.

He scoffs instead, stepping back. "Everyone in this house is stuck on RJ's nuts," he mutters before storming off, disappearing down the hallway.

My grip tightens on the counter.

The words sit heavy in my chest, pressing against something raw.

Gideon's always been resentful. Always felt like the outsider in his own home. But this? This felt... different.

I exhale, rubbing my arms as a chill runs down my spine.

For the first time, I let myself think it.

145

What if Gideon killed Violet just to hurt RJ? Just to get back at Ryan?

I take a slow sip of my wine, but it doesn't settle the unease slithering through me.

For the first time, I'm truly afraid of my own son.

CHAPTER
TWENTY-THREE

NOW - CAMILLE

I HATE that we need a lawyer. Hate that we have to treat our boys like criminals before the police do it for us. But I'm not stupid—I know they're suspects. The cops will be back, sniffing around like vultures, and when they come knocking, I want us armed and ready.

The overhead light flickers, casting sharp, jagged shadows across the marble countertops, the kind that make everything feel colder, heavier. The laptop screen glows in front of us, bright and clinical, illuminating every twitch of Gideon's face like he's already under interrogation. I sit next to him, close enough to feel his body tense, but not touching. Not comforting.

Ryan is slouched beside me, a ghost of the man he once was. His head hangs low, his hands trembling just enough for me to notice. He's not here—not really. His body is in the chair, but his mind? Somewhere else, drifting, lost in whatever fog his illness has wrapped around him today. I can feel it, the disconnect, the absence. And I hate it.

Across the screen, the bank-breaking attorney, Xavier

Witherspoon watches Gideon the way a lion watches wounded prey—calculating, assessing, waiting to see if he'll make a fatal mistake. He's not a man who wastes time, and I can already tell he's not buying what my son is selling.

And neither am I.

Across the screen, Xavier Witherspoon stares at Gideon through sharp, calculating eyes. He's not a man who wastes time. Everything about him—his clipped tone, the way his pen taps against his notepad, the impatience in his posture—tells me that he's already forming opinions, already assessing whether or not my son is a problem he can fix.

I already know what his answer will be.

"Alright, Gideon," Xavier starts, his voice even but firm. "Tell me exactly what happened the night of the party. Walk me through it, step by step."

Gideon shrugs, leaning back in his chair. "RJ and I got there around nine-thirty," he says. "As soon as we walked in, RJ left to go drink with his friends."

I hate that RJ ditched him, but I understood. However, I imagine that could've ticked him off even more and made him want to kill her.

"And you?" Xavier asks, watching him closely.

Gideon runs a hand over his face, exhaling loudly, like this is all some exhausting inconvenience. "I walked around. Grabbed a drink eventually. Played some beer pong."

"Time?" Xavier presses.

Gideon shrugs again. "Dunno. Maybe an hour into the party?"

Xavier's face doesn't change, but I can feel the shift in his energy. That's not a good enough answer.

"Gideon, the police are going to ask you for a timeline," he says, voice sharper now. "If you can't give them one, they're going to fill in the blanks themselves, and trust me, you don't want that."

I drape an arm around Gideon, rubbing his shoulder. "Baby, try to think," I say softly.

He stiffens under my touch and jerks away. "I am thinking," he snaps.

The rejection stings, but I don't react. This isn't about me.

Gideon shifts in his seat. "I think it was around ten-thirty when I started playing beer pong. Hunter said something dumb and I corrected him. He was drunk, got in my face, started talking crazy. Next thing I know, we're fighting."

Xavier leans forward. "You got into a fight at the party?"

"Yeah," Gideon says, rubbing his jaw like he can still feel the hit. "He punched me first. Tyler and Max broke it up. I left after that."

"You left?" Xavier repeats.

"Yeah," Gideon says, shifting in his seat. "I was pissed. Didn't wanna come home yet. So I wandered around for a while, ended up at the park. My phone died, so I just… I don't know, watched the stars and the moon, contemplating the meaning of the life. Fell asleep. Didn't get home till eight in the morning."

Ryan's head turns slightly at that, his unfocused eyes squinting like he's just now processing what's being said. He's so useless.

Xavier doesn't look convinced. "Did anyone see you leave?"

Gideon shakes his head. "Nope."

"You didn't tell anyone you were leaving?"

"Nope."

A pause.

Xavier's fingers tap against his notepad. "That doesn't sound good."

I inhale sharply. I know exactly what he means.

Gideon rolls his eyes. "What do you want me to say? That's what happened."

Xavier's voice cools, but there's a razor-sharp edge to it. "Let me be clear—you need someone to confirm your whereabouts that night. Without a witness, your story sounds like an excuse. People go to parks all the time but they don't fall asleep in them overnight unless they're homeless or hiding from something."

Gideon tenses but doesn't say anything.

Xavier sighs. "Tell me the truth. All of it. What was your relationship with Violet Kowalski?"

Gideon's lips press into a thin line. "I liked her. Asked her out during Mean Girls rehearsals. She said no, I moved on. No big deal." He leans back in his chair, voice flat. "I'm used to rejection."

The room is silent.

I watch Gideon's face, watch the way his fingers tap against the table, the way his shoulders are just a little too tense. He's lying. I know it. I know my son.

Xavier exhales through his nose. "Alright, you can go."

Gideon smirks, throwing up two sarcastic thumbs-up. "Can't wait to do this again tomorrow with the cops."

"Fix your attitude before then," Xavier says coolly. "Answer only when I tell you to answer. Keep it short. Do not get cute with them."

Gideon doesn't respond. He just leaves.

I let out a slow breath, my pulse still racing.

Xavier looks at me, and I already know what he's thinking.

He doesn't trust Gideon's story.

Neither do I.

I always knew this day would come.

Not exactly like this. Not with a high-priced attorney staring down my son across the kitchen table, drilling him for details about a dead girl. But in some deep, unspoken part of me, I always knew.

You don't raise a boy to be the golden child, the savior, the one who's supposed to pull the entire family out of the mud, without wondering—what if he cracks? What if all that pressure, all those expectations, all the sacrifices I made to get him to this point, turn him into something else? Something dark. Something dangerous.

Or what if his sibling grows jealous and decides to set him up for murder. Has Gideon cracked? No matter what, I can't let either of them go to prison. If Gideon did this, it's my fault. I've poured so much into RJ that he probably feels rejected.

Well, now it's RJ's turn.

"Alright, RJ," Xavier says, voice clipped, professional. "Tell me exactly what happened the night of the party."

RJ exhales slowly, dragging a hand down his face. "We got there around nine-thirty. As soon as we walked in, I took a shot with Tyler and some of the guys."

"Then what?"

He hesitates.

Just for a second.

I catch it. Xavier catches it.

"Violet found me around eleven," RJ finally says. He shifts in his chair. "We talked."

Xavier leans in. "About what?"

RJ clears his throat. "She wanted to be my girlfriend, like out in the open. I told her I wasn't looking for anything serious. That I couldn't claim her right now because I needed to focus on getting into college."

A chill licks up my spine.

Xavier doesn't react. Just nods, waiting.

RJ's voice drops, like he's ashamed of what he's about to say. Good. He should be.

"She got mad. Started yelling, accusing me of cheating. I told her to come upstairs so we could talk in private but..." He rubs his palms together. "We had sex."

The room goes silent.

Then a small sound from the doorway.

I whip around. Olivia.

She's standing there, eyes wide, her lemonade glass trembling in her hands.

"Go to your room," I snap.

She hesitates, looking from me to RJ, then scurries away.

I turn back to my son. My perfect son.

The one I built. The one I sacrificed for.

And I feel like throwing up.

Xavier keeps his voice even. "What happened after?"

RJ slumps forward, bracing his elbows on his knees. "She told me she loved me." His laugh is bitter, humorless. "I said 'yeah right.' She threw a shoe at me."

A sharp pain stabs through my temple.

Oh, RJ.

"And then?" Xavier prompts.

"I left her there in the bed. Went downstairs. Saw Hunter icing his knuckles. Someone told me to go get Gideon. I looked around, couldn't find him. Called him, no answer. Then I went back to the party, played some drinking games. After midnight, PJ, Nick, Raheem, and I went to IHOP. Got home around two."

His hands drag down his face.

"That's it?" Xavier asks.

RJ nods, eyes heavy with exhaustion. "That's it."

Xavier watches him for a long beat. Then he sits back. "Alright."

RJ stands, drags himself toward his room, shoulders hunched.

The second he's gone, I exhale a breath I didn't know I was holding.

Xavier doesn't sugarcoat it. "It doesn't look good."

My stomach turns.

"But it depends on what the police have. The autopsy will tell us more. Right now?" He shakes his head. "Both boys are suspects. It all comes down to evidence."

My pulse pounds in my ears. I look over at Ryan, who has fallen asleep.

"I'm sorry that you have to handle this on your own," Xavier says when he notices me look at Ryan.

I should have just let him rest in the bedroom because he

was of no help. I just wanted him to be involved. We're at this point because of him. RJ is his son.

But RJ can't go to prison.

He can't be a murderer.

I won't let him be.

CHAPTER
TWENTY-FOUR

THEN - CAMILLE

IT'S BEEN FOUR MONTHS, two weeks, and six days since I left my husband for impregnating a weave-wearing whore with an Instagram sponsorship deal and an ass built by Miami's finest plastic surgeons.

Not that I'm counting.

I miss the way he used to look at me before this mess. I miss waking up next to him in our ridiculous California king bed that's bigger than most New York apartments. I miss the way we'd sit on the couch and pretend to watch a movie while I scrolled through my phone and he absentmindedly rubbed my feet.

I miss my life. Our life.

And he knows it.

Ryan has been relentless. Flowers arrive at my condo every single morning, the scent of overpriced peonies and roses suffocating me before I even finish my first sip of coffee. Jewelry boxes litter my nightstand—Cartier bracelets, diamond studs, a watch so heavy it feels like I'm wearing handcuffs. Guilt gifts.

Because nothing says sorry I impregnated a video vixen like a fur coat in the middle of a Miami summer.

I drape it over my shoulders anyway.

Ricki watches me from across the couch, her arms folded tight, eyes narrowed into slits. "Camille, what the hell are you doing?"

"What does it look like?" I lift my wrist, admiring the way my new diamond bracelet catches the light. "I'm being romanced."

Ricki lets out a groan so deep it sounds like it came from her soul. "You cannot be serious."

I am serious.

I'm *very* serious.

I have spent four months, two weeks, and six days punishing Ryan. Making him suffer. Freezing him out. And in those four months, two weeks, and six days, I have realized one thing: I am not built for this.

Ryan has been my lifeline since we were in high school. Loving him isn't just something I do—it's *who I am*. It's in my bones, woven into the very fabric of my being. It's in my muscle memory, as automatic as breathing. Even when I hate him, even when I *should* walk away, my heart still beats in rhythm with his.

When my parents cut me off, I had nothing. No family. No home. No safety net. Just a void where my old life used to be. It was supposed to be a punishment, a lesson in obedience, but all it did was push me deeper into Ryan's arms. He and Ricki were all I had left, and between the two of them, only one made me feel wanted.

Ryan made me believe that choosing him was worth losing everything else. And maybe, back then, it was. He held me through the nights I cried over my mother's cold rejection, promised me we'd build our own family, one that no one could take from us. He told me that we were bigger than their judgment, stronger than their disapproval.

He made me feel invincible.

So, of course, I stayed. Of course, I forgave. Over and over and over again. Because when you've anchored your entire existence to someone, letting go doesn't feel like freedom. It feels like drowning.

So, I am not built to be without him.

I am not built for lonely nights in a condo without the man I love. I am not built for eating takeout alone. I am not built for falling asleep without the sound of Ryan breathing beside me.

And most of all?

I am not built for watching Tiffany's pregnant ass galavanting all over TMZ like she's some sort of basketball wife.

She is loving this. She's doing interviews, taking maternity photos, cradling her stomach like she's the first woman in the history of humanity to carry a child. And the worst part? People are eating it up.

Meanwhile, I have been in exile, waiting for the moment when it will all be over.

Ryan needs me.

And I need him.

Ricki shakes her head, pacing the room like she's the one with high blood pressure. "Camille, he's gonna do it again. That man could have a thousand furs delivered to your doorstep, and he'll still end up in somebody else's bed. He's just like Daddy!"

"He won't," I say, smoothing the coat over my shoulders.

"Oh my God. And you're just like Mama."

"He's learned from his mistakes." I ignore her comparisons to our parents. We were nothing like them. I knew how to put the women in place that Ryan messed with. My mother let it slide. Tiffany was going to pay, eventually.

Ricki cackles. Actually cackles. "Has he? Or has he just learned how much money it costs to get you to come back?"

I roll my eyes. "Ricki."

"No, Camille. You are better than this." She throws up her hands. "You have a whole baby inside of you! His baby! And he's got a matching set with a woman who probably can't even spell 'paternity test'! You really think this is gonna end with you two playing house again? This isn't some Hallmark movie."

I rub my stomach absentmindedly, a small smile tugging at my lips. It's a boy.

I found out last week.

And when I go back, when I make things work with Ryan, we are going to name him Ryan Jr.

Because *I* am Ryan Bell's wife.

Not Tiffany.

Not some chick from an old Jay Z music video.

Me.

And when I come back? She'll know it.

I glance at my phone, where Ryan's latest text sits unanswered.

"Come to dinner. Let me fix this."

I stand, shaking off the coat and turning toward Ricki, who looks so disappointed in me.

She doesn't get it.

She doesn't know what it's like to build a man from the ground up, to put all your energy, your love, your entire future into someone, only to watch them make a mistake that threatens to ruin it all.

She doesn't understand that Ryan is mine.

And I intend to keep him.

I grab my purse and my keys.

Ricki's mouth falls open. "You're really gonna do this?"

I glance back at her. "I love him."

She snorts. "You love a lifestyle."

I don't argue.

I don't have to.

I just smile. "Same thing."

And with that, I leave.

CHAPTER
TWENTY-FIVE

NOW - CAMILLE

I HAVE SPENT years carefully constructing the image of the perfect family, the perfect life. And now I'm sitting in a police station, gripping the armrest of a chair that smells like cheap disinfectant, while two detectives tell me that my sons are suspects in a murder investigation.

The irony is not lost on me.

I should be at home right now, sipping a glass of Sauvignon Blanc while avoiding my inbox full of invoices for the cleaning business. Instead, I'm here, in this godforsaken, fluorescent-lit hellhole, pretending that I'm not two seconds away from completely losing my shit.

Ryan is at his adult day care program—a place I use on the days when I just need to breathe without worrying about him wandering off or staring at the wall for hours. Olivia is at school, blissfully unaware that her family is on the verge of making the evening news. And my boys? My boys are sitting across the hall, while these detectives circle them like hungry wolves.

They've informed us that Violet was bludgeoned to death but they can't find the murder weapon. They suspect the murderer has taken it. They were super graphic in letting us know whoever killed her would have gotten blood splatter on them. And blood is impossible to clean.

Detective Winters clears her throat, and I snap back to the present, to the conversation that is spiraling further and further out of my control.

"We're going to need the clothes they wore that night," she says, her voice smooth and even, like she's ordering lunch instead of trying to dismantle my entire life. "And we'd like DNA samples. There was skin under Violet Kowalski's fingernails."

I feel my stomach lurch. Skin. Under her nails.

I keep my expression neutral, but my brain is screaming. Gideon had blood on his shirt that night. I had told myself —*forced* myself—to believe that it was all from the fight he had. But what if it wasn't? What if it really was *her* blood?

Xavier doesn't even blink. If this news rattles him, he doesn't show it. That's why we're paying him an ungodly amount of money. Because he's the only one keeping me from throwing myself across this table and demanding to know what the hell they think they know.

"You'll need a warrant for that," Xavier says, his tone almost bored. "My clients have already given their statements. That's all they're giving."

Detective Joseph leans back in his chair, folds his arms, and looks at us like we're personally wasting his time. "So, let me get this straight. You're refusing to cooperate with a murder investigation?"

Xavier smiles, a slow, condescending curve of his lips. "No. I'm simply reminding you that my clients have rights. If you want their DNA, get a judge to sign off on it. Otherwise, this conversation is over."

Winters lets out a slow breath, like she's trying not to roll her eyes. "You know, people who have nothing to hide usually don't need a lawyer to answer basic questions."

"And yet, here we are." Xavier leans back, completely at ease. "Either charge them or let us go."

Joseph taps his fingers against the table, his jaw tight. "You don't find their behavior suspicious?"

Xavier lets out a short laugh. "You know what's suspicious? A bunch of detectives trying to pin a murder on two teenage boys without a single shred of evidence."

Joseph opens his mouth to argue, but Winters shoots him a look, cutting him off before he can speak.

She turns her attention back to me, and for the first time, she speaks directly to me, not the lawyer, not the boys, but me. "Mrs. Bell," she says, her voice softer now, almost sympathetic. "I know this is hard. I know you want to protect your sons. But if one of them did this, wouldn't you want to know the truth? Wouldn't you want to make sure the right thing is done?"

I force a tight-lipped smile, even as my nails dig into my palms beneath the table. "Detective Winters, I *do* want the truth. I want to know who killed that girl just as much as you do. But I also know that the police don't always get it right. And I'll be damned if I let you railroad my boys without cause."

Her gaze lingers on mine for a beat longer, assessing, weighing. Then she nods. "Fair enough."

She closes her notebook, slides it into her folder, and stands. Joseph follows her lead.

"We'll be in touch," she says, and with that, they're gone.

As soon as the door shuts behind them, I let out a shaky breath that was caught in my chest.

Xavier turns to me, his expression unreadable. "We need to prepare. They're going to come back with that warrant."

I swallow hard and nod. "I know."

Because they're not done with us. Not by a long shot.

And I have no idea if my sons are innocent.

The car ride home is suffocating. I grip the steering wheel so tightly my knuckles ache, the skin stretched taut over my fingers and my pulse pounding in my ears. RJ sits in the backseat, slumped forward, his jaw tight, his hands fidgeting restlessly in his lap. Next to him, Gideon stares out of the window, his hoodie pulled up, his knee bouncing in irritation. Xavier exhales sharply, tapping his fingers on his leg. I sense his anxiety.

"Listen to me—neither of you talk to the detectives again without me present," he says, his tone leaving no room for argument. "I don't care if they show up at school, at the house, wherever. Do not say a word until I'm there."

RJ doesn't respond, just swallows thickly and keeps his gaze locked on the window.

Gideon mutters under his breath, "I don't have anything else to say to them."

"They'll get the warrant," he continues. "It's only a matter of time. And once they do, the clock is ticking. We need to start looking at other suspects because there's a strong possibility one of the boys will be arrested."

A thick, suffocating silence fills the car.

RJ shifts uncomfortably. Gideon exhales loudly. My stomach clenches into a tight knot.

Xavier turns slightly, his sharp gaze flicking between the two boys. "And if that happens, it'll most likely be RJ."

RJ visibly tenses. I can see his hands tightening into fists, his whole body folding inward like he's bracing for impact. Olivia, who must have heard us pull up, is already standing in the doorway when we arrive, her face lined with concern.

The moment we step inside, RJ barely makes it to the couch before collapsing into it, burying his head in his hands. Olivia follows behind, hesitating for only a second before placing a hand on his arm. "It's going to be okay," she whispers, like she believes it.

That's when Gideon scoffs.

Loudly.

The sound slices through the room, dripping with amusement, like this whole situation is one big joke to him.

"I refuse to go to prison because RJ murdered his girlfriend."

The words hit like a slap. Hard. Sudden. Stinging.

RJ's head snaps up. Olivia stiffens.

My pulse kicks into overdrive as I turn to Gideon, barely able to keep my voice level. "Excuse me?"

Gideon shrugs, arms crossing over his chest. "I mean, come on. Everyone is so focused on protecting RJ like he's some delicate little prince." His voice turns mocking. "Oh no, poor RJ! RJ is stressed! RJ is sick!" He rolls his eyes. "Nobody gives a damn that I had cops up my ass too. That I had to sit through the same questions."

RJ pushes himself up from the couch, his jaw clenched so tightly I can see the muscle ticking. "You really think I did this?" His voice is raw, shaking. "You think I—"

"I don't think anything," Gideon cuts him off. "I just know I'm not going to prison for some shit I didn't do."

A heavy silence spreads through the room like a thick fog.

I look between my sons—RJ, tense and desperate, searching for something in Gideon's face. Gideon, defensive and cold, his lips curling in something close to disgust.

Because I don't know who to believe.

But I do know one thing.

One of them is capable of murder.

And maybe—just maybe—Gideon set RJ up.

CHAPTER
TWENTY-SIX

THEN - RYAN

THE MIGRAINES ARE GETTING WORSE. At first, they were just an occasional inconvenience—something a couple of painkillers and a few hours of sleep could fix. Now, they creep up on me in the middle of practice, pounding behind my eyes like a relentless drum. They mess with my vision, my focus, my timing. They make me sluggish. Slow. Weak.

And in my world, weakness is a death sentence.

I don't tell Camille how bad it's gotten. I can't. I've already put her through enough. She's carrying my son, still dealing with the aftermath of everything I put her through with Tiffany, and I can't throw another burden on her back. She needs to see me as strong. As dependable. As the man who's going to fix all of this.

So I swallow the pain, push through training, and pretend like I'm fine.

But today, I'm not fine.

I'm sitting in Tiffany's penthouse, rubbing my temples as I try to will away the dull throbbing in my skull. The place is immaculate—floor-to-ceiling windows, sleek furniture, fresh-cut flowers arranged on every available surface. It smells expensive. It is expensive. And I know her life is about to get even better now that I'm officially on the hook for child support.

She's always lived well, but this? This is different. This is next level.

She glides into the room, wearing a fitted lounge set that clings to her body like it was painted on. She's still stunning—smooth dark brown skin, full lips, those hypnotic eyes that got me in trouble in the first place. But whatever spell she once had on me is broken. There's nothing between us anymore. No desire. No heat. Just the cold, hard reality of what we did.

And now, the proof of it is swaddled in a soft blue blanket, nestled in the crook of her arm.

"Do you want to hold him?" she asks, her voice unreadable.

I hesitate for a split second. Then I nod.

She steps forward, carefully placing the tiny bundle in my arms. He's warm, impossibly small, his tiny fingers twitching as he lets out a soft sigh in his sleep.

Damn.

He looks like me.

The same nose. The same mouth. Even in sleep, there's something familiar about him, something that makes my stomach twist in ways I don't know how to explain.

"You pick a name yet?" I ask, keeping my voice neutral.

She smiles, slow and deliberate. "I have the perfect name."

I nod, waiting.

"Ryan," she says.

I glance up, confused. "Yeah?"

She tilts her head. "No, Ryan. That's his name. Ryan Junior."

For a second, I think she's joking.

And then I laugh because she *has* to be joking. "Come on.

We already talked about this months ago. Camille is naming our son Ryan Junior."

Her smile doesn't falter. "And? Mine was born first."

The words hit me like a slap.

I stare at her, waiting for her to break, to crack a smirk and say she's messing with me. But she doesn't.

"You can't be serious," I say, shifting the baby slightly in my arms.

She leans against the counter, arms crossed, watching me like she's enjoying the show. "I'm dead serious. It's already on the birth certificate. You just need to sign."

I shake my head, my grip tightening on the baby, like that alone will undo this insanity. "Tiffany, that's not happening. Pick another name. Anything else."

"No," she says simply.

"Tiffany," I warn.

"It's done," she says, shrugging. "The paperwork is official. You want to fight me on it, go ahead. But just know I have no problem running to the media. 'NFL Star Ryan Bell Refuses to Sign His Own Son's Birth Certificate'—that's got a nice little ring to it, don't you think?"

My jaw clenches so tight I feel my teeth grinding together.

I look down at the baby—*my* baby—and my stomach churns. I don't deserve him. I don't deserve either of them. And now? I have to tell my wife that she can't name our son Ryan. She's going to kill me. And to be honest, I deserve it.

I feel sick.

Slowly, carefully, I hand the baby back to Tiffany.

"You're an evil bitch," I mutter under my breath.

She smirks, cradling the baby against her chest. "No, I'm the mother of your first born."

I don't have a response for that.

I just grab my keys and walk out, slamming the door behind me.

I don't remember driving home.

One second, I'm storming out of Tiffany's penthouse, my

head a mess, my stomach twisted in knots, my entire body vibrating with frustration and something close to panic. The next, I'm pulling into our driveway, gripping the steering wheel so hard my knuckles ache.

I sit there for a second, my forehead resting against the leather-wrapped wheel, my breath coming in shallow, uneven drags. Camille is inside. My wife is inside. And I have to tell her that the worst thing I could have ever done has just gotten even worse.

I step out of the car and walk up to the door, my body heavy, my legs unsteady. When I step inside, Camille is sitting on the couch, cradling her stomach, her eyes flickering to the TV with amusement. Her skin is glowing, stretched tight over her belly, a cushiony bathrobe swaths her, her long legs curled under her like she's been resting.

She looks peaceful.

And I'm about to ruin that.

She glances up when I walk in. "Hey," she murmurs. "You okay?"

No.

Not even close.

I swallow the lump in my throat and sit next to her, taking her hand. It's warm, soft, her fingers naturally lacing between mine like they always have.

She looks at me, brows knitting together. "*Ryan*. What happened?"

I open my mouth. Then close it. I don't know how to say it. How to package it in a way that doesn't completely break her.

But there's no way to soften this.

I take a deep breath. Then, quietly, I say, "Tiffany named her son Ryan Junior."

She doesn't react at first. She just stares at me, unblinking, the words sinking in, twisting around, taking root.

Then, a short, breathless laugh. "That's not funny, Ryan."

"I'm not joking," I say, my voice hoarse. "It's on the birth certificate. She—" I run a hand down my face, feeling sick just saying it out loud. "She's refusing to change it."

Her entire body stiffens.

Her hand slips from mine.

The silence between us thickens, swells, becomes unbearable.

Then she lets out a sharp breath, one that sounds like it *hurts* to push out of her lungs. "So you're telling me… that the son I'm carrying—the one I've spent months preparing for, the one I've chosen to name after you—isn't going to be the first to carry your name?" Her voice shakes, low and fragile, like it could break at any second.

I reach for her hand again. "Camille—"

"Don't," she snaps, snatching her hand away.

And then, like a dam bursting, the reality of it slams into her.

Her breathing goes ragged, her body folding forward as if she's trying to hold herself together, her arms wrapping around her stomach. Her shoulders start to shake, and when she looks up at me, her eyes are wild with grief, betrayal, disbelief.

"Ryan," she gasps, her voice cracking, her hands pressing into her stomach. "It hurts."

A bolt of panic shoots through me. "What?"

She grips her belly, her face twisting in pain. "I—I don't know. I think I'm cramping."

My heart starts pounding. This isn't normal. This isn't okay.

I jump up, patting my pockets. "Shit—okay, okay, we're going to the hospital. Let me grab the keys—"

I rush to the kitchen counter. No keys. I check the hooks by the door. Not there either. My breath quickens as I retrace my steps, my mind scrambling. I swear I left them—wait. Where did I put them?

I can hear Camille's breathing behind me, shallow, uneven, pained.

"Ryan!" she cries, her voice laced with panic.

"Hold on, I'm looking—" I open a drawer. Nothing. My vision goes blurry for a second, my head pounding, the migraine from earlier roaring back to life. My hands are shaking. My mind is slipping, slipping, *slipping*.

Why can't I remember?

My memory has been bad lately—more gaps, more fog, more static where there should be clarity. But now? Now it's failing me when I need it the most.

I rush back to her, dropping to my knees beside the couch.

Her face is pale, her breathing shallow, beads of sweat forming along her hairline. "Ryan," she whimpers, her hands clutching her stomach like she's trying to hold the baby inside.

I can't find the fucking keys.

We need to go. Now.

Fuck it.

I grab my phone and call 911.

Everything after that is chaos.

The paramedics arrive in what feels like both seconds and an eternity. Camille is crying, moaning in pain as they lift her onto the stretcher. My hands are shaking so badly I can barely text Ricki to tell her what's happening. I ride in the ambulance with her, gripping her hand, watching her face contort in agony, hating myself more and more with every passing second.

"It's too soon," she whispers, her voice wrecked with fear. "He's not supposed to come yet."

I press my forehead against hers. "He's going to be okay," I say, even though I don't know if that's true.

She's sobbing when they wheel her into the hospital.

They take her straight to the OR.

And then I'm left standing there, useless. Helpless.

Praying to a God I haven't spoken to in years.

CHAPTER
TWENTY-SEVEN

NOW - CAMILLE

YESTERDAY'S INTERVIEW with the detectives plays on a relentless loop in my mind, the weight of their questions pressing down on me like a slow, tightening vice. They're coming back. It's just a matter of time before a judge signs that warrant, before the police are tearing through my house, rummaging through my boys' rooms, digging for something —anything—that will damn one of them. And I don't know what they'll find.

That's what keeps my stomach twisted in knots, my nerves stretched thin like frayed wire. I don't trust either of them. I don't trust what they've told me, what they've left out. RJ swears he's innocent. I want to believe him, I do—but my faith is cracking under the pressure of everything piling up against him.

And then there's Gideon.

Gideon, with his sharp tongue, his cold stares, his smug indifference. It's like he doesn't even care. Like he's untouchable, watching the walls close in on his brother with an amused little smirk, waiting for me to pick a side. I hate that I have to pick a side. I hate that, deep down, I think Gideon is far more culpable.

But am I really willing to throw my own son under the bus? Even to save RJ?

No. I can't do that. No matter how much my heart aches for RJ, no matter how badly I want to protect him from whatever is coming, Gideon is my son first.

I need a break from it all. The suffocating weight of it, the tension curling in my shoulders, the endless ticking clock counting down to when my life blows up in my face.

But fate isn't on my side today.

Another one of my employees called off, so now I'm stuck cleaning an office myself. It's not so bad—mindless work, the kind that lets me slip into a rhythm, lets my body move without thinking too hard. And, more importantly, it gives me a break from Ryan. From the house. From the investigation.

At least, that's what I tell myself.

But scrubbing a stranger's desk, wiping down fluorescent-lit conference rooms, and vacuuming up remnants of corporate life doesn't do much to keep my mind from spinning back to where it always goes—what if one of my sons is guilty?

What if I'm just biding time before I lose them both?

The walls are closing in.

When I finish cleaning the office, I yank my phone from my pocket, expecting to see nothing but missed calls from Olivia or an automated message from the bank reminding me of bills I already know are due. Instead, Maci's name stares back at me, bold and unread. A text. Short. Ominous.

"Tell me this isn't true."

Attached is a screenshot.

I feel the blood drain from my face before I even open it, my gut already twisting with the kind of dread that settles in deep, heavy, suffocating. But I force myself to look.

It's a comment under an article about Violet's murder, buried under a thread of gossip and speculation.

"Camille Bell threatened my cousin on the day of her death."

A cold, electric jolt shoots through my spine.

The office around me feels suddenly smaller, the air too thick, the silence stretching out unbearably. My stomach clenches so tightly I have to grip the edge of the counter to steady myself. I knew this was going to catch up to me. I just didn't think it would be so soon.

I was careful. I made sure no one saw me. But of course, of course, Violet told someone.

And now the world knows.

My mind races, colliding with a thousand worst-case scenarios at once. What if she told RJ? What if he knew this entire time and has been keeping it from me? What if she confronted him after I cornered her in that bathroom? What if I was the final push that made him snap?

No. No.

RJ wouldn't kill her.

Would he?

My throat tightens, panic squeezing the air from my lungs. I don't even bother responding to Maci. There's no point. If she's seen this, the cops have seen it too. My vision tunnels, my body going into autopilot. I need to get home.

The drive is a blur. My foot presses harder against the gas pedal than it should, my hands gripping the steering wheel so tightly I can feel my pulse hammering through my fingers. My mind won't shut up, spinning through every possible scenario like a sick roulette wheel. The cops are going to come. It's just a matter of time. If this story has already hit the blogs, they're probably already drafting up their next move.

I don't have time to think about what I'll do next. I only know that I need to get Ryan.

When I get to the adult daycare center, I don't even bother parking properly. I throw the car into park, shove open the door, and make my way inside, moving fast, my nerves sizzling under my skin. The staff greets me like they always do, their polite smiles in place, but I don't have the patience for small talk today. I need to get him and get out.

Ryan is slouched in a chair by the window, his face blank, eyes distant. He looks up when he hears my voice, but there's no recognition in his expression, just that same vacant emptiness that's been there ever since the stroke. His hands tremble slightly when I take his arm, guiding him to his feet. He grunts—his version of a question—but I don't answer. I just lead him to the car, my patience hanging by a thread.

Getting him inside the house is like dragging dead weight. His movements are slow, sluggish, and his aphasia makes him grunt out sounds instead of full words. He's babbling, low and under his breath, fragmented syllables that mean nothing, and even more so than usual, I don't have the patience for it.

I just need him to shut up.

I hurry him inside, locking the door behind us, every second feeling like a countdown. The pressure in my chest builds as I pour water into a glass. My hands shake, my nerves shot, my pulse erratic. I don't even think as I crush up the pills, watching them dissolve into the water, stirring it just enough to make sure it's evenly distributed.

It's harmless. Just something to calm him down.

I hand him the glass, my face blank, my heartbeat loud in my ears.

He takes it. He drinks.

And then—

A knock at the door.

I freeze.

The glass slips slightly from Ryan's grip, water sloshing onto his trembling hands. My stomach drops to the floor.

Another knock, louder this time.

They're here.

I take a deep breath, my hands clenching at my sides. I knew this was coming.

I just didn't think it would happen this fast.

The moment I open the door, I regret it.

Detectives Winters and Joseph stand on the other side, their expressions unreadable, their presence intrusive, like a bad omen looming on my front porch. They don't belong here —not in my home, not in my world, not in my carefully constructed life that is already cracking at the edges.

I don't like them here.

I don't like the way Winters tilts her head slightly, her sharp eyes scanning me like she's searching for a loose thread to pull until everything unravels. I don't like the way Joseph stands with his feet planted firmly, his hands on his hips, like he's already made up his mind about me.

I grip the doorframe tighter, my nails pressing into the wood. "What do you want?"

"We'd like to speak with you for a moment," Winters says, her voice deceptively smooth. "Off the record."

I arch a brow. "I don't speak to cops without my lawyer present."

Joseph lets out an exasperated sigh, rubbing his temple like he has an actual headache dealing with me. "Camille, it's just a conversation."

It's never just a conversation.

I could slam the door in their faces. I could call Xavier and let him deal with it. But that might make me look guilty, and right now, I need to look like anything but that.

I exhale sharply through my nose. "Fine. But make it quick."

I step aside, letting them in, leading them into the kitchen. The house feels different with them inside it—tainted, like they're tracking in something I won't be able to scrub out.

Ryan is still at the kitchen table where I left him, his head dipped forward, his mouth slightly open, a thin line of drool escaping the corner of his lips. He looks like a lifeless doll someone forgot to put away. I don't even bother wiping his face.

The detectives scan the room, their eyes flickering over the messy countertops filled with dishes the kids left behind. I was too tired to deal with it, knowing I had to clean that office today for work. The kids could handle it when they got home.

Detective Joseph's eyes land on Ryan, and he lets out a low whistle. "You have a lot on your hands."

I give him a humorless smile. "Tell me something I don't know."

Winters crosses her arms, her gaze locking onto mine. "You threatened Violet Kowalski the day she died."

I blink. "Excuse me?"

Joseph pulls out his phone, swipes, then turns the screen toward me. It's a screenshot of an online comment, the kind of thing that spreads like wildfire once someone gets their hands on it.

"Camille Bell threatened my cousin the day she died. Said she needed to stay away from her son, *or else.*"

My stomach tightens.

"We already spoke to this cousin, Alyssa. She said that Violet called her right before she left for the party. Said you threatened her."

I knew this would catch up to me. Knew the moment I cornered that girl in the bathroom and told her she wasn't good enough for my son that it would come back to haunt me. I couldn't stop myself.

And I can't let them see that.

I tilt my head slightly. "Did someone see me do that?"

Winters watches me closely. "No."

"Then it's a lie." I shrug, crossing my arms. "Why would I threaten a little girl?"

Joseph leans against the counter, his arms folding over his broad chest. "That's what we'd like to know."

I force myself to exhale slowly. Keep my voice even. "I had

174

no reason to threaten her. She was just another high school girl dating my son. That's all."

Winters doesn't blink. "You didn't approve of her."

I let out a short laugh. "Of course not. I don't approve of most of RJ's choices. He's seventeen."

"You called her a distraction," Joseph presses.

I wave a hand dismissively. "And? That's not a crime."

"No, but murder is."

My stomach clenches, but I keep my expression neutral. "Are you actually accusing me of killing Violet?"

Joseph doesn't answer immediately. Instead, he taps his fingers against the counter, slow, rhythmic. "Where were you the night she died?"

I don't hesitate. "Right here," I say smoothly, turning my head toward Ryan.

Both detectives glance at Ryan, still slumped in his chair, barely conscious.

Winters' lips press together, her sharp gaze returning to me. "No one can corroborate that, though." They know about Ryan's CTE, the stroke, the dementia.

I lift a shoulder. "You asked where I was, and I told you."

Joseph tilts his head. "Does your Ring camera work?"

The question makes my pulse spike, but I keep my face impassive. "Of course."

Winters watches me for a beat longer, then nods. "We'll be back very soon."

I don't respond. I just open the door, motioning for them to leave.

When the door finally shuts behind them, I let out a slow, steady breath.

But I don't get a second to gather myself before I hear it—Ryan's voice, low, groggy, but somehow clearer than it's been in a while.

"Where were you that night?"

My entire body locks up.

Slowly, I turn.

Ryan isn't asleep like I thought. His eyes are open, staring at me, glazed but focused. And for the first time in a long time, there's something behind them.

Awareness.

Realization.

He knows.

He remembers I stepped out that night.

And now he's asking me about it.

CHAPTER
TWENTY-EIGHT

THEN - CAMILLE

EVERYTHING IS HAPPENING TOO FAST.

The ambulance speeds through the city, sirens wailing, the rhythmic whoop-whoop cutting through the night air like a knife. The back of the rig rattles with every pothole, every sharp turn, every swerve. My body jerks with the motion, but nothing—nothing—is as violent as the pain ripping through me.

It's unbearable. My stomach is rock-hard, twisting, contracting. I grip the sides of the stretcher, nails digging into the slick plastic as I let out a ragged scream. The paramedic beside me adjusts an IV, his voice calm and detached, like I'm not coming apart right in front of him.

"Your blood pressure is high," he says. "We're going to give you something to—"

I don't hear the rest. Another wave of pain surges through me, and I scream.

Ryan is here. He's in the ambulance, sitting to my left, his deep brown skin unusually pale, his hands trembling in his lap. Useless. He's watching me like he's the one in agony, like he's the one about to fall apart.

I turn my head toward him, my vision blurry from the sweat stinging my eyes, from the pure rage bubbling up between contractions.

"This is your fault," I grind out through clenched teeth.

His mouth opens and closes, like he wants to say something. Like he can say anything that will make this better.

Another contraction hits, and I nearly come off the damn stretcher. A guttural sound rips from my throat, half pain, half fury. The paramedic tells me to breathe, but I can't. There's no air. No space. No relief.

Ryan tries to touch my hand.

I slap him away.

"I hate you," I gasp, shaking, my entire body coated in sweat. "I swear to God, Ryan, I'm going to kill you."

He flinches, like I actually punched him. Like my words aren't justified.

The ambulance jerks to a stop, the force sending my head knocking against the thin pillow. A moment later, the back doors burst open, and suddenly I'm being wheeled out, the cold night air slapping my burning skin. Voices shout over each other. Someone barks out a list of my vitals. The sound of gurney wheels against pavement is deafening.

I barely register the bright, blinding lights of the emergency room before I'm inside, rushed down a long hallway that seems to stretch for miles.

Doctors. Nurses. Machines. I hear them before I see them.

"She's thirty-one weeks," one of them says. "Severe preeclampsia. We need to move fast."

My brain latches onto those words. Severe preeclampsia.

Something is wrong.

I shake my head, trying to lift my hand, but the contractions are too strong. I squeeze my eyes shut as another one rips through me. I'm going to split in half. I know I am.

A woman's voice, gentle but firm, cuts through the chaos. "Camille, honey, we need to do an emergency C-section."

My eyes snap open. "No—"

"It's the only way," she says, her face swimming into view. A doctor, mid-forties, kind eyes. But kind eyes don't mean shit right now. "Your blood pressure is dangerously high. You're at risk of seizures, stroke, organ failure—"

Organ failure?

My heart pounds so hard my head aches.

"The baby's heart rate is dropping," another voice cuts in. "We need to go now."

I shake my head again, violently. "No—he's not—he's not ready! He's not supposed to come yet—"

Ryan is here, standing to the side, his hands in his hair like he's about to pull it out. "Just—just save them both," he says, voice hoarse, broken. "Do whatever you have to do."

I whip my head toward him, and even through the agony, the chaos, the fear—I feel it. That unrelenting rage.

"I swear to God," I whisper, voice shaking, eyes locked on his. "If anything happens to my baby, I will kill you."

A nurse presses a mask over my face. The last thing I see before the anesthesia pulls me under is Ryan's pathetic, devastated expression.

Then—

Darkness.

Learning that Ryan gave his name away to Tiffany nearly killed me and my baby.

Literally.

The rage, the betrayal, the sheer insult of it was too much. It poisoned my blood, made my heart race, sent my body into a spiral it couldn't control. My baby was cut out of me too soon because of what Ryan did. Because of what Ryan took from me.

And now?

Now my son—*my* Ryan Jr.—is in the NICU, hooked up to tubes, fighting for every breath.

And I am in this hospital bed, numb, stitched up, medicated into submission.

The days blur together. Nurses come and go. Machines beep. The scent of antiseptic clings to my skin, my hair, my everything. The drugs they've given me keep me calm, which I know is their polite way of saying *sedated*. I barely remember yesterday, but apparently, I attacked Ryan.

I have no memory of it.

But I hope I hurt him.

The only thing I do remember is the weight pressing on my chest, suffocating me from the inside out. The quiet but loud kind of grief. The kind that turns everything gray.

I can't go see my baby right now. Not in this state. Not with the way my hands are shaking, not with the way I ache in places that have nothing to do with my incision. The doctor told me I can visit once I'm strong enough to get out of bed on my own.

Strong enough.

I want to laugh at that.

I gave birth four days ago, nearly bled out on the table, had my body split open so they could yank my son into the world. But this? This is the thing that breaks me? A name?

No.

It's not just a name.

It's what it represents.

Ryan Bell Jr. was supposed to be *mine*. The heir. The legacy. My son was supposed to be the one carrying that name forward, the proof that I was the woman Ryan built his life with. And Tiffany? She stole that from me. She took something sacred and *cheapened* it, turned it into a damn check with a cute little bow on top.

And Ryan?

Ryan let her.

He didn't fight her hard enough. He didn't stop her. He came home, sat at my bedside, and told me like he expected me to just... what? Accept it? Swallow it like it was just another one of his mistakes?

He took something from me.

And for that, I hate him.

I shift in the bed, wincing as a fresh wave of pain spreads across my abdomen. It's a sharp, stabbing kind of pain, like the doctors left something inside of me—something jagged, something wrong.

I think about the way Ryan looked at me when I woke up yesterday, his face battered, his lip swollen, his eye bruised.

I did that.

I don't regret it.

The door creaks open, and I don't have to look to know it's him.

Ryan steps in quietly, moving like he's afraid of setting me off again. He's still healing from whatever I did to him. His eye is a little less swollen, his lip no longer split, but there's something else in his face now. Something hollow.

"Camille," he says carefully, like he's approaching a wild animal.

I don't answer.

He lets out a slow breath, stepping closer to the bed.

"I went to see him," he says.

I tense.

"Our son," he clarifies. "I—I spent some time with him today. He's strong, Camille. He's doing better."

A lump rises in my throat, but I swallow it back.

Ryan shifts awkwardly, rubbing a hand over the back of his neck. "The doctor says if he keeps improving, they might take him off the ventilator soon."

I squeeze my eyes shut. *Good.*

But it doesn't change anything.

I still hate him.

"I know you don't want to see me right now," Ryan continues, his voice softer, almost pleading. "And I don't blame you. But I need you to know that I'm sorry. I—I never wanted to hurt you like this."

I open my eyes, staring up at the ceiling. I feel empty. Cold.

I should be crying. I should be screaming. I should be something.

But the drugs keep me still. Keep me calm.

My voice comes out quiet, emotionless. "You gave *her* my son's name."

Ryan flinches. "Camille—"

"You let her take something that belonged to me," I whisper. "And now my baby is in the NICU, and I can't even hold him, and all I can think about is how much I hate you."

Ryan exhales sharply. I don't look at him, but I hear the pain in it.

Good.

He should hurt.

Because I do.

And I don't know if I'll ever forgive him for it.

More days pass, and I barely feel them. Time is a shapeless, endless thing in the hospital. There is no morning, no night—just the rhythmic beeping of machines, the antiseptic sting in the air, the hushed voices of nurses, and the suffocating weight of waiting. Always waiting.

Waiting for my baby to be strong enough. Waiting for my body to stop aching. Waiting for the rage inside me to cool.

I've spent hours researching names, trying to find one worthy of him. My son—*my* son—is a fighter. A warrior. He is fragile but unbreakable, impossibly small yet filled with a strength I can feel in my bones.

Gideon.

It means warrior. And my baby will need to be one to survive this.

But I am not out of the woods. We are not out of the woods.

Ryan hasn't left the hospital. He lurks in the background,

pacing the hallways, hovering outside the NICU like an unwanted shadow. I hate him, but I can't do this without him. And I hate that even more.

Because I have nothing.

No money. No career. No plan. No way out.

For years, my whole life has been built around Ryan. He was the dream, the man who was going to take me to the top, the one I sacrificed everything for. I stood by him through every scandal, every betrayal, every wound he carved into my heart. And now, even after this, after the ultimate sin—after watching my baby fight for every breath because of him—I am still stuck.

The reality tastes bitter in my mouth.

I don't have a job. I've never had to work a day in my life aside from waiting tables back in college. My resume is empty except for charity galas and being the perfect, smiling wife at football banquets. If I leave Ryan, where do I go?

Back to what?

Back to who?

As if conjured by my spiraling thoughts, the door creaks open, and I freeze.

My mother steps inside.

I haven't seen her in years. Not since my father forbade her from speaking to me, not since she turned her back on me when I was at my lowest.

Her face is older than I remember. Her hair is grayer, her body smaller, but her eyes—the same sharp, knowing eyes I inherited—pierce right through me.

For a long moment, neither of us speak.

Then, finally, she exhales, stepping closer to the bed. "Ricki called me," she says softly. "She told me about the baby. She told me about...everything."

I swallow, my throat tight. "So that's what it took for you to care?"

Her expression doesn't change. "You know that's not fair."

I want to fight her. To claw into her for the years she let me rot, for the silence, for the way she turned her back and stayed gone when I needed her most.

But I don't have the energy.

I'm too tired.

Too broken.

She sits down beside me, her hands folding in her lap, and for a second, I remember being a little girl, sitting beside her on the pews at church, listening to sermons about sin and redemption, about love and loss.

"I was you once," she murmurs.

I scoff. "No, you weren't."

Her eyes flick to mine, sharper now. "I was exactly you."

I shake my head, looking away.

"You think you can't leave him," she continues. "That you need him. That without him, you have nothing. I know that feeling. I know what it's like to pour into a man and want to reap the benefits. I built that church. I wrote his sermons. And took care of home. You saw me do it all. And I couldn't leave what I had built."

I close my eyes. I don't want to hear this.

"I stayed with your father because I believed I couldn't do it on my own. Because I had no money, just a teacher's salary, no way to take care of you girls without him." She leans in closer, her voice lower now, steady, certain. "And one day, I looked in the mirror and I didn't recognize myself anymore. That's what men like him do. They turn you into someone you don't recognize."

My breath catches.

"Ryan will do that to you," she says.

I open my mouth, but nothing comes out.

She squeezes my hand. "And if you're not careful, one day, you'll wake up and realize he already has."

CHAPTER
TWENTY-NINE

NOW - CAMILLE

CHRISTMAS USED to be our favorite time of the year.

Ryan used to go *all out*. I mean *all out* like he was in a competition with every overachieving dad in the neighborhood. Even back when we had the mansion, he'd pay professionals to turn our home into something straight out of a Hallmark movie. Lights lining every inch of the house, twinkling in synchronized patterns, giant nutcrackers guarding the front door, a 12-foot Santa that waved at passersby, a mechanical sleigh on the roof—he even had a damn snow machine blasting flurries in the driveway. Never mind that we lived in Georgia, where a white Christmas was a literal miracle. Ryan wanted magic, and money made magic happen.

Inside, he was just as ridiculous. A tree in every room. Stockings embroidered with gold thread, garland dripping from every banister. One year, he even had custom wrapping paper printed with our family photo, because, according to him, "presentation is everything, Camille."

It used to drive me crazy, but I loved it. Those were the good days.

Now? Now I have to ask the boys to get the Christmas lights out of the attic, and they act like I'm asking them to carry a cross up Calvary. RJ mumbles something about being tired. Gideon straight-up pretends he doesn't hear me. And Ryan?

Well, Ryan's lights are out.

Not a single bulb flickering in that head of his.

I dust the mantle above our fireplace, where the decorations will go. On the mantel sits an empty vase, a brass monkey we bought on our trip to Bali—meant to symbolize protection and harmony, neither of which we ever truly had. And then there are the framed pictures of our family, lined up in a neat row.

One photo stands out: Ryan dressed as Santa, holding Olivia when she was four. I keep this picture up all year because it's her favorite. This was the Ryan I missed. The one who lit up our home, who made everything feel safe, solid.

I lift the picture, tracing my fingers over the glass, before glancing back at the man slumped on the sofa.

He was gone.

I've been on edge ever since the detectives came to speak to me about Violet. They have no proof that I actually threatened her, but what if they find out I wasn't home that night? It would make me look guilty. But I can't tell them where I really was—because that truth would shatter too many lives.

I call out to the boys, my voice cutting through the heavy silence of the house. "RJ, Gideon—meet me in the living room!"

Christmas is two weeks away, and we haven't so much as looked at a decoration. With everything going on—the police breathing down our necks, the whispers at school, the fear gripping this house like a vice—getting festive has been the last thing on my mind. But I need it now. Desperately.

Maybe a little seasonal joy will make the fact that we're living under a microscope feel less suffocating. Maybe twinkling lights and garlands can distract us from the undeniable truth—that it's been a week since Violet was murdered, and the rumors are getting worse. Every day, the speculation grows louder. It's only a matter of time before the cops show up with some damning evidence against one of the boys. Maybe both.

RJ is the first to appear, looking exhausted like he just finished running suicides on the football field. "What's up, Mama C?"

Gideon follows, slower, dragging his feet like just existing is an inconvenience to him. He rolls his eyes the second RJ calls me Mama C. He hates it. Thinks the title of "Mama" should be reserved for him, because he's the one I actually birthed. But RJ's been calling me that since he was little—his way of distinguishing me from the train-wreck who gave birth to him.

I fold my arms, looking between them. "I need you boys to get the tree, the lights, and all the decorations from the attic."

RJ sighs sadly, tilting his head toward Ryan, who is slumped in his chair, eyes vacant, lips parted like he's forgotten how to close them. "That was Dad's job."

I glance at Ryan, my stomach twisting. He's worse this week. It's like his dementia has sped up, like his brain is shutting down in real-time. There's no recognition in his eyes, no flicker of awareness. Just blankness. Perhaps the drugs are working. Soon he should kick the bucket.

"Well, now it's yours," I say, shaking off the unease, refusing to let this turn into another depressing moment. "So, chop chop!" I clap my hands twice, ushering them along.

They groan, but they go. Because like it or not, someone has to hold this family together.

And I'm all we've got left.

"The boys are going to get the lights. I guess you can watch as Olivia and I put them on the tree. Maybe you're feeling up to putting a bulb on?" I ask Ryan. He looks up at me and grins. Yep, he's as vacant as a foreclosed house with the lights still on.

No one home. No thoughts behind those eyes. Just an empty grin, like he's responding to some long-forgotten memory rather than the words I just said.

Eventually, the boys start trudging down from the attic, their arms loaded with dusty boxes, grumbling under their breath like I've just sentenced them to hard labor. Gideon slams his box onto the floor with unnecessary force, while RJ sets his down with more care.

"Thank you. But Gideon, you act like I asked you to haul bricks," I mutter, dusting my hands off and turning to Olivia, who has just entered the room.

Gideon rolls his eyes and storms away. He hates me and can't wait to get away from me. I can't wait for him to go away too. I'm starting to think that it won't be so bad if prison is the place where he gets away from me.

Olivia eyes the boxes with a mix of excitement and exhaustion. "Finally." She's still my precious little girl who loves to spend time with me.

"I'll leave you to it," RJ says just before he walks off.

"You don't want to help us?" Olivia asks. She would've never asked that of Gideon. It breaks my heart that all three kids weren't that close but I know I play a role in that.

"Nah, there's an MMA fight about to come on. We can watch a movie when that goes off."

"Cool. Okay, Mommy, let's get to work," she says.

Together, we start unpacking. Olivia and I take the lead, carefully sorting through years' worth of ornaments, tangled strings of lights, and a wreath that smells faintly of last year's cinnamon-scented spray. The living room starts to transform, bit by bit, as we wrap garlands along the banister and hang stockings over the fireplace. The Christmas tree, now standing tall in the corner, is still bare, waiting for its moment of glory.

Ryan watches from his usual spot, his eyes occasionally

flickering toward the decorations but never fully focusing. He used to be the one who insisted on a perfectly balanced tree, making sure no two ornaments of the same color were too close together. Now, he just stares with that half-empty look, as vacant as a storefront on Christmas Eve after everything's been picked clean.

I glance at Olivia as she untangles a string of lights, her delicate fingers working quickly. "What's the talk at school?" I ask, keeping my voice casual, though my stomach knots in anticipation of her answer.

She sighs, keeping her eyes on the lights. "People are talking. A lot. Some think RJ and Gideon did it."

My breath catches. I knew this was coming, but hearing it out loud from my daughter makes it real in a way I wasn't prepared for.

Olivia straightens up, frowning. "It's ridiculous. RJ would never murder anyone," she says, her voice firm, like she's ready to fight anyone who dares say otherwise.

I nod slowly. "And Gideon?"

She hesitates.

That's when I know.

Olivia's voice drops to a whisper as she leans in closer, glancing toward the hallway like she's afraid Gideon might appear at any moment. "I don't know, Mama," she admits. "I think... I think it could be him."

A sharp chill moves through me, and for a moment, I can't speak. My own daughter—Gideon's full-blooded sister—believes he could be capable of something this dark.

I swallow. "Why would you say that?"

She bites her lip, twirling a silver ornament between her fingers. "He's just... off, you know? He's always been different. He doesn't react to things the way other people do. And he had a thing for Violet, right? She rejected him. He barely talked about it, but I could tell it messed with him."

I shake my head. "Olivia, rejection doesn't turn someone into a killer."

"Maybe not," she says softly, "but what if it was more than that? What if he was jealous of RJ? He's always felt like he's in his shadow. And now everyone's saying RJ and Violet were a thing. What if that was enough to push him over the edge?"

I don't know what's more unsettling—the logic in her words or the fact that I've had some of the same thoughts myself.

"Listen to me," I say firmly, gripping her wrist. "Don't repeat that to anyone. Not to your friends, not at school, not even to RJ. Do you hear me?"

She nods quickly, her face serious. "I won't."

I release her, standing up straight and looking around the half-decorated room. The twinkling lights, the scent of pine, the stockings hanging from the mantel—it should feel warm, festive, full of holiday cheer. Instead, the walls feel like they're closing in.

I used to think nothing could ruin Christmas.

Now, I'm not so sure.

When we finish decorating, Olivia scampers off to find her brother so they can watch a movie in one of their rooms—because apparently, spending time with me, their devoted, long-suffering mother, is just too much to ask. Fine. Whatever. I've got bigger things to worry about.

That leaves me alone with Ryan, who's sitting in his chair looking as vacant as ever, blinking up at the twinkling Christmas tree like he's waiting for it to introduce itself. I sigh, bracing myself for the nightly ordeal of getting him upstairs. It's a slow, agonizing process, like escorting a drunk toddler up Mount Everest. By the time I've wrestled him through his night routine—teeth brushed, face washed, pajama pants on the right way—I'm sweating. When he finally collapses into bed, I tuck the blanket around him like a nurse patting down a hospital bed, muttering a half-hearted, "Goodnight, Ryan," before flicking off the light.

Then I head straight downstairs to pour myself a very large, very necessary glass of wine.

I sink into the couch, swirling the deep red liquid in my glass, letting the quiet of the house settle over me. It should be peaceful, but my mind won't shut up. It's buzzing, jumping from thought to thought, like a frantic little hamster on a wheel powered by dread. And, as usual, all roads lead back to Gideon.

I wonder... is he capable of killing someone? Did he inherit that from me?

And the real question that lingers, the one I can't shake no matter how much I sip at my wine—is murder genetic?

Maybe there's a little strand of DNA somewhere, curled up tight like a coiled snake, that dictates who has the capacity to kill out of jealousy, out of rage, out of whatever sick, twisted impulse makes a person take a life. And if that gene exists, then Gideon has it. I know he does, and I know where he got it.

I know what's lurking just beneath the surface, waiting for the right moment to strike. And if he had the chance, the right push, the right amount of anger... maybe he wouldn't hesitate. Maybe he already didn't.

I take another sip of wine, but it doesn't calm me the way I want it to. Instead, the thought just sits there, growing, taking root in my mind.

If the police come knocking for Gideon instead of RJ... will I stop them?

Or will I open the door and let them take him? I swirl the wine in my glass, watching the way the deep red liquid clings to the sides. My thoughts won't settle. The idea of letting the police take Gideon—it lingers, poisonous, like a splinter I can't dig out. I know I shouldn't think this way. But how much more can I take? How much more of his sneering, his anger, his quiet, calculated resentment?

. . .

A shrill ping cuts through the silence, snapping me out of my thoughts. My phone buzzes on the table beside me. I grab it, unlocking the screen to see a new message waiting.

Him: Can you get away tonight? Meet me at our spot?
Me: I can't
Him: I miss you so much.
Me: I'll let you know when we can see each other.

CHAPTER
THIRTY

THEN - RYAN

IT'S BEEN two months since we brought Gideon home. Two months since the NICU doctors finally said he was strong enough to leave, though not without a list of warnings, precautions, and follow-ups that made my head spin. Born at thirty-one weeks, my son had to fight for every breath, his tiny chest rising and falling with the help of machines, tubes taped to his fragile skin. The first few weeks were hell—his lungs weren't fully developed, his body struggled to regulate temperature, and he barely had the strength to suckle. There were apnea spells, terrifying moments where alarms blared because he'd stopped breathing, and endless nights where Camille sat by his incubator, whispering to him, begging him to keep fighting.

And he did.

Somehow, through the chaos, the infections, the jaundice, the late-night emergency calls—he fought. And eventually, the doctors told us what we had been waiting to hear: You can take your son home.

We should have been relieved. We should have celebrated.

Instead, we walked out of that hospital as two people who

had aged decades in weeks, carrying a baby who still felt too small, too fragile, too breakable. And at home, reality set in.

Gideon needed constant monitoring. Feedings had to be scheduled down to the minute to make sure he was gaining weight. His body was still catching up, weaker than other babies his age, prone to exhaustion from something as simple as crying too long. Camille barely slept, hovering over his bassinet, making sure his tiny chest rose and fell, waiting for something—anything—to go wrong.

And me?

I watched.

I watched Camille unravel, little by little, every day.

At first, she was just tired. We both were. But then, exhaustion turned into something else. She didn't laugh anymore. Didn't crack jokes. Didn't throw little digs at me the way she used to. She just existed. A mechanical version of herself, moving through the motions of motherhood like she was checking off a list, each task another weight strapped to her back.

She held Gideon, fed him, changed him, rocked him, but there was a distance, like she wasn't fully there. I would catch her staring at the wall sometimes, her eyes glazed over, her arms limp at her sides while Gideon wailed in his bassinet. I would find bottles left half-mixed on the counter, her forgetting where she had put them down in the middle of the night.

And when she did sleep, she had nightmares.

Violent ones.

I woke up once to her thrashing in bed, gasping, clawing at her throat, her whole body drenched in sweat. I tried to shake her awake, but when her eyes finally flew open, she looked right at me and whispered, "I hate you."

It shouldn't have cut as deep as it did.

But it did.

I sit across from her now, watching as she rocks Gideon, his tiny body curled against her chest, his breath slow, steady. It's the middle of the afternoon, but she's still in her robe, her hair piled on top of her head in a mess of curls she hasn't bothered to detangle. She doesn't look like the woman I married. Not because she isn't still beautiful—she is. She always will be. But because she looks...empty.

Like the best parts of her have been gutted out.

Like *I* gutted them out.

My jaw tightens as I force myself to say what I've been thinking for weeks. "Camille... you're not okay."

She doesn't look up. Doesn't react.

I lean forward, elbows on my knees, watching her carefully. "You barely sleep. You barely eat. You don't talk to me anymore." I hesitate, my voice lowering. "Do you even want to be here?"

Her grip on Gideon tightens just slightly. "Where else would I be?"

"That's not what I mean," I say, exhaling hard.

She finally looks at me, and for the first time in weeks, I see something behind her eyes. Not exhaustion. Not apathy. But anger. "I don't have a *choice*, Ryan." Her voice is low, clipped, dangerous. "Where else would I go? What else would I do? I have no job, no money, no way to raise *your* son without you."

I flinch.

She shifts in the rocking chair, her fingers ghosting over Gideon's back. "You have no idea what it's like, do you? To be completely dependent on someone who destroys you? To hate someone and still need them in order to survive?"

I don't respond.

Because what the hell am I supposed to say?

She shakes her head, looking back down at Gideon, brushing a thumb over his soft curls. "I love my son. But if I'm being honest, Ryan... I don't know if I *like* being a mother."

Something cold slides through me.

And the worst part?

I get it.

I see it every day.

She didn't get the baby she imagined. She got hospital rooms and feeding tubes, panic attacks at two in the morning because he felt too cold, weekly doctor visits with specialists who never had reassuring things to say. She got *this* version of motherhood—the one that no one posts about on Instagram, the one that doesn't come with cute baby showers or picture-perfect newborn photo shoots.

And I?

I failed her.

Again.

I should have given her a husband who didn't cheat. A marriage that didn't involve the humiliation of another woman carrying my firstborn. A pregnancy that was filled with joy instead of stress, rage, and betrayal. I should have given her a healthy baby, one she didn't have to worry about surviving every single day.

I should have given her everything she deserved.

Instead, I gave her *this.*

Camille's gaze flicks back to me, exhaustion laced in every feature. "You're just sitting there. Watching me. But you can't fix this, can you?"

I rub a hand over my jaw, staring at the floor, my throat tight. "No. I can't."

She nods, like she already knew that. "At least you're honest."

We sit in silence. The only sound in the room is the slow creak of the rocking chair and Gideon's soft, even breaths.

I should hold her. I should apologize again, even if it doesn't mean anything anymore. I should tell her that I will spend the rest of my life trying to make it up to her.

But I don't.

Because I know she won't believe it.

And for the first time in my life, I don't either.

CHAPTER
THIRTY-ONE

NOW - CAMILLE

I PEEL out of the parking lot of Serene Horizons Adult Facilities, the adult daycare, gripping the wheel tighter than I need to, my pulse still hammering from the ordeal of getting Ryan inside.

The drop-off is never easy. Some days, he goes willingly, eyes blank but compliant, letting the nurses guide him inside. Other days, he fights me, confusion twisting his face, his hands shaking as he grips my wrist and begs to stay home. Today was one of the bad days.

He struggled to say something with his eyes wide with something like fear. I could tell he wanted to say, "Don't leave me here."

But I had to.

Because I needed this. I needed a break.

So I'd kissed his cheek, forced a smile, and handed him over to the care of professionals who could do what I no longer had the energy to. And now, as I speed toward Atlanta, I try to ignore the guilt pressing down on my chest, suffocating and relentless.

I turn up the radio, let the city skyline come into view, and remind myself: Ryan is safe. Ryan is taken care of. And for the next few hours, I get to be just Camille. Not a wife. Not a mother. Not a crisis manager for a family unraveling at the seams.

Just me.

Atlanta has always been my escape, my temporary oasis. And today, I need it more than ever.

The drive to Atlanta is smooth, the kind of easy, mindless trip where my body moves on autopilot while my thoughts drift into darker places. I roll down the window slightly, letting the cool air whip against my face, hoping it will do something to shake off the heavy cloud that's been looming over me for the last week. The weight of this investigation, of Ryan's decline, of everything.

I'm listening to the podcast Bring Her Home, hosted by Taylor Tillman. Inspired by the disappearance of her little sister, she started this true crime podcast about missing Black girls. It's good background noise as I reach my destination.

I need this. I need a break from the walls of my house closing in on me. From the exhaustion of being a full-time caretaker, a full-time mother, a full-time business owner, and a full-time crisis manager trying to keep my family from completely crumbling.

That's why I'm here.

Atlanta has always been a breath of fresh air. And Ricki? My little sister, the only person who still sees me as me—not as the wife of a man falling apart, not as the mother of two potential murder suspects. Just Camille.

I pull up to the café in Buckhead that Ricki has picked for lunch, a trendy little spot where everyone wears oversized sunglasses, where the servers bring out overpriced avocado toast on rustic wooden boards and call it an experience. I spot Ricki immediately, sitting at the front by the window, already sipping a hot matcha latte, the picture of ease and independence. She looks good. Radiant, even.

Her hair is cropped short now, dyed copper, her skin glowing like she just stepped out of a damn skincare commercial. She waves when she sees me, her gold bracelets jingling on her wrist, and for the first time in weeks, I feel something close to peace.

"Damn, Cami," she says when I sit down, eyeing me over the rim of her glass. "You look—" she hesitates, choosing her words carefully, "—tired."

I huff out a dry laugh, setting my bag down. "That's an understatement."

She doesn't push. Not yet. She lets me order, lets me take a few bites of my food, lets me settle into the moment before she leans in, resting her chin on her palm. "How are you really holding up?"

I glance away, focusing on a group of women at a nearby table laughing over mimosas, their biggest concern of the day probably being whether or not they should get the peach Bellini or the lavender spritz.

"I'm fine."

Ricki gives me a look. The kind that says, *Don't bullshit me.*

"I know things haven't been right ever since Ryan had that stroke—"

I hold up a hand. "I don't want to talk about Ryan. Or the kids." My voice is sharper than I intend, but I mean it. For once, I want to exist outside of them.

Ricki watches me for a beat before nodding, accepting the boundary. "Okay. No Ryan. No kids." She picks up her fork, pointing it at me. "Just me and my favorite sister."

I arch a brow. "I'm your only sister."

"Exactly," she says with a smirk.

And just like that, the tension eases.

For a while, it's almost like old times. Like when I first got married, before I became trapped in a cycle of caretaking and survival. We sip on cocktails, eat overpriced salads, and talk about nothing and everything. I listen as Ricki vents about the annoying billing hurdles at her therapy practice, about how her condo association is raising fees again, about a trip to Mexico she and Leah are planning.

I'm proud of her.

She's built a life for herself completely separate from the dysfunction we were raised in. She has her own thriving business, a beautiful home, a healthy relationship with a woman who adores her. She broke the cycle. The same cycle of codependency that has swallowed me whole.

I should feel jealous.

Instead, I feel something close to relief. At least one of us got out.

"So," she says, stirring the last bit of ice in her glass, "Leah and I have been talking."

I raise a brow. "Oh?"

She hesitates, a small smile playing on her lips. "We're thinking about making things official. Getting married and having a wedding."

For the first time in a long time, I feel genuine joy bubble up in my chest.

"Ricki, oh my god!" I reach across the table, grabbing her hand. "That's amazing. I'm so happy for you."

She beams. "Yeah, we've been together for a while now, and it just feels right. We want something small, nothing too extravagant, but—"

My phone rings.

I ignore it.

Ricki continues, "We were hoping you could help with the planning. I know you have a good eye for this kind of stuff, and—"

The phone rings again.

I sigh, pulling it out of my bag. *Thurgood Marshall High School.*

I freeze.

Ricki notices immediately. "What's wrong?"

My stomach tightens as I swipe to answer. "Hello?"

"Mrs. Bell?" The voice is professional, measured, but there's an edge of tension beneath it. "This is Principal Kipton from Thurgood Marshall High. We need you to come in right away."

Everything inside me goes cold.

"Why?" I ask, my grip tightening on the phone.

There's a pause.

"I think it's best if we discuss this in person."

I already know.

"I'll be there soon." I hang up, my pulse thudding in my ears.

Ricki is watching me carefully. "Camille?"

"I have to go." I'm already pushing back from the table, grabbing my purse.

"What happened?"

I shake my head, throwing a few bills onto the table. "I don't know. But it's about the boys."

Ricki stands, grabbing my arm before I can rush off. "Do you want me to come with you?"

I hesitate. Just for a second.

Then, I shake my head. "No. I got it."

I don't *got it*.

But I don't have a choice.

I rush to my car, the afternoon sun beating down on me, the warmth doing nothing to thaw the ice that's settled deep in my bones.

Something's wrong.

And I have a feeling my entire world is about to shift.

Again.

The drive to Thurgood Marshall High School is a blur. My hands are tight on the wheel, my breath short and clipped. I don't even remember turning onto the highway, don't register the stoplights, the speed limits. All I know is that my heart is hammering, and my stomach is in knots.

I should be used to this feeling by now.

The dread. The panic. The bone-deep exhaustion of knowing that no matter how hard I try to keep my family together, to protect my boys, something always comes along to rip another hole in the seams.

When I pull up to the school, I barely throw the car into park before I'm out, slamming the door shut behind me. My heels click against the tile floors as I storm through the halls, my pulse thrumming in my ears.

I know this isn't about murder. If it were, they wouldn't be calling me here—they'd be hauling RJ off in handcuffs. But that doesn't make it better. It just makes it different.

Principal Sherry Kipton's office is at the end of the hall, past the administrative desk where the receptionist barely glances up as I push through the door.

And there he is.

RJ.

Slumped in a chair, looking stunned, his hands balled into fists in his lap.

And across from him, Detectives Winters and Joseph.

A plastic evidence bag sits on the principal's desk.

Inside? Syringes. And a small bottle of medication.

My stomach drops.

"What the hell is going on?" I demand, my voice sharp, my body already moving toward RJ like I can shield him from whatever fresh nightmare this is.

Winters leans back slightly in her chair, always the picture of calm authority, her eyes flicking to me, unreadable. "Mrs. Bell, take a seat."

I don't. I cross my arms instead, glaring at the baggie. "What is that?"

Principal Kipton clears her throat. She's an older woman, firm but fair, always measured in her responses. But right now, she looks as irritated as I feel.

"We got a warrant to search both RJ and Gideon's lockers," she says. "And we found this inside RJ's locker."

RJ snaps his head up, his face twisting in disbelief. "That's not mine!"

His voice cracks, pure desperation, but Kipton doesn't react.

"What am I even looking at?" I ask, turning to Winters, because I'm sick of the slow-drip method of giving me information.

"It's trenbolone," Joseph says. "A powerful anabolic steroid."

I blink.

I literally have to blink, because for a moment, I don't understand what I'm hearing.

"Steroids?" My voice comes out hollow, like it doesn't belong to me.

I turn to RJ, searching his face, looking for... what? Guilt? Shame? A confession?

Something clicks in my mind, something that's been lingering in the back of my thoughts for months.

Ryan was an excellent athlete. A natural. A powerhouse. But RJ? RJ is better. Stronger. Faster. More dominant. More explosive.

And I thought—I thought—it was just because he trained harder. Because he wanted it more. Because he had all the advantages Ryan didn't have.

But now?

Now I wonder.

Now I know.

My stomach twists. "RJ," I whisper. "Are you taking steroids?"

His face crumples. "Mom—no! I swear, that's not mine!"

I don't know if I believe him.

Kipton sighs, rubbing her temple. "Regardless, he's suspended for five days while we investigate further. I may take it to the board and have him expelled permanently."

RJ stiffens. "Expelled?" His voice cracks.

"You're damn lucky I'm even considering a five-day suspension first," Kipton says, unimpressed.

RJ looks like the floor is being ripped out from under him.

I rub my temple, my own breath shaky. "This isn't happening." The only reason they are even considering expelling him is because they think he killed Pretty Eyes.

"I assure you, it is," Winters says, standing.

RJ turns to me, his eyes wide. "Mom, please. You believe me, right?"

Do I?

I don't know anymore.

I should be defending him. Should be tearing into these people for accusing my son of this.

But I saw what was in that bag. And I know what it means.

Before I can say anything, Winters and Joseph exchange a glance. Then, she pulls a piece of paper from her folder and places it on Kipton's desk.

I recognize what it is before she even speaks.

"A warrant," she says smoothly, looking at me now. "To search your house. We need the clothes both RJ and Gideon were wearing that night. And their phones."

I inhale sharply, closing my eyes for a second.

Of course. Of course, they do.

"You already talked to my boys," I snap. "They gave their statements. And now you want to raid my house?"

"That's how investigations work, Mrs. Bell," Joseph says. "The sooner we get the evidence, the sooner we can rule things out."

I know what that means. They think they're ruling in my boys.

I close my eyes. My head is spinning. This is too much. This is too much.

I open my eyes and glare at them. "Fine. Then let's get this over with."

I turn to RJ, who still looks like he's in shock, and grab his arm. "Come on. We're going home."

He stands, moving like a zombie, eyes glassy. I grip his arm tighter, grounding both of us.

Because I know what's about to happen.

The detectives are following us.

The search is about to begin.

And I have no idea what they're going to find.

CHAPTER
THIRTY-TWO

THEN - RYAN

I DON'T KNOW what's worse, the migraines or the fear of what they mean.

For months now, the headaches have been relentless. Not the dull, nagging kind that go away with painkillers and sleep, but the kind that feel like someone is taking a hammer to the inside of my skull. The kind that make my vision blur, my ears ring, my body sluggish. The kind that make me forget things, little things at first—where I put my keys, what day it is, names that used to be second nature. And then bigger things. Gaps in conversations. Entire moments lost, like someone hit delete in my brain.

I know what this is.

I've known for a while.

But today, I get confirmation.

The doctor's office is tucked away in a quiet part of Atlanta, one of those private practices meant for people like me—athletes who can't afford to have their medical records leaked. The waiting room was empty when I came in, the nurse barely sparing me a glance as she led me back. Now, I sit on the exam table, tapping my foot, waiting for the verdict I already know is coming.

Dr. Abrams is an older man, maybe mid-sixties, his salt-and-pepper hair combed neatly to the side. He looks like he's been giving bad news for a long time, and he's learned to do it without an ounce of emotion. He flips through my file, his expression unreadable, then sets it down on the counter before looking at me.

"Your scans came back clear," he says. "No tumors, no bleeding, no structural abnormalities."

For a second, I exhaled, thinking the worst was over.

Then—

"However," he continues, "given your history, your symptoms are strongly consistent with early-stage CTE."

My stomach drops.

CTE.

I knew it.

I knew it before I even walked in here. Before the headaches got this bad. Before the memory lapses, the impulses, the irritability, the mood swings that don't feel like me but something *else*—something I can't control.

Dr. Abrams leans back against the counter, folding his arms across his chest. "Ryan, you've played football most of your life, correct?"

I nod slowly.

"And before that, you mentioned head trauma as a child?"

I exhale through my nose. I don't want to have this conversation.

Dr. Abrams watches me carefully. "Can you tell me how many concussions you've had?"

I hesitate. "I don't know. Maybe five or six?"

His eyes narrow. "And those were all documented?"

I glance away.

He sighs. "So, probably more."

Yeah. Probably more.

"Ryan, Chronic Traumatic Encephalopathy isn't something we can officially diagnose while a person is alive. We don't have a definitive test for it. But we do know that repeated head injuries increase the risk significantly. And from what you've told me—" he gestures at my file, "—you've been taking hits since you were a kid. We usually don't see these symptoms creep up until later."

I clench my jaw.

Each hit compounds the last.

I think about my mother's backhand, the force of it enough to send me sprawling. I think about the time she shoved me so hard my head cracked against the wall, the way my vision went black, the way I woke up on the floor, confused, my ears ringing. I think about the times she yanked me by the hair, shaking me until my head felt like it was rattling inside my skull. I think about the time she hit me in the head with a wine bottle.

I think of Camille saving me from my mother and her wine bottle.

Then I think about the field. The hits. The tackles. The sound of helmets colliding, the way I'd see stars after a rough game but still push through because that's just what we do.

Dr. Abrams exhales. "CTE is a degenerative condition. Over time, the symptoms will likely get worse."

The room feels small. Suffocating.

I swallow hard. "How much worse?"

"Cognitive impairment, memory loss, emotional instability, depression, aggression. Over time, it can lead to dementia."

The word dementia slams into me like a freight train.

I blink at him. "That's... that's years from now, right?"

He doesn't answer right away.

And that tells me everything.

I sit back, exhaling slowly, running a hand over my face.

CTE.

I always knew this game would take something from me. But I thought I had more time.

Dr. Abrams shifts, his voice softer now. "I know this is a lot to process, Ryan. I want to start you on a mild antidepressant. It might help stabilize your mood and control some of the impulsivity."

I scoff. "Impulse control?"

He nods. "It's common in players with head trauma. Difficulty regulating emotions, making reckless decisions, engaging in compulsive behaviors—including infidelity."

I let out a humorless laugh.

"Oh, so it's not my fault," I say dryly. "I didn't cheat because I'm an asshole. I cheated because my brain is broken."

Dr. Abrams doesn't flinch. "It doesn't excuse your choices. But it does explain why you struggle with control."

I press my lips together, staring at the prescription pad in his hands.

Another thing to add to the list of things that are broken inside me. I thought of all the other impulsive decisions I've made the last few years. Especially the gambling and investing in businesses without properly vetting them.

I glance back up at him. "And football?"

His silence is deafening.

I nod once. I already knew. But knowing doesn't make it hurt any less.

I leave the office with a prescription in my hand and a death sentence weighing on my shoulders.

I sit in my car for a long time, gripping the steering wheel, staring at the paper bag in my lap.

I have to tell Camille.

But not today.

Not yet.

Because if I tell her I'm sick—really sick—she'll never forgive me for everything I've done to her.

And maybe she shouldn't.

———

I sit in my car, gripping the steering wheel so hard my fingers ache. The prescription bag rests in the passenger seat, an unbearable weight for something so small. The air inside the car is thick, heavy with the reality I can't outrun—CTE. Dementia. A slow, inevitable decline that no amount of money, fame, or sheer willpower can stop.

I should go home. Camille and the baby are waiting. But how the hell do I walk through that door knowing that everything I built—everything I swore I'd provide for them—is about to crumble? How do I look my wife in the eye and tell her that the man she married, the man she sacrificed everything for, is already slipping away?

My phone buzzes against the console, jolting me from my thoughts. I glance at the screen.

Kevin - 2 Missed Calls

Shit.

I hesitate before answering. The last time my cousin called me twice back-to-back, I found out one of my investments had tanked overnight. Something about the way my stomach twists tells me this isn't a social call.

"What's up?" I answer, my voice rough.

"Cuz…" Kevin exhales sharply. "You sitting down?"

A fresh wave of dread slams into me. "Just tell me."

"There was a fire at the resort."

Silence.

My grip tightens on the wheel. "What?"

"Shit went up in flames, man. Whole place is done."

My heart pounds against my ribs. I blink, trying to process. "How the fuck did this happen?"

"They're still investigating, but word is… it's bad, Ryan. Real bad."

I press my fingers against my temples, the migraine from earlier threatening to split my skull in half. The resort—the one I put millions into, the one that was supposed to be my way out of football, my safety net—gone.

I can barely wrap my head around it when Kevin keeps going.

"And listen, it's worse than that," he says, voice tight. "They're saying safety protocols weren't in check. Some of the workers are talking about suing. And the city? They're coming for you too."

I suck in a breath. "No. No, no, no. We *had* safety measures in place."

"Apparently not enough," he mutters. "City's saying the project was rushed, corners were cut. If they find negligence, you're looking at more than just fines."

I shut my eyes. "Jesus Christ."

Why did I trust Kevin to handle this? He was supposed to be my main on the island to oversee this while I focused on playing ball. This can't be happening. First my health, now my money? My whole damn future slipping through my fingers in real time?

"How much am I on the hook for?" I ask, already bracing.

Kevin hesitates. That's never a good sign.

"Ryan... between this, the failed property in Miami, and the bad tech investment last year? You're bleeding, man. I don't know how much longer you can hold on before—"

"I *know* what's at stake, Kevin," I snap, rubbing a hand down my face. "Just give me a number."

Kevin sighs. "If this lawsuit goes through? You're looking at at least eight figures."

I let out a harsh breath, staring at the dashboard. Eight fucking figures.

I'm running out of money.

My football career is coming to an end.

My body is breaking down.

And now, I might be on the verge of losing everything.

"I need to go," I say abruptly.

"Ryan—"

I hang up.

The car feels too small, too damn hot. My pulse pounds in my ears, and for a second, I swear my vision tilts.

I force a slow breath through my nose. I need to pull myself together. I have to get home. Camille's waiting, and the last thing she needs is more stress. She's still struggling with Gideon. The postpartum, the antidepressants, the way she flinches when the baby cries—she doesn't need to know about this. Not now.

But eventually, I'll have to tell her.

Eventually, she'll realize that the life I promised her is crumbling.

And when that day comes?

I don't know if she'll still be there when the dust settles.

CHAPTER
THIRTY-THREE

NOW - CAMILLE

THE SECOND we pull into the driveway, my stomach knots so tightly I think I might be sick. The detectives' car rolls up behind me, their presence looming, inescapable. RJ is stiff beside me, his face pale, his jaw tight, his hands fidgeting like he doesn't know what to do with them. I don't either.

The moment I shift into park, I pull out my phone and call Xavier Witherspoon. I don't even give him time for pleasantries.

"They have the warrant," I say, voice clipped, sharp, my pulse hammering in my ears. "They're about to search the house."

"I'll be there in ten," he responds without hesitation.

I don't thank him. There's no time.

By the time I step out of the car, the officers are already moving. A fleet of them. Too many for just a clothes search. They march up my driveway like a firing squad, the warrant held up like a damn trophy.

Detective Winters greets me with a practiced, polite nod. "Mrs. Bell, as I mentioned at the school, we have a warrant to search the premises for the clothing RJ and Gideon were wearing the night of Violet Kowalski's murder, as well as their phones."

Her tone is light, almost casual, but there's something in her eyes—something sharp. Calculating.

Xavier's sleek black car pulls up just as I open my mouth to argue. He steps out, straightening his tie, moving toward us with the kind of practiced confidence that makes even the detectives pause.

"We're not here to argue, Detective," he says smoothly. "We'll comply, but I'll be watching everything your people do. And if they overstep, if they so much as move a sock they don't have permission to touch, I'll have a suppression motion on your desk before the ink on that warrant dries."

Joseph lets out a slow exhale through his nose. "Nobody's overstepping."

"We'll see," Xavier says with an easy smile.

RJ and I step inside, the detectives and their team right on our heels. Gideon is sprawled across the couch, hoodie up, one hand flipping through the TV channels like he couldn't care less that his house is about to be torn apart.

The second he sees them, though, his lazy posture straightens. His expression darkens. "What the hell is this?"

"The warrant," Xavier says, his tone patient, but firm. "Give them the clothes from that night."

Gideon scoffs, shaking his head. "You gotta be kidding me."

"Just do it," I say tightly. "Now."

He mutters under his breath but pushes off the couch and stomps up the stairs. RJ follows, moving slower, more reluctant. I don't know if it's because he's innocent and terrified, or guilty and terrified.

Either way, I can barely breathe.

The next ten minutes are a storm of motion. Officers move through my house with methodical efficiency, rummaging, digging, peeling back layers of my life one room at a time. Olivia comes downstairs, wide-eyed, clinging to the banister as she watches them, her little fingers curled into fists. I don't have time to comfort her. I don't even know if I have it in me.

Xavier stays close, his presence grounding, his every move calculated. He watches the officers like a hawk, his eyes flicking to every drawer they pull open, every closet they search.

RJ is the first to return. He hands over the neatly folded bundle of clothes with the reluctance of someone passing over a death sentence.

Then Gideon returns.

He doesn't hand his clothes over neatly.

He tosses them at Detective Joseph's feet like he's a servant.

"Knock yourself out," he says, smirking.

Joseph glares at him but doesn't rise to the bait.

An officer crouches, carefully unfolding Gideon's shirt. And there, stark against the fabric—

Blood.

A dull red stain.

Winters and Joseph exchange a look. The tension in the room spikes, thick, suffocating.

Xavier shifts beside me, his body language carefully unreadable, but I know what he's thinking. What I'm thinking.

This is bad.

But Gideon?

Gideon just laughs.

The sound is sharp, biting, utterly unimpressed. He looks at the detectives like they're idiots.

"That's not Violet's blood," he says, rolling his eyes.

Joseph arches a brow. "No? Then whose is it?"

Gideon leans in, a slow, smug smile stretching across his face. "Wouldn't you like to know?"

My breath catches.

"Enough," Xavier says sharply. "No more questions. If

you want to test the clothes, do your job. My client has nothing else to say."

Gideon shrugs, utterly unbothered, then flops back onto the couch like he doesn't have a care in the world.

RJ, on the other hand, is pale. Silent. Staring at the blood on his brother's shirt like he's seeing it for the first time.

Like he doesn't know what to believe anymore.

I know the feeling.

Because as I stand there, watching the officers bag my son's clothes, watching my lawyer try to stay five steps ahead of them, watching RJ start to unravel, watching Gideon smirk like none of this means a damn thing—

I realize I don't know what to believe either.

And that terrifies me.

I should have known they weren't done.

Detective Winters shifts her weight, exchanging a brief glance with Joseph before reaching into her folder. She pulls out another piece of paper, crisp and damning, and holds it out toward Xavier.

"A warrant for DNA samples," she says smoothly. "Both boys. Since Violet had skin under her nails, we need to determine if either of them was in direct physical contact with her at the time of her death."

For a moment, everything stills. My ears ring. My breath hitches in my chest, but I force my face to remain impassive, blank.

Xavier, ever the picture of control, takes the paper between two fingers like it's something diseased, skimming it with the same detached professionalism that makes him such a dangerous lawyer in the courtroom. His jaw tightens, just slightly, but his voice is as steady as ever when he speaks.

"I assume you'll be collecting the samples today?"

"As soon as possible," Winters confirms.

I steal a glance at RJ, expecting him to lash out, to shake his head, to tell them to go to hell. But he just stands there, frozen, his hands clenching and unclenching at his sides. His chest rises and falls in sharp, stilted breaths.

Gideon, on the other hand, reacts instantly, his signature arrogance cutting through the tension. He lets out a low, incredulous scoff, shaking his head. "This is a joke."

Joseph shrugs, ever the condescending bastard. "If you've got nothing to hide, there's no problem, right?"

Gideon rolls his eyes. "You won't find my DNA on that slut's body."

Xavier exhales sharply, pinching the bridge of his nose. "Gideon." His voice is steel, sharp, a warning.

But Gideon just smirks, shaking his head. He's playing this off like it's funny, like it's some kind of sick game. But I know my son. I know when he's faking. And beneath that smirk, I see it—the flicker of something else.

Guilt?

No. Not guilt.

Deflection.

Like he knows something he's not saying.

RJ, though?

RJ is breaking apart right in front of me.

His breathing has gone shallow, uneven. His fingers twitch at his sides like he wants to grab something—maybe punch something, maybe run. His jaw is clenched so tightly I swear I hear his teeth grinding, his eyes darting wildly between me, Xavier, and the detectives, like he's calculating something in real time, like he's trying to figure out *what comes next*.

And then—

Winters clears her throat.

"Oh," she says casually, almost as an afterthought, as if she's been saving this little bomb just for the right moment. "By the way, she was pregnant."

The air is sucked out of the room.

The words don't register at first. They hit like static, white noise in my head, impossible to process.

Pregnant.

Pretty Eyes was *pregnant*.

RJ flinches like he's been hit, his whole body locking up, his hands balling into fists at his sides. The blood drains from his face, his chest rising and falling in sharp, ragged bursts.

No.

No, no, no.

This can't be happening.

I barely process what she just said. My mind refuses to wrap around the words, refuses to make them make sense, refuses to let them land.

But then—RJ reacts.

It's visceral. Immediate. He looks like he's going to be sick. His whole face twists, his mouth opens slightly, like he wants to say something but can't form the words. His eyes widen, flicking wildly between me and the detectives like he's drowning and looking for a life raft.

Winters watches him. Carefully. Calculated. Like she was *waiting* for that exact response.

And that's when I realize—

They're not just looking for anyone who killed Violet.

They're looking for him.

Pregnant teenage girl. Pretty, young, dead. The media will eat this up. The world loves a tragic story, especially one that comes wrapped in innocence. They will put her face on every screen, in every article, on every news segment.

They will make her a saint. A victim of the worst kind of crime.

And they will do whatever it takes to find her murderer.

A slow, sick feeling coils in my gut.

I don't think. I move.

I step in front of RJ, instinct taking over, shielding him with my body. I don't even realize I've done it until I feel his ragged breath against my back, his whole body still locked in place behind me.

Winters raises a brow, like she expected nothing less. "Mrs. Bell—"

"Are you done?" I cut her off, my voice ice. My hands are shaking, but I keep them clenched at my sides, refusing to let them see it. "Or do you have more bombshells to drop?"

"We can do the cheek swab here for DNA," she responds.

I roll my eyes and wave her off. "Get it over with so that you can get out of my house."

Winters takes a slow step forward, pulling out a sterile swab kit, her gloved fingers working methodically as she preps the test. RJ's entire body is coiled tight, like he's bracing for impact, his breaths sharp and uneven. His eyes flick to mine—desperate, searching.

I don't look away.

The swab slides into his mouth. A quick, clinical swipe. Over in seconds. But the weight of what it means lingers, heavy in the air.

Winters seals the sample, turning to Gideon.

He smirks, pops a piece of gum into his mouth, and opens wide like this is all one big joke. The swab barely fazes him. If anything, he looks *amused*.

RJ, though—he's still frozen. Still staring at the little plastic vial that now holds the one thing that could determine the rest of his life.

Winters tucks the samples away, then steps back, brushing invisible dust off her coat.

"One more thing," she says, almost casually. "We'll be in touch soon, Mrs. Bell. But in the meantime, don't make any plans to leave town."

Her eyes flick to RJ.

"*Any* of you."

A thick, suffocating silence falls.

RJ swallows hard, his Adam's apple bobbing, his pulse visible in his throat.

And then—

The moment they step out, the door clicking shut behind them, RJ turns to me, his voice hoarse, almost broken.

"Mama C," he whispers, his face pale, his hands trembling.

But it's not what he says that makes my blood turn to ice.

It's what he doesn't say.

Because in his eyes, I see it.

The kind of fear that isn't about being wrongfully accused.

But about being caught.

CHAPTER
THIRTY-FOUR

THEN - CAMILLE

IT'S BEEN a year since Gideon and Ryan Jr. were born, a year since my body was ripped open, a year since I thought I would never recover. But I have. In some ways, at least.

I smooth Gideon's curls with my fingers, rubbing a little coconut oil between my palms before massaging it into his soft, springy strands. He squirms in my lap, restless as always, but I hold him steady, whispering quiet shushes into his ear. He's grown so much since those terrifying early days in the NICU, his tiny body hooked up to more tubes than I could count. Now, he's strong, sturdy in my arms, his round face full of life, his big brown eyes filled with a curiosity that makes my chest ache.

I love him. I have always loved him, but for a long time, I couldn't *feel* it. It was like trying to reach for something underwater, like watching someone else mother him while I floated outside of my own body. But I'm here now. I'm present. The weight of postpartum depression has loosened its grip, and I can finally breathe again. I can finally look at my son and feel the kind of love an abundance of acceptance and love. The kind of love that used to feel impossible.

But Ryan?

That's a different story.

I glance over my shoulder, catching sight of him in the reflection of the mirror above the dresser. He's standing by the window, rolling the cuffs of his shirt, his head tilted slightly like he's lost in thought. His hair is cropped low, the grays creeping in at his temples. He looks good. He always has. But I don't see him the same way anymore.

He was supposed to be invincible. Untouchable. But in the end, he was just a man. A man who got old too fast. A man whose body betrayed him before he was ready.

It's been a year since he retired. A year since we lost everything.

We had to file for bankruptcy to stop the lawsuits from bleeding us dry. The fire at the resort, the failed real estate investments, the business deals that fell apart before they could even get off the ground—it all came crashing down at once. One moment, we were standing on a mountain of wealth, and the next, we were clawing through the rubble, trying to salvage whatever was left.

But Ryan was smart in one way. Before things got too bad, before the city came after us, before the workers threatened to sue, he tucked some money away. A trust. One for Gideon and one for RJ, something to keep them afloat when they turned twenty-five. He knew there wouldn't be much left for them otherwise.

So here we are, sorting through what we still have, deciding what gets sold and what gets left behind. For now, we're still in the Augusta mansion, but not for long. Soon, it will belong to someone else, and we will be somewhere else. Somewhere *less*.

And yet, Ryan has never been more present. More *here*.

He's a different man now. Retirement has changed him. Maybe it's the guilt, or maybe it's the knowing—knowing that it's only a matter of time before his mind starts slipping away for good. The forgetfulness has already started, creeping in like a slow leak. Small things, at first—where he put his phone, the name of a coach he worked with for years. Then bigger things. Blanking out entire conversations. Staring into the distance, lost, until I have to shake him back into the present.

But for now, he is lucid.

And for now, I am beginning to forgive him.

I hate it.

I hate that it's happening so slowly, that it isn't a single moment, but a gradual unraveling of anger I've held onto like a shield. I don't *want* to let go of my resentment. I don't want to forget all the ways he failed me, all the ways he hurt me.

But he was there for me.

When I couldn't get out of bed, when I couldn't hold my own son, when I sat in the nursery staring at the wall while Gideon cried in the bassinet beside me, Ryan picked him up. Ryan held him. Ryan fed him when I wouldn't. Ryan rubbed my back when I curled into myself and whispered over and over that I wasn't a bad mother.

And now, he watches me with something soft in his eyes, something patient, something that almost feels like an apology.

I don't trust it.

But I feel it.

I lift Gideon onto my hip and press a kiss to his temple. His skin is warm, his scent sweet like baby lotion and the little bit of apple juice he had earlier. I let my eyes close for a second, just breathing him in.

Behind me, Ryan clears his throat. "You ready?"

I turn. He's watching me carefully, his expression unreadable.

I nod, adjusting Gideon in my arms. "Yeah."

We're heading to RJ's first birthday party.

One year ago, I was drowning.

One year later, I am still gasping for air.

But at least I can feel the ground beneath me again.

For now.

The second we step into the venue, I feel it—that simmering heat curling in my gut, that slow, insidious burn that has become far too familiar over the past year.

It's elaborate. Over-the-top.

A Godzilla theme, complete with an ice sculpture, green smoke machines, and some massive, animatronic monster looming over the partygoers, roaring every few minutes. Expensive catering, fully stocked bars, designer-clad guests who have more plastic in their faces than emotion.

This isn't a one-year-old's birthday party.

This is a spectacle.

And Tiffany?

She's thriving.

I can see it in the way she moves through the crowd, basking in the attention, her BBL frame poured into a skintight neon-green dress that leaves nothing to the imagination. She's laughing, tossing her sleek, jet-black hair over her shoulder as she clinks glasses with a group of women who look like they were cut from the same mold.

The child support is doing her well.

A sick, hot jealousy claws its way up my throat. I swallow it down.

I have nothing.

Everything Ryan and I built together, all the money, all the investments, the mansion, the security—it's all gone. And yet, here she is, still winning.

It's disgusting.

I force myself to focus, inhaling slowly as I adjust Gideon on my hip. I don't let the jealousy show. I don't let the rage simmering in my stomach spill onto my face. I've perfected the art of masking. A polite smile. A neutral expression. A carefully placed nod as I acknowledge the familiar faces in the room.

But I hate being here.

About a month ago, Ryan, Tiffany, and I sat down to

discuss how we'd move forward—how co-parenting would work now that things had settled between us.

Ryan Jr. was going to start spending more time with us.

At first, I fought it. I told Ryan I wasn't ready to have that woman's child in my home, that the wounds were still too fresh, that I needed more time. But deep down, I knew it was inevitable. RJ wasn't going anywhere.

And the more I watched Tiffany, the more I saw how she lived—this gaudy, chaotic, reckless life—the more I realized...

RJ needs a more stable home.

I glance around, taking in the party again.

There are too many adults.

Too many people without kids here for a toddler's birthday.

Reality stars, influencers, athletes, industry people—drinking, smoking, talking too loud, too wild, too inappropriate.

The air is thick with the scent of marijuana, masked only slightly by the cloying perfume of Chanel and Versace. Someone pops a bottle of champagne, the cork flying across the room, landing in the punch bowl. Laughter erupts.

This is not a party for a baby.

This is a party for Tiffany.

And RJ is just the excuse.

I exhale slowly, steadying my grip on Gideon, who squirms in my arms, reaching toward my necklace. I press a kiss to the top of his head, running my fingers through his soft curls to soothe him.

Then—

I see him.

RJ.

He's running.

I can't take my eyes off him.

There's an effortless strength in his tiny body, a confidence in the way he moves. At only twelve months old, he's steady on his feet, laughing as he dodges between guests, his short little legs carrying him with purpose.

And Gideon?

Still crawling.

Still struggling.

Still behind.

My stomach clenches as I grip Gideon tighter.

"Look at him go!" someone beside me says, their voice bright with admiration. "He's gonna be playing football just like his daddy."

My chest tightens.

"Yeah," another voice chimes in. "He's been walking since nine months."

The words slice through me.

Something in me cracks, splintering so fast and so violently that I have to bite the inside of my cheek to keep from reacting.

Nine months.

RJ has been walking since nine months.

And my baby?

My baby is struggling to even stand.

I look down at Gideon, my beautiful boy, my baby who fought to be here, my baby who was born too soon, too small, too fragile. He presses his tiny hands against my chest, babbling, oblivious to the war raging inside of me.

I know it's not his fault.

I know prematurity causes delays. I know some babies develop at their own pace. I know Gideon is still perfect, still whole, still mine.

But as I watch RJ run across the room, full of strength, full of life, full of promise, something ugly, something dark, something I've been swallowing for years—finally takes root.

RJ should be my son.

Not hers.

Tiffany doesn't deserve him.

She didn't struggle. She didn't fight for him the way I

fought for Gideon. She didn't carry the weight of loss and sacrifice. She didn't sit in a hospital bed, bleeding, broken, drugged into submission while her child clung to life in an incubator.

She didn't suffer.

And yet, she gets the strong one. The thriving one. The one who carries Ryan's name, Ryan's genes, Ryan's legacy.

And me?

I get the sick one. The slow one. The struggling one.

A sickness coils in my stomach, thick, inescapable.

It isn't fair.

It isn't fucking fair.

I clutch Gideon closer to me, pressing his tiny body against mine, my fingers gripping the fabric of his shirt so tight that my knuckles ache.

And for the first time—

I think about how easy it would be to make it right.

To take back what should have been mine all along.

CHAPTER
THIRTY-FIVE

NOW - CAMILLE

THE HOUSE IS A DISASTER. Furniture is slightly out of place, drawers left ajar, footprints smeared across my freshly mopped floors. The officers have turned this place inside out and left just enough evidence of their presence to remind me that they have the power to do so whenever they damn well please.

Xavier stands near the fireplace, adjusting his cuffs, his expression unreadable. "Now, we wait," he says, his voice even, professional. "They'll go through the Ring footage. To see the comings and goings of that evening to verify times with the statements the boys gave. And if RJ is the baby's father, if that's his DNA under Violet's nails—" He exhales through his nose, shaking his head. "They'll arrest him, Camille."

My stomach clenches, my nails pressing into my palms.

"No, they can't." My voice is sharp, desperate, like saying it out loud will make it true.

"I'm afraid that's what it's looking like. But an arrest is not a conviction." Xavier gives me a pointed look. "We need other suspects. Even if the evidence is circumstantial, it's still damning in the eyes of a judge. And I know you don't want to go to trial with this kind of heat."

I swallow hard. I know what he's saying is right.

But desperation makes people irrational.

I turn away, staring at the mess the cops left behind. The broken frame on the floor, the chair pushed away from the dining table at an odd angle, the kitchen counter cluttered with things they had no business touching. A vase tipped over, its contents spilled.

It looks like a break-in. Like we've already been violated.

Like we're guilty.

Then, before I can think better of it, I say, "What if I'm the suspect?"

Xavier goes still. "Excuse me?"

I turn back to him, crossing my arms over my chest, feigning confidence even though my insides are unraveling. "You said we need to introduce other suspects. What if we introduce *me* as a suspect?"

He gives me a long look, as if trying to figure out if I've lost my mind. "That's not how this works, Camille."

"Why not?" I shoot back. "The cops already have a story they're working with. I can give them another one. One that isn't RJ."

He exhales sharply, rubbing his temple. "You do realize that making yourself a suspect doesn't just *introduce* reasonable doubt, it puts a target on your damn back, right?"

I ignore his warning and push forward. "I threatened Violet that night." The words taste bitter in my mouth. "Just hours before she was murdered."

His jaw tightens, but he doesn't say anything, so I keep going.

"She told someone," I admit. "A cousin. I know it's hearsay, but I can confirm I threatened her. I have motive. There's not a shred of evidence that can convict me, What if Gideon killed Violet just to hurt RJ? Just to get back at Ryan?

I take a slow sip of my wine, but it doesn't settle the unease slithering through me.

For the first time, I'm truly afraid of my own son. but it can get the heat off of RJ. "

Xavier exhales. "Jesus, Camille."

"And there's something else."

I brace myself for this next part because once I say it, there's no taking it back.

"I left that night," I say finally, staring at the mess in front of me so I don't have to look at him. "The Ring camera will show it. They'll *see* that I wasn't home the whole time."

The silence that follows is suffocating.

Xavier takes a slow step toward me. "Where did you go?"

I say nothing.

He waits. Still, I say nothing.

His voice drops lower, a quiet edge to it now. "Camille."

I look up at him, my heart pounding in my ears. "Maybe I went to the party," I whisper. "Maybe I snuck in and killed Violet myself."

Xavier narrows his eyes, studying me. "You're lying."

"Am I?"

His lips press together, his jaw flexing, but then—he nods. "That could work." He exhales, raking a hand over his head. "It's risky, but if we frame it right, it gives the jury someone else to look at. Someone the prosecution can't pin down. But it can't just be you. We need real suspects. People who had motive. Opportunity."

He takes a step back, already shifting into defense mode, already working through his next steps. "I'll start pulling together names. We need people who had a reason to want Violet dead."

The weight in my chest lifts, just a fraction.

Xavier looks at me one last time. "If you think of anything else—anything at all—you call me."

And then, just like that, he's gone.

I stand there, staring at the door, listening to the sound of his car pulling away. My head is spinning, my stomach churning, my breath unsteady.

I turn back to the disaster zone that was once my home.

The cops don't just take evidence. They leave things behind, too.

A sense of invasion. A reminder of what they can do, what they will do, if I don't fix this.

My eyes flicker over the mess, and I shudder.

I have to clean this up.

All of it.

And I have to do it alone.

By the time I grab my purse, I'm so exhausted that I nearly forget to check the mail. The pile is thick—mostly bills, a few junk letters, and then—

The report cards.

The kids' names printed neatly on white envelopes.

I pause for a moment, staring at them. Timing couldn't be worse.

With everything going on, grades feel like the least of my concerns. But I leave them on the kitchen table anyway, placing them in a neat stack before heading out the door.

Because right now, I have something far more important to deal with.

I have to pick up Ryan.

And somehow, I have to make it through the rest of this evening without falling apart.

I guide Ryan into the house, moving slowly, carefully, as if he's made of glass. Some days, he walks fine, shuffling toward the couch without a second thought. Today, though, he's sluggish, his eyes unfocused, his body moving like he's wading through water.

I sit him down in the kitchen, pulling out the chair for him before pressing my hands against my lower back, exhaling slowly.

"You hungry, baby?" I ask, even though I already know the answer.

Ryan blinks up at me, the expression on his face distant, unreadable. He grunts something unintelligible, shifting in his chair. I sigh.

Lately, chewing has been hard for him. His jaw gets tired, and he loses interest in eating halfway through a meal. So, I do what I've always done—I adapt. I reach into the cabinet, grabbing the blender, then pull out a protein powder from the pantry.

A green smoothie.

I used to make them for him back in college, back when he was in his prime, back when he *had* a future. He would chug them after practice, thanking me with a kiss on the forehead, promising that I made them better than the team's nutritionist.

I scoop the powder in, add some almond milk, a handful of spinach, a banana, and of course—the pills. The familiar hum of the blender fills the kitchen, a rhythmic noise that drowns out the mess inside my head.

But as I pour the thick, green liquid into a glass, my gaze drifts back to the living room. The mess. The chaos. The overturned cushions, the displaced furniture, the sense of violation that lingers in the air like an unwanted guest.

My head throbs.

A sharp, pulsing pain that starts at my temple and radiates outward, wrapping around my skull like a vice.

It's just like Ryan's.

The thought makes my stomach turn.

I push through it, setting the glass in front of Ryan. He stares at it blankly, his fingers twitching slightly before he wraps them around the cup. I force a smile, brushing a hand over his shoulder.

"Drink up, love. It'll help."

Ryan grunts again, then lifts the glass, his lips pursing slightly before he sips. I stand there for a second, watching him, waiting to see if he rejects it, if he pushes it away like he sometimes does.

But he drinks.

That's one thing under control.

The pounding in my head intensifies. I rub my temple, wincing slightly as I straighten.

I need medicine.

I head upstairs, moving slowly, trying to steady my breathing. The kids are cleaning their rooms, doors slightly ajar, the faint sounds of movement coming from inside. I pass Olivia's door, RJ's. Then—

I stop.

Gideon's door is open, but barely. Just enough for me to see inside.

And what do I see?

A bag.

A bag with syringes.

My breath catches.

I step inside without thinking, my hands reaching for the bag before my brain can process what I'm about to do. I unzip it, my fingers brushing over the contents, my heart slamming against my ribs.

Syringes. A small vial of liquid.

It looks exactly like what the principal had in her office.

Trenbolone.

A rush of cold spreads through me, ice-cold realization settling in my bones.

I whip around, storming out of the room. "GIDEON!"

Footsteps. His door swings open wider, and there he is—his expression unreadable, but his posture stiff.

"What?" he asks, his voice thick with annoyance.

I hold up the bag, shaking it slightly. "You want to explain *this*?"

His gaze flicks to it. And for a split second—just a second—I see it.

Guilt.

But then, it's gone, masked by indifference. "I don't know what you're talking about."

I shake my head, my grip tightening on the bag. "You planted this in RJ's locker."

He scoffs. "That's ridiculous."

"You wanted him kicked out of school. You wanted him to look *aggressive* because steroids make people aggressive."

Gideon doesn't move, doesn't flinch, doesn't deny it.

And that's all the proof I need.

"You set your brother up," I whisper, my voice shaking. "You did this."

"Wow." Gideon folds his arms, letting out a dry chuckle. "You're really reaching, Ma."

"You planted it," I repeat, my voice louder now. "Because you hate him."

"I don't—"

"Because you've always hated him."

"Shut up," he snaps.

"You wanted to ruin him."

"I SAID SHUT UP!"

"Gideon, what the hell is wrong with you?"

And then—

"Because he deserves it!"

His voice is sharp, cutting through the tension like a blade.

"Yo, you planted that?" I turn just as RJ appears in the doorway, his fists clenched at his sides, his face twisted in anger.

His eyes—red-rimmed, furious—are locked onto Gideon.

"I know it was you," RJ says, stepping forward. "You set me up."

For a moment, Gideon just stands there. Then—

He laughs.

A short, sharp sound, filled with something bitter. "Oh, you know it was me? Did your little golden boy instincts tell you that?"

RJ lunges.

It happens fast.

Too fast.

A blur of movement—RJ's fist slamming into Gideon's jaw, the sharp sound of impact echoing in the room.

Then chaos.

They're on each other in seconds, fists flying, bodies crashing against the furniture, grunts and snarls filling the air. I don't think—I move.

"STOP!" I scream, trying to get between them, trying to grab at someone, anyone.

Gideon shoves me.

Hard.

The force of it sends me stumbling backward. My foot catches on the edge of the dresser, and then—

I hit the ground.

Pain explodes across my hip, sharp and immediate.

"Ma!"

RJ is at my side before I can blink, his hands gripping my shoulders, his breath heavy, fast. "Mama C, let me help you—"

I blink up at him, my heart racing. I see his concern, his panic, the way he's looking at me like I might break.

And then—

"WHAT THE HELL HAPPENED?"

Olivia.

She's standing in the doorway, her eyes wide, darting between me, RJ, and Gideon.

And I—I don't think. I just blurt it out.

"Gideon is trying to set RJ up!"

RJ helps me to my feet, his grip steady, but my attention is locked on Gideon.

He doesn't deny it.

Doesn't even pretend to.

"So what?" His voice is venomous, his jealousy dripping from every syllable. "He gets everything."

A heavy silence crashes over the room.

Gideon lets out a sharp breath, his hands curling into fists. "You and Dad have always loved RJ more than me."

His voice cracks.

And then—

He turns and storms out of the house.

For a long moment, none of us move.

I press a hand to my chest, trying to steady my breathing, trying to process what just happened.

RJ sniffles, and I glance over—

His nose is bleeding.

"RJ, you're hurt—"

"I'm fine," he mutters.

But Olivia isn't convinced. She rushes to his side, her hands fluttering, her voice soft, comforting. "Come here, let me help you."

And as I watch my children, my family, unravel right in front of me—

I wonder if any of us are going to survive this.

CHAPTER
THIRTY-SIX

THEN - RYAN

THE MIGRAINE STARTS before I even open my eyes.

A dull, gnawing pressure at the base of my skull, radiating outward, clawing its way behind my eyes, threatening to split my head open before the day even begins. I exhale slowly, pressing the heel of my hand against my forehead, willing it to pass.

But it won't.

It never does.

Still, I push through. I have to. Today is important.

Today is Gideon's day.

The last birthday party we'll have in this house. The last time this mansion—the one we built, the one that was supposed to be our forever home—will be filled with balloons and cake and laughter. The last time the walls will hear the echoes of celebration before we sell it off, another casualty of my mistakes.

I force myself out of bed, ignoring the throbbing in my skull, the way the light slicing through the curtains makes my vision blur. I move on autopilot, splashing cold water on my face, popping two ibuprofen, inhaling deep breaths until the worst of the nausea passes.

Camille is already moving downstairs, a force of nature, as always.

She moves through the kitchen with effortless efficiency, checking the food, setting up decorations, arranging gift bags on the dining table. She makes it all look so easy.

It's not.

I see the strain in her shoulders, the tight way she holds her jaw, the fatigue lingering behind her beautiful green eyes. But she doesn't stop. She never does.

Not for one second.

She's in her element.

And for a moment, I just watch her.

She's come so far from the woman I had to pull out of bed every morning, the one who used to stare at Gideon like she didn't know what to do with him. The one who used to look at him and see failure, loss, disappointment.

Not anymore.

Now, she is his fiercest protector.

She leans over the high chair, adjusting the little paper crown on Gideon's head, whispering something that makes him giggle, his chubby fingers reaching for her face. She laughs softly, pressing a kiss to his cheek before smoothing a hand over his curls.

She loves him.

Fully. Completely. Unquestionably.

And as I watch them, something in my chest clenches—something heavy, something sharp, something dangerously close to relief.

She's come back to us.

She's come back to me.

"Ryan, can you bring out the cupcakes?" Camille calls over her shoulder, breaking me from my thoughts.

I clear my throat, shaking off the moment. "Yeah, I got it."

The scent of vanilla buttercream fills the kitchen as I set

the tray onto the table, my movements slow, careful. The migraine hasn't let up, but I can't let that ruin today.

Gideon babbles happily in his high chair, kicking his legs, smacking his little hands against the tray. My boy. My fighter.

He's behind, yeah. But he's strong. He'll catch up.

He always does.

"Hey, big man," I murmur, crouching down so we're eye level. "You ready for your big day?"

He grins at me, his face lighting up in that way that makes everything worth it.

I stroke a hand over his curls. "You're gonna have a great birthday, G. I promise."

His giggle is soft, warm, pure.

I won't let him feel like less.

Not for one second.

I know Camille struggles with the comparisons. I know she sees RJ sprinting across a room while Gideon still wobbles, struggling to stand. I know she hates how easily people point it out, how they whisper about it when they think we can't hear.

But I don't care.

Gideon is mine.

My son. My blood. My legacy.

And he is perfect.

The doorbell rings, and the house fills with movement, voices, laughter.

Ricki is the first to arrive, wrapping Camille in a hug before heading straight for Gideon, cooing at him as he kicks happily in his high chair.

More guests trickle in—friends, family, people who have stuck by us even after the bankruptcy, after the scandals, after the fall.

I shake hands, nod, try to ignore the persistent pounding in my head.

Then—

Tiffany walks in.

And everything in me tenses.

She steps inside like she owns the place, her confidence effortless, her hair sleek, her makeup flawless. She's wearing white, because of course she is—because Tiffany doesn't give a damn about etiquette or subtlety.

But I don't care about her.

I only care about the little boy walking beside her.

RJ.

He's dressed in a tiny little designer tracksuit, sneakers fresh, too clean, like he hasn't spent a single second playing outside today. He looks around, taking in the decorations, the balloons, the cake, the warmth of the home.

And for a split second, I see it—

The hesitation.

The way his little body leans toward me.

The way his eyes search for something familiar.

Then, just as quickly, it's gone.

Tiffany nudges him forward, and he glances up at me, expression unreadable.

"Hey, buddy," I say, forcing a smile, crouching down. "You happy to be here?"

He hesitates—just for a second—then nods.

I reach out, ruffling his hair. "Good. We're happy to have you."

Tiffany sniffs, tossing her hair over her shoulder. "Yeah, well, let's just make sure we don't overstep today, huh? I wouldn't want him to get confused about where he really belongs."

My jaw tightens.

I could say something. I could remind her that half the trust I built is for RJ. I could remind her that if it weren't for me, she wouldn't be able to afford the lavish birthday parties, the designer bags, the goddamn house she's living in.

But I don't.

Because today isn't about her.

I glance over Tiffany's shoulder, noticing the woman she brought with her—Giselle.

She's one of Tiffany's close party friends. One of the women she goes out on the prowl with, looking for athletes.

Tiffany always does this.

Always brings someone, always keeps herself surrounded, as if she's too important to ever show up alone.

I exhale, rising to my feet, my headache pounding now.

The house is crowded, the voices too loud, the light too sharp.

But none of it matters.

Because today is for Gideon.

And I will not let anything ruin that.

Tiffany moves through the party like she's the guest of honor. Head high, steps slow and deliberate, making sure everyone sees her, making sure the world knows that she's here. That she still holds some kind of power.

I see the moment she spots Camille. I don't move right away, just watch. Camille is near the dessert table, adjusting one of the decorations, her posture too stiff, too controlled. Tiffany approaches, her heels clicking against the polished floors, her voice dripping with that fake-ass sweetness she's perfected.

"Camille, did you get the list of Ryan's allergies I sent over?"

Camille turns slowly, her face perfectly neutral.

"Absolutely," she says, voice even. "There's no shellfish or peanut butter on the menu."

Tiffany hums, smiling like she won something. "Great. Wouldn't want my baby to have a reaction at his own brother's party."

She lingers for a second, as if waiting for Camille to react. Waiting for a slip, a crack, anything.

But Camille doesn't give her one. She just smiles back.

Polite. Controlled. Lethal.

Tiffany nods, satisfied, and struts away, her hips swaying, already moving on to the next conversation.

But Camille—

Camille stays frozen. Her hand clenches around the napkin she's holding, crumpling it like she's imagining Tiffany's throat instead.

Her eyes, though. That's what gets me. There's murder in them. Pure, seething rage barely held together by the thinnest thread of restraint.

I feel it from across the room.

I see it in the way her chest rises too sharply, too unevenly.

And I know—

If I don't do something about Tiffany, Camille is going to explode.

One day.

Maybe not today.

Maybe not tomorrow.

But soon.

And when it happens?

There will be no putting out that fire.

The party is going well.

Better than I expected, given the circumstances.

Gideon is in his high chair, happily smashing handfuls of cake into his mouth, frosting smeared across his chubby cheeks. Camille, despite the tension simmering beneath her surface, moves with effortless grace, greeting guests, checking in with the caterers, making sure everything is perfect. And for the most part, it is.

The house is alive in a way it hasn't been in a long time—full of laughter, warmth, celebration. It almost feels normal. Like old times. Like before.

I try to focus on that, on the good.

I sip a glass of water, ignoring the lingering headache pulsing behind my eyes. The pain has dulled to something manageable, a background hum of discomfort, but it's still there, a reminder that my body isn't what it used to be. I push the thought aside and lean against the kitchen counter, watching Camille move across the room.

She's in her element—hosting, orchestrating, making sure everything goes smoothly. But I can see the edges of her control fraying. Every now and then, her smile slips. Her fingers tighten around a glass just a little too hard. Her eyes flicker with something dark when she watches Tiffany float around the party like she belongs here.

She's barely keeping it together.

And I don't blame her.

Tiffany has been making a spectacle of herself all afternoon, parading RJ around like a prize, ensuring everyone sees how advanced he is, how strong, how fast, how he already walks and runs with ease. The constant comparisons between RJ and Gideon have been subtle but insidious, like little needles piercing Camille's skin, one after the other.

I know it's killing her.

But she hasn't said a word.

Not yet.

The hours stretch on, the party winding down, guests slowly filtering out. I exhale, rolling my shoulders, letting myself believe—just for a moment—that we might actually get through this unscathed.

And then—

A scream shatters the air.

Not just a scream. A woman screaming.

My body goes rigid. My head snaps up.

I know that voice. It's Tiffany.

I push off the counter and move fast, weaving through the dwindling crowd, my pulse spiking. The moment I step into the backyard, I see them.

Tiffany and Camille.

Tiffany is livid, her face twisted in rage, her hand gripping RJ's tiny wrist so tight his skin is turning red. Camille stands across from her, frozen, Gideon still in her arms. Her face is a mask of carefully controlled fury, but I know her. I know that look. She's unraveling.

"You tried to kill my baby!" Tiffany shrieks, voice shrill, hysteria dripping from every syllable. "Are you insane? What the hell is wrong with you?"

The air in my lungs turns cold.

"What the hell is going on?" I demand, stepping between them. My voice is sharp, cutting, and Tiffany immediately turns her wrath on me.

"Ask her!" She jabs a manicured finger at Camille. "Ask your crazy-ass wife why she tried to poison my son!"

My stomach plummets.

I turn to Camille, searching her face, waiting for the denial, the outrage, something.

She lifts her chin, her grip tightening on Gideon. "That's not what happened," she says, her voice cold, even. "I would never—"

"I saw you!" Tiffany cuts her off, eyes wild, voice cracking. "I saw you handing RJ peanut butter! You knew he was allergic, and you gave it to him anyway! Were you trying to kill him? Were you hoping he'd go into shock so you could finally get rid of him?"

Camille flinches like she's been struck. The accusation hangs heavy in the air. Around us, the remaining guests have gone silent, all eyes locked on the unfolding disaster.

I step forward, lowering my voice. "Tiff, you need to calm down."

"I am not calming down!" she shrieks. "My baby could have died!"

RJ sniffles, his big eyes darting between us, scared, confused.

Camille takes a breath, but I can see it—the shake in her shoulders, the tremor in her fingers. She's close to breaking. "Tiffany, I didn't give him peanut butter. Someone brought Reese's Cups. I saw him reach for one, and I stopped him. That's it."

"Bullshit!"

"It's the truth," Camille snaps. "You walked in right as I was grabbing it from him. You didn't see what actually happened."

Tiffany lets out a sharp, humorless laugh. "You expect me to believe that?"

"I don't care what you believe!" Camille's voice rises, her composure cracking. "I stopped him. I made sure he didn't eat it. You should be thanking me, not accusing me of trying to kill him!"

I put a hand on Tiffany's shoulder, trying to ground her, trying to stop this before it gets any worse. "Tiff—"

She shoves my hand off.

"I'm done," she seethes. "I'm done playing nice with your wife. I don't want that woman anywhere near my child. Do you hear me, Ryan?"

Her words land like a hammer to my ribs.

"Tiffany, let's be reasonable—"

"No," she cuts me off. "You always defend her. Always make excuses for her." She shakes her head, her chest heaving. "I should've fought harder for full custody. I knew this was a mistake. I knew she was jealous, and I knew she'd try to hurt him."

Camille laughs—a short, bitter sound. "Oh, please. You live for this kind of drama. You want me to be the villain so you can keep playing the victim."

Tiffany's eyes narrow. "Oh, I play the victim?" She takes a step closer, lowering her voice to a lethal whisper. "At least I didn't bankrupt my family. At least I didn't lose everything because my husband couldn't keep his dick in his pants."

Camille stiffens.

For a second, I think she might hit her.

The energy between them is crackling, dangerous, one wrong move away from turning violent.

Then—

RJ lets out a small, broken sob.

And just like that, the fight drains out of Camille.

Her face crumbles for the briefest moment before she steels herself, turning away.

Gideon, sensing her distress, starts to cry, little wails bubbling up from his chest. Without hesitation, Camille lifts him higher, pressing his face into her shoulder, rocking him gently, soothing him even as her own body trembles.

The sight of her like that—shaking, holding onto Gideon like a lifeline—does something to me. Something that makes me want to wrap her up and get her away from all of this.

But Tiffany isn't done.

She grips RJ's wrist, tugging him closer. "Come on, baby. We're leaving."

"Tiffany, wait," I try.

She ignores me, turning to Giselle. "Let's go."

Giselle, who's been standing back watching with wide, delighted eyes, smirks before following her out.

Just like that, they're gone.

The silence they leave behind is suffocating.

I exhale sharply, rubbing my temple.

That could have been worse.

It was bad, but it could have been worse.

Camille is still holding Gideon, her fingers running over his back, her jaw clenched tight. She won't look at me.

And for the first time, a horrible thought creeps into my mind.

I don't think Camille would ever hurt RJ.

Not really.

But when Tiffany accused her—when she said those words out loud—Camille's reaction wasn't outrage.

It wasn't horror.

It was something else.

Something I can't quite explain.

And for the first time, I wonder—

Am I really so sure?

CHAPTER
THIRTY-SEVEN

NOW - CAMILLE

MY HEAD IS POUNDING and I need some rest after all that's happened.

There's still blood drying on RJ's face, shattered trust bleeding across every wall, and the stinging echo of Gideon's voice replaying in my mind like a curse I can't shake.

"You and Dad have always loved RJ more than me."

He's gone.

Out the door. Into the street. Into God knows what.

And I can't breathe.

I've called him five times—six, now. Each one goes to voicemail. Each one is met with the same hollow beep, the mechanical coldness of "Leave a message after the tone," like that'll be enough to keep my baby safe tonight. Like that'll tether him to this house he just tore himself from.

I rush down the stairs, phone still clutched in my hand, my mind spinning with worst-case scenarios—him running into traffic, getting picked up by the police, finding another innocent girl and killing her. That happened the last time he stormed away from me. I can't let that happen. I won't.

It hits me that I really think Gideon did this. He had to, right? He planted the steroids to get RJ in trouble. Did he plan this as soon as RJ asked him to go to the party that night? Or was it the fight he had that triggered it?

I grab my keys from the counter with trembling fingers, already halfway to the front door when I see Ryan.

Still sitting in the kitchen. Same chair. Same slouched posture. The smoothie glass is empty in front of him, sweat from the cup pooling in a perfect circle on the wood. He hasn't moved.

Not once.

He looks up at me, and for a second, there's something helpless in his eyes. Something childlike. His mouth opens slightly, like he wants to say something. Maybe "Are you okay?" Maybe "Where's Gideon?" Maybe just "Camille."

But I don't want to hear it.

I see red.

All of it—everything—boils up and spills out of me like lava I've kept contained for years.

I march straight toward him, my breath ragged, my voice rising before I even know what I'm going to say.

"This is all your fault!"

My hand moves before I can stop it. The crack of skin meeting skin echoes louder than the silence that follows.

The slap reverberates through me like a shot fired. His head jerks to the side, his body folding slightly from the force of it. The sound is sickening. Final.

And still, he doesn't say a word.

He just stares at me.

Wide, wet eyes. Shocked, yes—but not angry. Not indignant. Not defensive.

Afraid.

But also…

He understands.

That's what guts me most.

Because deep down, I know—I've always known—he

wants to be punished. He's been waiting for it. For this. For me to finally unload the weight of everything he's done, everything he's broken, everything we lost because of him.

The woman I used to be.

The life we used to have.

The future we were supposed to build.

His lip trembles. Just slightly. And he swallows hard, nodding once. A silent admission. A silent *I deserve that*.

And it should satisfy me.

It should ease something. Vindicate me.

But it doesn't.

It just makes the pain worse.

Because it doesn't fix it. It doesn't rewind time. It doesn't bring Gideon back through that door or scrub the blood from RJ's face or glue together the shattered bones of this broken family.

I feel myself unraveling right in front of him, my fists clenched, my chest heaving. I can't be here right now. I can't look at him. I can't sit in this house and wait for another phone call. Another knock at the door. Another piece of my world to fall apart.

So I turn.

Without another word, I storm out the front door, keys in one hand, phone in the other, and rage humming beneath my skin like a live wire.

Because if I don't find my son tonight—

If something happens to him—

I will never forgive Ryan.

And I will never forgive myself.

The night air is sharp and biting, the kind that seeps into your bones and lingers long after you've come inside. Christmas lights twinkle from every corner of the neighborhood—soft blues and reds blinking against frosted windows, inflatable Santas bobbing gently in the wind, nativity scenes glowing under porches like they're guarding peace itself.

But peace feels a thousand miles away.

I've been driving around for nearly an hour, my hands stiff on the wheel, my breath fogging the windshield. Every few blocks, I roll down the window and call his name into the darkness. Nothing.

It's only when I cut through one of the adjacent neighborhoods—nicer, quieter, the kind of place where people walk their dogs in Patagonia fleeces and call the cops if someone blinks too long at their mailbox—that I spot him.

Gideon.

Hunched shoulders, hands jammed deep in his hoodie, walking slowly down the sidewalk like he's got nowhere to be and no one to answer to. His breath clouds in front of him, visible in the glow of someone's glittering reindeer display.

I pull up beside him, tires crunching softly over the frost-laced street. My heart pounds as I lower the passenger-side window.

"Get in," I say.

He doesn't stop walking.

"Gideon," I repeat, sharper now. "Get in the car before somebody thinks you're casing houses and calls the damn police."

That gets him.

He hesitates, glancing over his shoulder, and for the first time I get a good look at his face.

My stomach twists.

His cheek is swollen and red, lips split, a smear of dried blood along his jaw. Worse than RJ, and that's saying something.

But still, he's got that expression. That same defiant scowl he wore the day he learned to say *no* and decided he liked it.

He opens the door slowly, slides into the passenger seat, and slams it shut without a word.

We ride in silence.

I don't ask where he's been. I don't ask what he was thinking.

I don't ask if he's okay.

Because I know he's not.

He's angry. Wounded. A ticking bomb of resentment and shame.

And for a second—for just a flicker—I think about asking him to go to Principal Kipton. To confess what he did. To take responsibility. Clear RJ's name before it's too late.

But I glance over at him—at his bruised face, the tremble in his hands, the fury simmering just beneath his skin—and I know now's not the time.

So I drive.

The world outside the windshield is quiet and festive, all plastic joy and mechanical twinkle. But inside the car, the silence is thick enough to choke on.

When we pull up to the house, the porch light is on. A single strand of Christmas lights flickers across the awning, half the bulbs dead. Another forgotten thing.

We step inside, both of us still silent, and that's when I hear it—soft voices coming from the living room.

I motion for Gideon to follow me, and we round the corner.

And there they are.

Ryan and RJ.

Sitting together on the couch like nothing is broken. Like everything is still okay.

RJ is holding a piece of paper, his voice excited and full of pride. "And that's my final GPA—3.8. I almost got a 4.0, but Mr. Devers gave me a B on that poetry analysis."

I pause in the doorway, watching, barely breathing.

Ryan stares at the paper. At first, there's nothing. Blankness. That terrifying, soulless fog that's started to take him more often than not. The kind that empties him out like someone blew a hole through the middle of his mind.

But then...

He smiles.

Not big. Not strong.

But a real smile.

Lopsided. Slower than it used to be. But real.

RJ doesn't flinch. Doesn't make it awkward. He beams. "You always said grades mattered, right? Gotta be smart *and* strong."

I watch him, my heart thudding, a strange weight blooming in my chest. Because the truth is—I never had to write *any* of RJ's essays. Never had to beg for extensions or do his work for him like I did for Ryan in high school and college. The essays I stayed up writing just to keep Ryan eligible. All those years carrying his potential on my back.

RJ earned this.

All of it.

He's an upgraded version of Ryan. A better design. And I didn't birth him. I nurtured him but I couldn't take full credit.

"Why are you talking to him?" Gideon's voice cuts like a blade. "He's not even here!"

RJ flinches, paper falling slightly from his hand. Ryan's eyes drift again, back into that vacant middle distance.

He turns and storms up the stairs, his footfalls hard and furious.

I don't stop him.

Because the truth is, I know why he's lashing out.

Gideon hasn't spoken to Ryan in weeks. Barely looks at him. He can't stand the blankness. The pauses. The forgetfulness. He doesn't have the patience for it. The grace. And he thinks this is his father's karma for bringing RJ into our lives.

But more than that?

He still believes Ryan always loved RJ more.

But he's wrong. Ryan has always gone above and beyond to show that he loved them equally. Even though he's had to love them differently, since they were very different.

That's what's tearing him apart.

As Gideon's bedroom door slams shut upstairs, I stand

frozen, the Christmas lights from the window casting colors across the living room floor. Red. Green. Blue.

But everything inside this house?

Is black and white.

Split clean down the middle.

And we are barely holding together.

CHAPTER
THIRTY-EIGHT

THEN - CAMILLE

IT'S A QUIET SUNDAY MORNING. The kind that floats soft and slow through the windows, golden light spilling across the floorboards of our new, smaller house just outside of Atlanta. There's no sound but the low buzz of the heater and the occasional rustle of Olivia's footsteps as she toddles down the hall in her fuzzy socks, her curls bouncing with every step. She's singing something off-key, something only she understands, and it wraps around my chest like a balm I didn't know I needed.

This house is modest—bare bones compared to the mansion we left behind. No marble counters, no winding staircases, no floor-to-ceiling windows. Just four bedrooms, two and a half baths, and a kitchen that smells like lavender dish soap and family.

But it's enough.

It's more than enough.

And it's quiet. Peaceful. Safe.

We moved here about a year after Olivia was born. Ryan found the listing, sent me the pictures while I was still recovering in bed, baby in my arms. He'd said, "It's not flashy, but it's got good bones." I didn't care about bones. I just needed somewhere we could start over. Somewhere the walls weren't still haunted by the echoes of a life we lost.

We're still sorting through the financial wreckage—paperwork, legal settlements, whatever scraps our lawyer and the financial advisors have managed to salvage from the bankruptcy—but we're not drowning anymore. And that's something.

Olivia, in all her light and softness, brought a peace into our lives I didn't think we'd ever feel again.

That pregnancy was different.

I don't know how to describe it. Maybe it was the fact that we knew this would be our last chance. Or maybe it was because I was finally starting to see Ryan again—not the broken version of him we all lived with after the scandals, but the man I married. The man who used to sing to my belly and kiss my shoulder in the mornings. The man who brought me mint tea when I was too nauseous to eat, who rubbed my feet at night even when he was exhausted himself.

He was present. More present than he'd ever been.

And when Olivia came into the world, screaming and beautiful, it was like the universe had pressed pause just long enough for us to catch our breath.

Gideon didn't take to her—at least not right away.

He was two when Olivia was born, old enough to notice the shift, to feel the loss of being the only child. Already quiet and serious, he grew colder, watching from a distance as she cried, as we doted on her. He never acted out, but the resentment was there—in the way he avoided eye contact, the way he went silent around her.

She adored him instantly, smiled at him like he was her whole world. He barely looked at her.

It's only recently that he's started to soften. A toy he shares without being asked. A juice box handed over. A quiet kind of trying.

But for all the joy we've found here, there are shadows too.

That day—Gideon's birthday—left a wound in this family that hasn't fully closed. Especially where RJ is concerned.

After the incident, Tiffany went full scorched earth. Screaming, threatening, documenting. She stopped all communication with me, demanded legal boundaries. Now, Ryan only sees RJ alone and only once a month. A few supervised hours in a neutral space—usually a park, sometimes a family center. He's not allowed to bring RJ here. Not allowed to take him around our children.

And me? I haven't seen RJ since that day.

Sometimes I wonder if he remembers it—remembers how I reached for his hand, how I snatched the candy from his grip before he could unwrap it. Remembers the panic in my voice, the urgency in my eyes. I wasn't trying to hurt him. I was trying to protect him. But Tiffany didn't care. She was waiting for that moment. She wanted a reason. Needed a reason.

The child support payments were slashed after Ryan's finances took the hit. Suddenly, her designer bags slowed down. Her "Mompreneur" brand dried up. And just like that, she was back on the scene—back at the lounges, back in full makeup by noon, always with a "girl's night" excuse in her captions. I can't prove it, but I know she's looking for a new baller. Someone younger. Someone with a longer career and less baggage.

Meanwhile, Ryan shows me pictures.

Every time he comes back from one of their visits, he slides his phone across the kitchen table like he's afraid I might not look. But I always do.

RJ is growing so fast. Taller than Gideon. Thicker, too. His face is expressive—curious eyes, quick smile, that same dimple Ryan has on the left side of his cheek. He's got Ryan's build already, that natural athleticism you can't teach. There's a sharpness to him, though. An edge I don't remember from before.

I watch the kids play from the patio while sipping an iced tea and eating grapes. Ryan walks outside, beaming, looking out at his children before he opens his mouth to speak.

There's a kind of hurt that doesn't make a sound when it enters the room—but you feel it settle in your chest like smoke, thick and invisible.

That's what I felt the second Ryan said it.

"RJ! Come here, son!"

Gideon froze mid-laugh. The joy drained from his face so quickly, it felt like a power outage. One second light. The next, hollow darkness.

My stomach dropped.

I knew he didn't mean it. Knew the dementia was getting worse, that his memory was glitching more often, slipping when he was tired or overwhelmed. But that didn't matter in the moment. Not to Gideon. Not to me.

"I'm Gideon," he shouted, his voice cracking as he turned to face his father. "I'm not RJ!"

Ryan blinked like he'd just been slapped. Confused, disoriented. His hand went up to shield his eyes again, but it didn't matter—he was already too late. The damage was done.

"I—wait, Gid... I didn't mean..." Ryan trailed off, shaking his head. "I know who you are, buddy. I just—my brain—"

I stood there for a beat too long, watching my son's face harden, watching the wall go up behind his eyes. He turned and stomped back toward the playhouse, brushing Olivia off when she tried to grab his hand.

And I snapped.

I crossed the yard and stepped up to Ryan, my voice low, sharp, trembling with all the weight I've carried for years. "You looked your son in the eye and called him by your other child's name."

Ryan's expression collapsed in on itself. "Camille, please—"

"You didn't even hesitate," I said, my voice shaking. "You don't even see him."

"I did. I *do*." Ryan reached out, but I flinched back.

"You don't know what that does to him." I shook my head, fighting the well of emotion in my throat. "He's already spent his whole life thinking you love RJ more. You just proved it."

Ryan looked like he wanted to cry. Like he would, if he had the strength left. His shoulders slumped. "I said the wrong name. It's the dementia, Camille. I didn't mean—"

"That doesn't matter to Gideon," I cut in. "That moment will live in him, Ryan. Like a bruise no one else can see."

Silence.

I exhaled slowly, swallowing down the scream rising in my throat. "You need to go inside."

Ryan looked toward Gideon, then back to me, guilt carved into every line of his face. He nodded, said nothing, and shuffled back toward the house like a man twice his age.

When I turned around, I saw Gideon sitting in the grass, arms folded, staring at a crack in the sidewalk. Olivia was next to him, babbling something about lions and jungle trees, trying to make him laugh.

He didn't.

And I wondered—for the hundredth time—how much more this boy can take before he closes for good.

I know it's not his fault.

I know his mind is breaking because the world broke him first.

Ryan didn't wake up one day and forget how to say our son's name. He didn't choose this unraveling, this slipping into fog. And I—I shouldn't have taken it out on him. Not today. Not like that.

But that's the thing about pain—it doesn't always know

where to go. It leaks, spills, lashes out at the person standing closest. And today, that person was him.

I know Ryan deserves some mercy. Even his cheating has been a result of poor impulse control from brain injuries. I've always known that he simply couldn't help himself. Some people with poor impulse control fight. Others cheat. I know he loves me.

And he didn't get like this on his own.

It wasn't just football. Not just the years of tackles and concussions and blackouts under stadium lights. This didn't start on the field.

It started in a house with no light, no warmth, no softness.

With a woman who birthed a special boy and raised him like he was nothing.

Ryan's mother never saw what treasure she had. She looked at her son and saw a target. A punching bag. A shame she couldn't drink away. I used to wonder how someone so vicious, so mean, could've created Ryan. And I wondered why he never fought back.

I remember the first time I really saw him—saw what he was living through. We were in high school, and he had a knot at the back of his head that didn't come from football. It wasn't football season. He finally confessed that his mother beat him but he still loved her. She was having a hard time being a single mother and an immigrant. Excuses. I hated her from the moment I learned what she did to him.

One night when my parents were asleep, I snuck over to his house so we could spend some alone time together. These moments were rare. His mom was supposed to be working the night shift at the nursing home. She was a CNA, barely holding onto her job because she smelled like gin half the time and called in sick the other half.

We were lying on his twin bed, the TV low, his hand warm in mine. I was tracing the scar on his bicep, one I already knew better than my own, when we heard the front door slam.

Ryan went still.

I'll never forget how fast the color drained from his face.

His mother stumbled into the room less than a minute later, reeking of liquor, wild-eyed, ranting about how he left a bowl in the sink and didn't put her laundry in the dryer. Like that was enough reason to beat her only child bloody.

And then she did.

She slapped him so hard his head jerked to the side.

I moved in front of him before I even realized it. I stood between them, yelling, pushing her back, trying to get her out of the room. She wasn't hearing a thing. Just screaming and swinging. And Ryan—he just stood there.

Frozen.

Like this was normal.

Like this was how things always went.

We ended up in the foyer, still shouting, her stumbling over her own rage, still reaching for him. And that's when something in me broke.

When I saw her turn, saw the way she moved toward him like a snake winding up to strike again—

I pushed her.

I didn't think about it. I didn't aim to kill. I just wanted her to stop. Just wanted to protect him.

But the push was harder than I meant.

She lost her balance.

And then she was gone.

Tumbling backward down the stairs.

Her neck hit first.

I heard it snap.

Then came the blood.

A pool of it, blooming like ink across the tile. Her body crumpled, twisted in a way I'll never forget. Her eyes still open.

Ryan dropped to his knees. He didn't speak. Didn't scream. Just stared.

And me?

I knelt beside him. Put a hand on his back. Whispered in his ear, calm as anything, "You didn't see anything. You were asleep. She must've come home drunk, fell down the stairs. Everybody knows what she's like. Nobody's going to question it."

He didn't respond.

He just kept staring.

So I took his face in my hands, forced him to look at me. "Do you understand me? You didn't see anything. You don't say anything. Not until the morning."

He nodded, eventually. Shaking. Pale.

I slipped out of the house like a shadow, careful not to step in the blood. I left him alone with her body, and yeah, it gutted me to do it—but it was necessary. It had to look clean. It had to look *believable*. No trace of me, no trace of the truth.

I remember pausing at the bottom of the stairs, looking down at her crumpled form, blood pooling beneath her like a dark halo. And I smiled.

Because no one—*no one*—hurts Ryan and walks away unscathed.

She thought she could break him. Keep him small. Crush whatever light was left in him. But she didn't see what I saw. She didn't understand that Ryan was destined for more. He was supposed to be great. He *will* be great.

And anyone who tries to get in the way of that?

They go.

Even though Ryan and I wouldn't marry until years later, that night tied us together in a way no ring ever could. We shared something deeper than vows. We shared blood. We shared silence.

We shared a secret that could bury us both.

And I don't regret it.

Not even a little.

CHAPTER
THIRTY-NINE

NOW - CAMILLE

I DON'T REMEMBER FALLING asleep last night.

Only that I woke up with my jaw clenched, my neck stiff, and the ache behind my eyes that always comes from too much thinking and not enough peace.

The house is quiet—eerily so. Gideon and Olivia are at school. Ryan is in the living room, the TV flickering in front of him, but I'm not sure he's actually watching. And RJ?

Still upstairs.

Still angry. Still nursing that sense of betrayal I can't seem to reach past. I don't blame him. What Gideon did was cruel and unfair, but I'm going to make it right.

I'm in the kitchen, nursing lukewarm coffee I don't want, when a firm knock rattles the front door.

It's Xavier. Punctual as always, standing there in his tailored coat like he's not about to step into a house held together by fraying nerves and secrets.

"Morning," he says when I open the door.

I step aside to let him in. We head straight to the kitchen.

He doesn't waste time.

"I talked to the school," he says, setting his phone down

on the table like it's a warning or a promise. "They're willing to let RJ come back. On one condition."

"What is it?"

"A drug test. Full panel. They want proof there's nothing in his system, especially steroids."

I exhale, pressing the mug to my temple like the warmth might ease the ache behind my eyes. "And if he passes?"

"Then he's back by Monday. Clean record. No disciplinary action."

Relief rises in me—sharp, fleeting.

"Thank you," I murmur.

"We're still deep in the trenches of this investigation," Xavier says, his voice low and measured. "The police are planning to test the boys' clothes to see if there's any blood evidence. When I saw the pictures from the crime scene…I was astonished. Violet was attacked with rage, not just force. They still haven't located the murder weapon—which, for now, is a good thing."

I tighten my grip on the mug.

"What about the blood on Gideon's shirt?" I ask, my voice barely above a whisper.

"We'll see," he says, tapping the edge of his phone. "Gideon claimed he got into a fight, and several kids at the party backed that up. They said it got physical. Could explain the blood."

He pauses, gives me a look. One I don't like.

"There's no visible blood on RJ's clothes," he continues. "And with the nature of Violet's injuries…whoever did it would've been close. There would've been splatter. There should have been *something*."

I swallow the lump forming in my throat.

"What are you thinking?" I ask carefully. "Who do you think could've done this?"

Xavier leans back in the chair, folding his hands slowly, deliberately.

"Well, first of all," he says, "if I'm going to act as your

attorney in any capacity—if I'm going to protect this family—I need you to tell me where you were that night."

A chill moves through me, settling in the hollow of my chest.

"It's only a matter of time before the police ask," he adds, watching me closely.

I look down into my coffee, now cold and untouched. "I can't tell you that," I mutter.

It's not defiance—it's fear. If anyone knew where I really was that night… if that truth came to light, it wouldn't just ruin everything. It would unravel other people too. It would burn down what little is left standing.

"Camille." Xavier's voice sharpens. "I don't care how bad it is. I don't care how complicated. I need to know before they do. Otherwise, I can't help you. I can't run interference, I can't protect RJ, and I sure as hell can't protect you if they decide to widen the scope of this investigation."

He's right.

But I stay silent, chewing the inside of my cheek until the metallic taste of blood blooms on my tongue.

Because if I tell him the truth…

He'll never look at me the same.

And neither will Ryan.

"I hope you change your mind," Xavier says as he heads for the door, pausing just long enough to give me that look—the one that says he knows more than he's letting on. You said you wouldn't mind being a suspect…" I wouldn't mind because I thought it would be saving RJ. But the more I think about it, I'm starting to think Gideon is the one who killed Violet. Murder is in his DNA because I implanted it there.

With that he's gone.

I sit there in the silence he leaves behind, trying to untangle the knots tightening in my chest. Trying to figure out what comes next. How to fix what's broken—if it's even fixable.

Hours pass. The sun begins to dip, casting long shadows

through the windows, and then I hear the front door creak open.

The kids are home.

Gideon stomps in without a word, his energy dark and coiled. He doesn't look at me, doesn't look at anyone. Just charges up the stairs and slams his bedroom door. Olivia enters in behind him but even she keeps her distance. She's always been cautious with him. I wish they were closer. I wish he had someone in this house who understood him— who could reach him when I can't. Because right now, I think Gideon feels completely alone.

"Hey, Daddy!" Olivia calls out brightly, her voice slicing through the tension like a beam of light.

Ryan, still in the living room, turns to her with a slow smile. That child loves him in a way that's so pure it almost hurts. And despite everything—his decline, his distance—he lights up when she enters the room. Like she's the only thing he remembers how to hold onto.

I let them have their moment and quietly head upstairs. I stop outside Gideon's door and knock gently.

"How was your day?" I ask.

There's a pause. Then, muffled but sharp: "Please leave me alone. Go check on your favorite son."

I press my lips together, forcing down the sting.

I *have* checked on RJ—multiple times today. And he is not okay. He's being framed for murder. He lost his girlfriend. His school nearly suspended him over something he didn't do. Everything is falling apart around him.

I sigh and walk away from Gideon's door, retreating to my bedroom. I sink onto the edge of the bed and reach for my phone.

There's a new text waiting.

"Let me see you tonight. It's been too long."

My heart skips.

"No. We need to keep it cool for a while. Things are crazy for me."

The reply comes fast.

"Let me relieve that stress."

I hesitate.

Temptation is a dangerous thing—especially when it comes wrapped in understanding and the promise of escape. But I can't afford escape right now. I can't afford anything that could make this worse.

I lock my phone and set it on the nightstand, just as I hear a soft knock at the door.

Olivia's voice follows.

"Mommy?"

I sit up straighter. "Come in, baby."

"I have a question," she says, closing the door softly behind her. "Is RJ going to jail?"

The question slices right through me. Her voice is small, barely more than a whisper, but the weight of it lands hard in my chest.

I sit up straighter, pat the spot next to me on the bed. She climbs up without hesitation, curling into my side.

"No, baby," I say gently, smoothing a hand over her hair. "He's not going to jail."

"But everyone at school says he will," she mumbles. "They're all talking about it. On Snapchat. On TikTok. It's everywhere."

My jaw tightens. I try to keep my face calm, measured, but my pulse is racing.

"He didn't do it," Olivia adds quickly, almost as if she's afraid I might believe them. "He would never do something like that."

I nod slowly. "I don't think he did either."

She pulls her phone out of the front pocket of her hoodie and unlocks it with a swipe. "Look."

She scrolls through a barrage of stories and screenshots, all flashing by in rapid succession, videos, memes, reposts of blurry screenshots from local news articles. There's RJ's face, taken from an old football post. His name, circled in red.

"Suspended." "Under investigation." "Tragic loss." "Blood evidence." Kids reposting it for clout. Making jokes. Cracking dark one-liners in the captions.

Then I see it.

The comment.

@Adeline_Sherwood

That whole family is crazy. Camille Bell did something to my shampoo in college and it made me bald. I still haven't grown my hair back. Evil runs through those people.

My stomach knots so hard I have to press my hand against it.

Addie. Of course it's her. I snatch the phone gently from Olivia's hands and quickly close the app.

"Don't look at that garbage," I say, my voice sharper than I intend. "People will say anything online."

But my hands are already trembling.

It's been years—but her voice, her face, the smug tilt of her chin, the way she carried herself like she was untouchable—it all comes back like it never left. Adeline Sherwood. She used to walk around GBU like she owned it. Like her pretty face and whisper-thin waist gave her immunity. She flirted with Ryan. Followed him around like a groupie. And when he finally gave in—when he betrayed me with her—that was her mistake.

Touching what was mine.

She thought she could get away with it. They always do, girls like her. Smiling wide with teeth too white, acting like rules don't apply to them. But I warned her. I gave her a chance. And when she didn't back off?

She paid for it. It was easy to slip in her room at the dorms while she was away. To my luck, she shampooed with a peppermint shampoo, I remembered because I had smelled it when she tossed her hair in my face. I mixed lye and extra peppermint oil in her shampoo and conditioner.

When I first saw Violet, I felt it—that same smug confidence, that same flirtatious little laugh. She didn't remind me of Addie. She mirrored her. And that was a problem.

Because the moment Violet got too close to RJ—too comfortable, too possessive—I saw it happening all over again. Another Addie. Another girl who thought she could take something that didn't belong to her.

And just like I warned Addie, I warned Violet too.

But they never listen.

And that's why they have to be dealt with.

CHAPTER
FORTY

THEN - RYAN

IT'S BEEN a long time coming. For years, I've had to walk on eggshells just to get a few hours with my son. Tiffany made sure of that. Visitation wasn't official, but she controlled the terms. If she was in a good mood, I got a weekend. If she was feeling petty, I got silence. No explanations. No callbacks. Just the cold shoulder and an Instagram post of RJ at brunch, captioned like she was doing it all alone. Like I didn't exist. Like I hadn't built half the life she was still clinging to.

But lately, she's softened—just enough to let me breathe. Just enough to give me hope. She agreed to let RJ come home with me this weekend. To finally visit the house I share with Camille. To be with his brother and sister like a real family. She texted me his school schedule and even packed his bag ahead of time. It felt like progress.

Until I saw the bruise.

It's faint, but unmistakable. Right beneath his eye, just starting to yellow. A fading fingerprint of pain. And RJ? He's quieter than usual. Withdrawn. His eyes dart away when I ask what he wants for dinner. His shoulders tense when I touch his back.

"What happened to your face?"

"I got in trouble for not cleaning my room."

We've just entered my car and I'm ready to take him home.

"Wait right here," I tell him.

He nods without asking why. Doesn't even look at me. I hop out of the car and head back to her door.

I knock on the door, jaw tight. She answers on the second try, barefoot in an oversized T-shirt, phone in one hand, attitude in the other.

"What?" she says, like I've interrupted something. Maybe a selfie. Maybe nothing at all.

I get straight to the point. "Why does RJ have a bruise on his face?"

She doesn't flinch. Doesn't blink. Just tilts her head, pretending to be confused. "What are you talking about?"

"He said you hit him. Because he didn't clean his room."

Her expression shifts, only slightly—amusement edging into irritation. "Oh, please. I popped him. It wasn't even that hard."

I step closer. "You hit him."

She shrugs. "Boys need discipline and you're not here to do it."

"He's a kid."

"He's my kid."

I can feel it rising in me—that familiar, bone-deep anger. The kind I've spent most of my adult life trying to outrun. The kind that used to live in my mother's house. The kind that took me years to unlearn.

"You think that gives you the right to put your hands on him?" I ask, voice low, steady.

"You act like I beat him with a belt or something," she snaps. "I told him to clean his room, and he didn't. He got slick with his mouth, and I corrected it."

"No," I say, stepping in just enough to make her pause. "You hit him. Just like my mother used to hit me."

She rolls her eyes. "Oh, here we go."

"You know what that does to a kid? The damage it leaves? You think I don't see what's happening here?"

"Ryan." She laughs, mocking. "You barely even see what's in front of you anymore. You think you can raise him better? With your memory? With whatever's going on up there?" She taps her temple with one manicured finger, the gesture cutting deeper than anything she's said.

"You're unraveling," she adds, voice venomous now. "No judge is gonna give you custody. So go ahead, act outraged. But we both know how this ends."

I stare at her, something hardening in me I haven't felt in a long time. It's not fear. It's not even rage. It's clarity.

Because now I see her for what she is—not a mother protecting her child, but a woman who's losing control and panicking. Lashing out. Grasping for whatever leverage she has left.

"I'm taking him," I say quietly. "And I'm going to fight for him. You won't be able to stop me."

She opens her mouth like she wants to say something else, some last dig—but I don't wait for it. I turn and walk away.

RJ is already buckled in the backseat, staring out the window like he's somewhere far, far away. I get in the car, start the engine, and drive.

I don't say a word. Not yet.

But in my chest, something is shifting.

I have to get my son out of that house.

I have to undo the damage before it becomes permanent.

Before RJ starts believing that pain is love.

Before he becomes what I used to be.

After we leave Tiffany's house, I don't take RJ straight home.

There's a knot in my chest that won't settle, no matter how tightly I grip the steering wheel. The bruise on his face keeps flashing in my mind—every time I glance at him in the rearview mirror, it's there, like a shadow stamped into his skin. He hasn't said much since we left. Just stares out the window, fiddling with the hem of his hoodie, lost in that quiet, heavy way I know too well. I used to do the same thing. Back when I was a kid. Back when I was getting beat for leaving dishes in the sink or forgetting to lock the door.

I pull into the ice cream shop without saying anything.

RJ looks over, surprised. "We're getting ice cream?"

I nod. "Yeah. Thought we could use a treat."

He doesn't smile, not right away. But he softens. And when we get inside and I tell him to get whatever he wants, he picks cookies and cream with rainbow sprinkles. Something sweet. Something soft to smooth out the edges Tiffany left behind.

When we get home, the front door swings open before we even reach it.

Gideon's standing there, arms crossed, eyes sharp. "Why does he get ice cream and I don't?"

He sees the cone that tightly RJ is gripping. The words hit before I have a chance to brace myself.

RJ stops in his tracks. I can already see the guilt creeping in, like he did something wrong just by accepting a scoop of sugar from his father. He looks at me, unsure.

"Gideon," I start, but Camille appears in the hallway, her eyes narrowing as she takes in the tension. She says nothing, but the message is loud and clear—*we talked about this.*

We agreed: no favorites. No special treatment. No cracks in the foundation that could grow into resentment.

Camille lets out a breath and grabs her keys from the hook.

"I'll go get some for everyone," she says. "Nobody's gonna be left out."

She doesn't wait for a reply. The door closes behind her, sharp and final.

In her absence, the air feels thick.

To break the silence, I nudge RJ's arm. "Wanna race?"

RJ perks up immediately. "Like a real race?"

"Yeah. Backyard. You, me, and G."

Gideon doesn't say anything at first. But after a beat, he huffs and mutters, "Fine."

We step outside, and Olivia follows, arms full of dolls. She plops down on the deck steps, eyes wide with curiosity, already narrating the moment like she's the announcer at the Olympics.

I line up with the boys at the edge of the yard. It's just grass and a small shed at the back fence, but to them, it might as well be a stadium.

"On your mark," I call.

RJ bounces on his toes.

"Get ready…"

Gideon tenses like a spring.

"Set…"

"GO!"

They bolt forward, legs pumping, laughter breaking loose in the wind. I hang back just enough to let them lead, my steps easy, my body holding back what it can still do. It's their moment.

RJ sprints ahead—fast, confident, effortless. He hits the finish and turns around, already throwing his hands in the air. "I win! I win!"

Olivia squeals, dropping her dolls and running off the deck to wrap her arms around him. "Winner!" she shouts, giggling. "You're the fastest!"

Gideon crosses the line seconds later—panting, red-faced, trying not to show how winded he is. He's not just slower. He's struggling. His eyes flick to RJ and Olivia, already celebrating like he doesn't exist. And I see it—the way his shoulders tense, the way his jaw tightens. That look in his eyes I've seen more and more lately.

He doesn't say anything.

He just storms back inside.

I start to follow him but stop at the door, watching through the glass as Olivia wraps her arm around RJ and leads him to the porch like he's some kind of hero. And in a way, he is. He's charismatic, athletic, smart. He's got my smile, my drive—hell, maybe even my future if things don't fall apart.

But Gideon?

He's different. And I don't know if different is enough.

I lean against the doorframe, running a hand over my face. The jealousy brewing in Gideon is only going to get worse. And I don't know how to stop it.

Because the truth is...

RJ is a star.

And no matter how much I love both of them—

Gideon doesn't have his shine.

CHAPTER
FORTY-ONE

NOW - CAMILLE

THE SHEETS ARE warm with the weight of him. His hand traces slow circles along my spine, his breath steady against the back of my neck, and for a second—just a second—I forget what waits for me at home. The tension. The silence. The blood-stained questions.

I close my eyes and let myself feel it—his mouth against my shoulder, his fingers brushing the edge of my thigh, the low murmur of *I missed you* whispered into my skin like a secret.

It's been so long since someone touched me like this. Ryan can't anymore. Not really. Not since everything started slipping from him. And I'm not just talking about the sex. I mean the presence. The focus. The man I married.

This? This is something else entirely. Something I needed more than I want to admit.

I haven't seen him—not since that night. The night Violet was murdered. Prior to Violet's murder, I was able to sneak away at least two times a week for our rendezvous.

I shift onto my back, watching the ceiling, the hotel fan kicking on with a soft hum. Guilt lingers somewhere beneath my ribs, but I push it down. I've been carrying too much lately. A little pleasure isn't a crime.

Eventually, I sit up and slide out of bed. My head is starting to throb, slow and mean. I reach for my bra, and he watches me dress, still tangled in the sheets.

"You okay?" he asks, voice low.

"Headache," I say, reaching for my blouse.

He leans over, opens his bag, and pulls out a gel capsule. "Here. This'll help."

I stare at it in his palm. "You know I hate swallowing pills. I'll take some BC powder when I get home."

He grins a little. "That's the only thing you hate swallowing," he murmurs, slipping it back into the bottle.

I laugh but I shudder inside. I don't know who I am right now. Just a woman cheating on her husband while her house implodes and one son might be a murderer and the other might go to jail.

I shake the thoughts off. I'm hoping for the best but it's looking to be the worst.

I finish getting dressed in silence. He does the same, pulling his shirt over his head, smiling as if we didn't just cross another line.

When I kiss him before we leave the room, it's not full of fire or frenzy—it's soft. Familiar. Like slipping into an old sweater that still fits a little too well.

We take the elevator down, him checking his watch, me adjusting my earrings. The lobby is quiet, understated. A fake pine tree decorated with red and white garland leans against the wall. There's jazzy Christmas music playing softly from somewhere near the lounge. It should be nothing.

But then I see them.

Two detectives—Detective Joseph and Detective Winters —standing at the front desk. Talking. Laughing, maybe. I can't hear. My stomach drops before my brain catches up.

They turn as we step into view.

"Good evening, Ms. Bell. Mr. Diggs."

My heart stops.

Quenton flinches. My stomach twists.

"Are you following me?" I ask, voice tight, but low enough to keep from drawing attention from the desk clerk now watching too closely.

Detective Joseph smiles, calm as ever. "Yes, ma'am. We've been looking into everyone connected to the case. You weren't home the night of Violet's murder, and that raised questions."

Detective Winters steps forward. "But now we know you were here. The hotel staff confirmed it. Time-stamped key card. Surveillance. That rules you out."

Relief doesn't come.

It can't. Not when Quenton stiffens beside me, eyes darting from me to the detectives.

"I'll call you later," I say to him quickly, keeping my face neutral, my tone light.

But he doesn't move.

He doesn't nod.

He doesn't say goodbye.

Instead, Quenton directs his attention toward the detectives, his jaw clenching. "Please don't tell my wife about this."

Detective Joseph shrugs. "Can't guarantee that, sir."

Winters adds, "Once an investigation widens like this, we don't always have control over what surfaces."

Quenton's face darkens. His entire body coils tight with rage, shame flickering behind his eyes.

He storms out without another word, his footsteps echoing sharply through the marble-floored lobby.

I'm left there alone. With them.

Joseph tucks his notepad away. "Once the DNA results come back, we'll be making an arrest. We've got the samples. The techs are already working on it. Whoever's under Violet's nails—that'll give us what we need."

Something sinks in me.

Low. Heavy.

They nod politely, like this is just another routine conversation, and walk away without ceremony. As if they didn't just upend what little I was trying to keep stitched together.

I don't say goodbye. I don't move until they disappear behind the glass doors.

And then I run.

Into the nearest restroom, through the swinging door, into a stall where the walls feel like they're closing in on me.

I drop to my knees and vomit into the toilet—violently, bitterly, until there's nothing left but dry heaves and tears.

Because I know whose DNA they're going to find.

And I know exactly who that arrest is going to destroy.

And worst of all?

I can't stop it.

CHAPTER
FORTY-TWO

THEN - RYAN

TIFFANY'S FUNERAL was a week ago.

Open casket. Grandiose flowers. Cameras parked outside the church like vultures. Reporters angled their lenses, hoping to catch RJ crying, or me cracking. They didn't get either. RJ didn't shed a tear. Just stood stiff in his black suit, staring at the floor like if he blinked, the whole world might fall apart.

I was glad when it was over.

Glad the headlines would move on. Glad I wouldn't have to drive to that house again and feel the heat rise in my chest every time Tiffany looked at me. Glad RJ was finally where he belonged. His mother was my greatest regret but RJ was one of the best parts of me. I couldn't wait for him to live with his siblings.

The suitcase barely made it past the threshold before Gideon started in.

"He's not playing with my video games," he snapped, arms crossed, eyes narrowed.

Camille gave him a warning look, but he didn't back down. He stormed upstairs and slammed his door before RJ could even step out of his shoes.

RJ didn't say a word. He looked around the living room like it was a museum exhibit—too clean, too still. His fingers twitched by his side like he didn't know what to do with them.

Then Olivia swooped in, bright as ever.

"Come on," she said, tugging his sleeve. "You can hang with me. We can stream anything in the basement."

She didn't wait for an answer. Just yanked him down the hallway, already talking about which movie they should watch. RJ followed, like a shadow being pulled by light.

I watched them go, something tight in my chest loosening a little.

Camille and I found each other in the kitchen, moving like a couple years removed from joy, but still trying. She poured two glasses of wine—her version of exhaling.

We leaned against the counter in silence.

"He doesn't even argue with Gideon," I said finally, nodding toward the stairs. "He's too tired to fight back."

"He just lost his mother," she said. "It'll get better. It's just an adjustment period."

I nodded, but didn't say what I was thinking. That he lost her long before she died. That he never really had her. She was just like my mother. Selfish and abusive. So, I had to fix it for him. He deserved a mother like Camille. Someone who would do anything for the ones she loved. It was her love that got me into the league. I messed it up but that's because I was messed up before I met her. She'll fix him though.

I swirled my wine and looked at my reflection in the glass.

"He's got talent," I said. "Football-wise. I've seen it. Quick feet. Good instincts. Coach is already watching him close."

"That's gonna be hard on Gideon."

"I know."

She took a sip, then set the glass down harder than necessary. "We're gonna have to try harder with him. You know that, right? He's already pulling away."

"I know."

I meant it. I did.

I loved Gideon. God, I loved that boy.

Even if he didn't have RJ's shine. Even if the world didn't clap for him the way they would for RJ. Even if the only way he knew how to stand out was by pushing people away.

"I hate that this is what it's come to," I said quietly. "I did this. I let it get this far."

Camille didn't say anything at first. Then: "Yeah. You did."

"Gideon will find his stride but I know I'm the reason he's different from RJ. He's deficient."

That one stung. But she wasn't wrong.

Gideon was different because of me. Because of what I let happen. Because I didn't stop sooner. Because I was too wrapped up in Tiffany, too consumed by guilt and lust, confusion and impulses. Because my damn brain's been slipping through my fingers like sand and I didn't know how to hold on.

I forgot Olivia's name last week. Stared her in the face and called her "baby girl," hoping she wouldn't notice. Sometimes I get halfway down the block and forget where I was going. Sometimes I look at Camille and mistake her for my mother. Once, I screamed at her because I thought she was about to hit me.

I cried after that. Not because I was scared. But because I knew—deep down—I was slipping. That the part of me that remembers is thinning out like worn fabric. I don't know how much time I have left. But I know I want to spend it with them. All of them.

The laughter from the basement floats up the stairs, muffled and light.

For a second, things almost feel normal.

Then I hear the floorboard creak behind us.

"Deficient?"

Gideon's voice cuts through the kitchen like a blade.

Camille turns fast, wine glass forgotten.

He's standing in the doorway, fists clenched, eyes rimmed red.

"I'm deficient?" he says again. "That's what you think of me?"

"No—G, that's not—" I start, but he's already gone.

Camille chases after him, calling his name, her voice breaking.

I stand there, frozen. I only meant as far as his athleticism, which isn't everything. But he's been compared to RJ since he was born. It's not my fault that he was born prematurely and didn't develop the way RJ had. It's only in those physical areas that he's deficient. But I hate that Gideon feels different, and I hate even more that I just reaffirmed it.

And still—God help me—I love them both. I would do anything to protect my sons. And my daughter.

I already have.

I slipped the fentanyl into her vodka the last time I dropped off RJ. She was in the shower. She never saw it coming. A few drops. That's all it took. She collapsed right there in her bedroom the next night. RJ was the one who found her.

I hated that it happened like that.

But I couldn't let her keep hurting him. Keep abusing him. Keep turning him into someone I wouldn't recognize. I did what I had to do.

And I would've done the same to Camille... if she ever hurt Olivia. Or Gideon.

But she didn't.

She's been the only thing holding this house together. Even when she's unraveling. Even when she's scared of me. She still stays. Still tries.

I pour another glass of wine, my hands shaking just a little.

And I pray—silently, like a man who's already been damned—that I'll have enough time left to make all this mean something.

Before the rest of me disappears.

CHAPTER
FORTY-THREE

NOW - CAMILLE

IT'S BEEN two days since the detectives discovered my secret. That I've been sleeping with Quenton Diggs. We started shortly after Ryan's stroke. One night he dropped RJ off after a game, the next thing I knew we were kissing and booking a hotel room.

After all these years of being lied to, disrespected, and left to carry the weight of this family alone, I finally stepped out on my husband. And so what? Who cares? At least I waited until he could no longer please me. At least I waited until he wasn't even Ryan anymore.

Because the truth is—Ryan cheated on me when I was still warm. Still willing. Still able to meet his every need and then some. I was loyal when he wasn't. I kept this house clean, the kids fed, my body tight, and my mouth shut while he dipped into the filth of groupies and video vixens. He humiliated me, and I took it like a good wife. Like a fool.

I try to remind myself that his brain injury has been chipping away at him for years. That it's not all his fault. That it's impaired his judgment, his impulse control, his memory, his patience. But lately, none of that feels like enough. Sympathy used to come easy. Now all I feel is disgust.

And now, thanks to some front desk clerk trying to earn a quick buck, the whole world knows about me and Quenton. As soon as those detectives showed up, it became a story. A scandal. Something for bored housewives to tweet about and small-town gossip pages to run with.

HEADLINE: SCHOOL COACH & SUSPECT'S MOTHER CAUGHT IN AFFAIR—MURDER INVESTIGATION HEATS UP

The comments section is a battlefield. They're calling me a Jezebel, a whore, a murderer in disguise. Saying I probably killed Violet to protect my side piece. That I'm unstable. Unfit. Evil.

And maybe they're not entirely wrong.

I glance over at Ryan. He's slouched in the chair at the kitchen table, blinking slow and heavy like he's somewhere between this world and the next. His eyes are fogged, distant, but when they settle on me, something shifts. A flicker of something that looks like fear. Or hate. Or both.

He looks at me like he doesn't know me.

And maybe he doesn't.

Maybe he's forgotten who I am. Or maybe—God help me—knows that I cheated on him. I only let him have his phone when he's lucid enough to communicate. He hasn't been lucid lately.

His green smoothie sits untouched on the side table. I make one every morning, packed with crushed pills—some to calm him, some to help him sleep, some to keep him docile enough not to burn the house down or wander off into the woods. But more importantly, some to speed up the process of him dying. Sleeping pills, caffeine, blood-clotting agents. And now that I've discovered my son's steroids—the ones I made him throw away, then fished out of the trash—I've been adding those too. Anything to induce another stroke.

Today, he eyes it like it's poison.

Like he knows.

Like maybe, on some level, he can sense that I finally crossed the line.

"Drink," I say, more command than suggestion.

He doesn't move.

"Ryan," I snap. "I said drink."

His hand reaches for the cup, trembles slightly—and then, with one swift motion, he hurls it to the ground. The glass shatters, green liquid pooling across the tile like vomit.

"What the hell is wrong with you?" I shout.

He flinches. I can see the panic in his eyes, the confusion twisting his features. He's somewhere else again. Somewhere trapped in the past, where I'm not Camille—I'm his mother. And he thinks I'm here to hurt him. I am here to hurt him. I'm ready for him to die. I've been ready.

"I'm not her," I say, stepping forward. "I'm not your mother."

But he's already curling into himself, whimpering like a child.

My chest aches. Not with pity—but rage.

"You want to act crazy?" I mutter, yanking open the pill bottle on the counter. "Fine. Let's do crazy."

I crush two tablets in my palm and grab a fresh cup of water. When I turn back to him, he's trying to push himself up, trying to get away. I shove him back down.

"You're gonna take your medicine, Ryan," I hiss. "Whether you want to or not."

He shakes his head, lips clamped tight.

"Open your mouth," I growl.

He doesn't. So I slap him as hard as possible

The sound cracks through the room. His face snaps to the side. I take advantage of the moment and shove the powder in, then the water, holding his mouth closed until he swallows.

"Good boy," I whisper, brushing the side of his face like I didn't just slap him seconds ago.

He stares at me, eyes glassy, defeated.

I back away, chest heaving, hands shaking.

This isn't who I wanted to be. But it's who I am now. And I don't have the luxury of regret—not when the detectives are closing in. Not when my own children are slipping through my fingers. Not when the boy I protected—the one I raised like my own—might go down for taking Violet's life. When in reality, I'm almost certain it was my envious son, Gideon. Gideon, who has hated his brother since they were toddlers. Gideon, who has always known there was a difference between them—a difference I'm sure he's sensed I resented him for, no matter how hard I tried to hide it. RJ was the child I was supposed to birth, and I've never been able to get over that.

I grab a mop to clean up the mess and catch my reflection in the dark oven door.

Eyes wild. Hair out of place. Lip curled.

I don't recognize her either.

And just like Ryan…

Maybe I don't want to.

I'm scrubbing the green mess off the tile when my phone buzzes on the counter. I ignore it at first, focus on the trail of broken glass and bitterness streaked across the floor. But the buzzing doesn't stop.

Three, four, five notifications.

I grab it with a sigh, expecting another headline or cruel comment.

But it's not a stranger.

It's Maci.

Maci Diggs.

Her text slices through me faster than I can brace for it.

I've been in your corner since Ryan got sick. I've looked after your kids when you couldn't. And this is how you repay me?

You sleep with my husband.

We were friends! You Bitch!

Olivia is never allowed over my house again.

I stare at the screen, stunned. Not for myself—for Olivia.

If I'm honest, I was only friends with Maci out of convenience. Our daughters have been inseparable for years, and somewhere along the way, that turned into birthday parties, family dinners, emergency pickups. The kind of friendship that forms when your kids grow close and you're forced into the same spaces.

So no, I don't feel the loss personally. But for Olivia? My heart breaks.

Quenton and I had been careful. We knew the risks. But this Violet situation cracked everything open—and now, the judgment is pouring in from every direction.

I think about the void the Diggs family will leave behind. Not just the friendship, but the fallout at school. The whispers. The side-eyes. The cruel jokes Olivia won't be able to outrun.

And there's something else I've lost too.

Maci had been my quiet source of sleeping pills ever since she decided to wean off. She handed them to me casually, no questions asked. But now? That lifeline is severed.

I scroll back through the message. It's all there, sharp and final—Bailey and Olivia's friendship? Done. My access to Maci? Gone.

The betrayal doesn't sting on its own. It's what it means for my daughter. Olivia loves Bailey like blood. And now, the one place that still felt like safety is gone.

But then another fear creeps in—darker, heavier.

Because those pills? I don't have many left.

CHAPTER
FORTY-FOUR

THEN - CAMILLE

IT HAPPENED FAST.

One second, I was washing dishes. The next, a glass shattered against the wall inches from my head.

"Don't you ever talk to me like that again!" Ryan bellowed, eyes wide, mouth twisted into something feral.

I froze, hands still dripping with soap. For a moment, I thought I'd misheard him. Thought maybe he was venting about a game, a bad memory, something from the past.

But then he said it.

"Always trying to humiliate me. If you hit me again, I'm going to hit you back!"

And I knew.

He wasn't talking to me.

He was talking to his mother.

"Ryan," I said slowly, carefully. "It's me. Camille. I'm your wife."

"No, no, no—you're not," he muttered, pacing, fingers clawing at his hair. "You're lying. I'm too young to get married. You are evil and I hate you. You just hit me with that bottle!"

"Ryan, baby. Please—listen to me."

He lunged forward, knocking a bowl off the counter. I screamed.

That's when RJ came running in, followed by Gideon. RJ got to him first, grabbing his father's arm while Gideon went for the other. They were scared but focused, two boys moving like a team. This wasn't their first time calming a storm.

"Dad! It's us! It's RJ and Gideon!"

"Let go of me! Don't touch me!" Ryan thrashed, but they held tight. "She's gonna hit me—she always hits me!"

I backed out of the room, my hands trembling so badly I could barely find the doorframe. I turned, fled down the hall, and collapsed into a heap in the corner of the family room.

My sobs came in gasps. Gut-deep. Ugly.

The kind of cry that doesn't feel like it's coming from your throat—but from your bones.

Olivia came in right after me. She didn't say anything. Just sat next to me on the floor and wrapped her arms around me.

"It's okay, Mommy," she whispered. "It's okay."

But it wasn't.

Because this was our life now. Living with a man who used to be a rock and now broke everything he touched.

It took two hours for the quiet to settle back in. I don't know how the boys did it—how they managed to calm him down, or whether he wore himself out. But eventually the shouting stopped. The crashing. The footsteps.

I stayed curled up on the couch, a blanket pulled around my shoulders even though I wasn't cold.

Then I heard it.

Soft, measured footsteps.

And Ryan's voice.

"Camille?"

I turned slowly.

He was standing in the doorway, eyes clear, shoulders slouched with something that almost looked like shame.

"Can I... can I come in?"

I nodded, wordless.

He moved toward me cautiously, like I was the one who might break next.

"I'm sorry," he said, his voice cracked with fatigue. "I didn't mean it. The boys told me what happened. I just get so confused lately.."

"I know," I whispered. "I know."

He dropped to his knees in front of me.

"I didn't mean to scare you. Or the kids."

"You did."

He flinched, but nodded.

"I'm trying, Camille," he said, his voice cracking. "I'm trying so hard to hold on. I wish I could just die. I wish something would just take me out and you could collect that insurance policy… so I'd stop being a burden to you and the kids."

And he was a burden.

He wasn't always. Once, I could handle it. Once, there were more good days than bad, and I thought I could ride it out—wait for a breakthrough, a miracle, some shift in the universe that would make it all make sense again. But it never came.

I stayed home with him in the beginning. We were managing, barely, with what we'd salvaged after the bankruptcy. But then he got worse. The memory lapses. The paranoia. The violence. And the kids? They were growing up, needing more by the minute.

Olivia's dance classes became expensive. The costumes, the travel, the out-of-state competitions.

RJ's football? A whole other world of equipment, clinics, showcases, private training.

We even sent Gideon to a theater camp in New York—an elite one. That cost more than we had any business spending, but I didn't want him to feel left out. I didn't want him to believe he was less than his siblings. Not because of us. Not because of what we couldn't give.

I didn't want any of them to suffer because their parents mismanaged their lives.

Well—because Ryan mismanaged everything.

And then there were the treatments. The alternative therapies. The out-of-pocket meds. The rotating nurses I had to hire whenever I had to leave the house. It all piled up until we were drowning in it.

I started the cleaning company to stay afloat. At first, it was just a side hustle. Then it became the thing that kept the lights on. The thing that paid for Olivia's pointe shoes. For RJ's cleats. For Gideon's headshots.

But God, I was tired.

I wanted him to die just as badly as he wanted to.

"I'm sorry," he said again, lower this time.

"It's okay," I whispered, because that's what I was supposed to say. "It's not your fault."

But it wasn't okay.

And it was his fault.

And I was tired.

So damn tired.

It had been years of bending over backward for him. Of patching the holes in his mind and the cracks in this house and pretending it didn't cost me pieces of myself every single day. I didn't want to do it anymore. I wasn't even sure why I did it in the first place. Maybe I thought it made me a good wife. A good woman. Or maybe it was just the codependency my mama passed down to me like a curse.

This is what I got for hitching myself to him all those years ago. For choosing *love* over sense. For thinking my looks would carry me further than a degree ever could. This was the price.

And then he leaned in and kissed me.

"If I could drop dead right now, I would, Addie."

My body went cold.

"What did you just say?" I whispered.

He blinked at me, confused. "What?"

"You called me Addie."

He shook his head, already backpedaling. "No—I didn't. Camille, I didn't mean—"

I slapped him.

Hard.

The sound cracked through the room like a gunshot. He stumbled back, eyes wide, lips parted.

"I'm CAMILLE!" I screamed. "You don't get to forget that! You don't get to forget ME!"

He reached for me, desperate now. "Camille, I'm sorry—I didn't mean—"

But it was too late.

With one name—just one slip of the tongue—he'd flipped a switch inside me. The same one that flipped when I pushed his mother down those stairs and watched her skull split against the edge of the banister. That same exact fury. That same release.

He was right.

He was better off dead.

And I was going to make sure of it.

CHAPTER
FORTY-FIVE

NOW - CAMILLE

IT'S Saturday morning and my head is pounding like a drum in the back of my skull.

I wake up with my tongue stuck to the roof of my mouth and a sour film coating my teeth. The room spins just slightly, enough to let me know I drank too much last night. The air in the bedroom is heavy, stale, and it smells like sweat and disappointment.

Ryan is beside me, curled on his side, snoring softly. His face is slack, peaceful in a way he hasn't been in days. I stare at the back of his head and try not to feel anything.

The kids aren't speaking to me.

Not a word since the story broke. Not about breakfast. Not about school. Not even Olivia, my sweet Olivia, who once cried if I didn't kiss her goodnight.

I deserve it. I know that. I slept with Quenton Diggs, and now our family name is a hashtag. I thought I was being discreet. Careful. I thought what Ryan and I had already died years ago. But now it's official. Our infidelities have come full circle, rotted through everything we built. We're two sides of the same tarnished coin—him with his groupies, me with my secrets.

The bedroom is dim, light filtering through the heavy curtains. My temples throb. My throat burns. I start to shift out of bed when—

BANG. BANG. BANG.

The knock is sharp. Violent.

Ryan jolts upright, eyes wide and glassy, like a frightened child waking from a nightmare. "Whaaa?" he gasps, voice hoarse. Then he slurs something unintelligible.

I reach for the pill bottle on the nightstand. My fingers are shaking, but I get the cap off. "Here," I whisper, placing one in his palm and handing him a glass of water. "Just take this, okay? It's probably nothing."

He swallows, his hands trembling as the glass clinks against his teeth. His eyes keep darting to the door like he's waiting for it to burst open.

"Rest," I say. "I'll handle it."

But even as I say it, dread rises up my spine like cold water.

I wrap my robe tighter around me and pad down the stairs barefoot. My breath feels tight in my chest. The pounding comes again—louder this time, more urgent.

I reach the bottom step and my heart drops.

Through the glass panel, I can see them. Two detectives. Several uniformed officers behind them. Patrol cars lining the curb. Flashing lights pulsing red and blue across the lawn. Neighbors standing outside in robes and sweatpants, clutching coffee cups and gawking like it's a damn show.

Detective Joseph shouts, "Camille Bell? Open the door. We have a warrant."

My hand fumbles with the lock. My voice barely works. "A warrant? For what?"

"For the arrest of Ryan Bell Jr.," he says. "Please open the door, ma'am."

My fingers go numb.

I unlock the door and step back, heart hammering in my ears. The cold morning air rushes inside, but I barely feel it. I'm already texting Xavier with trembling thumbs:

Come now. They're arresting RJ. Please.

The officers pour in like a flood. Heavy boots on hardwood, the sound echoing like gunfire in my chest. Upstairs, I hear feet—quick ones. Then RJ's voice.

"What's going on?"

"Stay where you are!" an officer yells. "Hands where we can see them!"

"Wait—wait! Don't touch him!" I scream, pushing past one of the officers, my robe flying open at the legs.

RJ appears at the top of the stairs, confused, shirtless, a pair of sweatpants hanging low on his hips. His eyes are wide, bloodshot. He hasn't been sleeping. He hasn't been eating. He's a child. My child.

"I didn't do anything," he says, his voice cracking. "I swear—"

The officers surround him.

And then Olivia is there. She rushes from the living room barefoot, hair wild, face blotchy from sleep.

"No!" she screams. "No, please! Don't take him!"

They grab RJ's arms. Cuff him.

Olivia throws herself at them, screaming louder. Kicking. Hitting. Crying so hard she's choking.

"He didn't do this! It was Gideon! IT WAS GIDEON!"

The whole room freezes.

Even the officers pause.

And that's when I see him.

Gideon. Standing at the top of the stairs, just behind where RJ had been. He's in his pajamas, arms folded, face blank. But behind his eyes... there's something smug. Something cruel. A twist of his lip that no seventeen-year-old should be able to make.

A smirk.

My breath catches in my throat.

Olivia's screams break again, louder, wilder, her body trembling in my arms as I pull her back.

"RJ," I call out, my voice hollow. "We'll fix this. I promise you. I'll get you out."

He looks down at me as they lead him out the front door, his eyes wide with fear, with betrayal.

Then he's gone.

Taken.

My son.

The front door slams shut behind the cops and my knees buckle, but I don't fall.

Not yet.

I stand there, holding my daughter, staring at the empty space where my boy just stood.

The front door still swings slightly on its hinges. The cold air is creeping in, curling around our ankles like smoke.

I can't breathe.

But Olivia? She can't even stand.

Her knees buckle, and she slips from my arms, collapsing onto the floor like a rag doll. Her breath comes in fast, shallow gasps, each one quicker than the last. Her fingers claw at her throat, and her eyes are huge—wild and glassy, darting from the door to me and back again like she's looking for a way to rewind time.

"No," she sobs. "No, no, no, Mommy, they took him. They took RJ—he didn't do anything!"

Her voice cracks like glass underfoot.

She curls into herself, rocking back and forth, fingers digging into her scalp, nails scratching against skin. "I can't breathe. I can't breathe. Mommy, I can't—I can't—"

"Olivia." I drop to my knees beside her, grabbing her hands, trying to still them. "Baby, look at me. Look at me. Breathe with me, okay? In. Out. In. Out—"

But she can't. She's gone under. Hyperventilating. Writhing. Her eyes don't see me anymore—they're locked on that door, on the memory of her brother being ripped away like he was nothing. Like we didn't just spend a decade building this family.

I wrap my arms around her and pull her into my chest, rocking her like she's a toddler again. I whisper to her. I sing to her. I press my cheek against her forehead and beg her to breathe.

"Breathe, baby. Please. Come back to me."

Her little fists are trembling in my hands. Her face is wet with snot and tears, and her chest keeps hitching, like her lungs are fighting to remember how to work.

And all the while, from the corner of my eye...

Gideon.

He's still at the top of the stairs, watching. Silent.

Until he laughs.

A dry, bitter chuckle that slices through Olivia's sobs like a razor.

"If that were me," he calls out, loud enough for the whole house to hear, "she wouldn't even care."

My head snaps toward him.

"She just threw me under the bus," he continues, shaking his head like the whole thing is a joke. "I'm her *full-blood* brother, and I'm the one she's accusing."

I rise slowly from the floor, Olivia still trembling beside me. My body feels like it's moving through molasses—heavy, unsure. But my voice is sharp when it comes out.

"Did you do it, Gideon?"

He smirks.

"Did you kill Violet?"

He leans against the railing, arms folded across his chest, eyes glinting with something cold and poisonous.

"You need to tell the truth," I say, stepping closer. "It's not fair for RJ to go to prison for something he didn't do."

Gideon shrugs, like this is all theoretical. Like we're talking about some story on TV. "If I *did* do it, there's nothing you could do about it."

My stomach drops.

"I would've gotten rid of the murder weapon a long time ago. Burned it. Or maybe I buried it. Who knows." He shrugs again. "And that bitch would have had it coming. Rejecting *me* for him? A deep, artistic soul for a shallow-ass jock? She didn't see me. Nobody ever does."

His voice grows sharper now, slicing into the room like glass.

"I'm glad he's gone. Maybe now this house can finally breathe without all his arrogance hanging in the air."

"Gideon—"

"This is *my* family," he growls, jabbing his thumb into his chest. "Not his. He was never supposed to be here in the first place."

The words ring out like a gunshot.

And for a split second, he looks triumphant. Like he's been waiting to say this all his life.

And maybe he has.

Because there's no fear in his eyes.

No remorse.

Just the twisted satisfaction of watching everything fall apart.

CHAPTER
FORTY-SIX

THEN - RYAN

THE PLACE LOOKS NICER than I expected.

At least from the outside.

Serene Horizons. That's what the sign says. Soothing blue letters on a white stone wall. Sounds like a spa. A retreat. But I know better. I know what this is.

An assisted living facility.

For people like me.

Camille parks the car, but neither of us moves. Her hands stay locked on the steering wheel like letting go might shatter whatever resolve she's managed to build on the drive over. Her face is unreadable, but I know her too well. She's biting down on something. Hard.

Finally, she kills the engine.

We get out and walk toward the doors, side by side but worlds apart.

Inside, the place is... pleasant.

Big open windows. Pale blue walls. That strange soft lighting that tries too hard to feel like natural sunlight. There are fake plants in every corner—plastic leaves that almost pass for real if you squint. The whole place smells like lemon polish and something faintly sweet. Muffins, maybe.

It's clean. Calm. Quiet.

I glance around and wonder if this is what the end of the road looks like. If this is where they send the strong ones when they stop being useful.

And I wonder if Camille's already made up her mind.

I try to lighten the mood.

"So… this place got a gym?" I say, glancing over at her. "'Cause I plan on being the fittest stallion in the stable."

It earns a small smile from her—tight, tired—but it's something.

"You'll definitely be the youngest," she says.

And I catch it—the flicker of unease in her eyes. The way her fingers clench just a little tighter. That's how I know this is real. Not just some information-gathering tour. Not just a "just in case." She's thinking about it. Planning. Preparing.

And honestly? I don't blame her.

There's soft jazz playing from hidden speakers, and a woman behind the counter greets us like we're there to sign up for a cruise.

"We're here for the 11:00 tour," Camille says, smoothing her coat. Her voice is steady, but I know her tells. The slight shift in her posture. The way she keeps one hand on her purse strap, like it's an anchor.

The woman checks us in and soon enough, we're following a perky young coordinator named Lydia. She's got that bright, overly rehearsed tone—like she's read too many brochures and thinks positivity can cure anything.

"This is our recreation lounge," she says, gesturing to a room where a few older folks are playing cards and watching an old western on TV. "We do game nights, music therapy, even pet visits on Fridays!"

I nod, but my mind drifts.

I used to be *somebody*. A man with a name. With muscle

and presence. With purpose. Now I'm being shown around like I'm already half-dead.

We keep walking. A hallway with rooms—small, clean, too quiet.

"We encourage personalization," Lydia chirps. "Pictures of family, mementos, anything that helps with memory anchoring."

Camille nods. I don't say a word.

We pass a little gym—two treadmills, a stationary bike, some yoga mats.

I give her a look. "Told you," I say under my breath. "Fittest stallion."

She doesn't laugh. Just exhales and glances away.

We finish the tour. There's a calendar on the wall filled with activities—bingo, chair yoga, storytelling hour. It feels like I'm visiting someone else's future. Not mine.

Outside again, the air feels colder. Or maybe that's just the dread sinking deeper into my bones.

Camille walks to the car in silence. I follow, my steps heavy.

We sit. Quiet again. The same silence as before—but different now. Thicker.

"I don't want to do this," I say finally.

She turns her head toward me, slowly. Her eyes are soft. Wet.

"I know."

"I don't want to be a burden either. I don't want to keep scaring you. Or the kids."

Her lips press together again. Her hand reaches over and rests on mine. Warm. Steady.

"You're not a burden," she says.

But we both know that's not true. I've thrown things. Screamed things. Forgotten things. I've mistaken her for my mother. I've put my own family in danger—without even knowing it.

I stare out the windshield at the swaying trees, wondering

how I got here. How I went from carrying teams on my back to needing help remembering my daughter's name.

"If I could just... die," I say, barely above a whisper, "you wouldn't have to carry all this. You could move on. The kids would be safe. You'll have the insurance money."

"Don't," she says sharply. "Don't say that."

I shake my head. "It's how I feel."

She doesn't respond right away. Just looks out the window. Her profile looks older today. Not aged—just worn. Like something that used to shine but got dulled from overuse.

I don't know what we'll decide. Whether I'll be here next month. Whether the next time we visit, I'll be carrying boxes instead of questions.

But I do know this: I've already lost pieces of myself.

And if this is where the rest of me goes to die—

I hope she doesn't come with me.

This is a good day for me.

Later that night, after the kids are asleep and the house has finally gone quiet, Camille brings me a glass of water and sits beside me on the edge of the bed. Her face is softer now. The tension from earlier has eased. Or maybe she's just tired. We both are.

She leans in and kisses my forehead. Not in a pitying way. Not in that careful, distant way she's done the past few months. This one is full. Present. Intimate.

I close my eyes and let myself feel it. Let myself feel her.

"It's been a long time," I murmur.

She nods slowly. "Too long."

And then she kisses me again—this time on the mouth. And something wakes up in me, something that hasn't stirred in months. Not just desire. Not just hunger. But the need to feel alive. To be wanted. To feel like a man again.

She undresses me slowly. Methodically. With purpose. Her hands don't tremble.

Then she reaches into the closet and pulls out the drawer

from my old dresser. I hear the clink of metal—the slide of silk. Neckties.

She climbs on top of me, straddling me gently, and ties one wrist to the bedframe. Then the other.

I chuckle low. "Getting kinky on me?"

She leans in close, her mouth just over mine.

"Just making sure you don't float away."

She kisses my neck. My chest. My shoulder. Every touch is careful. Like she's memorizing me.

I don't notice the needle until I feel the sting.

Sharp.

Deep.

Instant.

"What—" I start to say. My voice catches in my throat. "What was that?"

She presses her lips to my ear. Her breath is warm.

"I'm granting your wish," she whispers. "You said you wanted to die."

My body stiffens.

"Camille?"

I'm trying to move, trying to pull against the ties, but my limbs feel slow. Heavy.

"What did you do?" My tongue is thick in my mouth. "Camille—baby—please…"

She strokes my hair. Calm. Tender.

"You said it yourself. You didn't want to be a burden anymore."

My heart pounds. My eyes blur. I blink fast, but everything feels like it's moving sideways. A high-pitched whine builds in my ears, louder than any sound in the room.

I try to shout but the words won't come.

Then—

It happens.

The stroke hits like a lightning bolt.

At first, it's just my right hand. It curls in on itself, tight and twitching, like it's trying to vanish. Then my arm. Then my leg. My face feels wrong. Drooping. Like someone turned off gravity on one side.

I want to cry out but my mouth doesn't work. It's just wet gurgling. My vision tilts. My chest is shaking. A burning erupts behind my eyes.

Everything inside me is screaming, but no sound leaves my throat.

She leans over me, watching. Her hand presses softly against my chest.

"You're okay," she whispers, like I'm a child having a nightmare. "It'll be over soon."

Darkness blooms at the edges of my sight. The ceiling drifts farther away.

My body jerks once.

Then again.

And then—

Everything stops.

CHAPTER
FORTY-SEVEN

NOW - CAMILLE

THE HOURS since they took RJ have been brutal.

The house is too quiet. Not peaceful—just empty. Like something's been ripped away and the silence is what's left behind. Olivia's finally asleep on the couch, buried under two blankets. I gave her half a Valium to get her there.

I shouldn't have. I know that.

But I didn't know what else to do. She wouldn't stop crying. Couldn't catch her breath. Her body shook so violently I thought she might break apart in my arms. And every few seconds, she whispered his name—RJ, RJ, RJ—like a prayer. Like a curse. Like if she said it enough, it might bring him back.

So I gave her the pill.

And now I just sit here, watching her chest rise and fall, wondering when everything slipped this far. Wondering how it all managed to rot so quietly.

Xavier called about twenty minutes ago.

His voice was low. Clipped. Calm like always—but there was weight in it. Gravity.

"The DNA under Violet's fingernails matched RJ."

I didn't breathe.

"And the autopsy confirmed that was RJ's baby."

The room spun.

He kept talking, even as the floor dropped out from under me.

"Her friends told the cops she'd already told RJ about it. That he didn't take it well. That he was upset. Saying he wasn't ready."

Motive. That's what the cops are running with. Motive.

I think I stopped listening for a full minute, just staring at the wall. Did he do it? I was so confused. I refused to believe it. Gideon was so smug. He did it. I know he did.

"He says Violet scratched him during sex," Xavier added. "That it was consensual. That she liked it rough sometimes. But Camille... they're building a case."

He said they're filing for emergency bail. Said we might get him arraigned by morning if we're lucky.

But I don't feel lucky.

I feel like the sky is closing in.

Gideon left not long after. Said he was going for a walk. Didn't ask where. Didn't look me in the eye. Just slipped out the back door like his sister hadn't just screamed his name in front of half the damn neighborhood.

And I wanted to follow him. I wanted to grab him by the neck and scream: *Why? Why did you do it?*

Because I know.

Deep down in the rot of my marrow, I know it was him.

But there's no proof.

And without proof, my golden child sits in a holding cell while the monster gets to take a walk in the moonlight.

I go upstairs, legs heavy, stomach knotted with dread. The door to our bedroom is cracked open. The light's off.

Ryan's in his chair by the window, slouched in the dark. The blinds are drawn, but moonlight still cuts through, throwing silver across his slack face.

He sees me.

Tilts his head.

Slow. Careful. Like he's not sure who I am tonight.

"Cam…ill…" he slurs.

That voice. That ragged, shredded thing. I remember when it used to be smooth. Rich. Capable of soft talk and shouting matches. Capable of everything.

Now it sounds like pain made human.

I move toward him.

And the rage rises.

"I hate you," I whisper.

He frowns. Tries to sit up. Can't.

I step closer, fists clenched.

"I hate you so much."

He blinks. Confused. "Wha… what…?"

"This is your fault," I say. "All of it. The cheating. The lies. Your brain turning to soup. RJ wouldn't even be in this house if it weren't for you."

He flinches.

"I carried this family. While you forgot my name and drooled through appointments. I covered your rage. Your paranoia. I smiled when people asked how you were doing. I said you were fine when I knew you weren't. And now our family is in hell."

I'm pacing now. Breathing hard. My voice rising with every word.

"You ruined everything!"

I hit him.

He gasps.

"WHY WON'T YOU JUST DIE?"

I hit him again.

"DIE."

Again.

"DIE."

My fists go limp, but I can't stop crying. It's pouring out of me now. Years of it. Years of holding everything together with duct tape and prayer.

Ryan curls in on himself, barely able to lift his hands. He wheezes. Tries to speak.

"S…sor…ry… Cam…ill… I… sor…ry…"

It's pathetic.

And it shatters me.

Because I used to love this man.

Now? I don't even know what's left of him.

I step back, breathing like I ran a marathon.

He's still slumped, listing to the side, face slack. One eye drooping lower than the other. He lifts a hand, but it trembles and falls.

I stare at him.

Then I turn and walk out.

And I don't know who I'm more afraid of anymore.

My son.

Or myself.

I wander the house like a ghost in my own skin.

The walls feel too close. The air too thin. Every creak of the floorboards feels like it's pressing on my nerves. I keep hearing Olivia's screams from earlier, echoing between the walls like some kind of warning.

I feel like I'm losing my mind.

Maybe I already have.

I end up in front of Gideon's room. The door is closed, but not locked. Of course not. Gideon's careful. Quiet. A master of blending in. I twist the knob and step inside.

It's tidy. Too tidy. The bed is made, the floors are vacuumed, the desk wiped clean. Nothing looks out of place.

But I know better.

I start tearing the room apart—pulling open drawers, ripping his mattress off the bed-frame, dumping out bins and flipping through notebooks. I claw through everything, looking for a sign, a clue, a weapon—anything to prove what my gut's been screaming for days.

That he's the one who did it.

That RJ is innocent.

That I'm not crazy.

But there's nothing. Just the neat little life of a boy who plays the victim so well, you start to believe it.

The cops already searched this house. They didn't find anything then. And I don't find anything now.

I leave the room with my chest burning and go straight to RJ's.

It still smells like him—body spray, sweat, detergent, something boyish and warm and familiar. The bed's unmade, a duffle bag sits by the closet still half-zipped. I sink down onto his mattress, bury my face in my hands, and sob.

I've always loved him more. I hate myself for it, but it's true. Even when I tried to hide it, the love I had for RJ was different. I never meant to make Gideon feel less than. But he did. And maybe that's what broke him.

And now? RJ is sitting in a jail cell for something I know he didn't do. And I can't save him.

I wipe my face, about to stand, when something catches my eye.

An envelope, on the floor peeking outside from under the bed. Like he tried to hide it but didn't do a good job. Perhaps the arrest disrupted the hiding. I picked up the envelope and it has slanted handwriting on the front reads:

To RJ. From Pretty Eyes.

My stomach twists.

I walk to the desk and open it with trembling fingers.

Inside is a folded piece of paper, soft at the creases from being read over and over again. I unfold it.

I can't wait until we can run away together.

Soon. I promise. I love you.

The handwriting… it's too familiar

My breath catches.

I reach into the envelope again and find something else—an SD card.

Panic flares hot and sharp behind my ribs.

I race back to the bedroom, digging through the closet

until I find it—our old digital camera. Ryan's eyes follow me from his chair, wide, frantic, flickering with some deep, buried awareness. Like his broken mind knows something is about to be unearthed.

I slot the SD card in, scroll through the images—

And I almost drop the damn thing.

My heart stops.

The screen flashes photo after photo.

Olivia.

Nude.

Some in front of her mirror. Some lying on her bed. Some with RJ in them.

They're touching. Kissing.

His hand is on her thigh in one. Her mouth near his ear in another. A tangle of limbs. Skin. Familiarity.

Like lovers. They were lovers.

My knees go weak. The room tilts.

I stumble into the bathroom and vomit into the sink. Violently. Until my throat burns and nothing is left inside me but air and bile and the kind of horror that doesn't wash off.

No.

No no no no no.

Not Olivia.

Not my daughter.

I lurch into the hallway, stomach twisting, bile clinging to the back of my tongue.

I feel sick. Dizzy. Like I'm floating outside my body.

I reach the living room, gripping the walls to keep from falling.

"OLIVIA!"

My scream is guttural. Raw. Like something animal clawed its way up my throat.

She appears from the hallway a moment later—groggy, blinking, rubbing her eyes. Hair messy, pajama top hanging off one shoulder.

"Mom?" she mumbles. "What's wrong?"

I don't answer.

I just step forward, camera still clutched in my shaking hand.

"What were you and RJ doing?" I rasp.

She freezes.

"What?"

I hold up the camera. "Don't lie to me. The photos. The envelope. 'Pretty Eyes'? That's you, isn't it?"

Her eyes widen in horror. Her mouth opens. Closes. She starts to shake.

"Mom, I—I didn't mean to—I didn't think it would be like that—"

"You were sleeping with him?" I shout.

Her whole face crumples.

"I'm sorry!" she sobs, collapsing to her knees. "It was my fault—I started it—I just wanted him to love me. Please, please don't hate me. He didn't force me, I swear—"

"He's your brother." I'm in disbelief. I can't believe I've just said those sequence of words.

She's trembling now, every word hitting me like a hammer to the chest.

"I didn't mean for it to go this far," Olivia sobs, her arms wrapped tight around herself, rocking slightly like a little girl. "He wasn't supposed to be the one to pay for what I did."

My entire body stills.

"What are you talking about?" I whisper.

She won't look at me.

Her bottom lip trembles as the words pour out, raw and frantic.

"I found out Violet was pregnant when I went through RJ's phone," Olivia says. "I wasn't supposed to see it. But I did. And she wasn't getting rid of it."

My blood runs cold.

"What…?" I whisper.

"I saw the texts," she goes on, voice shaking. "She said she was keeping it. That it was *hers*. That she didn't care what RJ thought. She was *going* to have it."

I stumble back a step, my mind reeling.

"I thought Violet was Pretty Eyes," I murmur. "I thought it was her…"

Olivia laughs, but there's no joy in it—only bitterness.

"She wasn't. I was. He called *me* that."

The floor feels like it's slipping out from under me.

I shake my head. I can't process it. I don't *want* to process it.

"No," I whisper. "No, you're confused. You're—"

"I'M NOT CONFUSED!" she screams, her voice shrill, body trembling. "She was going to ruin everything. She was going to *trap* him."

She presses her hands to her temples, squeezing her eyes shut like the memory is stabbing through her.

Her voice dissolves into a sob.

"After Ms. Maci and Bailey went to sleep, I snuck out. I went to the party. I found her in that bed, passed out from drinking. Who drinks while they're pregnant?! I hit her with a candle holder, over and over again. There was blood. So much blood. I didn't know what to do. I panicked. I ran."

I stagger back against the wall, breath punched out of my chest.

"You let him take the blame," I whisper, the rage beginning to rise like acid. "You watched your brother get arrested. You let him sit in a cell while you—"

"I thought it would go away!" she yells, sobbing harder. "I thought if I said nothing, it would all just… go back to normal. I didn't know they'd find DNA. I didn't know it would get this far."

I want to scream. I want to hit something. I want to reach out and hold her and shake her all at once.

"I'll confess," she says suddenly, her voice eerily calm. "I'll go to the police. I'll tell them everything. RJ doesn't deserve this."

She turns toward the door.

"Olivia, wait," I say, stepping forward. "We need to think. We'll call Xavier—"

She spins to face me, eyes sharp and gleaming.

"No! I have to get him out now!"

"Olivia—"

Before I can stop her, she lunges toward the fireplace. Grabs the Balinese brass monkey statue from the mantel.

My heart seizes.

"Olivia, no—"

She lifts it, tears streaming down her cheeks.

"I'm sorry, Mommy."

She swings.

The metal collides with my skull.

White-hot pain.

Then nothing.

Just the sound of her sobbing—fading—into black.

I drift in and out of consciousness, completely unable to move. Somewhere in the haze, I hear Ryan's footsteps shuffle down the hall. I pray he has the mind to call 911. But I just beat him—I just took my rage out on him—so maybe he'll let me bleed out.

Then, I hear the front door open.

"MOM!? MOM?!"

It's Gideon.

I know he hates me.

I'm definitely about to die.

CHAPTER
FORTY-EIGHT

NOW - CAMILLE

THE FIRST THING I register is pain. A low, dragging throb in the back of my skull, like someone is peeling the inside of my head with a butter knife. My eyelids are heavy, crusted with sleep and pain and whatever they pumped into me. The lights are too bright, even through closed lids. The air smells like bleach and sadness.

I try to move my hand. It's sluggish. Numb.

"You're awake."

The voice floats to me, familiar. Warm. A tether pulling me back.

I blink slowly, the room swimming into view like something underwater. Pale walls. Monitors. IV drip. That faint mechanical beep-beep-beep that reminds you you're still tethered to this world.

It's Ricki, and she's sitting beside me, eyes glossy, hand wrapped gently around mine like it's made of porcelain.

"Oh my God," she whispers. "You scared the hell out of me."

My throat is dry. My tongue feels like sandpaper. I try to speak, but all that comes out is a rasp.

"Don't talk," she says quickly, brushing hair from my forehead. "You've got a concussion. Pretty bad one, too."

I try to nod but regret it immediately. The pain sharpens, ricocheting across my skull like shattered glass. I groan.

"Easy, easy," Ricki murmurs. "You're okay. You're safe. Just rest."

I don't feel safe. I feel like I've been hit by a truck. Or—

The monkey.

It rushes back in pieces. Olivia's eyes. Her voice. The weight of the brass. The blow. The blackness.

I flinch.

Ricki tightens her grip on my hand. "Hey, hey. You're okay. You're in the hospital. You've been out for a while, but you're stable. The kids are okay. I'm here."

The kids.

The word slices through me like a blade.

RJ. Olivia. Gideon. Ryan.

Oh God.

Tears press at the corners of my eyes, but I'm too weak to cry.

I squeeze Ricki's hand instead. It's all I can do.

And silently, behind the pounding in my head, one question keeps screaming.

Where is Olivia?

Ricki starts to rise. "I'm gonna go get the nurse. Let them know you're awake."

I squeeze her hand weakly. "Wait."

She pauses mid-step, looking back at me.

I gather every ounce of strength I have. My throat is raw, my chest tight, but the question burns in me. "Where... is Olivia?"

Ricki's face changes.

Just the flicker of it is enough to tell me.

She looks away. Down. Anywhere but at me.

"Ricki," I whisper, voice cracking. "Tell me."

She hesitates—then slowly, quietly, lowers herself back

into the chair beside me. Her eyes are glassy again. She swallows hard, like she's trying to get the words past a lump in her throat.

"Camille…" Her voice is soft. "She's been arrested."

I blink, like the words don't quite land.

"What?"

"After she attacked you," Ricki says softly, "she ran out of the house and went to the Diggs'. She left her bloody clothes and the murder weapon in their shed. Then she went straight to the police station and confessed. She told them everything, Camille. About the affair. The pregnancy. The fight. All of it."

I'm staring at her, but the world is tilting sideways again. I can't breathe. Can't move.

I start to cry. No warning. Just sobs ripping through my throat like claws. It's a kind of crying I haven't done in years. Messy. Loud. Childlike.

Ricki wraps both arms around me and holds tight.

"She's just a little girl," I whisper into her shoulder. "She's just a baby."

"I know," she whispers back.

"She was my baby."

"I know."

My body shakes so hard the IV line tugs against my arm. My tears soak through Ricki's shirt. She doesn't move. Doesn't flinch. Just holds me like she's the only thing left keeping me tethered to earth.

When the crying dulls to hiccups and shallow breaths, I pull back and wipe my face with trembling fingers.

"Where's Gideon?" I ask, voice hoarse.

Ricki sighs. "He's the one who found you. Called the ambulance. He stayed with you until they got there."

I stare at her.

"He's at my house now," she adds. "I didn't want him back in that house. Not after… everything. He's safe, Camille."

Safe.

But for how long?

I close my eyes, a new wave of grief rising behind my ribs.

My daughter is in jail.

My son is missing from me in a different way.

And the house that was supposed to hold us all together has become the thing that swallowed us whole.

"Where's Ryan?" I ask, my voice hoarse and scratchy. My throat aches. My head pounds. But the question tumbles out before I can catch it. "Is he here? At your house?"

Ricki stills.

The warmth drains from her face. Her expression shifts into something I can't name—grief... pity... dread.

"Ricki?" I press, sitting up despite the ache behind my eyes. "What is it? Where is he?"

She hesitates.

Then lowers herself into the chair beside me, taking my hand like she's about to deliver the worst kind of news.

"Camille," she says softly. "Ryan is dead."

The words don't land at first. I blink at her, confused. "What? He died last night?"

"No, Camille. He died three years ago."

My stomach drops.

No.

I shake my head. "No, no. He's sick. He's sick, but he's still alive. He had a stroke—don't you remember?"

"Camille," Ricki says again, firmer now. "We buried Ryan three years ago. He had a massive stroke. There were complications. You were there. You gave the eulogy."

My mouth opens, but nothing comes out.

She can't be right.

He was just in our room. In his chair. Slumped by the window with that faraway look. I *felt* him. I *saw* him. I—I...

But he already had?

I was trying to kill a ghost.

I can't breathe.

I feel like the bed is collapsing underneath me, folding me inward. I see him. I hear him. I feel him.

"Oh my God," I whisper.

Because if Ryan's been dead this whole time—if he's been dead for three years—then who the hell was I talking to every night?

What did I see?

"You've been under so much stress," Ricki is saying gently. "Everything with RJ and Olivia... and now this concussion... Camille, you're not okay."

But I'm not listening anymore. My ears are ringing. My vision is closing in.

I thought I was holding this family together.

I thought I was the only sane one left.

But if Ryan is dead—and has been all along—then maybe I'm not sane at all.

Maybe I've been gone longer than I realized.

My chest starts to convulse.

The lights flicker in and out.

I reach for Ricki, but I can't feel her hand anymore.

"Camille?" she shouts, her voice rising. "Camille?!"

My body jerks, violently, and the world tilts sideways. I can hear Ricki screaming for help, feel her turning me on my side. There's pressure in my head, sharp and searing, like something's exploding behind my eyes.

And then—

Black.

Total and complete.

Like someone just pulled the plug on my mind.

Like I never woke up at all.

CHAPTER
FORTY-NINE

THEN - CAMILLE

AT SOME POINT, I broke. The resentment in my heart exploded and I could no longer take any more. So, I injected his veins with air. An air embolism. I'd seen it on a show about nurses once. That if you inject air into someone's veins, they would die.

To do research, I drove a few counties over after borrowing Ricki's library card. Wearing a jet-black wig and a baseball cap I snuck into a library and Googled how to administer one. Then I wiped the search history as well as my fingerprints.

Syringes were easy to get hold of. And oxygen, well that's freely abundant. I didn't even debate with myself about whether I should end his life.

I was sick of the humiliation and embarrassment. My codependency had run its course. I was ready to be independent of him and collect that insurance check.

He didn't die right away. Of course not. That would've been too easy. Too clean. Too merciful.

No, Ryan survived the stroke I gave him. He held on—barely, pathetically—for three more days. I thought it would be quick. I thought that once the air hit his veins, once that syringe emptied, it would be over. I tied him up with neckties, whispered death like a lullaby, and watched the stroke tear through his body like a firebomb. I was sure that was the end.

But his body refused to let go. And that was just like Ryan, wasn't it? Always staying too long. Always hanging on past the point of usefulness.

The doctors called it "massive but survivable." That's the phrase they used. Massive. But survivable. His right side was paralyzed. His face sagged on that side like melting wax. His mouth hung open, wet and twitching, and his eye wouldn't close all the way, just stared—dry and red—like he was half-dead already.

And the aphasia.

They tossed that word around like it meant something soft. Like it was a gentle misfiring of the brain. But there was nothing gentle about it. It was watching him struggle to remember our children's names. Watching tears slip down his cheek while his lips flapped uselessly. He couldn't speak. Couldn't hold a spoon. Couldn't wipe his own mouth. The man who used to take up so much space in this world had been reduced to a slack, breathy thing. And it made me furious.

Because I had meant for it to end.

Not to drag on.

Not to turn into some long, torturous coda that stretched out our misery and forced the kids to see him like that.

They came to the hospital. All three of them.

Olivia sat by his bed for hours, stroking his hand, crying until she couldn't breathe. She whispered things to him—things I couldn't make out—but I recognized the tone. The desperate, aching kind of love that clings to what's already slipping away.

RJ didn't say much. He sat in the corner, elbows on his knees, hands clenched so tight they shook. His eyes never left the machines. He hadn't cried, but the grief was all over him—tight jaw, twitching muscle, breath he kept trying to steady. I could tell he didn't know what to feel. Anger. Sadness. Relief. Maybe all three.

And Gideon... Gideon didn't cry either.

He stood at the edge of the room like he didn't belong to us at all. Like he was there as an observer, not a son. His face was blank. His posture too straight. When the nurse asked if he wanted to hold his father's hand, he shook his head like she'd offered him something disgusting.

Three days later, Ryan died.

Blood clots, they said. One to the lungs. One to the brain. Silent killers. They moved fast—faster than I ever could've planned for. I got the call in the middle of the night. The nurse said it gently, like I might break. Like I hadn't already shattered.

I didn't cry.

Not then. Not at the hospital. Not at the funeral.

I felt... light. Not happy. But unburdened. Like something I'd been dragging behind me for years had finally been cut loose.

We buried him in his navy suit. The one Olivia picked. She said it made him look like "Dad again." I nodded, because that's what you're supposed to do. Nod. Agree. Pretend the worst parts of someone dissolve when they die.

The service was tasteful and appropriate. Polite lies whispered into floral arrangements. Friends, coworkers, people who hadn't seen him in years—everyone had something nice to say. "Great man." "So strong." "He loved you all so much." I said thank you. I smiled. I played my role.

None of them were there when it got bad. When the money ran out. The fame ended. They all disappeared. I wanted to curse them and force them to leave. But I smiled and hugged them.

And after all that, I waited.

For the money.

For the only thing that made any of it worthwhile. The payout. The insurance policy I'd held onto like a secret promise. That all this suffering, all this sacrifice, would mean something.

Except it didn't.

Because Ryan, in his endless brilliance, had let the policy lapse.

No payout. No check. No relief. Just bills. Just debt. Just me, staring at the life we built and realizing it was all for nothing.

I wanted to scream. I wanted to dig him up and kill him all over again. I wanted to shake him back to life just so I could slap him, curse him, make him understand what he'd done.

You left us with nothing, Ryan.

You let yourself rot.

You let us rot with you.

And now you're dead, and I'm still here.

Still standing.

Still cleaning up your mess.

But at least now… you're out of the way.

CHAPTER FIFTY

NOW - CAMILLE

A TEMPORAL LOBE TUMOR. That's what's been camping out in my skull, screwing with my sense of reality and rewriting the past like it's a Netflix reboot.

The doctors say that's what caused the hallucinations. Not just tactile—like the times I swung my hand to slap him in the face. The times I pinched him. The times I drugged him. It was visual and auditory, too. I saw him, clear as day. Slouched on the sofa in the living room, or sitting at the kitchen table. I heard him breathe. Heard him mutter my name. Sometimes I'd hear the creak of the floorboards upstairs and swear it was him pacing. His shadow in the corner of my eye. His voice in the back of my head. All of it. Every inch of him—alive in my mind, long after he was cold in the ground.

I wasn't grieving.

I was malfunctioning.

It wasn't sorrow that kept Ryan in the house—it was my brain tumor. It was my inner resentment made flesh.

I screamed at a dead man. Hit him. Drugged him. Tried to

kill him—again. And the whole time, there wasn't even a him to kill.

I told Ricki everything once the fog started lifting. Once the tests came back and the scans were clear and the tumor was officially diagnosed. I expected her to lean into science, hard. Facts and figures and gray matter.

But no.

Ricki—who, mind you, is a *doctor*—gave me the most woo-woo, incense-burning, moonwater-charging theory I've ever heard.

"I think it was a manifestation," she said, dead serious, like she was diagnosing a demon. "The guilt. The shame. The anger. You never processed it, Camille. You stuffed it so far down, your body had to create something to carry it for you."

She said the tumor was grief and resentment in physical form. That my rage over Ryan's betrayal, the humiliation, the money, RJ, Tiffany—all of it—took shape in the one place I couldn't run from: my own brain.

"I think you summoned him," she whispered, like she was reading tarot.

I wanted to tell her she was out of her damn mind. But the truth is, some part of me believes it. Because what else explains it? What else accounts for how real it felt—the voice echoing from upstairs, the weight of his hand on mine, the way I hated him. The way I loved him.

How do you explain spending all this time trapped in a haunted house, only to realize the ghost was you?

It's been over a month since everything went down.

After the seizure, they ran a battery of tests—MRIs, CT scans, bloodwork, the works. That's when they found the tumor. Buried deep, quiet and insidious, like a splinter lodged in the folds of my mind. They suspect it had been there for years. When they asked how long I'd been hallucinating Ryan, I couldn't answer. I honestly didn't know. There was no defining moment. Just a slow blur where memory and madness melted together. A slippery slope into a world where the dead walked and the living were haunted.

They removed the tumor during surgery. I survived.

But I'm still recovering.

Alone.

I've been asking my sister to help me put the shattered pieces of my thoughts back together. Ricki didn't want to at first. She's a therapist, and treating family is an ethical no-go. But when I told her I caused Ryan's stroke, when I admitted I injected air into his veins and wished him dead long before the tumor ever bloomed... well, she agreed. She couldn't exactly refer me to someone else. I couldn't go blabbing to her colleagues that I had killed my husband.

The road to recovery isn't linear. It's not even paved. Some days I wake up in a fog so thick I forget which memories are real. Others, I feel everything too much. Like someone peeled back all my skin and I'm just walking around made of exposed nerve endings and regret.

Ricki's been pushing me to confront things I buried years ago.

She says I was codependent. That Ryan was my addiction.

But I was his, too.

We were each other's drug—familiar, toxic, impossible to quit. And maybe that's why I stayed so long. Maybe staying with him was some twisted reenactment of our parents' marriage. A sad little play where I could rewrite the ending, prove that if I just loved hard enough, I could fix the broken thing.

As I walk through this house—our house—the one I'm finally preparing to sell, I start to see the hallucinations for what they were. I can trace them now. I remember all the times I thought I saw Ryan. Sitting in the living room. Standing by the stairs. Muttering to himself at the table. And every single time the kids spoke to him—RJ and Olivia—they were really just talking to the urn and pictures on the mantel. The same urn I dusted weekly. The same photo frame beside it. Olivia used to say, "Goodnight, Daddy." And I thought... God help me, I thought he said it back. Sometimes Maci would say it after Olivia did if she were visiting.

My mind placed him there. As if he wasn't a vase of ashes on display. As if he hadn't already been reduced to dust.

Speaking of the kids...

Olivia has been remanded to psychiatric care. When she was arrested, she harmed herself in custody. They say she shattered. Completely. The reality of what she'd done—the incest, the murder—it broke her down. Xavier's working on the case, pulling every string he can. He thinks he can negotiate a deal with the DA. Maybe manslaughter. Maybe even avoid trial altogether if she's deemed unfit. And looking at her now... I'm not sure she isn't.

When I asked Ricki how I missed it—how I missed what Olivia and Ryan were doing behind my back—she didn't offer comfort. She offered a clinical analysis dressed up in therapist speak. Apparently, I'd been drugging myself this whole time. The crushed pills in Ryan's drinks? I was consuming them. Stimulants in the morning. Sedatives at night. Enough to keep me unconscious while my step-son and daughter slipped down to the basement together.

Gideon didn't hear anything—he sleeps with headphones.

And I? I was knocked out because prior to the pills insomnia kept me up at night.

I asked Ricki how something so vile could happen. How a brother and daughter could become something else. She explained it clinically. She said sometimes brain wiring gets crossed. That Olivia, having been separated from RJ for most of her formative years, didn't develop a proper sibling bond. That she internalized our obsession with RJ—mine, Ryan's, the world's—and turned that obsession into love. Romantic love. That she wanted to be seen. To be chosen. And RJ, being the attention-starved narcissist he was, gave her that validation. Gave her a mirror.

She used phrases like "eroticized attachment," "disorganized trauma response," and "developmental sexualization in the absence of consistent paternal boundaries."

All I heard was: You helped create this.

And she's right.

I did.

I will never forgive myself.

Not for what I did to Olivia.

And not for what I did to Gideon.

He saved my life that night. Called the ambulance. Stayed until they arrived.

But he hasn't spoken to me since.

He's living with Ricki now. Finishing high school online. He's cut ties, and I don't blame him. I suspected him. Accused him. Believed he was capable of murder. And he *did* give me reasons—God, did he—but still. I see it in his eyes: the betrayal. The ache.

I don't know if I'll ever earn his forgiveness.

But I'll try.

As for RJ... he's gone too. He's moved in with Tiffany's parents. The charges were dropped, but the rumors linger. People whisper. Coaches rescind offers. The words "murder" and "incest" hang over his future like a funeral veil.

And for once, I don't care about his future in football. Or scholarships. Or his image.

All I care about is the two kids I gave birth to. But I fear I've lost them. I did this to them.

Because this house? It wasn't a home. It was a pressure cooker. A stage. A coffin. And now I'm tearing it down brick by brick, memory by memory.

I just hope I can do the same to the version of myself that built it.

I wear a knit hat pulled low over my forehead to cover the shaved patch on the side of my head from the surgery. It's February, bitter and gray, the kind of cold that stiffens your bones and settles behind your eyes. The hat doesn't match my coat, but I don't care. It hides the surgical line above my temple. That's enough.

I pull out of the driveway slowly. The front lawn is dead, the grass brittle and pale beneath a thin film of frost. The For Sale sign leans slightly to the left, like even it's tired. Red and white. Blunt. Unforgiving.

The Kowalskis are suing me for wrongful death. That house is the first casualty.

I don't look back.

The drive to the hospital is quiet. Just the soft hum of the heater and the low crunch of tires on salt-stained roads. Trees blur past in shades of gray and brown, their limbs bare and sharp like ribs. Everything feels exposed. Raw.

At the facility, the walls are a blinding, institutional white. The air smells sterile. A nurse leads me to the visitation room, says Olivia will be in shortly, then leaves me alone with the cold chair and the weight in my chest.

When the door opens, I stop breathing.

She looks... smaller. Not just physically. Like someone deflated her from the inside. Her skin is pale, almost translucent. Her wild green eyes are dulled, haunted. But when they land on me, there's a flicker—something barely there. A twitch of familiarity. A ghost of a daughter I used to know.

She sits across from me without a word.

I search her face, trying to find a place to begin. An apology. An anchor.

"I'm sorry," I say softly. "That Gideon hasn't come yet. He... he needs time. But I'm here. I'm not going anywhere."

She doesn't nod.

She doesn't blink.

She just looks at me, silent.

And then, in a voice that sounds like it's traveled a thousand miles on broken glass, she asks:

"Where's RJ?"

EPILOGUE

THE ATLANTA JOURNAL-CONSTITUTION
March 8, 2023
BREAKING: Teen Guns Down Stepbrother in Shocking Suburban Shooting
By Dee Holloway, Staff Writer

DECATUR, GA — In a case already steeped in scandal, grief, and psychological unraveling, the Bell family saga has taken another devastating turn.

On Monday evening, 17-year-old Gideon Bell turned himself in to DeKalb County Police after allegedly fatally shooting his stepbrother, Ryan "RJ" Bell Jr., outside of RJ's maternal grandparents' home in the Glenwood neighborhood.

Witnesses say RJ, 17, was living with his late mother's parents when Gideon appeared at the home shortly after 5 p.m., armed with a handgun. According to police reports, Gideon fired five times, striking RJ in the chest and abdomen. RJ was pronounced dead at the scene.

What makes the case all the more harrowing is that Gideon reportedly waited for police to arrive, surrendering peacefully and handing over the weapon. In his signed statement, obtained by AJC, Gideon wrote:

"RJ ruined our family. He took advantage of my sister, broke my mother, and left me with nothing. No one protected me. So I did what nobody else would."

The murder comes just weeks after the shocking revelations surrounding the Bell family were made public. RJ, once a promising football star, was cleared of murder charges after his younger sister, Olivia Bell, was arrested and charged in connection to the death of her classmate, Violet Kowalski. Olivia is currently being held in a psychiatric facility following a suicide attempt and is reportedly undergoing competency evaluations.

Gideon, described by former teachers as "quiet," had recently withdrawn from traditional high school and was living with his aunt, Dr. Ricki Stafford, a well-known psychotherapist in the area. Sources close to the family say Gideon had become increasingly withdrawn after accusations surfaced that he may have been involved in the murder—claims which were later proven false.

"This is a tragedy stacked on top of tragedy," said Xavier Witherspoon, the family's longtime attorney. "The Bell family has endured unthinkable pain, and would appreciate their privacy while dealing with this matter."

RJ's paternal grandmother declined to comment.

Gideon Bell is being held without bond at the DeKalb County Juvenile Detention Center, though prosecutors have indicated their intent to try him as an adult. He has been charged with first-degree murder, unlawful possession of a firearm, and premeditated homicide.

A court date has not yet been set.

-The End-

FREE BOOK EXCERPT

BLACK GIRL GONE

Chapter 1

The road stretches out in front of me, endless and dark, and my feet keep dragging even though they're screaming at me to stop. Every breath tastes like smoke, sharp and bitter, like it's still clinging to my lungs. I can feel the fire behind me, even though I don't dare look back. The heat and the crackling wood is all in my head now, burned into my memory like so many other dreadful events.

"I did it," I whisper, my voice raw like I swallowed glass. "I finally did it."

The words sound hollow, like they don't belong to me. My hands are shaking, tucked deep into my sleeves to keep them warm. The air is frigid, biting at my face and burning my throat with every inhale, but it doesn't faze me. I don't feel much of anything except the weight of fear and guilt pressing down on my chest, threatening to crush me.

Then I hear it. A car.

The low rumble of an engine makes my whole body lock up. I stop dead in my tracks, my eyes darting to the headlights cutting through the dark. My stomach flips, and my legs scream at me to run, but where? It's just trees and this empty road. Nowhere to hide.

The car slows as it gets closer, and my heart starts pounding so loud I swear the driver can hear it. It's a police cruiser. The brakes squeal softly as it stops a few feet away, the headlights flooding over me, making me squint.

A tall, broad cop steps out, his hand resting on his belt. He's got the kind of face that looks tired but not unkind. His eyes are sharp, though, scanning me like I'm some puzzle he's trying to piece together.

"Miss, you alright?" he asks, his voice calm but firm.

My throat feels like it's closing up, but I force myself to speak. "I... I need help."

His eyes flick behind me, and his whole body goes tight. He's staring at the glow of the fire through the trees, his hand moving instinctively to his radio.

"That fire back there—" he starts, but doesn't finish. Instead, he speaks into the radio clipped to his shoulder. "Base, this is Unit 47. Got a structure fire about half a mile off Route 16. Looks like it's fully involved. Send the fire department and backup."

My stomach twists, but I keep my face blank. Don't blink. Don't move. Don't give him anything to work with.

"You coming from there?" he asks, his tone sharper now, his eyes cutting back to me.

I nod slowly, swallowing hard. "Yeah."

"What happened?" His voice softens again, like he's trying to coax the truth out of me.

I bite the inside of my cheek, tasting copper. "It was an accident," I say, my words stumbling out fast.

He glances down at my clothes, his eyes lingering on the dirt and soot smeared across my skin. His tone changes— gentler, but more pointed. "Is there anyone else in the house?"

My stomach drops. The words stick in my throat, and for a second, I can't breathe. Then I force myself to say it.

"Yes," I whisper. "The man that kidnapped me. He's still in there."

His eyes widen, his whole body stiffening. "The man that *kidnapped* you?" His voice is sharp now, the calm gone. "For how long?"

"Twenty years," I say, the words spilling out before I can stop them. "Since I was seven."

The radio crackles, and I hear another officer's voice responding to the fire call. But the cop isn't paying attention. His eyes are locked on mine, his face unreadable.

"Alright," he says finally, his voice quieter now. "Come on. Let's get you to safety.

I let him guide me to the cruiser, my legs shaking so bad I think they might give out. The seat is cold under me, and the door closes with a soft thud that is far too loud in the silence. He gets in on the driver's side, his hands steady on the wheel as he pulls back onto the road.

"What's your name?" he asks after a few moments of silence.

I swallow hard, the name hanging heavy on my tongue. "Charmaine. Charmaine Tillman."

Baba hadn't called me that the entire time he held me captive. He gave me a new name. *Nakia*, because it meant pure in Arabic. That name no longer fit me.

He picked up his radio again. "Base, this is Unit 47. Female in custody says her name is Charmaine Tillman. Requesting immediate verification."

My stomach tightens, but I keep my face blank, my eyes locked on the road ahead.

"Where were you taken from?" he asks while he awaits for confirmation.

"DC. I was at a school fair when I was taken," I respond.

The radio crackles again. "Unit 47, Charmaine Tillman is

an African American female who went missing in 2002. Presumed dead."

"Have special victims meet me at the hospital. I'm taking her there now," he responds.

The cop's hands tighten on the wheel, his jaw clenching. He glances at me, his eyes softer now, almost careful. "I'm sure you've been through a lot, but it's all over now."

I nod, my throat too tight to respond. I doubt it's all over. I'm sure this is just the beginning.

"I'll get you to the hospital right away," he says, his voice quieter now. "We'll take care of you."

I look out the window, watching the trees blur past. The fire's glow is gone now, swallowed up by the dark, but I can still see it in my head. I can still hear him, feel his breath on my neck, the weight of his hands holding me down. My chest tightens, and I press my fingers into the edge of the seat, trying to ground myself.

The hospital smells too clean, like bleach and chemicals, and it hits me like a wall as soon as we walk in. The lights are harsh, buzzing faintly, and the waiting room is too loud with the sound of phones ringing and shoes squeaking against the floor.

A nurse rushes over, her face all soft concern. She's older, with a no-nonsense vibe that reminds me of a teacher who always knew when you were lying.

"Sweetheart, are you hurt?" she asks, her hands fluttering like she's afraid to touch me.

"I'm fine," I say, the words automatic now. "Just tired."

She drapes a blanket over my shoulders and leads me to a chair. Her touch is light but firm, like she's trying to hold me together. The cops step away, their voices low as they talk to someone at the desk. My stomach flips again, but I keep my eyes on the floor.

The doctor comes in a few minutes later. She's a tall Black woman with a calm, steady presence that makes my shoulders relax just a little. Her badge says *Dr. Wallace*. She crouches in front of me, her hands resting on her knees.

"Charmaine, right?" she says, her voice soft but direct. "I'm Dr. Wallace. Can you tell me if you're hurt anywhere?"

"No," I say quickly. "I'm fine."

Her eyes narrow slightly, like she doesn't believe me, but she doesn't push. "Alright. Mind if I take a look at your arm?"

I glance down and realize for the first time that there's a shallow cut just below my elbow, dried blood flaking against my skin. I nod, letting her take my arm. Her touch is gentle, but the antiseptic stings, and I flinch.

"Sorry," she says quietly, her eyes flicking up to meet mine. "This happened tonight?"

"Yeah," I say, keeping my voice even. "It's nothing."

She finishes quickly, then leans back on her heels, watching me. "You're safe now," she says. "You know that, right?"

I nod, but the word feels heavy in my chest. Safe. It doesn't feel real. Not yet.

Dr. Wallace's hands are steady and sure as she checks me over, her touch light but clinical. She asks questions in that calm doctor voice..." Any pain, any dizziness, any injuries I can't see..." but I barely hear her. The harm she's looking for isn't on my skin. It's buried too deep for her to find. All that's left of the physical scars are the faint marks around my wrists, ankles, and neck from being leashed like a wild animal. The ones inside me? They're still raw.

She notes the ligature marks. She asks about the sexual abuse. It's still too soon to tell her everything I've been through. I'm not ready yet.

When she's done, she steps aside, her gaze lingering on me like she's trying to say something without words. I don't look at her. My eyes are on the two people coming toward me, their badges catching the hospital light.

Two detectives. The man is tall and broad-shouldered, his face lined with years of work that's probably shown him too much. The woman next to him is smaller, sharper, her gaze quick and assessing. They move like they've done this before, like they already know part of what I'm going to say.

The man crouches slightly so his eyes are level with mine, his tone low and careful. "Charmaine, right?" he asks, like he's trying the name on for size. "I'm Detective Callahan. This is Detective Monroe. We're from the Special Victims Unit. We want to help, but we need you to tell us what happened."

As soon as the man speaks to me, I avert my eyes from him like I was trained. Looking a man in the eye meant lashings. Just him being near me sends searing pain down my backside.

"I was at the cabin," I say, my voice slow and deliberate. "I've been there... for a long time."

The words hang in the air, heavy and sour, but Callahan doesn't blink. "How long is 'a long time,' Charmaine?"

I swallow hard, my chest tightening. "Since I was seven."

I glance up, fear tightening my chest. His jaw tightens just slightly, but his voice stays steady. "And who kept you there?"

"Baba," I say, the name catching in my throat like bile. "That's what he made me call him."

Monroe, the smaller one, leans forward, her elbows resting on her knees. Her voice is soft, but there's an edge to it, like she's trying to decide if I'm lying. "He's the one who took you?"

I nod, my gaze fixed on a crack in the floor. "Yeah."

"How did you get away?" she asks.

The lie comes easily, like I've been practicing it my whole life. "He fell asleep," I say, my voice small and shaky. "I... I knocked over a candle. It caught fire. Everything happened so fast. I ran."

Callahan's eyes narrow slightly, his head tilting as he watches me. "The fire started accidentally? From the candle?"

"Yes," I say quickly, nodding like it's the most natural thing in the world. "I didn't mean for it to happen. I just... I panicked."

Monroe doesn't write anything down. She just keeps watching me, her gaze sharp and unreadable. Callahan glances at her, then back at me. "Do you know if anyone else was in the cabin? Anyone besides Baba?"

I shake my head, the motion quick and definitive. "No. It was just me and him."

The silence stretches out, heavy and uncomfortable. I can feel their eyes on me, feel the weight of their thoughts even though they don't say them out loud. They're not sure if they believe me. I can tell. But they don't push. Not yet.

Callahan clears his throat, his tone softening. "You're safe now, Charmaine. We'll look into the fire and everything else, but right now, we just want to make sure you're okay."

The two of them step away, their voices dropping into whispers I can't make out. I sink further into the chair, pulling the blanket tighter around me like it can protect me from their questions. My stomach twists, my mind racing with everything I can't let them find out.

I did it. I killed him. But they can't know that. No one can.

Monroe glances back at me, her eyes sharp and curious. I drop my gaze, staring at the floor like it's the most interesting thing in the room. The glow of the fire flickers in my head, bright and consuming. My heart pounds, and I press my hands into my thighs, trying to ground myself.

The voices around me blur into nothing, and all I can hear is the echo of Baba's voice in my head, the sound of the gunshot, and the crackling of flames swallowing everything I left behind.

They keep me at the hospital for hours, poking and prodding like I'm some kind of specimen. Doreen, the nurse, brings me water and crackers, her face soft with pity.

"You've been through a lot," she says, her voice warm. "Just take it one step at a time, okay?"

I nod, forcing a small smile. "Thanks."

She pats my hand before walking away, and I let the smile drop. The room feels too bright, too exposed. Every time the door opens, my chest tightens like I'm about to be found out.

A knock sounds at the door, and I glance up to see the older cop standing there, his hat in his hands. "Charmaine, we're going to take you somewhere safe for the night. We've contacted your family."

My stomach flips. "My family?"

He nods, stepping into the room. "Your mom. She's on her way. And will get you tomorrow."

I stare at him, my pulse thudding in my ears. They're coming. The family I've been missing for years is finally coming for me.

The cop smiles, his expression kind but tired. "You're going home, Charmaine. It's finally over."

The words hang in the air, heavy and final. I nod slowly, my fingers tightening on the blanket. "Okay," I whisper, my voice barely audible.

But it doesn't feel over. Not yet. Not with what I left behind.

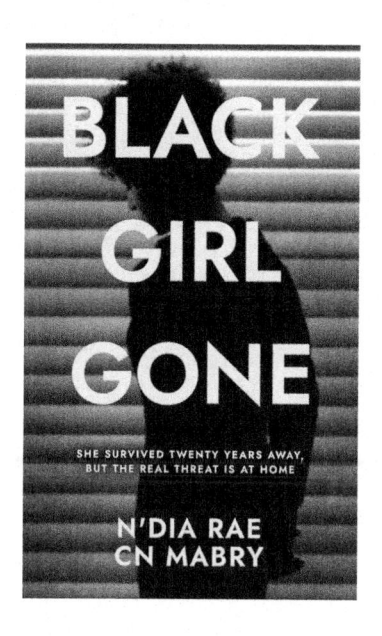

Read the rest today! This book is available in KU.

COMING SOON

Join the mailing list to be the first to know of this new release + upcoming sneak peaks.

Sign Up Here!

ABOUT THE AUTHOR

I write the kind of thrillers that keep you up at night, questioning everything and everyone. Psychological and domestic suspense is my sweet spot because I love digging into the dark corners of the mind and the messy, complicated nature of human relationships. I want my books to pull you in so deep that even after you turn the last page, you're still thinking about them.

My love for thrillers started with *Gone Girl*. That book (and movie) flipped a switch in me, and I've been obsessed with crafting twisty, unputdownable stories ever since. You can usually find me writing in a café, eavesdropping for inspiration, and drinking way too much coffee.

CN Mabry is my thriller alter ego. If you know me as N'Dia Rae, welcome to my darker side. Hope you survive the journey.

Printed in Great Britain
by Amazon